"DID YOU HAVE TO SCARE ME LIKE THAT?"

He sat down in the chair opposite her. "You should be more alert. After all, you are in a foreign country."

She narrowed her eyes at him. "How did you get in here? Ivar will not be pleased."

"Actually, Ivar told me where you were. Ivar considers me a friend now."

"I shall have to tell him otherwise."

"If you do, I will have to add another night to your tally of bedsport."

"Verily, your threats are becoming tiresome. Do you seriously think I will agree to let you sate your lust on me?"

He laughed. "First of all, I will not be sating *my* lust. It will be a mutual sating. Second, they are not threats. When you come to my bed, it will be willingly. Well, somewhat willingly."

She glared at him.

I am beginning to find her glares charming. How pitiful i

D0377272

Romances by **Sandra Hill**

THE NORSE KING'S DAUGHTER
THE VIKING TAKES A KNIGHT
VIKING IN LOVE
HOT & HEAVY
WET & WILD
A TALE OF TWO VIKINGS
THE VERY VIRILE VIKING
THE VIKING'S CAPTIVE (formerly My Fair Viking)
THE BLUE VIKING
TRULY, MADLY VIKING
THE LOVE POTION
THE BEWITCHED VIKING
LOVE ME TENDER
THE LAST VIKING
SWEETER SAVAGE LOVE
DESPERADO
FRANKLY, MY DEAR
THE TARNISHED LADY
THE OUTLAW VIKING
THE RELUCTANT VIKING

ATTENTION: ORGANIZATIONS AND CORPORATIONS
Most Avon Books paperbacks are available at special quantity
discounts for bulk purchases for sales promotions, premiums,
or fund raising. For information, please call or write:

Special Markets Department, HarperCollins Publishers,
10 East 53rd Street, New York, New York 10022-5299.
Telephone: (212) 207-7528.   Fax: (212) 207-7222.

SANDRA HILL

The Norse King's Daughter

AVON

An Imprint of HarperCollinsPublishers

This is a work of fiction. Names, characters, places, and incidents are products of the author's imagination or are used fictitiously and are not to be construed as real. Any resemblance to actual events, locales, organizations, or persons, living or dead, is entirely coincidental.

AVON BOOKS
An Imprint of HarperCollins*Publishers*
10 East 53rd Street
New York, New York 10022-5299

Copyright © 2011 by Sandra Hill
Excerpt from *Deadly Angels* © 2012 by Sandra Hill
ISBN 978-0-06-167351-1
www.avonromance.com

All rights reserved. No part of this book may be used or reproduced in any manner whatsoever without written permission, except in the case of brief quotations embodied in critical articles and reviews. For information address Avon Books, an Imprint of HarperCollins Publishers.

First Avon Books mass market printing: October 2011

Avon Trademark Reg. U.S. Pat. Off. and in Other Countries, Marca Registrada, Hecho en U.S.A.
HarperCollins® is a registered trademark of HarperCollins Publishers.

Printed in the U.S.A.

10 9 8 7 6 5 4 3 2 1

If you purchased this book without a cover, you should be aware that this book is stolen property. It was reported as "unsold and destroyed" to the publisher, and neither the author nor the publisher has received any payment for this "stripped book."

*This book is dedicated to
my granddaughter Jaden,
who is princess to the bone. She would
fit in perfectly with my five Norse princesses.
Plus she's got a bit of Viking in her blood.*

*As the mother of four sons, I somehow lost
the girlie gene. The desire to wear chiffon
and ruffles with sparkly shoes to school, and
the ability to pull it off. How to shop like
an Energizer Bunny, and find all the best
bargains. The love of a good cuddle, even
with your girlfriends, or especially with your
girlfriends. The talent for climbing a tree
one moment and dancing a delicate ballet
the next. The way you can say, "I love you"
without hesitation or fear of rejection.*

*So here's to you, Jado, may you always
be a princess in someone's life.*

A wench's word let no wise man trust,
nor trust the troth of a woman;
For on a whirling wheel their hearts are shaped,
And fickle and fitful their minds.

THE POETIC EDDA
HÁVAMÁL

The Norse King's Daughter

PROLOGUE

**Comes a time when all good Viking men
must bite the shield . . . and wed . . .**

"**T**oss the babe in the fjord. Or leave it on the cliff. Either way, the whelp will be dead afore morn."

Sidroc Guntersson, third son of Jarl Gunter Ormsson, was a noted warrior who had seen cruelty in all its forms, but his father's pronouncement about Sidroc's newborn child turned his blood cold. "How can you suggest such for your own kin?" *Why am I surprised? No doubt you wish you'd ended my life in the same manner.*

His loathsome father, who had the paternal sensibilities of a rock, shrugged and leaned back in the throne-like armed chair atop the dais in his great hall. Even as he spoke, one paw-like hand stroked the long, pale blonde hair of his latest concubine, a girl no more than thirteen. In all his twenty and six years, Sidroc had many times witnessed his father's lusty appetites appeased by the *more danico*, multiple wives, as well as numerous mistresses, bed thralls, and any serving maid of passable appearance. On occasion, all at the same time. The gods only knew how many by-blows he'd bred, along with his four legitimate sons and two legitimate daughters.

" 'Tis a split-tail," his father pointed out, as a defense for abandoning a newborn.

Sidroc bristled. "Yea, 'tis a girl, and the mother is dead." Sidroc's voice was raspy with emotion. He'd seen men cleaved from head to belly in battle, but the image that would stay with him forevermore was of Astrid lying in a pool of her own blood. With a bloody mass of squalling, flailing arms and legs lying betwixt her thighs, its cord still uncut.

Eydis, the wet nurse serving his brother Svein's one-year-old boy, had agreed to take his daughter to teat, but only until he hired another suitable maid, or until his brother found out. Svein did not share anything with anyone, especially not with him, ever since Sidroc thrashed him as a boyling, despite being five years younger. As he recalled, he'd been provoked by Svein's drowning a stable cat, just for sport.

Sidroc was full aware that it was the practice in some parts of the Norselands to put a newborn out to die when it arrived underweight or handicapped in some way. After all, living was difficult in the harsh northern climate, and survival was indeed best reserved for the hardiest. But to stand by and watch a child, one not handicapped in any way, be killed, well, it was something he could not do. Whether it be his child or some other's.

To be honest, he felt no strong connection with the baby, less than a day old now. But he would be less than a man to abandon its fate to others like his father.

" 'Tis not uncommon for a woman to die of the childbirth fever," his father remarked coldly. "You are too missish by half."

Missish? Sidroc shook his head at his father's perception of him. He was a far-famed warrior, adept with halberd and broadsword. But all his father saw was a man not in his selfsame mold of cruelty.

His wife had not been a love match for him; as in most noble families it was an arranged marriage for gain, but he had held an affection for Astrid from the start. Not that he'd seen much of her in the two years they'd been married, what with his a-Viking and fur trading. "I promised Astrid on her deathbed that I would care for the child."

His father shrugged again, and now his hand was groping his concubine's small breasts. The silly girl giggled and preened at the attention of her master, even such a public display.

Sidroc knew he did not have his father's full attention. Still, he persisted. "Signe deserves to live."

"You named the child?" His father made a tsking noise of disapproval.

It nigh gagged him to ask his father for favors, but needs must, he chastised himself. His much smaller keep at the edge of the Vikstead estates had burned to the ground last winter, along with a storeroom piled to the ceiling with precious furs intended for market. He and Astrid had been living with his father until he could rebuild. Even that favor had galled him. "All I ask is that Svein's wet nurse be permitted to continue caring for the baby here at Vikstead until I return from a commitment I have made to the Jomsvikings. Once I have regained my wealth—"

"If you care so much, take the babe with you."

"They do not allow women or children at the Jomsborg fortress."

"How long would you be gone?"

Someday, old man . . . someday! he seethed with tightly fisted hands. As a third son with two healthy older brothers, Sidroc knew he would never inherit the jarldom and that he must accumulate wealth enough to purchase his own lands, hopefully away from Vikstead this time. Joining the elite Jomsvikings had been his best option for increasing his fortunes. "Two years. Three at most."

"Pfff!" his father scoffed. "Find a wife then, a rich one this time, for Thor's sake! One with lands."

This was a refrain he'd heard from his father many times in the past, a demand he'd resisted mightily. No doubt he'd married Astrid in part because she carried no dowry, just to defy his father. At the time, he'd had wealth and property enough that it had not mattered.

"Six sennights I give you to find a bride and a home for the whelp," his father conceded. "At the end of that time, the babe goes. That is my final word."

How had this argument with his father snowballed from a disagreement to a battle of wills? How had he allowed himself to be backed into a corner? "I suppose you have someone in mind, even with Astrid scarce turned to ashes in her burial pyre," he gritted out.

"King Thorvald of Stoneheim has one more un-married daughter. Try her." His father gave him an evil grin. "Or not. It matters not to me."

Sidroc knew the woman his father referred to. Princess Drifa. Although she was long in the tooth for a woman—at least twenty-four years old—she was not unattractive. Being half Norse, half Arab, her features were exotic with slanted dark eyes, and her body was fine-boned. As he recalled, how-ever, she had an outlandish passion for growing things. There was ofttimes dirt under her finger-nails, dried leaves in her black hair, and she was known to bring flowers and bushes indoors. On one occasion she even reeked of manure that she claimed made her flowers sweeter.

Ah well, he supposed there were worse things. He would need to find a mother for Signe eventu-ally, in any case. Besides, it was good to have a ready bedmate when no other was available.

Thus it was that Sidroc Guntersson of Vikstead, instead of going a-Viking this springtime season, as was his norm, or rebuilding his home, went off a-courting. May the Norns of Fate guide him!

CHAPTER ONE

Beware of rogues with bad intentions . . .

Drifa, daughter of the Norse King Thorvald,
was being seduced, good and well.

After twenty-four years of resisting matrimony,
even when she viewed the good examples of her
four married sisters, Drifa was falling in love a little
bit. Or in lust, leastways. And after only three sennights of the man launching his game of pursuit.

And what a handsome rogue, he was! Sidroc
Guntersson was not much older than she. Perchance only twenty-six. She was of average height
for a woman, but he was at least a head taller.
With shoulder-length, chestnut hair, dark gray-
green eyes framed by thick, dark brown lashes, a
full sensuous mouth, and a battle-honed body, he
was pure Viking man at his virile best.

He had been wed before, not that that mattered to her. His wife had died. What was odd to
her, though, was that he refused to talk about her
death. "Later," he kept saying. "Not now."

On the one hand, she thought his pursuit of another woman was disrespectful so soon after his
wife's death. On the other hand, some men were

like that. If they loved hard enough, they wanted to replace that love with another. Not that he had said all this, but his silence on the subject was telling to Drifa. Who could not be drawn to a man who had loved so much?

"Open your mouth for me, princess," Sidroc murmured against her lips, which were already swollen from his numerous kisses. Somehow he had managed to find her in a secluded section of her herb garden, where he had her backed up against a stone wall.

"Why?" she asked, which gave him the perfect opening.

His tongue slipped inside and began to stroke her with an in-out motion that mirrored what he was doing down below. With his hands cupping her bottom and his thighs separating her legs, which were dangling off the ground, he undulated his hips against her. It was impossible not to notice the hard rod of his lust as it sought her woman-channel.

"My sap runs thick and hot," he rasped out. "Quench me, m'lady."

Oh! Oh! She began to swoon with utter ecstasy, especially when he sucked lightly on her tongue.

So this was what her sisters had sighed about.

So this was all the fuss the maids were always whispering about.

So this was why the gods had created men and women.

How could she have been so ignorant for so long? Was her sap rising, too? Did women even have sap? Was it this man alone, or was the time ripe for her to yield? Oh, good gods! Was she over-ripe? Nay, she did not think she would yield to just any man. *Holy Frigg! What is he doing now?*

"Tell me you will be my wife," he whispered against her ear, which he was also plying with wet-tipped tongue and hot breath. "I. Need. You."

"Why?" she asked again on a keening wail of torturous pleasure.

With a chuckle, he pressed the evidence of his need against her. If possible, it was bigger . . . and harder.

"Why *me*?" she elaborated.

"Because I want you above all others. And because you want me, too," he asserted with the usual arrogance of a Norseman.

She was confused. How could she answer when she was beset with so many conflicting emotions? She was unaccustomed to yielding to a man's attention. In truth, more than two dozen Norsemen, and a few Saxons, had offered for her in the past ten years. None of them had affected her like this. *What an understatement! My blood is boiling in my veins. My bones are melting. My brain is one big throbbing mass of sexual fog.* "I . . . I . . .'tis too soon."

"Nay. Betimes too much thinking clouds a person's thinking. Betimes a person must jump into a decision. Betimes a woman must wed or go barmy from lack of carnal bliss."

What? You are making that up. She had no chance to say that, though, because he was kissing her again. And caressing her breasts. And rubbing himself against her nether parts.

A flush of arousal swept over her in waves, and when he asked again, "Please, sweetling, be my wife," she answered, "Yea, I will."

Then—oh, praise the gods and all the goddesses!—he used his wicked, wandering hands and his thrusting hips to bring her to a peak that would have had her screaming her woman-joy if his tongue had not been firmly planted in her mouth.

For long moments she lay boneless against his chest, her face nestled in the crook of his neck, panting like a warhorse.

What just happened? Have I died? Was that what he meant by carnal bliss? Best I pretend that this was not a shocking happenstance for me, or he will laugh at me. "That was nice," she said in as calm a voice as she could muster.

He laughed. The brute just laughed at her. "We will go to your father this eventide," he told her between quick, nibbling kisses, as he helped her straighten her *gunna* and the long, open-sided apron worn by most Norse women.

Did I say him yea? I must have, but . . . "Mayhap I should approach him first, alone." *And mayhap I need to think this through in some quiet place far from his tempting self.*

He shook his head. "Together. We will go together. And we will be wed within a sennight so we may return to Vikstead and present you to my father."

That was not going to happen so soon, for the simple reason that the sixtieth anniversary of her father's birthday was to be celebrated in ten days' time. Everyone was coming, including three of her

sisters who lived in Britain. Her father would never
countenance her absence from such an important
event. "Why must we rush?"

His face flushed, but all he would reveal was
"'Tis not important, but you will understand in
good time."

**He'd landed in the royal barmy bin where
all the king's men . . . and women . . . were
missing a few stones from their turrets . . .**

Later that day, Sidroc sat on a bench on one
side of the hearth in the largest solar of Stoneheim,
surrounded by members of the Norse royal family
who had come from far and wide to celebrate the
king's upcoming sixtieth birthing day anniversary.
They were all that a family should be, and all he'd
never experienced himself.

After at least a dozen futile attempts, Sidroc had
yet to ask King Thorvald for his daughter's hand
in marriage. He supposed that he should have told
Drifa from the beginning why he must marry,
and with haste yet, but he was experienced in the
love arts, and he knew, sure as gammelost stinks,
she would have balked if he told her it was not so
much that he needed her, as that he had a newborn baby who needed a mother. Women wanted
to be courted. Later . . . he would tell all later. They
would both laugh about his craftiness.

For now, Drifa's sisters were eyeing him suspiciously. This family did naught but talk and laugh
and shout over one another, and the subjects they

discussed were outrageous. Like some experiments being done with honey on a man's staff to prevent conception, for the love of Frigg! "Now, if a man could lick his own cock, that would be another thing," the king had proclaimed, and they'd all laughed, even the women.

In truth, going by the glaring sisters, he would not be surprised if someone asked Drifa in front of one and all if she still had a maidenhead. Actually, he hoped they did. Mayhap then he would have a chance to make an offer of marriage and get it over with.

In the midst of his elation this afternoon over Drifa's acceptance of his proposal, he'd forgotten her having told him days ago of the planned feast, but she hadn't warned him of the deluge of guests who would arrive so soon. If she thought he was going to linger around this overcrowded castle for ten more days, without a wedding, he had news for her. "King Thorvald, can we speak in private?"

"Later, my boy, later," the king said jovially, turning back to a servant who was carrying a tray with goblets of mead.

Drifa, who sat on the bench beside him, squeezed his hand. "Have patience."

Patience! He gritted his teeth, trying not to appear overanxious. He'd already wasted three sennights in this drafty, hodgepodge, stone and wood castle, designed by one of the sisters, Breanne, who had a passion for building things. Chairs, tables, pigsties, castles, and whatnot. In fact, Breanne sat beside her husband, the Saxon Lord Caedmon, on an opposing bench whittling on a stick to amuse a child who hovered watchfully over her shoulder.

Another sister, Ingrith, was returning from the kitchen, where she'd been engaged in her particular passion. Cooking. As evidenced by the delicious aromas wafting through the air. Roast hare and honey oatcakes would be his guess. Ingrith's husband, another Saxon lord, John of Hawks' Lair, who seemed bemused by the whole situation, said near his ear in passing, "You are a dead duck, my good man, once these barmy birds get their claws in you."

Lord Hawk was the one doing the experiments with honey, cocks, and male seed caps. He had no room to complain of barmy birds, in Sidroc's opinion.

"I wish you would get your claws in me. Quickly. On the marriage bed," he whispered to Drifa.

"Patience," she said again, though she was now wearing a pretty blush on her face reminding him of how close to swiving they'd come today. Mayhap he would visit her bedchamber tonight, to seal the deal, so to speak.

"What did you say to Sidroc?" Ingrith inquired of her husband, who tugged her down to sit on his lap. You'd expect that of a newly wedded couple, but these two had been together for at least a couple of years.

"I was telling the man how fortunate he is to be in the midst of such intelligent Vikings, dearling," he assured his wife.

"Pfff! I can only guess—" Ingrith's words were cut off as the oldest sister, Tyra, approached with her husband, Adam the Healer. Another Saxon. What was it with these Viking women? Would a good virile Viking not do?

Tyra was a big woman. In fact, she'd trained to be a warrior at one time. Tyra stared pointedly at Drifa's blush and at her hand laced with his, resting on his thigh, then glared at him.

"Should I kill him, Father?" the bloodthirsty wench asked.

"Good gods, nay! We may have a husband for Drifa yet," said King Thorvald.

Drifa tsked her opinion.

Obviously the old goat was more aware of his intentions than he'd let on. In fact he winked at Sidroc, then leaned his massive body back into an armed chair, a horn of ale in hands propped on his lap, his legs extended to the fire. Although he was an old man, he appeared to be in fine physical condition, and although his hair and beard were white, they were finely groomed and adorned with precious jewels. The quality of his tunic and *braies* and boots attested to his high station.

Sidroc's best friend, Finn Vidarsson, ofttimes referred to as Finn Finehair, who had traveled here with him, was the only other man of his acquaintance who took grooming so seriously. In fact, Finn was known to trim his chest and man-hairs on occasion, a habit that he claimed women loved. Finn had never wed, claiming he'd never met a woman who matched his beauty. If Sidroc had not witnessed Finn's prowess in battle, he would question his manliness.

Calling himself back to the present, Sidroc demanded, "I must needs speak to you as soon as possible, King Thorvald. 'Tis urgent that I get home to Vikstead afore—"

"Did I tell you about the time Adam drilled a hole in my head?" King Thorvald asked him.

Only about a dozen times. "Did I tell you—?"

"Saved my life, it did," King Thorvald said, as if Sidroc hadn't spoken. "Made my cock get bigger, too, I warrant."

"Father! Such language!" five women protested, including Vana, who was married to Rafn, the Viking *hersir* who commanded all the troops at Stoneheim. Vana had a passion for cleaning and was scrubbing at a trestle table behind them while the family meeting was about to commence. Though why he would be included in a family meeting posed both good and bad possibilities in Sidroc's befuddled brain.

"Mayhap Adam should drill a hole in your head," the king suggested to him.

Sidroc sputtered. "My co— manpart is plenty big enough." Holy Thor! He hoped Finn didn't hear about this. He would no doubt have a dozen holes drilled in his fool head.

"Well, I hope so. I have been trying to get Drifa married for many a year. After all this time, she deserves something . . . big."

Drifa tsked some more.

Everyone laughed, except him. He was crossing his eyes with frustration.

"Since you apparently already know my intentions, King Thorvald, do you then agree to give your daughter Drifa to me?"

The king rolled his eyes. "I do not *give* my daughters to any man. They have the right to choose. A promise I made to their mothers long ago."

"What kind of lackbrained thing was that to do?"

Five women snarled.

"That does not mean like-minded men cannot influence them, however," the king added.

"Influence her," Sidroc sputtered. "Drifa has already accepted my suit. Have you not, sweetling?" he asked, picking her up and setting her on his lap. If Lord Hawk could take such liberties with his woman, so could he. Besides, if it was influence the king wanted, he was more than willing to . . . *influence*.

Drifa tried to escape, but he held on tight.

Everyone, even the women, stared at him, impressed at his finesse, no doubt.

"Let me up, you brute," she said halfheartedly.

"Stop squirming."

"Stop poking me with that . . . thing."

"Your father wants to drill a hole in my head to make it bigger."

"So I heard."

"Some folks think bigger is better."

"Some folks are lackbrained."

Tyra narrowed her eyes at him. "I thought you were already married."

He had hoped to avoid the subject, but 'twould appear he was not going to be so fortunate. "I was. My wife died," he replied, stiff-lipped.

"When—"

"Stop, Tyra. Sidroc does not like to talk of

his wife who has gone to the Other World." She squeezed Sidroc's hand.

He stared at Drifa with surprise. *Drifa is defending me?* He had conflicting feelings over that circumstance. A rather odd joy filled him that anyone, least of all a woman, would come to his aid. And he was filled with guilt that she did not know his true reason for being here. Ah, well, he would make it up to her later. He squeezed her hand in return.

He started to say, "It's not that I—"

"Nay, Sidroc," Drifa said. "It is for you to discuss if and when you choose." She silenced Tyra and her other sisters with a glare.

Who is this woman I am about to be betrothed to? Can she possibly be as amazing as I am beginning to believe?

"So, what think you, daughter, of a combined wedding/birthing day celebration ten days hence?"

Sidroc was about to protest the delay, but bit his tongue. That would still allow him another sennight for what should be only a two-day trip back to Vikstead.

Drifa nodded, and he kissed her thoroughly afore she could raise any objections. To his surprise, and pleasure, she sank into his kiss as everyone cheered their good wishes.

The Norns of Fate must be on his side after all.

Or not, he soon found out.

CHAPTER TWO

**The best-laid plans of mice and clueless
Viking men . . .**

Drifa was happier than she'd ever been in all
her life. Until, that is, Sidroc's well-laid plans
caused her heart to nigh break.

It all started later that day with Drifa's ill-timed
eavesdropping. Or was that good-timed?

Sidroc was at the lower end of the great hall
speaking to his comrade-in-arms Finn Vidarsson
as they shared horns of mead. Finn was a strutting
peacock of a man, vain to the bone, who had every
Stoneheim kitchen, chamber, and serving maid
aflutter.

She heard her name mentioned and decided
Sidroc must be announcing her father's consent to
their marriage.

"So, you have accomplished your goal, my
friend. Well done!"

Goal? What goal?

"And just in time," Sidroc agreed.

In time for what?

"She is comely enough, though not up to my
high standards," Finn remarked.

As if I would have you!

"No woman is comely enough to match you," Sidroc scoffed.

"Still, methinks bedding the princess will not be such a hardship for you, Sidroc."

Sidroc chuckled. "It took nigh tupping to get her to agree."

Oh nay! Please do not be discussing me so!

"And that would have been a problem?"

"Nay, but I needed to withhold that treat if I wanted her consent to wed."

Treat? You rat! You bloody, stinking midden rat! "I want you above all others." That is what you said to me. Liar!

"And now what?"

"I plan to swive her silly tonight. Then we will wed in ten days. After that, I will take her to my father's estate and leave her there whilst there is still time to join the Jomsvikings. The funds in her dowry should satisfy my father."

Over my dead unswived body!

"Dost think your father will indulge her zeal for plants?"

"I daresay he will let her do as she wills as long as it does not interfere with his drinking and whoring. She will have my baby to while away her time besides bloody roses and manure."

He expects to plant his seed and have it take immediately. The arrogant ass! But, oh, his words cut to the quick. *Apparently his interest in my occupation with growing things is as false as his supposed affection for me.*

"By then, you would have rebuilt your fortunes and can build a home wherever you choose. Mayhap even the Orkney Islands where many Vikings have settled."

"You make a good point, Finn. The Orkneys are out of my father's range and yet only a day's longship ride in good weather from the Norselands."

He has no home of his own? He would move to another country without consulting me?

"The binding ceremony cannot come too soon for me," Sidroc added, "but the most important thing is that she *will* wed me now. A betrothal is as binding as the actual wedding vows."

"Or so you think," Drifa said, stepping out from the corridor where she had been standing, holding a pottery jug of mead, which she'd brought to replenish their supply. Her heart was nigh breaking, but she must get through these next few moments before letting loose her tears.

"Drifa!" Sidroc said with alarm, staring back at her over his shoulder.

And so you should be alarmed, you lying, lecherous lout.

He stood and approached her.

She backed up and held up one of her hands to halt his progress. "There will be no wedding."

"I can explain."

She shook her head. "You thought to wed me and shed me, all in one swoop. What a foolish maid you must think me."

"I can explain," he repeated.

"I ne'er expected love from you," Drifa said,

hoping the twitch at the side of her mouth did not betray her foolish dreams, "but you said you wanted me above all others."

"I do." But then he dug his own grave, so to speak, when he tried to jest, "The only other candidate at the moment is Brunhilda of Lade."

Drifa's heart shriveled. Brunhilda was forty if she was a day and weighed as much as a warhorse. *And Sidroc views me in the same way. Even if he is jesting, I am not amused.* "Go! Leave Stoneheim and ne'er let me see your devious face again."

"We would suit, Drifa. You know we would."

She raised her chin haughtily. "Pigs will fly afore I accept you now."

"Is this a game you played with all your other suitors? Led them on to believe you will wed. Then cut off your favors at the last moment."

"Ooooh, do not try to lay the blame for this travesty on me."

"Travesty, is it?" He almost grinned.

The troll!

"You are a passionate woman, Drifa," Sidroc said, trying a different tack. "We would both benefit from this union."

I ne'er was before. Passionate, that is. And I ne'er will be again. Look what it has led me to. "You would swive me for coin?" she jeered. "What kind of man would do that?"

"A man who is desperate."

Does he imply that only a man who is desperate would want me? And why is he desperate? It mattered not. He was a *nithing*, withholding a swiving as if that was some grand prize. Implying that she was panting after him like a randy she-goat. "Stay away from me, you mangy dog," she warned as he drew closer.

He laughed.

Big mistake, that!

Before he could anticipate her next action, she raised the pitcher high with both hands and walloped him over the head. Not only did she knock him over, with mead flying everywhere, but the back of his head struck the edge of the bench on the way down. He landed on the rushes like a fallen oak, eyes closed.

"Oh my gods! I've killed the man I love . . . I mean, the man I hate . . . I mean, *help!*"

It was huge, as far as side effects went . . .

When Sidroc awakened, his skull ached as if it had been cracked open in the back, and his brain was seeping out. Slowly, so as not to jar his head and increase the pain, he stared about the small chamber where he was lying on a pallet.

He felt as weak as boar piss and could swear his stomach was shrunken inward. Yea, a quick scan of his upper body with his fingertips found his ribs protruding. He frowned with confusion. How could he have lost so much weight in such a short—

"You're alive!" Finn jumped up from the chair where he had been sitting, and Sidroc put up his hands to ward him off. He did not think he could

withstand a hug . . . if, indeed, that was what Finn
had intended.

With hysterical irrelevance, he noted that Finn
did not look his usual elegant self. His tunic
and *braies* were rumpled. His forked beard not
so forked. And his hair looked as if it had been
combed with a hay rake.

"Of course I am alive. Didst think a thump
on the head by a mere female would send me to
Asgard?"

Finn seemed confused and then thankful when
another man entered the room. It was Adam the
Healer, the Saxon husband of one of Drifa's sisters.

Speaking of Drifa, he hoped she was sorry
now. Knocking him out without allowing him to
explain! She was probably off somewhere weeping her eyes out with regret. He should probably
punish her in some way. After they were wed.

"Sidroc, my good man, you gave us a scare,"
Adam said as he gingerly sat on the edge of the
mattress and began to examine his eyeballs by lifting one lid, then another.

"I did?" he asked, running his furred tongue
over his furred teeth. He blew out and almost
knocked himself out again with his foul breath.
"How long was I asleep?"

"Asleep?" Finn chortled.

"You were unconscious for six sennights,"
Adam informed him.

"What?" he hollered and tried to sit up. Almost
immediately, he sank back down and had to fight
the blackness that wanted to overtake him again.
A sudden memory came to him, unbidden, of being

force-fed endless spoonfuls of gruel and water, most of which had run down his chin to his neck and chest. "Where is the witch who put me in this condition?" he demanded.

"Drifa has gone away." Adam's gaze shifted, not meeting his direct scrutiny.

"Away where?"

"I am not precisely sure. She went off with her sisters after King Thorvald's birthday on her personal longship, *Wind Maiden*. A short pleasure journey, they said. That usually means shopping. Probably to Birka."

"*Wind Maiden*? What kind of lackwit name is that for a longship?"

Adam just shrugged as he pulled aside the bed fur and examined the rest of his body, though how tapping Sidroc's chest with his fingertips could prove anything was beyond Sidroc's understanding.

"You allowed your wife to go away without you on a 'pleasure journey'?"

"The Stoneheim princesses do not ask permission."

Mine will. If we are still to wed, that is. But then another thought occurred to him. "Drifa left me here, unconscious?" he asked with disbelief.

"I assured her that you would recover in time to offend her again."

"Humph! Can I assume I am no longer betrothed?"

"That would be a good assumption, considering what Drifa overheard you say."

Really, women made too much of courting and

marriage. They expected men to fall over swooning in rapture at the possibility of gaining their favors, when in fact most men just wanted to get the ceremony over with so they could continue on as before.

But then the implications of his situation sunk in. Six sennights? Three sennights past his father's deadline. "Finn?"

Understanding the unspoken question, Finn shook his head. "I went back two sennights ago, and the babe was gone."

Rage filled Sidroc then. He sat up and despite the bindings about his head, he pulled at his hair and screamed out his fury. His anger was directed at his father, but also at Drifa for her part in this macabre play. And he wept for the baby he would never see grow into a girling.

His guilt was a heavy weight on his soul. And he did not accept failure easily.

But then his hysteria turned to laughter as yet another thought occurred to him. "Did you perchance drill a hole in my head, healer?"

Adam nodded. "It relieved the pressure inside your head and led to your recovery, I believe."

"I asked him to drill one in my head, too, but the healer would not oblige," Finn complained.

Sidroc, still laughing, lifted the laces of his *braies* and peered downward. "Bloody hell, the king was right."

And then Sidroc sunk into blessed unconsciousness again.

As he was sinking, sinking, sinking into oblivion, he decided, *Those damn Norns of Fate are fickle creatures . . . like all women.*

Some men just need a good thumping to keep them in place . . .

"What do you mean by 'He is gone.' He cannot be gone."

"Gone like the wind." Drifa's father made a whooshing sound, for emphasis. "Disappeared in the night with that foppish friend of his. His long-ship must have been kept sea-ready all that time. They took off the selfsame night that he regained consciousness. Must have been weak as watered ale. Adam says his seamen no doubt carried him out."

"Where did he go?"

"No one knows." Rafn spoke now. "We thought mayhap Jomsborg to join the Jomsvikings, something he had previously planned, according to Finn. But I sent some men there to check, and no one has seen him."

"He did not even thank me for drilling a hole in his head," Adam added with a grin.

She did not want to know what that grin implied.

"One of my men overheard his comrade-in-arms Finn mention Iceland," Rafn informed her. "Or was it that new country beyond Iceland discovered by Erik the Red?"

"Why would he rush off like that?"

"Uh," her father said.

Rafn and Adam exchanged glances.

"What?" she insisted.

"He might have been in a bit of a furor over your absence," her father confessed.

"Did you not tell him where I had gone?"

"How could I do that? I did not know where you went. No one ever tells me anything."

"Tyra mentioned a 'pleasure journey,'" Adam said.

"And you thought we swanned off like feckless maidens?"

He nodded.

Idiot!

'Twas true Drifa had not wanted to draw attention to the mission she and her sisters had taken upon themselves, but she should have known better than to leave their menfolk in the dark. Men could not find their way in a fog, let alone the dark.

Once Finn had informed them of Sidroc's need to rescue his baby, Drifa and her sisters grew outraged. In a family of five daughters, how could they not disdain a man like Jarl Ormsson who placed no value on a girl child? And so they decided to swoop into Vikstead and grab the baby. Bring it back to Stoneheim, where Sidroc would be overjoyed once he awakened to find the babe safe and sound.

But then they'd decided to go to Birka before returning home, to put any Vikstead followers off their scent, if there were in fact any who cared that the child was gone. They'd renamed the girling from Signe to Runa, as a precaution.

None of this was done with the intention of

her marrying the lout. But she did feel guilty for having struck him down, as deserving as her blow had been. And besides, what had the fool been thinking, keeping this information from a potential wife? How little he must have valued her to think she would let a baby die for lack of a husband's love. In truth, she probably would not have agreed to wed him if she'd known his motive, but she would have worked with him to save the child.

"But . . . but now I have his baby, and he is not here." Drifa wrung her hands with dismay.

"You have his baby?" her father asked gleefully, as if the squalling infant off in an adjoining chamber with the wet nurse was not announcing her presence to one and all. "Now you will have to marry, for sure."

"It is not *my* baby, Father. Even I could not plant a seed and have it flower in six short sennights."

Her father waved a hand dismissively. "*His* baby then. It matters not. If you have his baby, he will insist on marriage."

"You forget, Father, it is also Jarl Ormsson's granddaughter."

"Uh-oh!" the three men in the room said as one.

"That Gunter Ormsson is a mean buzzard. Good gods, we will have all the Vikstead warriors attacking us now," Rafn said.

"Why would the man attack us when the jarl did not want the baby to live?" Drifa asked.

Rafn shook his head at her. "Drifa, Drifa, Drifa, you do not understand men."

Well, that was obvious.

"A man may not want something for himself,

but he will fight to the death to hold that something if someone else wants it," Rafn explained.

"That is pure male drivel."

"Plus, pride may be involved, if Gunter thinks his honor is involved," Adam added.

"The man has no honor," she said hotly.

The three men in the room just shrugged.

"Well, that settles it then. Return the baby to Vikstead," her father said on a long sigh, his hopes for the marriage of his last daughter being dashed.

"I cannot do that. Ormsson plans to kill the baby," Drifa told him.

The king put fingertips to his forehead and rubbed. "All this thinking is giving me a head megrim." He turned to Adam. "Dost think I need another head drilling?"

"Nay. What I think you need . . . what I think we all need is," Adam said with an exaggerated pause, "a beer."

Soon she stood alone in the solar, wondering how she'd gotten herself into such a mess. This was almost as bad as the time she and her sisters had killed the earl of Havenshire and buried the brute in the bottom of a privy. Except now she was stuck with the evidence of her crime. Living, breathing, squalling evidence.

Just then, Rafn stuck his head back in the doorway and grinned at her. "Sidroc did have a message of sorts regarding you afore he left."

She arched her brows at his mischievous expression.

"He said, 'Bugger the bitch!' "

Drifa threw a ball of yarn at his retreating back.

Oh well. She was sure to find Sidroc soon and he would joyfully take the baby off her hands.

Oddly, she could swear she heard laughter in her head. Was it the Norns of Fate making mirth at her destiny?

Mayhap she was the one needing a head drilling.

On the other hand, mayhap not. One of her body parts might enlarge, or she might grow one she did not want.

Chapter Three

**FIVE YEARS LATER, ON THE WAY TO
BYZANTIUM**

**There are passions, and then there
are passions . . .**

"Wake up, princess. Time to smell the roses.
Ha, ha, ha!"

Princess Drifa turned over on her pallet under
the canvas shelter in the center of the longship, and
pretended to be napping.

"I smell *flowers*. Does anyone else smell *flowers*? Ha, ha, ha!"

Do not react, Drifa. Do not react.

"Mayhap it is your armpits, Arne. Seems to me I
saw *grass* growing there. Ha, ha, ha!"

*Oh, good gods! You'd think they were youth-
lings, not grown men.*

"I for one plan to *plow* a few *fields* once we
land, and I don't mean *grass*. Ha, ha, ha!"

*We have been too long asea if that crudity passes
for humor.*

"My wife has a *garden*. Betimes she likes me to
till it for her . . . with me *hoe*. Ha, ha, ha!"

Yea, way too long.

"You are so full of shit, but then *manure* is good for the *soil*. Ha, ha, ha!"

Do they think I will be shocked by their coarseness? If they only knew, I have heard far worse. Drifa had been raised in a keep of fighting men, ofttimes two hundred warriors in residence at one time. It was not the first time she had heard that word.

"When my *lily blooms*, it wants naught but a wet furrow to rest in. Ha, ha, ha!"

I have seen your lily, Otto, and it is naught to brag about.

"Someone best tell the princess to get up off her *flower bed* and come see what is on the horizon."

It did not matter that the seamen made mock of her with their floral jests. Better that than toss her overboard as had been threatened more than once when they'd been hit with one misery after another and the food supply had dwindled down to the hated lutefisk.

In their defense—not that they needed defending—although Njord, the god of the seas, had been kind to them with good weather, it had been a long, tiresome journey from the Norselands to Constantinople, or the city the Vikings called Miklagard, Great City. They had come by way of the Dneipr, where they'd had to weather sea storms, cataracts, sandbanks, and treacherous shoal waters. Not all the waterways were connected and portage had been necessary on occasion, requiring the seamen to carry the longships overland on their shoulders.

Also, in their defense, this was a trip that had been forced on them. They resented Drifa mightily.

She must have dozed off then because next she was aware there was a leather-clad toe nudging her hip. Glancing up sleepily, she saw Wulfgar of Wessex, commander of the small fleet, including her own *Wind Maiden*; he was one of the few Saxons aboard. "We are almost there, Princess Drifa," he announced in his usual dour way.

"Really? Truly?"

"Really. Truly." His voice reeked with sarcasm as he turned abruptly and walked away.

The grump!

Rising, she straightened her hair that lay in one long braid down her back and fluffed out her gown. And then she gasped at what she saw.

The sun was about to set as the four longship prow heads of fierce dragon, wolf, raven, and bear plowed through the rolling waves approaching Constantinople. The Golden City certainly earned its name this day as its onion domes and fanciful turrets, marbled facades and mosaic tiles sparkled like vibrant jewels.

And the gardens! Ah! Even from this distance, she could see that the vibrant colors of the terraced gardens added to the aura of precious stones.

For Drifa, who loved flowers, this journey was a long-held dream come to fruition. In fact, she'd been obsessed with plants from an early age. And where better to study them than the Imperial Gardens of Miklagard.

The specially made chest she carried with her everywhere contained sharpened quills, brushes made of silky sable and camel hair, and hundreds of parchment sheets displaying drawings of plants, listing their origins and characteristics. An expensive pastime, for a certainty, considering the rarity of parchment, except for that allotted the monk scribe illuminators, but then she had an immense dowry just sitting there these twenty and nine years. Leastways, that was how she justified her passion to her father and four married sisters.

Not that she hadn't been tempted to follow the path of most normal women. There had been that one man, of course. Sidroc of Vikstead. But, nay, she had forgotten about him long ago, or she tried to, which was nigh impossible with his daughter Runa prancing about Stoneheim like a young lamb. Drifa had to smile just thinking about the little imp and how she had ingrained herself in the hearts of all of them. Her only regret about this journey was how much she would miss the little dearling.

By some strange quirk of fate, the Norns of Fate no doubt, Drifa had gotten herself involved with the abduction of Sidroc's daughter. With good intentions, she'd brought the baby back to Stoneheim where Sidroc should have still been lying unconscious from her blow to his fool head, but, lo and behold, the dunderhead had gone, his whereabouts still unknown. He was dead for all she knew.

She had mixed feelings about that. She wanted Sidroc to be found, still living. Of course she did, though the prospects of that were dim after five years. But a true mother could not love Runa more. In fact, the child called Drifa Mother, despite Drifa's initial corrections. Above all else, Drifa feared that Sidroc, if he was alive, might take Runa away. Why would he not?

No one, other than her sisters, knew of the child's origins. Most folks just assumed Runa was an orphan child Drifa had adopted. Most of all, Drifa worried that Jarl Ormsson might discover the whereabouts of the child and make her a slave, just for spite.

She called herself back to the present with a shake of her head to clear it of unwelcome what-might-have-beens.

Unlike her, many of the sailors, mostly Vikings, had traveled to the wondrous capital of the Byzantine empire afore, some having served in the emperor's elite troop of Norsemen, the Varangian Guard. Still, this sight on arrival must surely amaze even their hardened souls. It would be a work of art if it could ever be conveyed to canvas.

She went over to the rail next to Wulf. "Sorry I am if I am responsible for your ill-temper."

" 'Tis not you. Well, not you entirely," he added with an unapologetic lack of grace. "I have been listening to the complaints and inane jests of not just two hundred seamen but my fellow *hersirs* since we left the Norselands three sennights ago." He motioned with his head toward the two well-dressed men on his other side. *Hersirs* were commanders of troops in their own right.

One of them, Jamie the Scots Viking, spoke up now. "Salt air gives me a rash, Wulf. I canna stop itching. A bath would be welcome to me braw body." Jamie's deep, rolling brogue was known to cause women to melt, according to his own assessment, and men to cringe . . . like fingernails scraping on a rock.

"I was going to tell you about that. Your *braw* body is ripe, m'friend," offered Thork Tykirsson of Dragonstead, the most untamed, outrageous Viking ever born to ride a longship. Thork pinched his nose as he spoke, giving his voice a nasal whine.

Jamie elbowed Thork, who elbowed him back. This went on for several long minutes. You'd think they were youthlings instead of grown men of twenty and more who happened to be seasoned warriors. Her father would not have entrusted her to their care if they were not. When her eyes connected with Wulf's, she could tell that he was thinking the selfsame thing.

But then Alrek, another Viking *hersir*, tripped over a coil of rope and got thrown betwixt the two dumb dolts at the ship's rail. The young man was not known as Alrek the Clumsy for naught. Luckily his sword was still in its scabbard and he had not stabbed himself in the leg, as he'd done more than once in the past. Or worse, had launched himself over the rail into the Sea of Marmosa. Drifa's sister Tyra, a woman warrior, had trained Alrek herself, and had scars to show for it.

Ignoring Wulf's continuing glower, Drifa said, more to herself than anyone else, "I cannot wait to see the Imperial Gardens."

"Huh?" Alrek said after straightening. "Me, I want to go to the chariot races at the Hippodrome. I heard they have teams of four colors who compete against each other for grand prizes. Gold coins usually, but betimes a solid silver helmet. Mayhap I could enter a race, though I have no use for a solid silver helmet. Mayhap it could be melted down."

Alrek's words seemed to stun them all. Alrek on a chariot with spiked wheels was a horrifying prospect.

"Och! I prefer to watch the dancing girls in the Pleasure Palace. 'Tis a fact, fair maidens, no matter the country, like to see what I wear under me *pladd*. Not you, of course, m'lady." This from Jamie, of course, who winked at her with mischief in his dancing eyes. He wore the traditional *léine* and *brat*—the *léine* being a saffron-colored shert that hung down to his knees, leaving bare his hairy legs, and the *brat* or *pladd*, which could only be described as a blanket attached at the shoulder like a mantle and wrapped around his body, leaving his sword arm free. It was secured with a thick leather belt around his narrow waist. Quite a sight! Especially when he now flicked up the back of the strange Highland garment to demonstrate, thus exposing the hard globes of his buttocks to the rowers who sat on their sea chests along both sides of the ship. Not to her, of course, but to everyone else.

While the crew burst out in laughter, and Wulf was still muttering about the reference to "fair maidens" in a "Pleasure Palace," Thork put in his two pence. "Forget dancing. 'Tis other body activity I have a yen for."

"A yen?" Jamie hooted. "Doona be daft, man. 'Tis more like a full-blown, goat-worthy lust."

"Goat? What goat?" Alrek wanted to know.

"Bloody hell! Have you men no sense, speaking

so coarsely in front of the king's daughter?" Wulf chastised the lot.

The three *hersirs* ducked their heads and mumbled their apologies.

Addressing Drifa, Wulf said, "I have ten years on these lackwits, but betimes it feels like fifty."

It was true that Wulf appeared much more serious than the others, but she knew that they shared a hatred for the Saxon king Edgar, fed by a long list of personal injustices and downright crimes. Rumor was that they had sworn a blood vow two years ago to make the monarch's life as miserable as possible, which they did by acting as outlaws on land and pirates on sea, doing whatever they could, barring murder, to harass the king.

Still addressing her, Wulf added, "We can spend three days here, at most, if we want to intercept any of the royal shipments being sent for Edgar's coronation." Wulf spoke freely to her of their "illegal" acts because he knew that her father supported him wholeheartedly.

"Coronation! Pfff!" exclaimed Jamie. "The scoundrel has been king for more than ten years now. Why he needs a crowning at this point is beyond my ken."

"Money, pure and simple," Thork proclaimed. "It always comes down to more coin and treasure for the royal coffers, which give him more power to continue with his brutal acts."

"Actually, he could not be crowned afore now. 'Twas a penance handed down by Archbishop Dunstan for one of Edgar's many lecherous sins. No crown on his head for ten years. Plus he picked a time when all the rulers of surrounding countries could come pay him homage . . . or else." Alrek might be clumsy but he had a sharp head on his shoulders, in Drifa's opinion.

"I wish my penances were so simple. I would gladly go without a crown . . . or a hat for a few years," Thork complained. "One little lecherous act and my family has exiled me 'til I get my life in order."

Many sets of eyes turned on him.

"All right. Several lecherous acts."

"We can attack Edgar where it hurts, but only if we are in time to waylay some of those emissaries." Wulf was back on the subject of his continuing gripe.

Drifa felt her face bloom with color. "This side trip to deliver me to Miklagard was not a side trip at all, I am well aware, but I had no idea how long it would take. It has caused you a huge delay."

She suspected that her father had issued a request that was more like a threat. Not quite "Do this or die," but close. "It is always good policy to have friends in high places," she asserted defensively.

"Me . . . I prefer friends in low places," Thork said, "if you get my meaning." He waggled his eyebrows at her with exaggerated licentiousness.

Wulf took her by the elbow and steered her away from the others. "It's not too late, Drifa."

Drifa was not offended by Wulf's using her name in such a familiar fashion. She'd known Wulf ever since her sister Breanne married his best friend, Caedmon. Although he'd only been to Stoneheim this one time, and then just to pick her up, she'd met him on occasion in the Saxon lands at family gatherings.

"I worry about abandoning you in the middle of that snake pit court in the Golden City."

"You aren't *abandoning* me."

"Regardless of whether you are there by choice or not, you are ill-prepared for the atmosphere of corruption."

"Wulf," she said, as if he were a youthling she was about to lecture, "all courts are like that, whether they be Saxon, Norse, Arab, or Byzantine."

"Your own sister Tyra was kidnapped whilst here years ago."

"That was under a different emperor."

Wulf threw up his hands in frustration. "I don't know what your father was thinking."

"He sent four of his trusted warriors to guard me. Do not worry. Once I have completed my studies, I will go home." *My father has ensured that. Did he not make me promise that in return for this boon, I would wed on my return? Gods only know what prospects he will gather this time! In truth, he has run out of prospects. Still, I should wed and provide a real home for Runa. 'Tis time.* "Believe me, Wulf, come winter I will be home."

"I wish I could believe that."

CHAPTER FOUR

Viking spiders are the deadliest of all . . .

Sidroc Guntersson was sick to his Norse gills of
Byzantium.

He lay back relaxing his battle-weary muscles in
the warm waters of the bathing pool, in his private
chambers at the Blue Palace. They had more palaces than fleas here in Miklagard. Occasionally he
used his big toe to turn a lever that allowed more
hot water to enter. You had to admire the skills of
the ancient Romans who first held Byzantium.

A slave girl had gone off to get him fresh drying
linens. Finn was in an adjoining chamber having
his nude body massaged with oil by an equally
nude houri; knowing him, he was probably having
her pluck his stray man-hairs, as well. And Sidroc's
mistress, Ianthe Petros, would soon arrive to take
care of his other needs.

Thinking on those needs, he smiled and reached
a hand down to his half-limp cock, giving it a quick
squeeze, like a promise of attentions to come. His
favorite appendage became immediately alert.
That was not surprising. What was surprising was
the size of the thickenings he got ever since that

bloody head drilling. Not that he was complaining, nor were the women who shared his bed furs.

One might think that, with all these pleasures, he would be content. Not so! Life was good at the moment, true, but Sidroc knew too well that it would not last.

After five long years serving in Emperor John Tzimisces's Varangian Guard, much of it under the direction of the wily General Sclerus, he had enough of greedy rulers, berserk commanders, and often unwarranted killings on a scale so massive and bloody it made even a Viking cringe. He would fight to the death to save himself, those close to him, women or children in peril, and rulers with just causes to fight. But that was it. No more!

He had just returned from yet another of the endless Byzantine battles, mostly against the Moslems, including the defeated powerful border emir Saif ad-Dawlah. If he never saw sand, camels, or tents again, he would be a happy man. Of course that had been only slightly better than his posting in the freeze-your-arse Balkans before that. Thank the gods, the Bulgarians finally surrendered, but then only after losing thirty thousand men in a five-year war.

Suffice it to say, he had well earned the vast treasure he'd amassed for his service as a commander in the Varangian Guard. Finally he would be able to purchase an estate, possibly in the Orkneys, where many Vikings had settled, only a day's longship ride from the Norselands. The best part was that the weather never got brutally cold, and it was far enough away from his father and brothers, though the other side of the world would be even better. On the other hand, he was a Viking, born and bred. The ice of the North was in his veins. 'Twas a hard decision to make when choosing a home. If it were not for his father . . .

The only question was how to broach the termination of his service to the emperor in a diplomatic way, one that would result in the release of his annual pay and not land him in prison, or dead. The Byzantines hated to lose their mercenaries—actually, any of their soldiers—because they feared that the secret of Greek Fire, which they'd invented, would leave the country. Sidroc and Finn had made sure never to associate themselves with the incendiary substance that ignited almost magically and could be used ruthlessly against enemies. It was once used against an invading force of ten thousand Russians, and they were all killed. Yes, the less they knew the better, he and Finn had always contended.

Another reason for diplomacy in resigning was that the emperor could be peevish and spontaneously vicious on occasion, without warning or excuse. Like the manner in which he and others before him castrated all royal illegitimate sons and sent the illegitimate daughters to convents for life. Betimes they plucked out an eye, just for good measure. At least the emperor left them living. Unlike Sidroc's father.

He still raged betimes over his father's cruelty and the loss of his baby daughter. The old man had married twice more since he'd seen him last and had five more children, only one of them to his wives, or so he had heard. He wondered how many of those he'd permitted to live, considering his lack of regard for Signe.

He smarted, as well, over the ill-treatment he'd suffered at Drifa's hand. Every time he got an aching head, he was reminded of her blow. He wouldn't have the bitch now if she were served up to him on a silver trencher, bare-arsed naked with an apple in her devious mouth.

He had to be thankful that Finn—and six seamen—had held him down on his longship when they left Stoneheim five years before, to prevent him from returning to Vikstead and cutting out his father's cold heart. As rewarding as that deed might have been to him emotionally, it would surely have resulted in his own death by his brothers and the Vikstead warriors, or at the very least being outlawed from his homeland by King Harald Bluetooth.

Despite his bad experience with Princess Drifa, he would seek a wife, but not right away. He could bring his mistress, Ianthe, with him, but he doubted she would be happy in colder climes, away from her Greek culture. There was a change of seasons here in Byzantium, even snow in the winter, but summers, like today, were very hot and humid. Winters in the Norselands were not for the faint of heart. Nay, he would settle a sum of coins on her, for which she would no doubt show her thanks in the way she knew best. He smiled at the erotic mind picture that prompted.

Someday he hoped to make his father—and Drifa—pay, pathetic and immature as that might be. He alternated the subject of his periodic tirades between Drifa and his father. Every time he had to suffer sand in every body orifice when on desert patrols, he muttered, "Someday, princess (Father), you will pay." Or when he was wet and shivering cold in Bulgaria, he muttered, "Someday, princess (Father), you will pay." Or when he had to maneuver his way amongst the bloodthirsty politics of the imperial family (they were wont to murder each other whenever an opportunity arose), he muttered, "Someday, princess (Father), you will pay." Or when he walked a tightrope of diplomacy between the court contenders-to-power and the military leaders out in the field, he muttered, "Someday, princess (Father), you will pay." Or when he was forced to don the ridiculously opulent uniform of the Varangian Guard for palace duty, he muttered, "Someday, princess (Father), you will pay." Or when the empress and her royal ladies sent him off on an errand to do this or that to appease their lusty appetites, he muttered, "Someday, princess (Father), you will pay." Or when he thought of his little daughter, long dead now, he muttered, "Someday, princess (Father), you will pay."

"Master," the slave girl carrying a stack of drying cloths said as she approached on silent, shoeless feet across the mosaic tiled, marble floor. "Would you like me to dry you now?"

Sidroc glanced up at the girl whose barely developed body was visible through her thin bathing shift. She bowed her head and stood still under his perusal. 'Twas obvious she would be willing if he was so inclined. He was not.

"Leave the linens and tell my mistress, Ianthe, to enter when she arrives."

With a sigh of relief, the girl scooted away. He should be offended, but he just laughed.

Just then Finn walked in, his nude body shiny with enough oil to boil a boar. He eyed the maid's backside as she departed.

"She is too young for you," Sidroc said as he stood and began drying his long hair.

"Dost think so?" Finn sank down onto a bench and braced one foot on the other knee, examining his toenails, which looked fine to Sidroc.

"Aren't you going to wipe off all that oil?"

Finn looked surprised. "Nay. The whole point is to keep the skin soft."

A Viking with soft skin? "You'll slip off your horse."

" 'Tis not a horse I intend to ride forthwith."

"Really, with all that oil, you'll blister liked a greased pig in the sun here."

"Speaking of that . . ." Finn stood and showed him his backside. "Lita pointed out to me that—"

"Lita?"

"The houri who just massaged me." He waved a hand dismissively. "She pointed out that I am not sun-bronzed all over." He pointed to his white arse. "She suggests I lie in the sun naked for a while to even out my bronzing, front and back."

"Finn, you are a lackwit."

His friend grinned.

Betimes Sidroc could not tell when Finn was jesting or not. "We are becoming too soft, Finn."

To his surprise Finn nodded and began to wipe

some of the oil from his body. "When we were in the Norselands, 'twas not uncommon to bathe in an icy fjord."

"Recall that one winter when we had to break the ice afore jumping in," Sidroc added. 'Twas odd the things one missed when far from home. When he was back in a smoky, drafty longhouse, he would no doubt miss the beauty and warm sun of Byzantium.

"I'm going to ask the emperor to release me from my duties," Sidroc informed his friend while he was dragging on a pair of *braies* . . . not those ludicrous big-legged *braies* the Varangians wore whilst at court.

"If you leave, so do I."

It was a subject they'd discussed numerous times before. Sidroc still kept a longship here in Miklagard with a minimal crew of seamen. Leaving would be no problem. Leaving with permission and an extra pouchful of gold was another matter entirely.

"You will ne'er guess who is coming to court," Finn said of a sudden.

"Someone is always coming to court," Sidroc said.

"Yea, but this someone is different."

Noting Finn's expression of impending doom, Sidroc braced himself, just arching a brow in question.

"Princess Drifa of Stoneheim is coming to the Imperial Court."

Sidroc's eyes went wide. "Here? To Miklagard?"

Finn nodded, gleeful with his news. "She has come to study flowers, of all things."

Sidroc cared not why Drifa was coming here. At last, at long last, he was to be given his opportunity. In a bit of fanciful musing, he imagined himself the spider and her the unwary bug about to be drawn into his web.

With a wicked grin, he closed his eyes again and murmured, "Princess Drifa, you are about to pay."

Fancy meeting you here, dearling . . .

The longships drew closer to the wharves lining the deepwater harbor. In fact, the city was built on an elevation surrounded on three sides by water— the Golden Horn to the north, the Bosphorus to the east, and the Sea of Marmosa on the south, all of which provided natural defenses against enemies.

A retinue of well-dressed Greek men could be seen approaching down the stone steps from the parapets in the sea wall of one of the many palaces. Their welcoming party, she assumed. Her father would have sent word ahead ensuring she would be treated according to her rank during her sojourn.

Once they emerged onto land, she, flanked by her four-*hersir* escort, was greeted with solemn ritual by a short, balding man wearing the most opulent jade silk robe she'd even seen on a man. It was edged and belted with gold. He wore rings on several fingers, one of them having a ruby the size of a pigeon egg. "I am Senator David Phocas, here on behalf of Emperor John Tzimisces, and this"— he motioned to the tall, ascetic-looking man in

regal church robes at his side—"is our most revered Patriarch Antony of the Hagia Sophia cathedral, the papal legate in Byzantium. We welcome
Your Highness, Princess Drifa of Stoneheim. May
your stay in our imperial city be one of peace and
joy."

Luckily Drifa had prepared well for her journey and had studied the Greek language this past
year with an elderly Greek slave her father had
purchased for just that purpose. Mina had been
supposed to travel with her to Byzantium but had
become ill a month past and was still recovering.

Drifa bowed her head to the senator. "It is my
pleasure to finally enter your wonderful country."
To the high priest, Drifa, according to prearranged
ritual, bowed from the waist with her right hand
touching the ground. When she rose up, she placed
her right hand over the left, palms up, and said,
"Bless, Your Grace."

The patriarch raised the fingers of one hand in
the shape of a Christogram. Holding that hand
toward her, he pronounced, "May the Lord God
of all people bless you."

She assumed that "of all people" was meant to
let her know that even Vikings were blessed by the
One-God. Drifa nodded and then pointed to each
of the men beside her in turn. "Accompanying me
are Lord Wulfgar of Wessex in the Saxon lands,
Thork Tykirsson, son of the high chieftain Tykir
Ericsson of Dragonstead in the Norselands, Laird
James Campbell from the land of the Scots, and
Alrek, a noted warrior who serves my father good
and well." She also turned to show the four war-

riors standing rigidly at attention behind her. "My guardsmen."

She hoped she gave her welcoming party pause: she did not come unprotected to an alien land. "We thank you for your warm greeting," she added. "I bring gifts for your emperor from my father, King Thorvald."

"An audience will be arranged for you," Senator Phocas told her, "though the court is very busy at the moment preparing for the emperor's wedding. We have assigned chambers for you in the Garden of Sun Palace."

This was news to her. That she would be housed in a sun palace was wonderful, of course, but she'd been unaware of a pending royal wedding. The former warlord had become a widower many years before and had chosen the unmarried state thereafter, unusual for a monarch whose duty was to provide heirs, none of which he had yet. She had always thought there must be a story there.

"Come, my lady, we have provided for you a special escort to take you to your rooms. There is a curfew in the city, and the palace gates close from late afternoon to dawn. Just a precaution to keep the peace," the senator said. Then he beamed as he announced, "Your guards will be your own countrymen, by the by. Varangian guardsmen."

If the emperor's representative and the church leader were dressed with opulence, the Varangians' attire could only be described as splendid, a far cry from the garments back home, even when they were made of fine materials. They wore tunics of soft red wool, long sleeved and so tight along the forearm that they must be sewn on. That tightness caused the excess fabric to billow out above the elbows. Rich embroidery decorated the neckline, hem, and wrists of the garments in panels showing intertwining leaves of gold and silver thread. The men, all exceedingly tall, mostly with blond hair, wore *braies* of brilliant yellow and blue and pearly white that resembled loose pantaloons down to the knees, where they met highly polished black leather boots. *Chalmys*, long purple cloaks denoting the imperial guard status, were fastened on the right shoulder with brooches bearing the military insignia of the emperor, leaving the right arm free for weapons.

"Good gods!" Thork murmured from her one side.

"Like peacocks, they are," Jamie murmured from her other side. "I'd like a pair of those breeches in blue."

"It must take them hours to get clothed in the morn," Alrek added.

"They are too pretty, by half," Wulf concluded.

Luckily, all their remarks were low enough not to be overheard, but she suspected that the smirks on her *hersirs'* faces told all.

The senator motioned for the Varangians to step forward. Anticipating her pleasure at meeting some of her countrymen in this foreign land, he smiled and stepped aside, giving her a first close-up view of the colorfully dressed men in the emperor's elite attire.

But she did not smile.

Standing at attention, dead center of the seven

Varangians, was a chestnut-haired man spearing her with luminous gray-green eyes, not unlike the much-loved girling, Runa, back at Stoneheim. It was none other than Sidroc Guntersson.

He, too, was not smiling.

CHAPTER FIVE

In the still of the night . . .

As they were led, Varangians to the front of them, Varangians to the back of them, through one street after another, then one palace corridor after another, Drifa's head swung right and left, like a copper weather vane of a rooster she'd seen one time atop a cotter's barn.

The senator and high priest had departed for the Imperial Palace, where some feast or other was being held, leaving her in the care of the emperor's guard. Apparently she was not invited, not that Drifa would have wanted to attend in her travel-worn garments.

A huge Nubian chamberlain with rings of keys hanging from his belt—a eunuch by the looks of his smooth-faced, almost feminine features—was leading them to their assigned rooms in one of the smaller palaces. It appeared as if many of the lesser palaces were connected to the central palace by opened-sided passageways, like spokes on a wheel. Everywhere there were fragrant gardens and tinkling fountains. Drifa couldn't wait to examine them.

"I feel as if I've entered Asgard, a paradise beyond description," Alrek whispered at her side.

"The only thing missing is a few dozen—" Jamie started to say.

"Valkyries," the rest of her group finished for him.

They all laughed, even some of the Varangians. Not Sidroc, though, she noticed, turning to peer at him over her shoulder. Mayhap he took his guardsman duties seriously, never daring to waver from watchfulness, and that was the reason for his sour demeanor. Probably not, though, because when she glanced to his side, his friend Finn winked at her.

Turning forward once again, her face flamed. She would need to talk to Sidroc soon, and how he would take news of Runa's—nay, Signe's—presence at Stoneheim boded ill for Drifa. Her greatest fear was not his fury over her striking him down, but that he would take Runa away from her. But she would not let that prospect dampen her spirits on this great adventure of hers.

Drifa's mind and all her senses boggled at the passing scenery. As dusk rose over the city like a gossamer cloak, colors swirled and changed on the marble, glass, and mosaic tiles. All the splendor was highlighted by the gold dome of the magnificent Hagia Sophia cathedral in the distance.

Finally they entered the Sun Palace, a structure of pink marble flecked with green malachite chips. It was three floors high and built in the shape of a cross, with a huge garden in its center, and a number of smaller gardens or grottos along each arm. She, her four guardsmen, and the four *her-*

sirs were assigned one whole arm of the cross on the ground level. If this was a lesser palace, as the apologetic senator had implied, Drifa could not imagine what would be grander.

"Look at those tapestries." Thork pointed to one of the walls. "My mother would swoon with envy." The enormous tapestry in question depicted the Last Supper, the One-God religion's Christ with his twelve disciples.

Drifa had met Thork's mother, Lady Alinor of Dragonstead. She was far-famed for her sheep and uniquely woven wool fabrics.

"Mayhap you could purchase a tapestry—a much smaller one—to take back to her," Wulf suggested.

"Me too. And some painted tiles. And cuttings from those flowers over there." Drifa smiled. "I fear my longship will be overflowing with goods when I return home."

"And this just your first day here," Wulf observed, a rare smile of indulgence on his handsome face.

"Perchance you will bring a new husband home with you, too," Thork added with a twinkle in his mischievous eyes.

She heard a snorting sound behind her, and knew with certainty that it was Sidroc.

"Nay, I have had enough of devious, full-of-themselves men. I much prefer digging in my garden and a good pile of . . . manure."

There was another snort behind her. And much laughter from her guardsmen and *hersirs*, although they could not know that it was a directed remark.

"I thought we had some fine castles in the Highlands, but they are huts compared to this," Jamie remarked. "If I brought any of these fine objects home to gift my parents, they would look out of place in the untamed, bare-bones surroundings. Like gold plating a pigsty."

"There is charm in the wildness of the Highlands," Drifa asserted.

"Yea, there is," Jamie agreed with a grin that implied there was wildness, and then there was *wildness*.

Wulf added his opinion. "A rich cream sauce on a breast of pigeon is welcome on occasion, but betimes a thick slab of bloody, hearth-roasted boar better suits."

"Wine is fine, but beer is better?" Thork asked.

"Precisely," Wulf said. "And, believe you me, wine flows in Byzantium like mead in the Norselands."

Once they had all been shown to their chambers and Drifa was introduced by the chamberlain to her new maid, Anna, a Greek slave girl, Drifa thought she was finally alone, but nay, Sidroc was outside in the corridor talking to Ivar, one of her guardsmen, an older man who was a long-time comrade of her father's.

Well, this was her opportunity. "Sidroc, I need to speak with you."

He held up a halting hand. "And I have things to say to you, as well, but not now."

"When?"

He smiled, and it was not a pleasant smile. "At my convenience, m'lady." On those words, he walked lazily after his comrades, his black polished boots clicking on the marble floor.

Sidroc seemed so angry with her. Why? She had rejected his suit, but surely he had to admit that he'd given her cause. Well, she had struck him over the head and he had been in a death-sleep for six sennights, but she had not meant to do him such harm. Still, that must be the reason for his fury. Once she informed him that his daughter was at Stoneheim and thriving, he would probably be thankful, and all would be well again.

Or not.

She would not think on it now. Later.

"What was he discussing with you, Ivar?" she asked.

"Just warning me of the perils to watch for here in Miklagard, and in the palace itself."

"Oh? Is there something in particular I need to worry about?"

Ivar shook his head. "Nay, as long as we guard you well, your safety is assured."

"Beware of snakes in the garden, however, princess," Wulf said, coming up to them. "And I do not mean the crawling-on-the-ground kind. I have warned you afore, and will do so again, there are devious men, and women, in this court who would slit a person's throat whilst offering words of welcome. The daughter of a Norse king would make a valuable captive for ransom."

Drifa rolled her eyes. All these warnings were becoming tiresome, but it was interesting that Sidroc was concerned for her safety. A good sign, surely. She held to that positive thought until later that night when she was enlightened to his true sentiments.

For hours she'd been restless, unable to sleep. A new bed in a new country. The unfamiliar sounds of water trickling in the fountain of the small garden separated from her bedchamber by only a latticed wall. A more secure wall could be pulled closed and locked at night, which she should have done, and, in fact, had promised her guards she would do.

Her mind was also occupied with the numerous things she wanted to see and do during her short stay in Byzantium, and, yea, three months was not nearly enough time, but longer than she wanted to be parted from Runa. Worry over Sidroc's obvious anger also kept her awake.

Mayhap she should get up and close that wall now.

But she did not.

So it was her fault that just as she'd slipped into a light slumber she heard a rustling sound in her room. Before she could open her eyes, thinking it was probably Anna, who'd already checked on her three times, a heavy weight landed on her and a hand pressed over her mouth, stifling her scream. A man, she decided.

Whoever it was said nothing as she squirmed, trying to dislodge him. He just lay on her like a dead weight, almost suffocating her. One hand held her wrists over her head. The other hand still pressed against her mouth. His legs were wrapped around hers. She was immobilized.

"I am going to lift my hand. When I do, if you make even a squeak, I swear, I will strip you naked and blister your backside with the flat of my broad-sword."

It was Sidroc.

"Do you understand, princess?"

Before she had a chance to respond, he released his hand over her mouth, and she began, "Are you demented? How did you get in here?"

"Uh-uh! Bad girling! Bad! I told you to remain silent. Well then, you must prefer I do this." He put a hand over her breast, and began to massage it roughly. She was wearing only a thin sleep rail, and it was as if he was touching her bare flesh. Even worse, she could feel his thickening against her thigh.

She made a whimpering sound.

"Does that mean you are ready to remain silent whilst I talk?"

She nodded.

"You will speak only when I ask a question. There is naught else you have to say of interest to me."

If you only knew!

He took his hands off her mouth and wrists and rose to a kneeling position, his rump resting lightly on her legs.

"You are in such trouble, Drifa. Why did you come to Byzantium?"

"To study flowers."

"Did you know I was here?"

"What?" That question surprised her. "Why would I come here if . . . oh, I see. You think I am chasing after you." She made a tsking sound of disgust.

"You were hot for me once," the cad pointed out. She started to say something and he wagged a forefinger at her. "Speak only in answering my questions. Remember."

She pressed her lips tightly together, but her eyes shot daggers at him.

He just laughed. "So, have you killed any more men since I saw you last?"

"I did not kill you."

"You tried."

"I did not! I merely tapped you on the head with a pitcher. How was I to know your head was eggshell thin and would crack so easily? Do you behave in this lackbrained manner because some of your brains seeped out?"

"Nay, but a part of me has grown larger. Foolish maid, did I not tell you to remain silent?" He leaned forward a bit so that the bulge beneath his *braies* touched her nether parts.

Noting with hysterical irrelevance that he wore typical Norse attire now, not the Varangian uniform, she gasped and tried to push against his chest. "You brute! You ignorant oaf. Leave off!"

Which only caused him to take her hands in his again, lacing them on either side of her head. Then in one fluid move, he hooked her ankles with his and spread her legs wide. Arching back on extended arms, his position made his hard rod fit itself into her woman-channel. Only his *braies* and her sleep rail separated them.

To her dismay, *it* seemed lodged against a part of her in such a way that even the slightest movement caused ripples of pleasure to sweep out to other parts of her body. "You have no right to treat me with such disrespect."

"Keep your voice down, lest one of your guards hear. See this knife in my belt sheath. It is sharp enough to split the hairs on a witch's whisker. I would hate to kill one of my countrymen on his first night in the Golden City."

"You would not!" It was hard to speak when she was trying to keep her body stiff and unmoving down below.

"I would. And it would be your fault for having a running tongue."

Whff, whff, whff, she huffed inwardly, fighting the rising arousal that just his body pressure was causing. If it were lighter in the room—there was only the moonlight seeping through the lattice-work—he would see that the skin on her face and other places was flushed. "Can I ask a question?"

"Just one."

"Why are you doing this?"

"Because I can."

She frowned with confusion. "One more question. Are you trying to seduce me into marriage again?"

"Are you being seduced?" He studied her closer and ran the knuckles of one hand over her breast, causing the nipple to peak.

The ripples turned into waves. Erotic waves.

"Marriage is no longer an option after your crimes," Sidroc continued.

His insult stopped her pleasure waves like a dam rising abruptly in a fjord. Fortunately. Then another thought came to her unbidden. "Are you already married?"

"Nay."

Yet another thought occurred to her as she puzzled his odd demeanor. *Crimes? More than one? Oh nay! Surely he does not know about Runa?* "Do you intend to wed, ever? Do you not want children?"

"Why are you speaking?" He ground himself against her. Once. Twice. Thrice.

She closed her eyes for a moment and almost wept at the joyful torture.

"If I do wed and, gods willing, if I fill my longhouse with babes, 'twill not be with the likes of a bloodthirsty wench such as you. I would sooner have a wolf than you to mother my sons and daughters."

That was cruel and unwarranted, and what did it say about Runa and what he would do if he discovered his daughter was alive and that she wanted—nay, intended—to keep the child in her care? Would he consider her an unfit mother, rather, caretaker?

She had to tell him.

Just not yet.

"But that does not mean I will not rut with you. By now you have surely lost your maidenhead."

"And if I have?"

"It matters not a whit to me. Your experience in the bed arts will be more appreciated than a fumbling virgin's lack of skill."

Just then there was a tap on the door, and Ivar

said, "Princess Drifa, are you all right? I heard voices."

Quickly, before she could say him nay, Sidroc rolled over to his back and tucked her in at his side, her head on his shoulder. A sharp knife was pressed at her breast on the other side. "Enter," he said.

Ivar opened the door hesitantly. "Princess?" Then noticing Sidroc, he drew his sword. "Guntersson! How did you get in here?"

"Princess Drifa let me in, did you not, sweetling?"

She nodded, feeling the sharp point of his knife cut through the cloth of her sleep rail. Turning her face away from him, she tried to gather her thoughts.

"My heartling is just shy," he told Ivar, then pressed a kiss to the top of her head. "Are you not, my little sweet cake?"

Sweet cake? Her head swiveled so that she could glare directly at him.

"Didst know that the princess and I were betrothed at one time, Ivar? We are . . . um, reconciling." He made the word *reconciling* sound lewd.

Ivar's eyes shot to her. With her scant clothing and her bruised lips that he would no doubt attribute to kissing, his indignation faltered. "This is the first I have heard of this. Tell me true, princess, do you want the knave gone, or not?"

She hesitated for only a second. "He will be leaving in a moment. Will you not, my big cow cake?" She batted her eyelashes at him.

Sidroc chuckled and told Ivar, "Leave us for a few moments, and I will be gone . . . for tonight.

We have a few matters to *discuss*." The implication was that they would get a quick swiving in yet.

The obnoxious dolt!

Now that the need for silence was gone, she turned on him. "Get up out of my bed. At once."

He rose, but just sat on the side of the bed, staring down at her.

She raised the bed linen up to her shoulders.

He laughed derisively before turning more serious. "You said earlier that you had something to say to me."

Hah! The time for that particular talk had passed. Still, there were some things that must be said. "I apologize for causing your injury. Not for the hitting, mind you. That you deserved. But I ne'er intended to do you such injury." She waited, expecting—nay, hoping—that he would accept her apology.

He did not.

"I did try to make reparations," she said.

He just arched his brows at her.

"We tried to find you. I mean, my father and Rafn sent longships hither and yon in an attempt to discover your whereabouts, but you disappeared." Again she waited for his acceptance of her words.

He said nothing. At first. Then he pointed out, "I lay abed, dying as far as you knew, and you went on a 'pleasure journey.' Do you wonder why I am so angry?"

"I can explain."

"Familiar words. Dost recall how many times I asked you to let me explain my rush to wed?"

She could feel her face heat. He was right. She

had refused to listen to his excuses. "I know now why you acted thus . . . your daughter."

He bristled. "How do you know about her?"

"Finn told us. Do not blame—"

He put up a halting hand. "I do not want my daughter's name to come from your tempting lips. Ever! She is dead and gone, and whilst you may not have wielded the weapon of her demise, you are partially responsible by keeping me from rescuing her in time."

"Wh-what?" she sputtered. *Holy Thor! The man thought Runa was dead. Now I really do need to tell him of her whereabouts.* "Sidroc, I have something important to tell you."

"There is naught of importance you could impart to me in my present mood. Now, continue with this lackbrained apology of yours."

She was the one who bristled now, even as her mind reeled with the news that he thought his daughter dead. "There was no excuse for the cold-blooded way in which you went after me."

He shrugged.

"Can I say one more thing about your dau— you know who?"

"Nay."

Despite his refusal, she blundered on, "What if others took matters into their hands whilst you were in a death-sleep?"

He stood abruptly and glared down at her. Nigh shaking with fury, he spat out, "You dare . . . you dare to blame me for Signe's death? You dare to imply that others did what I could not? I could kill you for that alone."

"That's not what I meant. I was merely—"

He waved a hand back and forth in front of his face.

"No more. I must needs leave afore you force me to kill your guardsman."

"What is it you want from me, Sidroc?" she asked tiredly.

"My father will pay one day for his perfidy, but you . . . It is not what I want, but what you will do. I lost six sennights of my life because of you, six extremely important sennights, and so much more. I intend to make you my bed thrall afore either you or I leave Byzantium. Six sennights. Forty-two nights you will pleasure me in the bed furs."

"Rape?"

"Nay. As I recall, your passions rode high when I touched you afore. They will again. Your embers will burn, believe you me."

He was deluded if he thought she would willingly accept him under that kind of threat. Even so, she asked, "In what halfwitted circumstances do you imagine that I would agree to be your anything?"

"Everybody has a weakness. I will discover yours, and then you will yield."

Drifa thought immediately of Runa and shivered.

"See, already I can see guilt on your devious face. What is it you hide, princess?"

"Not a thing," she lied, knowing she must change the subject, and quickly. "Assuming you could succeed, and I am unwilling to concede that you could, what if you breed a child on me?"

"I would take it from you. Like that." He snapped his fingers for emphasis.

Her blood turned to ice, but she could not let him see the effect his words had on her. *Think of something else, Drifa. Change the subject.* "You know, I have a gripe, too. Rafn told me what you said about me. 'Bugger the bitch.'"

"Appropriate, don't you think?"

"Nay, I do not. I could just as easily say 'Bugger the bastard.'"

"Go right ahead. Mayhap we can accommodate each other."

"You are such a vulgar man."

"A little bit of vulgarity adds spice to the sex act."

"I can't do this. I won't do this."

"You have no choice; princess or not, I will have you, and I will have you good and well, and often."

May the gods spare me from the arrogance of a Viking man! Not that it was ever going to happen, still she had to ask, "That will satisfy you?"

At first, he stared at her with contempt, but then he grinned down at her with blatant wickedness.

"I certainly hope so."

The more he learned, the more he fumed . . .

Sidroc was on a military exercise field within the Imperial Palace grounds the next morning when he was approached by one of the four *hersirs* who had accompanied Princess Drifa.

He recognized Wulfgar now, having met him one time briefly in Jorvik while Eric Bloodaxe had still been king of Northumbria. Wulfgar was a Saxon thane, heir to some vast estate in Wessex if he ever reconciled his differences with his estranged father, Ealdorman Gilford of Cotley. He knew this from Thork's uncle who was Lord Erik of Ravenshire, a half-Saxon, half-Viking nobleman who secretly supported Wulf's efforts against King Edgar.

"Guntersson," Wulfgar said in greeting, standing at the side of the arena where Sidroc had been in vigorous swordplay practice with Finn.

Swiping a forearm across his sweaty brow, Sidroc returned the greeting with "Cotley," and could see that Wulfgar was surprised at his knowing his full name.

"Call me Wulf," the man said, bristling. Obviously he preferred not to be known by his family name.

He could understand that. "Call me Sidroc."

The two men sized each other up. Of the same height and musculature, each recognized the other as an equal foe, if the need ever arose.

"Can you spare a moment?" Wulf inquired.

Sidroc nodded and walked over to the barrels of water. Taking a long draught from a cup that hung at the side, he motioned for Wulf to sit on a nearby bench. Joining him, Wulf observed his surroundings. " 'Tis an impressive display of military preparedness."

"You have no idea. This is only one of three fields where the Varangian Guard hone their skills, and there are three others for the tagmatic armies assigned to the palace. In addition, there are thematic armies throughout the empire. In all, tens of thousands of armed men, either off to battle, recovering from battle, or about to march off."

"I understand the emperor, John Tzimisces, is a former military man."

"He is. Well respected, too."

"And about to be married."

Sidroc rolled his eyes. "Wait 'til you see his betrothed. Her appearance will surprise you, but she *is* pious, you must credit her that. Was a nun most of her life."

"Piety is a requisite for marriage in Byzantium?" Wulf arched his brows at him.

Sidroc snorted. "Hardly. You will soon learn that, as religious as this nation purports to be— they have hundreds of churches in Miklagard alone—they are great practitioners of adultery. And fornication. But then they do penance. Most men of the upper classes have at least one mistress. Many have several."

"And you?"

Sidroc laughed, not at all offended by the question. "Only one."

"Have you enjoyed being a Varangian?"

Sidroc shrugged. "It has met its purpose for me. There is much wealth to be gained for good soldiers."

Wulf nodded.

"Are you interested in joining the guard?"

"Oh, good Lord, nay! I am engaged in another enterprise." He eyed Sidroc for a moment, as if wondering whether he could trust him, then told him about the pirate activities he led against King Edgar. "That is one of two reasons why I came here this morn. To see if you might be interested in joining us."

Ah, so that's why he approached me. Sidroc was surprised and, yea, flattered at the offer. "Mayhap later. In truth, I am about to resign from the Varangians, but I must needs build a home for myself. 'Tis time for me to set down roots."

"Where? Dost have a place in mind?"

"I'm considering the Orkneys, but I have not yet ruled out someplace in the Norselands. Wherever I choose, it will be far from my father's jarldom."

"I can understand the need to distance oneself from a father, believe you me," Wulf said. "At least consider it for the future."

"I will," Sidroc said. "You mentioned two reasons for approaching me. The other?"

"Stay away from Princess Drifa."

Sidroc stiffened. "Oh? And why would I do that? More important, why would you care? Are you interested in her yourself?"

"Nay! But she is under my protection whilst I am still here in Constantinople."

"And how long will you be here?" Sidroc asked coolly. He did not appreciate being bullied on personal matters, even in the guise of friendship.

"A few days. A sennight at the most. But Drifa has four guardsmen who will stay with her."

There was clear warning in Wulf's words, past the point of mere bullying, and he did not like it. Not one bit. "What makes you think I would harm her?"

"You entered her bedchamber in the middle of the night."

"And?" *Pray the gods that is all you know.*

"And I know that you were betrothed at one time."

"Drifa told you that?" *I would not think it was something she would be inclined to boast about.*

Wulf shook his head. "Her guard Ivar did. And he was not happy to discover you there."

"Still trying to figure out how I got in, is he?" He chuckled. "Do you know the circumstances surrounding that betrothal?"

"Nay."

"Why not ask Drifa?"

"I did."

And obviously had no success if his frown was any indication. Sidroc had to smile at that. The wench was stubborn with others, too. Not just him.

"What are your intentions toward the princess?"

By thunder, he sounds like her father. "That is none of your concern."

"It is if you mean her harm."

It depends on your definition of harm, my friend. "I will do naught without her consent."

"That is the worst non-answer I have ever heard."

And the best you are going to get. "Drifa is no longer a young maid. At twenty and nine years, surely she has the right to make her own decisions."

Wulf bristled. "Drifa is a princess with a powerful father. Her age has naught to do with anything. This is a great adventure to Drifa, one she will never repeat again, once she returns home to mother her child."

Her child? Sidroc jerked back as if he'd been slapped. "Drifa is married?" He tried to recall if he'd even asked that question since she'd arrived in Miklagard. Probably not. He'd just assumed.

"Nay, she is not married, and if you say one word defaming her honor, I swear you and I will engage in swordplay, and it won't be for practice."

"First you offer me work. Then you offer me threats."

"My apologies. I may have overreacted."

"Dost think so?" But then Sidroc decided to end the argument . . . for now. "Has she ever been married?"

"Not that I know of."

"How old is the child?"

"The child is irrelevant to our discussion."

"I beg to differ. How old is the child?" he gritted out.

Wulf shrugged, as if unsure. "Runa is four, I think, but I am not a good judge of children's ages. She could be three or six, for all I know." He threw his hands out in dismissal. "I have only been to Stoneheim once, and then only for a short time. I've never discussed the child with Drifa."

So the bitch let another man swive her, possibly soon after she rejected me. He hated the fact that he cared. Another misdeed to add to her list. *Oh, she will pay. She will surely pay.*

"Mayhap she adopted the child," Wulf offered.

And mayhap not.

"I expect she will wed on her return to Stoneheim," Wulf added. " 'Tis a promise she made her father in return for his permission to come to Byzantium."

"And is there a man picked out for that honor? Perchance even her baby's father?"

"I don't know. As I said, I don't even know if it is her birth child, although the girl does call her Mother." He eyed Sidroc suspiciously. "You were once close to the princess. Why not ask her yourself?"

"I intend to."

CHAPTER SIX

It was sort of a dinner date . . .

Drifa had a wonderful day, even though she chose not to accompany Wulf, Thork, Jamie, and Alrek to the Hippodrome for the chariot races. Instead she'd unpacked her travel chests and enjoyed the small garden outside her chambers.

She'd met one of the gardeners—there were seventy-five assigned to the various palace gardens—and he'd explained that hers was a butterfly garden. Already she'd taken out her parchments and sketched various plants and butterflies, noting which ones were attracted to which flower. Many of them would not prosper in the colder climates of the Norselands. She would certainly try, though.

Now she was heading toward the royal dining chambers for a feast to honor the soon-to-be queen. She had dressed with special care tonight, looking every bit a princess with her single braid, intertwined with pearls, coiled into a coronet atop her head like a crown. She wore Norse attire: a long-sleeved white undershift of gossamer-thin linen, ankle-length in front and dragging a pleated train in back. Over it was the traditional, open-sided, full-length apron of crimson silk, embroidered on all the edges with gold thread in a writhing wolf design, the same one as on the Stoneheim banner. The gold-linked belt about her waist and the rare bloodred amber pendant hanging from her neck were further demonstrations of her stature. She even wore light gold hoops over each ear, from which dangled thread-thin chains holding a dozen tiny rubies.

Her *hersir* companions had also dressed according to their high rank, complete with heavy, etched gold rings hugging their upper arms. Betimes appearances did matter, and this was one of them.

If she had been dazzled by the splendor of her surroundings yestereve, she was stunned by the demonstrations of wealth exhibited as they walked through the Imperial Palace. Fresco-painted plaster walls and ceilings, mosaic floors, marble fountains with bronze sculptures of animals spouting water, triptychs: the three-paneled, hinged, iconic paintings or carvings of the Christian God or his saints or the Blessed Mother, in little alcoves, furniture so finely carved and decorated, she feared they would break if anyone sat on them, and lighting fixtures hanging from the ceilings, some of which must hold a hundred candles, as well as oil lamps attached to the walls.

They were seated by the head chamberlain far down the great banqueting hall, on divans situated before low tables groaning under heavy gold plates, of such quality they could support a Norse family for several winters, beside which were silver knives and spoons. Until the meal would be served, the tables displayed sumptuous foods to be eaten with the fingers. Dates, olives, *botargo*—the eggs of salted mullet served on tiny squares of *paximadi*, a bone-hard Byzantine bread softened with wine—various cheeses, and some odd green nuts. Wine spiced with anise was poured into goblets of agate encrusted with colored stones. No rustic mead or drinking horns here.

It was no sign of disrespect that the princess was not seated closer to the dais, the chamberlain explained to her. There were so many heads of countries here to witness the emperor's upcoming wedding that it was difficult even to get everyone into the hall.

Almost immediately she realized that Sidroc, Finn, a few of the Varangians, and a beautiful Greek woman had followed them into the banquet hall and were being seated by the same chamberlain across their table.

Sidroc nodded his head at her.

"I hadn't expected to see you again so soon."

"The chamberlain probably thought to make you more comfortable with fellow countrymen. Little did he know I would as soon break your neck as break bread with you."

The woman who now sat beside Sidroc gasped at his rudeness, and Drifa's companions started to rise with outrage.

Drifa motioned for her defenders to sit down. "Pay no mind to the offensive boor. He is harmless."

Sidroc gave Drifa a look that said he would show her how harmless he could be.

The woman punched Sidroc in the arm with her little fist and hissed, "Behave," which struck Drifa as oddly intimate.

But then he surprised them all by saying, "My apologies, Princess Drifa. Betimes I have been out in the field with men too long, and I forget how to treat a lady."

What a load of boar droppings!

"Ianthe, this is Princess Drifa of Stoneheim," Sidroc began. Then to Drifa, he said, "And Princess Drifa, this is Ianthe Petros, my . . . friend."

Ianthe cast Sidroc a glance of consternation.

Clearly his mistress.

Sidroc also introduced Ianthe to Wulf, Thork, Jamie, and Alrek, who was staring at the Greek woman as if she were a goddess come to earth. In addition, he introduced Drifa and her *hersirs* to the three other Varangians with them, besides Finn.

There was some discussion then about what the men had witnessed at the Hippodrome that day. Apparently an unknown warrior had come on the scene to win an important race, for which he was awarded a Saracen stallion. One of the Varangians had participated in a chariot race recently and engaged them with harrowing tales of how close the spiked wheels came to each other and what happened when a spectator had fallen over the railing into their path. He'd also explained the whole system of racing at the far-famed Hippodrome, whereby teams of four colors entertained the crowds several days a sennight. And it was all free to the public.

Someone asked Drifa what she had done that

day and she told them about her garden and the intriguing manner in which certain flowers attracted certain types of butterflies. She planned to examine other gardens on the morrow after her scheduled audience with the emperor. The men were probably bored with her plant obsession, especially those with whom she'd traveled and had heard her prattle endlessly about this flower and that bush, but they pretended interest. One of the Varangians even mentioned that he'd seen a rose in Egypt one time that was so dark it appeared black.

"I would love to see that someday," Drifa said, on a sigh. As much as she knew about plants and flowers, there was so much she did not know or had never seen.

"Princess Drifa would as soon be gifted with a pretty weed as a fine jewel," Sidroc told his mistress with amusement.

Drifa would as soon lean across the table and clout the oaf with one of these gold plates, and she did not care if he was unconscious for another six sennights.

By the grin on his face, she could tell that he read her mind.

Ianthe watched the silent exchange between the two of them with interest. Then she addressed Drifa, "Princess Drifa—"

"Please, Ianthe, just call me Drifa."

"Speaking of jewels, Drifa," Ianthe began again with a smile, "what is that stone about your neck?"

"Ianthe is a jewelry maker," explained Finn, who had been occupied thus far with a woman on his other side . . . a woman whose husband was getting redder and redder in the face, either from excess wine or Finn's attentions to his spouse. In either case, 'twas best that Finn find another object for his affections.

"It is amber," Drifa told Ianthe, noticing for the first time the intricately crafted silver chain hanging from her neck like a spiderweb interspersed with pale blue stones. Pretty, loose wrist rings, also of silver, adorned both arms. She wore gold-braided sandals, the type of open shoe men and women alike favored in this warm climate.

Ianthe really was a beautiful woman, with golden eyes and light brown hair center-parted and coiled on either side of her head in the Greek fashion, all complemented by her long, sleeveless, green silk tunic in a style the Greeks called a *chiton*. Her skin had the olive cast of a true Byzantine.

In addition, Drifa noticed that the matching ear ornaments that Ianthe wore hung from pierced ears. Drifa did not know many women who put holes in body parts, in her part of the world, leastways. Some men did, though, especially sailors, which Vikings were. To some, it was a sign that they had traveled around the world. To others, it was payment for burial in the event they died at sea or in battle.

"Amber? Really?" Ianthe appeared fascinated. "I always thought amber was yellow or orange in color."

"Actually, amber comes in many colors," Thork interjected. "My father is a far-famed amber harvester and trader. I have seen amber clear as rain, yellow, orange, red, brown, green, blue, and even black, which is actually just dark shades of all these other colors."

Everyone looked at Thork with surprise. He was usually so frivolous. 'Twas hard to see him as a serious student of anything but play.

"We call it the Gold of the North," Drifa added.

"The most interesting amber has a small insect in it, or bits of a flower or leaf. Look at this one." Thork pulled an oval piece of amber the size of a flattened egg out of a side placket in his *braies*. It was yellow in color with flower petals inside forming a cross. "I carry it for luck."

"Like worry beads," Ianthe remarked.

"Exactly. I worry a lot," Thork said, winking at Ianthe.

Sidroc made a snorting sound of disgust, but Ianthe just smiled at Thork. The rascal.

"Actually, Ianthe, I have brought the emperor a gift of amber, a dozen stones of varying shades," Drifa said. "My meeting with him is not until tomorrow afternoon. Wouldst like to see them before that?"

"I would love to." Ianthe beamed at her offer. "But why not come to my shop so that I can show you my handiwork. It is located just outside the palace gates, walking distance. We can break fast and talk."

"That sounds wonderful."

Ianthe gave her directions.

Sidroc looked as if he'd swallowed a sour apple at the prospect of his mistress and former betrothed becoming friends.

Wulf and the others just laughed, except for

Alrek, who was still gaping at Ianthe with cow-eyed adoration. "I could accompany you, Princess Drifa," Alrek offered. Sidroc snorted again.

Alrek was a man who talked with his hands. He was also not known as Alrek the Clumsy for nothing. No one was surprised when one of his hands hit a goblet and wine flew everywhere, dousing his companions.

It was touching to see the way Alrek's friends covered for him, pretending not to see another example of his clumsiness. Would he ever outgrow it? Hardly, since he must have seen close to twenty and two winters already.

"Dost think you could arrange for your father to sell me some of his amber?" Ianthe asked Thork, trying to get attention away from red-faced Alrek, who was attempting to mop up his mess and making more of a mess of it. "I have worked with just about every stone there is, from crystals to diamonds, but not amber."

"Certainly," Thork said. "I will come to your shop with Drifa, if you wish . . . to give you more information."

He was fooling no one on the type of information he would like to convey, along with details about his father's trading merchandise.

"Me too," Alrek said again. "Princess Drifa will need extra protection in the busy marketplace."

Alrek, too, was fooling no one.

Oddly, Sidroc exhibited no jealousy over the men's interest in his mistress, although he did snipe, "Why don't we all come?"

"Are you being sarcastic?" Drifa inquired sweetly.

"Me?" He placed a hand over his heart with exaggerated innocence. He smiled at her then, and, oh, he had a very nice smile. She recalled in that moment why she had fallen for his seduction five years ago and braced herself to resist his dubious charms.

"Who other?" she snipped as Sidroc continued to play the innocent fool.

And, really, the oaf had some nerve threatening to make her a bed thrall when he already had a lovely mistress to satisfy his base urges. And sometime she was going to tell him exactly what she thought of his coming into her bedchamber in the middle of the night when he had no doubt just slipped out of Ianthe's arms.

Ianthe narrowed her eyes, studying the interplay between her and Sidroc, so Drifa quickly turned to Wulf and began talking about what he had planned for the next few days. The *hersirs'* stay in Miklagard had already been extended from a day or two to five as they saw and heard of more sights and activities they must witness.

When she glanced back again, Ianthe had her arm looped with Sidroc's and was leaning up to whisper something in his ear. He, in turn, whispered something in Ianthe's ear, which caused his mistress's cheeks to bloom with color.

Drifa felt an uncomfortable surge of jealousy, which was untenable to her. She didn't want the cad. She didn't!

The whole time they'd been talking, servers had been placing platter after platter before them.

They started with *kakavia*, a fish soup that had

mussels and chunks of white fish floating on top. Then there was a young goat, head intact, stuffed with garlic and leeks, as well as lamb and pork in many variations, roasted, and covered with sweet and savory sauces, a combination much favored by the Greeks. The Greeks, like the Vikings, enjoyed mustard with their meats, too.

Also, small wooden skewers held pieces of meat with vegetables, like carrots, onions, and something new to her, eggplant. Of course there was plenty of fish, fresh and saltwater, thanks to the nearby waterways, including snails and mussels still in their shells. Baby octopuses swam in leek butter garnished with parsley. Dolmades were rolled grape leaves filled with chopped meats and barley.

Many of the dishes were covered with *garos*, a fish sauce, or a white cream sauce called béchamel. Lentils were offered in many different combinations.

At the end of the meal, slices of fruit cleansed the tongue. Oranges, limes, grapes, succulent melons, figs, and pomegranates. Or for those few not yet filled to the gullet, servants carried in a tray of sweetmeats the Greeks had invented called marzipan, and *kopton*, a deliciously sweet confection made of baked layers of parchment-thin dough interspersed with butter, thinned honey, and walnuts.

Drifa promised herself to write down the names of some of these foods as soon as she returned to her chambers so she would be able to relate it all to her sister Ingrith. She also intended to purchase all the various spices she'd noted in these foods, like saffron, cloves, turmeric, cardamom, nutmeg, cinnamon, cumin, mastic, and rosemary, which would surely please Ingrith.

Some of the offerings were strange and not for the simple palates of the Norsemen around her, but overall it was a feast fit for a king . . . or, rather, an emperor.

Speaking of whom, even from this distance, John Tzimisces could be seen at the high table seated beside his bride under a golden canopy.

"Oh my!" she said, as she got her first good look at Theodora, the woman who would become empress. Actually, she had already been crowned empress days ago. In this country, oddly, a woman became empress even before the wedding ceremony. In any case, while the emperor was rather short and at least fifty years old, he was a finely built, handsome man with reddish-blond hair and neatly trimmed beard, and if she was not mistaken, piercing blue eyes.

But his bride was a different story.

"Yea, she is long in the tooth," Sidroc said, reading her unspoken surprise. "At least matching the emperor in age, would be my guess."

"It is interesting how fifty is long in the tooth for a woman, but no detraction from a man's virility," Ianthe commented.

"Hah! 'Tis the way of men throughout the world, whether they be Greek, Saxon, or Viking," Drifa agreed. "Once a man gets a bit of gray in his beard, he starts looking at girls scarce out of swaddling clothes."

The men all groaned, and Sidroc had the nerve to say. "Men age like good wine. Women age like vinegar."

"Idiot," she murmured. "Still, 'tis surprising that the emperor is marrying a woman past child-bearing years. I thought heirs were of great importance in royal circles."

"In this country, they castrate the younger boys in a family so they will not inherit, whether it be the crown or a family's wealth," Thork pointed out. "Can you imagine?"

All the men cringed at that image.

"No one would snip off my braw body parts, no matter my age," Jamie asserted. "Even coming from the womb, I would bite the hand that dared touch my claymore."

"Claymore!" the other men hooted with laughter.

"What is castrated?" Alrek wanted to know. "I know how horses are castrated betimes, but how . . . oh my gods!"

"Precisely," Wulf said.

"The reason that John marries is purely political. Theodora is of the powerful Phocas family, a direct line in the Macedonian dynasty. Furthermore, he is merely the regent emperor holding place for the young Basil and Constantine until they are of age," Sidroc explained. "Having no love for court life, he is a military man at heart and that is where he would rather be.

"What is surprising to me is that a man of power and high regard, such as John, would wed a woman homely as a squashed bug," observed Finn.

"Finn!" she and Ianthe protested.

"Oh come, you must admit she is not at all comely. And that is being kind."

True, but it seemed mean to say it aloud, even if they were speaking in the Norse tongue that the Greek servers could not understand. Wulf was able to speak and understand the language because Norse and Saxon English were so similar, and Ianthe must have been with Sidroc long enough to learn his language.

And it was rude, of course, to make mock of the guest of honor for whom the feast was being held. But these were men, and men ofttimes cared little for the niceties, like politeness.

"Apparently beauty is not one of the criteria that the emperor seeks in his new consort." If Wulf was trying to be kind, he failed miserably.

"Obviously. After all, he could have wed the beauty Theophano, the previous empress, long ago, if he chose. In fact, he led her to believe he would as he openly visited her bedchamber nightly," Sidroc said. Then in a whisper, he added, "Why else would she help him kill her husband, Nicephorus, John's uncle, to help him gain the throne?"

"In a most brutal fashion, by the by. Stabbing and decapitation in his bedchamber," another of the Varangians disclosed, also in a whisper.

Finn and Sidroc nodded.

"And then he exiled her to a convent," the Varangian added.

"No doubt she walloped him over the head with a pottery pitcher or promised him one thing or another, then reneged," Sidroc decided. "Not to be trusted, like some other woman we know."

He and Finn both turned to stare at Drifa on that happy note.

"Hey, I had good reason," she protested.

But no one was listening.

"I heard that Polyeuctes, the church patriarch at the time, levied a huge penance on John for all his sins, which included the political marriage and the exiling of his mistress," Wulf said, demonstrating what Drifa already knew. Court gossip spread faster than chaff on the wind. "Theodora is after all the daughter of Constantine VI and aunt to the two young emperors Basil and Constantine. The churchman would not allow John to enter his church and be crowned until he complied."

"Personally, I think beauty should be its own dower," said Finn, who was far-famed for his vanity.

"I agree, I agree," piped in Thork and Jamie, who did not suffer from an excess of humility, either.

"How would that work?" Alrek wanted to know. His question was met with groans from the rest of them.

"I'm glad you asked, Alrek," Finn said. "Methinks beautiful persons should not require a dowry, whereas ugly persons should have to pay someone to wed them."

"Mayhap you should wed yourself, Finn," Drifa remarked.

"I would if I could," he replied with unabashed conceit, not recognizing, or choosing to ignore, the sarcasm of her words.

The subject was changed as the entertainment

began. There were musicians, who moved from one spot to another so that all might enjoy their talents. Acrobats flipped and jumped here and there. Contortionists bent their bodies in such a manner that they appeared boneless. And dancers, both male and female, drew ooohs and aaahs. In some cases the men linked arms over the shoulders and did these joyful moves that required great agility as they bent their knees at the same time they kicked outward. Then there were the partners, male and female, who did dances where they moved seductively about each other, casting sultry glances, teasing and then touching, teasing and touching.

Because of all the wine consumed, some of the men went off to the lavatories, where communal facilities allowed them to piss to their hearts' content, with the waste water being immediately washed away.

Then Ianthe was called over to another table by a friend, leaving Drifa alone, which she did not mind. She relished this solitary moment when she could observe the vast wonders around her.

But then the biggest wonder of them all eased himself down to the divan beside her, thigh to thigh. With a smile, which did not reach his eyes, he said, "So, Drifa, I understand you harbor a secret."

# CHAPTER SEVEN

It was a sticky subject . . .

Sidroc leaned back on the divan, one arm across the back behind Drifa, and watched with interest the abject fear that crossed her pretty face.

Whoa! What is this? He could understand a little embarrassment over his discovery that she'd borne a child outside of wedlock, but not terror. In fact, she backed away from him a bit as if she feared he might strike her. *Who or what has made her fear physical attack?*

"Secret? What secret? I have no secret." The wringing of her hands in her lap and a tic at the side of her mouth told a different story.

You lie like the rushes on a longhouse floor. "Not even Runa?"

She gasped, and her face flamed. "You know about Runa?"

He nodded. "I learned today that you had a child without the benefit of marriage."

"Oh," she said with what he could swear was relief. "*That* Runa."

What is going on here? What did I say that would cause her relief? "You know that many Runas?"

"A few."

She no longer appeared frightened, and that puzzled him even more. He sensed somehow that solving this puzzle was important to him. "Have you thought any more about my plans for you? I certainly have." He touched his knuckles to one soft cheek as he spoke, and felt the same attraction that had drawn him to her five years ago. She truly was a beautiful woman, even at her advanced age.

"Your plans are of no interest to me, you rat." She swatted his hand away.

He moved the hand to her thigh, and felt her stiffen. It was not entirely a stiffening of affront, but rather one of stimulation. He had been with enough women to know when one was fighting her attraction to him . . . and losing the battle. "Now that I know you are no longer a maiden, I have no reservations about my plans." *Not that I had many afore. Well, a few. Mayhap this rat is just playing with you, little mouse.*

"Oh please! Spare me from the ego of a windy man."

"Windy, am I?" He grinned at her. And saw her fight a return grin. "We will be good together, Drifa. You know we will."

"And what of your mistress?"

It was his turn to stiffen. "Ianthe has naught to do with us."

"I beg to differ. I would never mate with a man who was mating with another woman at the same time."

"Mate? Is that a woman-word for tup, or swive?" *Or fuck?*

"There is no need to be coarse."

M'lady, you have not heard coarse yet. Good thing I didn't say fuck *aloud.* "Let me put it this way. If Ianthe were no longer my mistress, then you would come willingly to my bed furs?"

"Nay! That is not what I meant."

I thought not. "Meet me tomorrow after dusk at the Madonna fountain. 'Tis just past the entrance to the Sun Palace. You cannot miss it. It is alight with candles night and day."

"Why would I do that?"

Do not play games with me, you saucy wench. "To begin to pay your debt."

"This is ridiculous. I owe you naught."

"You owe me plenty. Either meet me there, and I will lead you to my chambers in the Varangian Palace, or I will come to your rooms. Believe you me, my rooms are preferable for what I have in mind."

He could tell she did not want to ask, but curiosity won out, causing him to bite his lip to hide a smirk.

"Why?"

"Because I plan to make you scream your ecstasy, and it might embarrass you to have your guardsmen overhear." *Good gods, I am arousing myself.*

She shook her head as if he were a hopeless case.

Betimes he was.

"Dost really think my guardsmen are so ineffective they would not follow me, or forbid me to leave my rooms?"

"A devious woman like you can always come up with a likely story."

"You defame me, Sidroc. You really do. There are things you do not know that would change your mind."

A likely story! "Tell me then."

"I cannot. Not now. Not here."

Surprise, surprise! "Secrets?"

She nodded.

He spat out a particularly foul word.

She merely appeared saddened by his opinion of her, but he could not allow himself to soften with pity. Instead he told her some of the things he planned to do to her once he had her naked. With each description, her breathing heightened. He was not sure if she was panting with insult or arousal.

And he was beginning to wonder if he was serious or not.

Just then he noticed that the men were sauntering back to their seats; so Sidroc stood and began to move to the other side once again. Soon Ianthe would be returning as well.

But Thork—the rascal—said with a mock-serious face, "What was that I heard you say about licking?"

With an equally straight face, Sidroc replied, "I was telling Princess Drifa that the problem with honey on those lemon cakes over there is that you must keep licking your fingers for a long time after eating to remove the stickiness."

Not one single man at the table believed him.

You could say it was a good-bye tup . . .

"I did not mean to show you disrespect, Ianthe. I am so sorry," Sidroc said as they left the Imperial Palace.

"Sidroc! You have never mistreated me. In truth, you have raised me up, and you know it."

"You deserved my full attention tonight, and I let my animosity toward Princess Drifa cloud my judgment."

Even though the palace gates closed at night, because of the imperial feast he'd been given special permission to escort Ianthe to her home above her jewelry shop. He nodded to the guards as they passed through.

Ianthe, whose arm was looped with his, gazed up at him with question. "What do you have against the princess? Other than her breaking your betrothal? That is what happened, is it not?"

"How would you know that?" He would bet his finest arm ring that the princess didn't discuss the subject.

"Finn."

"Humph! Finn's mouth is bigger than his ego."

"Do not blame him. I asked."

"I am not so small-minded that I would begrudge a woman the right to change her mind. There is more to me and Drifa than that, but it is not a subject I wish to discuss now. There is something else I need to tell you."

Although she was clearly anxious to hear what he had to say, she waited until she'd unlocked her door and they'd gone up the stairs, where she unlocked yet another door to her home. Inside were cozy living quarters that doubled as both a bed-chamber and a salon, with the usual low divans on jewel-toned Persian carpets. Although there was a brazier, she had no need for a kitchen since she was able to purchase fresh-cooked meals daily down in the market. Besides, food spoiled quickly in this heat. In the winter, food could be stored in a cold cellar, but even then food stalls were open practically outside her front door.

He sat down in an armed chair, and she handed him a goblet of his favorite apricot wine with a slice of lemon in it. He'd been with her for two years now, and she knew his desires without asking. Desires of all kinds, by the by. Sidroc was a man of big appetites in the bedsport, and she matched him in enthusiasm, even when he asked her to do things that might make some women cringe. His tastes had been honed these five years of serving in foreign countries.

For some reason, he thought of Drifa then. Would she balk if he asked her to wear nipple rings? Or refuse to pose for him naked? Or be shocked if he told her to kneel on all fours?

Or how about near-public swiving? Behind this two-story building, a walled garden had been built that Ianthe cherished for its privacy and beauty. He liked the privacy, too, especially since they'd made some memorable love there a time or two. The possibility that a customer might walk in on them, though remote, gave an edge to their sexual activity.

"What troubles you, Sidroc? What is it you hesitate to tell me?" she asked, coming up to sit on his lap.

"I am leaving," he said bluntly.

"Tonight?" She gasped. "You have a new mission?"

He shook his head. "Nay, I mean to leave Byzantium, for good."

He saw the regret on her face, but no crushing blow of pain. They'd been apart far more than together these past two years.

"I knew our liaison would end eventually, but not this soon." Tears welled in her eyes and she blinked to stop them from overflowing.

He hugged her close and kissed the top of her head. "Nay, dearling, not tonight. What I should have said is that I am ready to end my Varangian duties. I intend to speak to General Sclerus as soon as possible."

"You must be careful how you approach him," she warned, swiping at her eyes.

"I know."

"My husband had a friend who wanted to resign after ten years of faithful duty so that he could move himself and his wife and children out of the city to the family farm. Instead of rewarding him for his service, the general sent him to a desert outpost where he still is today." Ianthe's husband had been a vintner with a small holding in Crete before he died suddenly of heart pains. His greedy kinfolk had pushed her out of the door right after the funeral. Sidroc had not known her then.

"I will be careful . . . as diplomatic as I can be," he promised, "but what I started to say is that 'tis time to settle on my own lands, probably the Orkneys. Would you want to come with me?" He threw the invitation out there, though he was not sure he wanted Ianthe with him for life, as fond as he was of her.

"Is it cold in the Orkneys?" she asked, pressing a forefinger to her lips, as if she actually contemplated such a move.

"Well, yea, I suppose it is, compared to Byzantium, but warmer than the Norselands where I grew up."

She sighed deeply. "I appreciate your offer, Sidroc, but this is my home. I wish no other. Besides, you know that I am barren."

He waved a hand dismissively.

"A man needs sons," she insisted.

"Not me." After failing to rescue one small baby, he had no wish for others. Even worse, he'd had time to deliberate these past five years, and he worried that he might treat a child the way his father and his brothers treated their children . . . with numerous thrashings and constant belittling. Mayhap it ran in his blood.

Nay, no children for him.

What a man needed was a good woman to warm his bed furs on a winter's night, and it mattered not that it be wife or concubine or passing fancy. He did not say that to Ianthe, though, for fear she would take offense.

"So, this will be good-bye for us then?" she asked, tears welling once again in her eyes. "I will miss you sorely, dear one."

"I am not leaving *yet*," he said, and ran a hand along her flank.

"But we must not drag it out, either. Let this

be our last night together. We started as friends before we became lovers. We should end as friends as well."

He wanted to argue with her, but she was right. Prolonging their farewells would be unwise. Oh, there were things to be arranged. Money to be settled on her. Making sure the deed to the jewelry shop was in her name. Renewing the annual trading permit with the powerful eparch, or prefect, of the city, who could make life hard for a single craftswoman, if he chose. Perchance Sidroc should hire a guard to stay with Ianthe for at least a year. That way she would not have to seek another protector, if she did not want to. But those things could wait until the morrow. For now, he had other things on his mind.

"If this is to be our last night together as lovers, I do not want to waste a moment," he said.

She smiled seductively and slid off his lap, going over to the far wall where she opened a chest and picked out a few items. When she returned, she knelt between his thighs and handed him the scarves.

"Ah, sweetling, I am going to miss you so much," he said, tipping her chin up to meet his kiss.

"Show me how much," she purred.

Like a good Viking warrior, he followed orders. In fact, he more than showed her.

And showed her.

And showed her.

And once dawn light crept over the Bosphorus, he showed her again.

CHAPTER EIGHT

In the garden of good and tempting . . .

Drifa was up at dawn, ready to begin a day of exploration in the Golden City, followed by her audience with the emperor.

But she had to wait a few hours to begin with her visit to the jewelry maker since she did not want to be pulling Ianthe from her bed. Gods only knew who would be sharing it with her. Well, actually, she knew, but chose not to have that image planted in her brain.

Suffering aleheads from overindulging the night before, all four of her *hersirs* declined her invitation to take her to visit with Sidroc's mistress, although Alrek promised to come later . . . once he stopped emptying the contents of his stomach into a chamber pot. Apparently someone had brought several barrels of mead up from the longships and they'd shown their appreciation in the way Viking men loved. A competition to see who could suck up the most brew in the shortest period of time. Men!

So it was with her four guardsmen that Drifa left through the huge bronze Chalke Gate, the main entrance to the Great Palace. Above the gate was an enormous mosaic icon of Christ. The first thing they noticed after passing through was the overpowering scent of flowers.

" 'Tis the perfumers," Ivar told her. "The law in Miklagard requires all makers and vendors of scents to be located within a stone's throw of the palace gates. Can you guess why?"

She looked at the dozens of shops and stalls, promising herself to buy some perfumes for herself and her sisters on her way back later, and then she looked toward the bustling city. Even with the scented "screen" of the perfumers, the stench of the city was overpowering. A fragrance wall. How . . . enterprising! She pinched her nose as they stepped forward, being careful where she stepped. "The interior of the palace is a marvel with terracotta pipes bringing in fresh water, and carrying away waste from the indoor privies. Why this?" She motioned toward the city.

"There are trenches along all the streets and underground drainage pipes, and aqueducts and cisterns, but hundreds of thousands of people are crammed into this city, along with their animals. It backs up. Not to mention slimy fish blood and rotting vegetables."

One of her other guardsmen said, "I would not want to take a bath in the shores of the Bosphorus or the Sea of Marmosa where all this waste is being dumped."

"They have public bathhouses throughout the city and privies where there are as many as fifty holes in a row," Ivar said with a gleam of humor in his eyes. "They even have sponges on a stick for wiping, to be shared by all."

"Whaaat?" Would men ever stop surprising her with the things they would discuss, even in the presence of women? Yea, Vikings were earthier than other peoples, but this was going a bit too far. "I cannot believe you mentioned that, Ivar."

"There are buckets for rinsing the sponge," Ivar conceded, "but I imagine it becomes rather rank after a while." Ivar, like many men, enjoyed shocking women with the coarser side of life. "Mayhap they dump it in the many flower beds I see about the courtyards, like the manure you put on your plants, Princess Drifa."

"Eeew!" But, really, was it any worse than using leaves or nothing at all back in the Norselands, or Saxon lands, too? At least Norse folks bathed often. "Well, it certainly puts a different light on the Jewel of Byzantium," Drifa decided.

"Humph! More like a grubby, unpolished stone if you ask me."

Drifa had to look up when talking to Ivar, as she did with the other Viking guardsmen. They were big men, and their size, as well as their weapons, was noted by many passersby as they walked on the raised pavement toward Ianthe's jewelry shop. Ivar's double-bladed battle-axe, which he had named Death Bringer, also drew particular attention.

Even as the guardsmen conversed with her, their eyes were ever alert for danger.

They headed toward the Augustaion, the public square, via the wide main thoroughfare known as the Mese. The Augustaion also served as a busy marketplace, with shops on both sides sheltered by colonnades. It was here they would find Ianthe.

Once they arrived at the jewelry shop, one of the guards stationed himself outside, next to one of Ianthe's daytime shop guards. Two others went around the side and to the back of the property, and the fourth, Ivar, came inside with her.

Ianthe greeted her at the door, giving her a kiss on one cheek, then the other. "I am so glad you were able to come."

"You are our first stop of the day. I hope we are not too early."

"Not at all. I am up every day at dawn to prepare my shop for opening. And good that you came here first. I will show you some of the sights you must not miss in Constantinople, although it will take you days, mayhap weeks, to see everything."

"I have time."

Ianthe showed her around the shop first, where an assistant was laying out various pieces of jewelry on silk cloths and short display pedestals. In the back, two young women were sitting at long tables, one of them constructing a necklace of silver beads interspersed with aquamarines, and the other making one of the spiderweb creations like Ianthe had worn last night, also with aquamarines.

"You work often with the blue stones?" Drifa asked.

"I love them, all the different shades of aquamarines. Are you familiar with the stone?"

"By the runes! Am I ever! We Vikings are

seamen at heart and there is a superstition about aquamarines that they keep a sailor safe and free from seasickness." She rolled her eyes. "Because they are named after seawater, some lackwits even think they are harvested from mermaid caves."

"I get mine from the Rus lands," Ianthe said with a straight face before breaking out into a grin. "You would not believe the stories I hear, too. That the stones can be used as antidotes for poison, that they cure throat, stomach, and tooth aches, that they bring good luck in battle to the wearer, even that they act as love potions."

"I know of seers who use aquamarine globes to see the future."

They both laughed. Then Ianthe said, "It matters not to me why they buy my jewelry, just that they buy it."

Despite Ianthe's protests that she had not invited Drifa as a customer, Drifa purchased three of the necklaces for Breanne, Ingrith, and Vana, and a set of delicate arm rings for Tyra.

She showed Ianthe the chest full of amber that she was going to present to the king, then asked her if she could complete a quick jewelry order for her, and dumped out a small leather pouch of tiny round amber stones the size of peas. "A necklace?" Ianthe asked.

"Nay, something else," she said with a smile.

Ivar followed her like a shadow, which was amusing, really, since he was so big and the shop so small. She could tell by his flushed face that he was embarrassed to be bending and shifting to avoid knocking anything over. When they went upstairs to Ianthe's private quarters, Ivar was convinced to stand outside the door.

Upon entering, Drifa clapped her hands with delight. "Oh, this is lovely."

"Really?"

"Really." Ianthe probably thought that being a princess, Drifa had been exposed to many more luxurious female living quarters. She had been, and the palace was a far cry from this relatively humble abode, but Drifa loved it for its beauty in such a small space.

A thick Eastern carpet covered the floor with warm colors of deep red and cream and azure blue. Situated about the room were several low couches and tables.

Of a sudden, Drifa wondered how long Sidroc had known Ianthe. And how well. *Oh nay! Surely he was not involved with Ianthe back when he proposed marriage to me. On the other hand, knowing the cad, mayhap he had been.*

Drifa's attention was drawn then to a far corner where incense was burning in front of a picture painted on wood of the Virgin Mary with the Christ child. "How pretty!" Drifa remarked.

"We Greeks venerate icons. Windows to Heaven, we call them. You will see them throughout the city, and not just in the palace or churches. Some of them are plain on wood, others are crafted out of enamel or ivory, even with precious jewels on them. They can be huge, like those in the Hagia Sophia cathedral, and others are portable." Ianthe put a hand over her mouth and grimaced. "I talk too much. Sidroc says that betimes I chatter like a monkey he saw one time in far-off lands."

Sidroc! Another reminder that the man who had been betrothed to her for a short time, the man who threatened to take her to his bed, the man who was father to a child she loved, was this woman's . . . what? Protector? Lover?

"I enjoy hearing all this, Ianthe. Please do not stop on my account." Or on the advice of he-whose-word-is-worthless.

Ianthe smiled sweetly and motioned toward a back door. "Since you love plants and flowers, I thought we might dine on the balcony overlooking my humble garden."

Drifa gasped at what she saw. The balcony on which they stood, protected by a black iron railing, overlooked a lovely courtyard down below. The area was not even the size of a large bedchamber, but every space was filled with trees, flowers, bushes, and walkways, all situated around a small fountain in the center. "Oh my gods and goddesses, this is exactly what I wanted to see here in Byzantium. The palace gardens are grand, but this is the type of setting I would like to construct back at Stoneheim. Not using the same plants, of course, since many would not survive our harsh climate. Still . . ." She turned to Ianthe and said, "See, you are not the only one who can ramble on."

"I enjoy your enthusiasm. Would you like to go down and look around? Irene is not yet done setting out our meal." She pointed to an elderly woman who was placing platters of sliced fruit, cheese, olives, and honey bread, along with the cups of some beverage, on a round table, beside which were several chairs.

"Oh, yea, I would," she said, and followed Ianthe down a set of steep steps, apparently the only entrance into the garden. Urns sat along the balcony and on every other step, spilling ivy and an aromatic type of trailing rose.

Although it was early morning, the air was already hot and very humid. Good for the plants but not so good for the body. Ianthe, her hair parted in the center and coiled off either side of her face, was dressed appropriately for the weather in a *chiton*, the traditional sleeveless, ankle-length tunic favored by Greek women, today in a pretty shade of sky blue. The garment appeared cool, with the shoulders, neck, and arms exposed. Drifa, on the other hand, was sweltering in her long-sleeved, ankle-length *gunna*, covered with an open-sided apron. Even though her hair was pulled off her face in a single braid, she could feel perspiration beading along her hairline and under her arms. She determined then and there to purchase cooler garments today in the marketplace, or buy fabrics to have them made.

The gurgling fountain and a flowering fig tree gave the garden a welcoming aura. In addition, on one side there was an odd tree with heart-shaped leaves. The tree was not much taller than one of her Viking guardsmen, with gnarled widespread branches as wide as it was tall.

As Drifa's brow furrowed studying the tree, Ianthe said, "We call this the Judas tree. Supposedly the same tree from which Judas Iscariot, the betrayer of Christ, hanged himself."

"I love the dark rose flowers." Some of the flowers grew right out of the trunk of the tree.

Ianthe pulled several pods, resembling long pole beans, off the tree and handed them to her, but not before opening one of them and showing her the seeds inside. " 'Tis said that the flowers of this tree were once white, but turned dark with shame after Judas sinned by taking his own life on it."

A fanciful story. If she took the seeds back to the Norselands, which she would definitely do, the Vikings would no doubt invent their own Norse myth, perchance involving Baldr, who was similar in many ways to the One-God religion's Jesus Christ.

As they walked about, Drifa noted lilies, roses, and many, many irises in colors from white to blue, purple, and bright yellow. Ianthe explained that she had a particular liking for the strong-rooted flower. Friends who traveled about the world often brought her roots from any new species they saw. As a result, she now had fifty or more varieties. "It occurs to me, Drifa, that this flower would grow well in your homeland. Once mine are done blooming, I could separate the roots and give you some samples of each different color to take home."

Drifa was touched by her generosity. "You would do that for me?"

"With pleasure."

Guilt swamped Drifa suddenly because of her association with Sidroc, even though it was Sidroc who was the guilty party. She squeezed Ianthe's arm. "I will come and help you dig them up. Let us say two sennights from now?"

"Oh, I do not know. It does not seem appropriate for a woman of your high station to be digging in the dirt."

Drifa put a hand on each hip. "Who do you think does all the digging in my gardens at home? Certainly not my father. And I would not trust the servants with my precious flowers. They do not know a rose from a radish."

They were back up on the balcony eating the lovely first meal, which was fortunately not too heavy in the heat, when Drifa brought up a subject that had been nagging at her. "Do not be offended, Ianthe, but are you able to support yourself independently here?"

Ianthe smiled. "You mean, must I depend on Sidroc's support? Nay, do not be blushing so. I'm sure others wonder the same."

" 'Tis not just curiosity on my part. I come from a family of independent women, and betimes I have wondered what it would be like to live on my own. I am no longer a young maid, obviously, but still my father pushes me toward marriage." She could have bitten her tongue for revealing so much.

"The answer, my dear, is that I can definitely support myself, and well, but that was not always the case. Sidroc set me up with this shop. He discovered me working as a jeweler's assistant three years ago. To say that the master jeweler was cruel would be an understatement. Sidroc beat the man bloody and took me away, on the spot."

"And you have repaid him by becoming his

mistress? Oh, please forgive me. I cannot believe I asked you that impertinent question. How rude of me!"

Ianthe patted her hand. "Friends can talk of intimate things, and I am hoping that you and I are becoming friends. The answer is that I went to Sidroc's bed willingly a year after we first met. He is a man of many passions. In truth, we share the same . . . um, tastes in lovemaking."

Drifa had no idea what she meant and wasn't about to ask. She did ask another question, though. "Do you love him?"

Ianthe thought a moment. "I do love him, but only as a good friend and an equally good lover."

"How about Sidroc? Is he in love with you?" Drifa really was being intrusive, but her tongue seemed to have a mind of its own.

"Pfff! I doubt he thinks of me once he leaves my bed. Forget I said that. Of course he cares about me, but I do not think he is capable of the softer sentiments."

His crass marriage proposal to Drifa had been proof of that.

"I make the distinction between loving some-one and being in love," Ianthe went on, "because I know what being in love is like. I was in love with my husband, who died four years ago. I doubt I will ever love another in the same way. Do not look with pity on me, though. I live a satisfactory life." She laughed then. "Well, satisfactory up 'til now. Since Sidroc has ended our relationship, I will have to find my satisfaction in other ways."

Again, Drifa wasn't about to ask her what she

meant by "other ways," but that was interesting
. . . that Sidroc had ended his relationship with her.
"Is this something new?"

"As of last night. Well, truth to tell, this morning." Ianthe blushed.

Drifa did, too, suspecting what she meant by
"this morning." The randy goat had stayed all
night, and not to eat grass, either. Clearing her
throat, she asked, "Why end your relationship
now?"

"He is leaving Byzantium."

"He is? When?" So much for the forty-two
nights of bedsport threats he'd made to her!

"As soon as he is able to gain a release from
his Varangian duties. It could be within days, or
months, I would imagine."

Oh. So forty-two nights might not be out of the
question. *Good gods! What am I thinking? Of
course it is out of the question.*

As if reading her mind, Ianthe said, "Sidroc is
a good man. He told me last night that you were
betrothed at one time."

Drifa made a decidedly unfeminine snort of de-
rision. "A betrothal of about three hours! Did he
happen to mention that?"

Ianthe shook her head, clearly puzzled by the ve-
hemence of Drifa's response. "Perchance you could
resume your betrothal? Mayhap God brought you
here to Constantinople at the same time Sidroc was
here because he wants you to be together."

Drifa was fairly certain God had no plans involving forty-two nights of sex, which was all
Sidroc had planned for her. "We are at cross wills

every time we meet. I daresay we would kill each other if forced to be in each other's company for more than a day." Or forty-two days!

Ianthe glanced at her skeptically, then turned when she noticed a young woman, the assistant who had been helping in her shop, standing in the doorway. "There is a Saxon seaman who wants to buy a spiderweb necklace, but he wants to know if you can make one up with pearls for a bride-gift when he returns to Britain."

Ianthe turned to Drifa. "Would you mind waiting until I return? I will have Irene bring you another cup of wine."

Drifa sat, relaxing in the shade of the roofed balcony, enjoying the chirping of birds and the sound of running water from the fountain. It was so tranquil, just what she hoped to accomplish when she got home to Stoneheim . . . or in her own home, wherever that might be, eventually.

She thought of all she had accomplished so far, and it was not yet noon. She'd seen the perfume stalls and would buy some scents on her way back to the palace. She'd bought jewelry for her sisters. She'd made a new friend. She'd found hardy plants that she could easily transport back to the Norselands.

Her visit to Byzantium could only get better.

CHAPTER NINE

He'd like to pluck her petals . . .

Sidroc stood in the doorway watching Drifa relax in the world she clearly loved best. A garden.

For the moment, she wasn't aware of him, her head tilted up toward the sun, the only sounds those of birds, the fountain, and, if you listened closely, the Sea of Marmosa, which was not so far away.

She truly was a lovely woman, even lovelier than she had been five years past. With her eyes closed, she did not have that exotic Eastern cast to her features, except for her skin, which had a slight olive tone. Her black hair when unbound would be like silk waves down to her waist. Her figure was delicate but voluptuous due to her full breasts contrasted with her slim waist and rounded hips.

Walking up to the table where she sat, he ran a fingertip along the portion of her neck exposed by her single braid and said, "How is my little flower today?"

Startled, she jumped, and the full cup of wine sitting before her almost tipped over. Thanks to his quick reflexes, he managed to catch it and move it to the center of the table.

"You boor! I am not your little anything."

"We shall see."

"Did you have to scare me like that?"

You do not know scared yet, sweetling. He sat down in the chair opposite her. "You should be more alert. After all, you are in a foreign country."

She narrowed her eyes at him. "How did you get in here? Ivar will not be pleased."

"Actually, Ivar told me where you were. It seems we have a common friend back in the Norselands. His cousin Snorri Straggle Beard and I fought side by side at the Battle of Blue Fjord. Ivar considers me a friend now."   •

"I shall have to tell him otherwise."

"If you do, I will have to add another night to your tally of bedsport."

"Verily, your threats are becoming tiresome. Do you seriously think I will agree to let you sate your lust on me?"

He laughed. "First of all, I will not be sating *my* lust. It will be a mutual sating. Second, they are not threats. When you come to my bed, it will be willingly. Well, somewhat willingly."

She glared at him.

I am beginning to find her glares charming. How pitiful is that? "I expect that it may take a little whetting to sharpen the blade of your passion. My blade, on the other hand, is already whetted." *Where do I come up with this stuff? Finn must be wearing off on me.*

"You must have a rock betwixt your ears. In

what circumstance could you imagine my giving free consent to mate with you outside of marriage? Not," she quickly added, "that I would want you for husband now."

He smiled, getting an inordinate amount of pleasure from baiting her. "Not that I would want you for a wife, either, but I am a soldier at heart, Drifa. I know how to fight battles on the field and off. As I told you before, everybody has a weakness. I will find yours."

Once again, she got that odd look of fear on her face, and he sensed that there was some secret she was hiding from him. Ah well, he would find out in due time.

"I have no weaknesses where you are concerned," she asserted, and was about to stand up.

He put a hand on her shoulder and shoved her gently back down. "Do not get your innards in a twist, dearling."

Her chin shot up at the use of the endearment.

So he used it again, of course. "I suspect, dearling, that the weakness I seek is already in you. I suspect that you have a passion for me that you are struggling to bridle. I suspect that even now your breasts are aching and there is a wetness pooling betwixt your legs." *Bloody hell! I am arousing myself here.*

She gasped and sputtered for something to say, something tart and biting, no doubt. Women fought their own passions betimes.

"And I suspect," he quickly added, "that you would like to pick up one of those urns and clobber me over the head. Again. But I have to warn you,

I will not allow another head drilling. My man-part is already too big." *And getting bigger by the moment.*

"You . . . you . . . you lusty, ignorant, full-of-yourself, deluded troll!"

"Tsk, tsk, tsk! Methinks you need some more expletives to add to your stock. Perchance I could take you through the marketplace and teach you some new ones. In different languages even. Yea, the marketplace is teeming with foul words." *And foul other things, too.*

"Oh, thank goodness!" Ianthe came through the doorway and blew some stray hairs off her forehead. "I wanted to lead you through the bazaar today, Drifa, to show you some special places, but now that Sidroc has offered I can get back to my very difficult customer."

"Oh, nay, that is not necessary, Ianthe," Drifa said. "I have Ivar and my other guards to go with me. We can just browse today. Perchance there will be another day when you and I can shop together."

"Of course," Ianthe said, "but still—"

"It will be my pleasure," Sidroc told Drifa. And it would be. There were places and things he would show her that no one else would. "I insist."

While Ianthe called for more wine, Drifa hissed at him, "Begone!"

He responded with honeyed cordiality, "Uh-uh, my thorny flower. I am going to be your very own bee, pricking you at every turn. Bzzzz!"

"My brother-by-marriage John raises bees at Hawks' Lair. You do know what happens to male bees, do you not, Sidroc?"

"If that smirk on your face is any indication, I do not want to know." In truth, it was a rather adorable smirk as far as smirks go.

"One prick, and the lusty bee is dead."

So much for my bzzzing plans!

You could say it was the Byzantine Mall . . .

Drifa was not happy. Ivar was not happy. Her other three guardsmen were not happy.

Her bodyguards did not like her being in such a crowded, dangerous place.

She did not like the unwelcome burr on her backside that had come along, uninvited.

But Sidroc, the burr, was enjoying himself immensely as they walked through the busy bazaar a short time later. She considered pushing him into that pile of horse droppings over there, but he would probably pull her down with him.

She was not going to let him ruin this marvelous excursion. Once one grew accustomed to the foul odors of the city, there were other smells that were more pleasant. All kinds of meat and poultry and fish were being grilled on charcoal braziers. Drifa mused at one point, "I swear every animal from the Christian Noah's Ark must be represented here in one form or another." And as for the fruits and vegetables sliced and split for inspection of the customers, "Could the Garden of Eden boast any better?"

"The only thing missing is the serpent," Sidroc agreed, then made a ludicrous hissing sound.

Wealthy patricians, men and women alike, were carried through the city on litters borne by well-attired slaves. A sharp contrast to other almost-naked, miserable slaves being prodded, along with goats, cattle, and other livestock, toward the auction square. Uniquely dressed dessert nomads with their turbaned heads led camels laden with Mongolian silks and Russian furs.

And the sounds! Cart wheels rumbling over stone and wood walkways, church bells pealing, a dozen or more different languages, shouts of merchants calling out their wares, and many colorful and unique expletives. Yea, Sidroc had been right about the latter. "Move that cart, you camel turd!" "Not a coin more, you thieving son of a goat herder's whore!" And *fuck* in various permutations. "Fuck your sorry arse!" "Fuck me if I'll pay that price!" And the ever-popular "Fuck, fuck, fuck!"

Drifa could feel her cheeks heat with embarrassment, and she turned to the side so that Sidroc would not see and say that he had told her so.

But he chuckled, and she knew he saw and was amused.

"Come, Drifa, over to this stall." He almost shoved her toward a cloth merchant who had some ladies' garments already sewn together. "You said that you wanted to buy some Greek apparel."

She rooted through the various piles and picked out several gowns and three ells each of silk fabrics in blue, red, and green, along with lengths of braiding and bands of embroidered, stiff brocade. Byzantine silk was among the most precious of commodities, valued as highly as gold in some cases, and she could see why.

"Back here, lily of my heart," Sidroc said, calling her to the rear portion of the tent. He had taken to calling her silly flower names, just to annoy her.

"Don't you have Varangian things to do?"

"I just returned from six months of Varangian things."

"Viking things then."

He winked at her. "I *am* doing Viking things."

She had no idea what he meant by that, but she felt the wink all the way down to her curling toes. "Un-luck shines on me today!" she murmured.

"Did you say *fuck*?" Sidroc asked with mock horror.

"I did not." She started to stomp away from him, but he grabbed her hand.

"Come here now. I have found the perfect attire for you."

I can scarce imagine. Actually, it turned out that her imagination didn't stretch that far.

He held up a garment that was made of sheer red cloth, which would leave the neck, arms, and abdomen bare, with triple layers of cloth over what would be the tips of the breasts and the nether folds. The bottom started at the hips, below the navel, and was actually a pair of *braies* of sorts, gathered at the ankle. It was the type of thing she imagined a harem girl might wear.

"Here is the best part, my shy violet." He shook the garment, and tiny bells that edged the ankles and wrists tinkled. In a voice low enough for only her to hear, he said, "Whene'er you walk about my bedchamber, I will hear you coming."

"Like a cow," she said with dry humor.

Which did not deter him at all. "More like my personal love slave." He waggled his eyebrows at her. "Also, when you dance for me, you will not need music. Your bells will make a special music."

"Dance? This is the first I've heard of dancing."

"All love slaves dance. Not that I know much about love slaves, but if I ever had a love slave, I'm sure she would dance. In any case, isn't this wonderful?"

"Yea, wonderful," she agreed, again with dry humor, which again he ignored. "I am not buying that thing."

"Of course not, my blushing rosebud. I will purchase it for you."

Meanwhile, her guardsmen stood at the outer perimeter of the tent, staring at them with bemusement, instead of the anger they should have exhibited. But then she realized why as two of the guardsmen went in and examined harem outfits, for their lady loves back home, she presumed. Men!

Her suspicions were proved true when Sidroc laughed. "Your wife will love you for that gift, Farle. And Gismun, your betrothed will want to marry you with haste if you dare to buy her one."

Good gods! Has the man befriended all my guards?

After the purchases were paid for, and, yea, Sidroc did buy the scandalous garment, she insisted, "For some other woman. Not for me. Definitely not for me."

He just waved her protests aside.

They were back in the marketplace, which now swarmed with musicians, jugglers, magicians, fortune tellers, and astrologers.

"Would you like to have your fortune told, peach blossom?"

That's all she would need. Some fortune teller guessing her secret and spilling it to Sidroc. "Nay, not today, and stop calling me those flower insults."

"M'lady"—Sidroc put a hand over his heart—"they are endearments."

"Well, stop endearing me then."

He just smiled.

In truth, she liked this playful side of Sidroc. Too bad he tossed his threats of bedchamber activities in betwixt every other nice thing he said or did. She felt like a fish on a Northman's line, being pulled in, bit by bit. If nothing else, Northmen excelled at fishing.

And always at the back of her mind were thoughts of Runa, and how Sidroc must be informed about his daughter. But how? And when?

As they walked, and somehow he'd managed to link his hand with hers, fingers entwined, she noticed statues interspersed throughout the city, mostly of the first Constantine, for whom Constantinople was named.

One of the most unusual sights involved men sitting atop tall pillars high above the crowds. Sidroc explained that these were ascetic monks known as stylites who chose to live up on the pedestals praying. Food and water were passed up to them by other monks. Drifa did not want to know how other bodily functions were handled.

At a shop featuring everything marble from statues to a game with tiny balls called marbles, Drifa bought a cylinder that was used for rolling out dough for various sweets. Ingrith would love it. In fact, she bought two. The other for the Stoneheim cook.

Whilst there, Sidroc of course had to do something outrageous. Somehow he discovered these long marble things, like cucumbers, of various sizes, bulbous on the ends. At first she did not know what they were until she realized they were replicas of men's phalluses. "This one is about my size . . . since my head drilling," he said, weighing it in one hand.

"You dolt!" She rushed from the shop, hearing his laughter in her wake. Her guardsmen stood at the front of the shop, unaware of his latest outrageousness.

Once he caught up with her, Sidroc said, "Do you not want to know what they are used for?"

"I do not!"

"Oh well, you do not need one whilst I am around."

She would not even look his way, having realized three verbal jabs ago that he deliberately baited her when he had shown her a stall with the testicles of every possible animal you could imagine, and another where the mandrake root was being sold. He had to explain to her that the mandrake root resembled a woman's female parts. As if she would know what she looked like down there!

So now she bit her bottom lip for silence. Glancing skyward, she saw that the sun was overhead. It must be about midday. "We should return to the palace if I am to prepare for my audience with the emperor." She directed one of her guardsmen to pick up the case of amber that she had left with Ianthe for her inspection.

"I would get it for you," Sidroc said, although she hadn't thought to ask him to, "but I have an appointment with General Sclerus. 'Tis best I be in uniform for what I have to say."

"Your request to quit the Varangian Guard?"

He tilted his head in surprise.

"Ianthe told me."

"What else did she tell you?"

Oooh, I like the look of worry on his sorry face. "Plenty."

When he waited and she said no more, good soldier that he was, he chose to attack from a different angle.

She should have been prepared. She should have had her drawbridge up and her defenses mounted.

"So, tell me about your child's father. The man you presumably bedded right after you abandoned me to near death."

"I did not . . . he is not . . . I will not . . ." she sputtered. *Oh gods, oh gods, oh gods! The web of my lies keeps getting bigger and bigger.* She calmed herself by inhaling and exhaling several times. "'Tis none of your concern." *How I wish that were true.*

"You lie," he said. "Believe you me, your face tells all when you utter falsehoods. But I wonder why."

"Leave off, Sidroc, I have too much on my mind to answer your questions." *And I need more time to polish my lies. Or polish the truth when I give it to you.*

"You lie again. All right. We will delay speaking of your lover, but what I want to—"

Just then they were interrupted by several little girls who ran in front of them, chasing after a goat that had gotten loose from one of the stalls. Laughing and giggling, they dodged this way and that, their long hair whipping about their sweet faces.

Drifa was reminded of Runa, of course, whom, of a sudden, she missed sorely. How Runa would love seeing the bazaar! Drifa vowed to buy the little girl many gifts to make up for her absence. Maybe even that marble game she'd seen. And a Greek gown in her favorite color, blue. Dozens of ribbons of every color in the rainbow.

She inhaled and exhaled to calm herself as they resumed walking. Only then did she realize that Sidroc was studying her closely.

"What now?" she asked.

"Tell me about your child?"

chapter ten

Viking James Bonds, they were not . . .

As he and Finn waited for their appointment with General Sclerus, Sidroc mulled an untenable, too-horrifying-to-contemplate prospect.

"Could Drifa's child be mine?"

"Whaaat?" Finn nigh shouted.

Sidroc hadn't realized he'd spoken his concern aloud. Well, too late now. "Every time I mention Drifa's child, she gets skittish. In fact, you could say she is downright fearful. And not once does she answer my questions about the girl . . . Runa by name, I think."

"Could you have forgotten having tupped her?"

"Holy Thor, nay! I am not demented enough, despite the hole in my head, nor so widely tupped, to forget such an event, especially with a Norse princess. But what if she swived me whilst I was in the death-sleep?"

Finn's eyes widened at the possibility, but then he pointed out, "I was there most of the time at your bedside."

"But there was that time when you went to Vikstead to look for Signe?"

"You have the right of it, but honestly, Sidroc, I have ne'er heard of such happening afore. Although 'tis a well-known fact that men's cocks sustain enthusiasms whilst asleep. In truth, one time my morning enthusiasm was so big I would have bronzed it if I could."

That was not a picture Sidroc needed in his head. "Is it so far afield to think a woman couldn't hop onto an erection and have her way with a helpless man?"

"Yea, it is too far-fetched." This from Finn, the master of far-fetched. "But we come back to the question: Why is she so scared?"

"I do not know." *You can be sure I will find out, though.* "Still . . . I cannot fathom it. *Drifa?* The princess of prim?"

"She did have a passion for you once."

A short-lived one that ended in a wallop over my head. "Why would she take advantage of me whilst I was in the death-sleep? If she wanted to swive, she only had to ask."

"Mayhap she yearned for a child . . . *your* child, and feared you would ne'er wake up to give it to her the natural way."

Impossible! It never happened!

Did it?

"Ahem!"

He and Finn turned to see a servant standing in the doorway. "The general is ready to see you now."

As they stood and prepared to walk into one of the smaller reception rooms, a half-dozen men in uniforms walked out. They were minor generals in both the tagmatic and thematic armies, each of whom Sidroc and Finn knew. Short greetings were exchanged by all.

Byzantium was divided into military districts called themes, each of which had its own armies, garrisons, and such. Then there was a whole other group of military men assigned to the palace in Miklagard. These were called tagmatic armies. General Sclerus was the commander-in-chief of them all.

But the presence of these generals together and the way they'd regarded Sidroc caused a prickling sensation to run up the back of his neck.

"Uh-oh!" Finn said.

"Definitely," Sidroc agreed.

More uh-ohs resounded in their heads once they entered the room where General Sclerus was studying a huge map spread across a table. He was not alone.

The emperor, John Tzimisces, wearing a simple tunic and *braies*—not his usual royal garb, though the garments were of what appeared to be silk or softest wool—lounged before a table, sipping at a goblet of wine. Also, there was Patriarch Antony sitting rigidly and somber, telling his beads in his lap; leastways, that's what Sidroc hoped he was doing with his hands in his lap. And even more ominous was the presence of Alexander Mylonas, the rodent-faced eparch of Miklagard.

While the emperor ruled all of Byzantium, the eparch, or prefect, controlled almost every facet of life and business in the Golden City. He was a man much feared by the merchants and common folks, with good reason. Ianthe had endured more than one encounter with the vile prefect.

"Your eminence," Sidroc said as he and Finn bowed from the waist before the emperor. They waited to straighten until the emperor replied, "Welcome Lord Guntersson. Welcome Lord Vidarsson."

Neither of them were lords by any stretch of the imagination, but they did not bother to correct the ruler. Not anymore. They had done so on several occasions in the past to no avail. If the emperor wanted to think of them as Norse lords, so be it.

Still standing, he and Finn parroted, "Your holiness," to the patriarch, who nodded at them. They also exchanged greetings with General Sclerus and Prefect Mylonas, both of whom acknowledged their presence but with no particular warmth.

Oh well. So that was how it was going to be.

"You wished to speak with me?" the emperor said right off.

Was it meaningful that he and Finn were not asked to sit and share a cup of wine?

Probably.

"Your majesty, we wish to resign from the Varangian Guard and return to our homelands," Sidroc said. No one in the room seemed surprised by the request, but as silence loomed, Sidroc went on, "Finn and I have served you well these past five years, but 'tis past time we settled our own estates." Not that they had any at the moment, but the emperor didn't need to know that.

The general glanced up from his map reading

and asked, "Do you have any grievance over the way you have been treated as Varangian guardsmen?"

"Not at all. We have been well paid and respected."

"Except for our pay for this past year's service, which is due about . . . oh, *now*," Finn added with the subtlety of a bull in a glass palace.

"Is there a reason why they have not been paid?" the emperor asked General Sclerus.

Red-faced, the general said, "So many men are to be paid from this last returning group. 'Tis just a delay." To Sidroc and Finn, he said woodenly, "If you go to the minister of finance today, you will be paid."

"Many thanks," he and Finn said.

"When would you like to end your service?" the emperor asked then.

"As soon as possible," Finn blurted out.

Sidroc shot him a glare of warning. "We have returned from a long mission only days ago. We would not like to delay our passage until the Norse fjords freeze over the winter months." A perfectly logical explanation. Now, if only they would accept it!

The emperor, the eparch, and the patriarch exchanged meaningful glances, which could only spell trouble.

He and Finn exchanged meaningful glances, too. Theirs spelled, "Uh-oh!" *Again!*

"There is a short mission we would ask you to complete before you leave," the emperor said.

"Both of us?" Finn demanded.

Sidroc was going to kill Finn for his rudeness, if someone else didn't do it for him.

"One would be fine, two would be better." The emperor's tone now was not as friendly as when they'd first entered.

"What is it you would have us do . . . if we agree?" Sidroc emphasized. It was one thing to be polite, another to be weak.

The emperor waved a hand for General Sclerus to explain.

"The muscle of the Byzantine empire has been increasingly in the strongholds we have in the borders, where our warlord generals have maintained a defense against the Moslems. But many of these warlords, the *dynatoi*, have grown too powerful. We cannot allow it to continue."

"Greedy. And ungodly," Patriarch Antony said, speaking for the first time. "They must be stopped lest Byzantium becomes another Sodom and Gomorrah."

The emperor raised his brows at that possibility, but did not correct the holy man. It was an exaggeration, Sidroc presumed. And really, didn't the emperor come from warlord stock himself?

Sidroc was familiar with that biblical story of Sodom and Gomorrah, and he would be damned if he was going to be the Greek's pillar of salt. As if reading his mind, Finn whispered to him in an undertone, "I would not look good in salt."

"What did you say?" the general demanded.

"Just telling Sidroc that we need more information," Finn lied.

"Precisely what do you want us to do?" Sidroc

asked, looking at the emperor, Sclerus, and the patriarch in turn. He had no idea what role the eparch played in all this.

"The border properties are not paying their taxes properly," the eparch said, "and we suspect they are harboring criminals who must be brought to justice."

The eparch was second in power only to the emperor in Miklagard. He enforced the law of the land, tracking down culprits and trying them in the courts. Sometimes criminals were flogged on the spot. He supervised all the people and goods coming into and leaving the country. Anyone who wanted to do business in the city needed to get a permit from him. He even set prices and wages for goods and services, and regulated taxes. Some said he had a thousand people working for him from his headquarters in the Praetorion, which also housed the prison, on the Mese halfway between the Augustaion and the forum. A man not to be trifled with, for a certainty.

So, seeing the eparch's involvement, Sidroc concluded that this was about money as well as fear of eroding power.

"I repeat, what would you have us do?" Sidroc was beginning to suspect they had been set up. Recognizing that he and Finn wanted to leave, they were using that as leverage. "Surely you do not expect us to lead troops into those areas. It sounds like a massive operation."

The general shook his head. "We are not looking for an outright fight. Not at this point, anyway. What we want is information."

"Spies? You want us to spy?" Sidroc was incredulous. He was a fighter, not a slyboots who could slip in and out of dark corners.

"Yes," the general answered, "but only on one warlord, Steven Bardas, and his holding, two days' ride by horse or camel in the mountains close to Byzantium. You would only be gone a week, or two."

The scorn in the general's tone was telling. It was a well-known fact that the Sclerus and Bardas families had been at odds with each other for generations. They were dynasties, really. Warring dynasties. And the connections were many and complicated. For example, the emperor's first wife, Maria, had been a Bardas.

"Would not Greek soldiers do better for this role?" Finn asked. "Sidroc and I do not exactly blend in." 'Twas true. They were taller than the average Greek and clearly Nordic in appearance, Finn more so with his blond hair.

"That is the best part," the emperor interjected. "Apparently Bardas is recruiting mercenaries, including my Varangian guardsmen."

"Won't he be suspicious?" Sidroc could not believe he was even considering another assignment, and one as a spy, at that. He was a soldier, not a sneak-about.

"You two can convince him otherwise," the general said. "We would not ask if we did not think you were capable."

Right. Why not just ask us to walk through fire, or put a sword through our own hearts? "If we undertake this one last mission," Sidroc addressed the emperor, "do we have your oath to release us from our duties, with bonus pay?"

The emperor stiffened at their demand for a promise, but then he looked to the patriarch and said, "I give my oath afore God."

That was good enough for Sidroc. When Finn started to say something, Sidroc stepped on his foot.

Specific details were given to them then as they all scanned the map of the region in question. Forget about horses or camels, they would probably need goats to climb that mountainous area. Or at the least, mules. How humbling was that for a Viking? *Gods, I need to be back on a longship again.* Thinking of that, he decided to send word to his men serving under him here in Byzantium to make ready his longship and bring it to Miklagard forthwith. It had been beached near a harbor outside the city gates these past five years.

Now that the meeting was over, the eparch looked at Sidroc and said, "What will your mistress, the pretty jewelry maker, do when you resign?"

The pretty jewelry maker? Flags of warning went up in Sidroc's head. "She will work as usual."

"She will not be leaving with you?"

Sidroc shook his head, warily. Mylonas's interest in Ianthe alarmed him. There was so much he could do to thwart her business and personal life, if he so chose. "Does Ianthe have reason to be concerned? Are her trade permits not in order? Is she behind in her taxes?"

"No. I was just asking."

He and Finn exchanged glances. Sidroc would definitely need to hire a guard or two for her, aside from the daytime shop guard. In fact, she might be better off living outside the city, making her jewelry there, and hiring someone to manage her shop.

He sighed. One more problem to resolve before he left the city that was beginning to feel not so golden to him.

But then he had still another problem to deal with.

"I believe I will be meeting one of your countrywomen shortly," the emperor said as his chancellor of the bedchamber helped him into formal robes. "A Norse princess."

"An Arab," Sclerus said scornfully. If there was anything the Greeks hated more than Arabs, Sidroc did not know what it was.

"An Arab? In the palace?" Mylonas's ears perked up with interest.

And the patriarch spat out, "A pagan? Is she a Moslem?" The priest's eyes were practically bugeyed with outrage.

"Nay, nay, nay! Drifa is a *Norse* princess. Viking to the bone. Her father is the powerful King Thorvald of Stoneheim." Sidroc could not believe he was defending the traitorous baggage . . . the woman who might very well prove to be the mother of his secret child. "Really, she has only a speck of Arab blood from her mother's side."

All three men gave Sidroc dubious assessments, as if to say, *We shall see.*

"In any case, 'tis time for me to hold audience," the emperor said, and all three men left the room.

"Holy Valkyries!" Finn said.

"My thoughts exactly."

"Dost think we should follow and see what Princess Drifa faces?"

Sidroc sighed deeply. *'Twould seem a Viking's work is never done.*

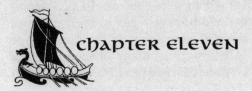 CHAPTER ELEVEN

And then the other shoe dropped . . .

Drifa had thought she'd seen every marvel in the world in her two days in Miklagard, but it was nothing compared to what she witnessed in the Hrysotriklinos, or Golden Hall, where visiting envoys and delegations were formally presented to the emperor and empress.

The long room that resembled a cathedral in its grandeur had marble and colorful mosaic floors. Like paintings, they were. Even the ceilings were adorned with frescoes, mostly biblical scenes. Off to the side were columns, between and behind which court visitors stood. In fact, everyone—at least two hundred people—stood. Only the emperor and empress sat during the lengthy court rituals. Now that the delegation from the Rus lands and some nuns from a mountainous convent in Crete had been heard, it was her turn.

The *logothete,* or chief minister, led Drifa and her contingent of four *hersirs* forward, each carrying gifts for the royal heads of state.

They proceeded down what felt like a gauntlet of visitors, as well as court officials and their assistants, many of whom were eunuchs. In a conversation her father had been engaged in one time with Rafn, he'd referred to eunuchs as the third sex of Byzantium. There were so many of them because they were considered trustworthy, without high ambitions.

Some members of the governing body known as a senate were there as well. And the empress had apparently brought with her numerous ladies-in-waiting, all dressed in finery to rival queens in other countries.

Drifa noticed Sidroc and Finn off to one side as she walked a center path through the long reception hall. Both were in uniforms but apparently not on duty. Finn winked at her, but Sidroc stared at her, grim-faced. *What has his* braies *in a twist now?* she thought, tired of the ups and downs of the brute's moods. First he railed at her, then he teased. No sooner did he smile her way than he was glaring. He made playful jests, then threatened her with vast bouts of sexplay. She would ponder those contradictions later.

Drifa had dressed to the highest standards today, befitting her role as an emissary of a Norse king. She wore a saffron-yellow linen *gunna*, long-sleeved and ankle-length with a train, tucked in at the waist by a gold-linked chain. Over it was the open-sided Norse apron in a deep apricot silk, so fine a quality were both garments they billowed when she walked. In fact, she needed the tight twisted rings about her wrists to keep the fabric from covering her hands. Gold brooches in the pennanular style sat on each shoulder, fastening the shoulder straps. Her black hair, newly washed, hung straight down her back, held off her forehead with a silver fillet made up of writhing wolves, whose jaws met in the center, holding an amber star. The wolves represented her father's standard, and the star represented the Star of the North. On her feet were soft white brocade slippers with silver and gold embossing. A heavy gold chain about her neck held a pendant matching the one on her fillet, a larger star set in gold. Rune rings adorned several fingers.

She was flanked on both sides by the four *hersirs* who'd brought her to Byzantium. They'd taken as much care with their appearance today as she had. More than one woman gave them double looks as they passed by, especially Jamie, who wore Scottish attire that left bare his muscular legs. Her four guardsmen were in the crowd behind them.

As they neared the dais where the emperor and empress sat, Drifa stumbled with shock over what happened before her very eyes. If not for Wulf and Thork, she might have fallen flat on her face.

The throne rose up in the air a little and the golden lions sitting on either side began to shake their tails and roar. Gold and silver trees embellished with precious stones, like diamonds and rubies, held life-like birds that began to sing. It was the most astonishing marvel she had ever seen. It must be magic, or the most incredible feat of some mastermind.

The emperor laughed at what must be stunned looks on their faces.

The *logothete*, who had led them forward,

stopped at a circle of purple marble, where he used
his staff to rap on the floor for attention from the
murmuring crowd. In a booming voice, he announced, "Your Serenity, I bring you Princess Drifa
of the Norselands and her companions, Lord Wulfgar Cotley of Wessex, Lord Thork Tykirsson of
Dragonstead, Lord James Campbell of the Scottish
Highlands, and Lord Alrek Arnsson of Stoneheim."
Drifa stifled a grin at the wincing men beside her,
none of whom claimed to be lords of anything.

Her men went down on one knee and lowered
their heads. Alrek almost tipped over, but Wulf
grabbed his arm and caught him in time. Drifa
merely bowed her head as befitted her high station.
If they'd been in closer proximity, she might have
been permitted to kiss the emperor's right hand. As
it was, they were at the bottom of three porphyry
steps that led to the pedestal on which the thrones
rested.

"Rise and welcome to Byzantium. Your presence
at this blessed time is an honor to both me and the
empress," the emperor said, looking toward the
stone-faced woman at his side, who would be his
wife in a few days. In truth, Drifa felt a shaft of
pity spear her for the Empress Theodora, who appeared out of place and miserable.

The emperor and empress sat on the double
seat of an ornate, double-cushioned throne under
a canopy of purple silk hangings. Purple was the
color reserved for royalty because its dye was made
from the scarce murex shell.

The emperor wore a long-sleeved tunic of purest
white with jeweled embroidery around the neck-

line and a straight line down from chest to feet. Around his neck was a purple *chalmys* cape adorned with golden squares, the edges of which held jeweled pendants hanging from gold chains. If that wasn't enough glitter, on his head the emperor wore a gem-studded crown that had a fringe of gem pendants hanging from chains down the nape. Her father and his men would have a good laugh over the crimson shoes.

Like peacocks, the females were not so colorful. Empress Theodora wore her mostly gray hair pulled tautly off her face into coils above each ear. She wore no jewelry, except for her diadem, which was a smaller version of the emperor's crown. Her *chiton* was pale blue silk with no embroidery or adornment of any kind. And she wore no face paint, like many women of the court did . . . kohl, rouge, powder, and such.

With ritualistic fanfare, the *logothete* took the parchment roll of credentials from Drifa and handed them to an aide standing near the throne.

"Your Majesty, I bring you gifts from my father, King Thorvald." Drifa motioned with her hand for each of the *hersirs* to step forward one at a time. "Here," she said, opening a carved wooden case with a satin lining, "are samples of some of the most precious amber harvested by Vikings in the Baltics. As you see, they are all colors and sizes, suitable for display or decoration or to be made into fine jewelry." The emperor leaned forward with avid interest.

"For you, Empress Theodora, I have a special gift." Thork handed her a small, silk-lined leather pouch. Having learned that the empress had been in a convent at one time, Drifa had commissioned Ianthe this morning to quickly make up a set of prayer beads, which the Greeks called *komvos-koini*. Hers were made of tiny amber balls on a silver chain with a silver amulet containing a relic of St. Sophia that Ianthe had provided. A simple job for Ianthe's assistants, just a matter of stringing the beads, really.

You would have thought Drifa had handed Theodora a sack of gold, so pleased was she. In fact, tears welled in her eyes as she said, "I thank you for your gift, Princess Drifa." Then the empress added, "I understand you are interested in flowers. Would you care to see my private garden?"

Drifa nodded, and the empress said that one of her ladies would contact her for a time and place.

The empress was no less homely than she had appeared the night before, but she was a kind woman, Drifa realized, and that was more important. To her, leastways.

She also gifted the emperor with rare white furs from the North Bear, a tun of mead, and a finely crafted sword perfected in the pattern-welded style, its hilt of solid silver embossed with gold.

After the presentation of gifts, the emperor gave her a formal invitation to the wedding and bid her stay in the palace as long as she was in the city. He raised his hand and made the sign of the cross in the air, a signal of dismissal. The *logothete* backed them away from the throne, calling out, "So be it! So be it!"

As they turned a short distance away, she noticed General Sclerus, chief commander of all Byzantine armies, who had been pointed out to her the night before. He was talking, head to head, with a rat-faced man who stared at her suspiciously.

She soon found out why.

"I am Prefect Mylonas," he said, putting a hand on her forearm to halt her progress.

She tried to shrug off his insolent hand, but the rodent just squeezed.

"I noticed the products you gave the emperor. I wonder what other goods you have brought into our country. I know for a fact that you have declared none. No one trades in Constantinople without my permission, not even royal personages."

"Trade? What trade?" she sputtered.

"That is what we will discuss. Come to the Praetorion tomorrow before noon. Do not force me to send my men for you."

"Are you threatening me?"

He shrugged. "And here's another bit to ponder, m'lady. I noticed you have Arab blood in your pretty body. Do you perchance act as spy here in Constantinople for our Arab enemies?"

"That is an outrageous suggestion. I have only ever known one Arab in passing in my whole life, and he was a medical comrade of my Saxon brother-by-marriage."

"Be there. Tomorrow. That is all I will say for now."

The exchange took only a moment, and her guardsmen had not yet caught up with her. Her *hersirs* had not even noticed the man, so much were they gaping at their surroundings.

But Sidroc had noticed.

When they were outside in a corridor, he stomped up to her and demanded, "What did Mylonas want with you?"

"Mylonas? The rat-face?"

"Precisely."

"He wants me to prove that I am not here to trade goods. Or spy."

"That is not all he wants."

"What?"

Sidroc motioned for Ivar, her other three guardsmen, and the four *hersirs* to follow him into a side chamber. It opened onto a long garden that ran in terraced ledges all the way down to the sea wall.

"Finn and I must leave the city in the morning—"

"I did not think you were leaving so quickly," she interrupted. For some reason, her body hummed with alarm. She did not want him to go.

"Not home, princess. A mission. A short military mission that will take us out of the city for a sennight or so. Ivar," he said then, turning away from her, "you must take special care to stay with the princess at all times, and to alert others where she goes. People disappear in Miklagard, ofttimes under the directive of Mylonas." Addressing Drifa again, he said, "I would not want to be forced to rescue your sweet arse from a desert harem where you have been sold as a slave."

"Do not be ridiculous. That would never happen."

He arched his brows.

"It has happened more times than I can count.

And, clearly, you have come to the attention of the eparch. Not to mention General Sclerus, who has a hatred of anything Arab."

"I am not Arab," she said with consternation.

"Part Arab," he corrected dryly.

Ivar put a hand on Sidroc's shoulder in a manly way. "Thank you for the warning. We will take special care."

Sidroc turned to her *hersirs*, who stood listening to the information intently. "Wulf, how much longer will you be in the city?"

Wulf shrugged. "No more than a sennight, but if there is that great a danger, we will take Princess Drifa with us."

And cause them further delay. I would ne'er hear the end of it.

"I would accompany Princess Drifa to the meeting with the eparch but I must leave the city afore dawn," Sidroc continued, ignoring her totally. "Would you accompany her, Wulf? In fact, all of you?" He indicated her *hersirs* as well as the guardsmen.

That seemed a bit of an overreaction to her, but she had more to be annoyed over. "I am standing right here, Sidroc. You do not need to speak as if I am invisible. And let it be known, Wulf, I make my own decisions, and I am not leaving Miklagard until I am ready."

The men rolled their eyes in the manner men did when they thought their women were acting illogically. In other words, when they did not agree with them.

"I have a bad feeling," Sidroc insisted in the end.

"I am not your problem," she asserted, concluding the meeting. Or so she thought.

"Unfortunately, that appears not to be true." Before she could question that odd statement, Sidroc turned to the others. "I would speak to the princess in private for a moment. Ivar, you can stand in the doorway and watch if you are concerned about the impropriety."

"I have no interest in—" she started to speak, but Sidroc took her upper arm in a vise-like clasp and nigh dragged her into the garden and past the ever-present fountain. With no doubt panic-stricken irrelevance, she noted that this must be a bird garden. Dozens of different kinds seemed to be chirping and singing. When they were far enough from curious ears, he inhaled and exhaled several times.

"Well, spit it out. 'Tis obvious you have something stuck in your craw. Again."

He glared at her. "I'm trying to find the words."

She arched her brows and tapped her foot impatiently.

"Is Runa mine?"

The things women do to hide their secrets . . .

Sidroc watched with increasing fury as Drifa's face went bloodless and she put a hand to her heart, swaying on her feet. What had seemed like an impossible idea a short time ago was becoming possible.

"What do you mean by such a question?" she demanded in her haughty princess voice, raising her chin and pretending ignorance.

Hah! She was as innocent as a cobra in a privy. Well, her lies were about to come back and bite her in the arse.

"What do you think I mean? Every time I mention the child or its father, you get scared. You ne'er answer any questions about the girl. And you just about fainted now when I asked if Runa was mine. You are hiding a secret, M'lady Liar, and I would know what it is. The logical conclusion would be—"

"—that I birthed a child of your seed? For the love of Frey! When you asked if Runa was yours, you meant *ours*?" she asked with wide eyes and dropped jaw. And then relief, of all things. "What was it? An immaculate conception? A long-distance tupping? I swear you are the dunderhead of all dunderheads." She dared to laugh at him.

His jaw hardened with anger and he fisted his hands to keep from throttling her. "Did you or did you not have your way with me when I was in a six-sennight sleep? Did you birth my child? Was Runa born, oh, let us say, almost exactly four years ago?"

She stared at him with seeming incredulity.

"Answer my bloody damn questions?" he roared.

He could tell she wanted to hit him, but instead she asked in an irksome voice of calmness, "Exactly how would a woman go about having her way with a sleeping man?"

"As if you do not know! She would wait until he was in a death-sleep, and when he had a nighttime erection, or mayhap she would have brought him to enthusiasm with her hands or mouth, she would climb atop him and hump until his seed shot into her womb."

Her eyes got wider and wider with his words. "Mouth . . . enthusiasm . . . hump?" she sputtered. "You think I did those things?"

He nodded. "Mayhap more than once."

"Runa is not a child of my womb."

She was lying, or at the least there was some secret she was withholding. "Do you swear the girling Runa is not of my blood?"

"She is not our child, Sidroc. But just for the sake of curiosity, what would you do if she was? You are a soldier. You have no home. You have no wife."

"I will soon have a home, and I would have my child under my shield, regardless. If you bore my child and kept it from me, I would take the babe in a trice and not look back."

Her lips quivered and her hands shook as she sank down onto a marble bench. He followed and turned toward her, knee to knee.

"Sidroc, I have never lain with a man, and Runa is not our child."

He was still suspicious. "So, if I asked your men about the girl . . . the color of her hair or eyes, her facial features, they would not say reddish-brown hair, gray-green eyes? If I went to Stoneheim and saw the child, there would be no resemblance?"

"Nay, do not be questioning my men. And I

definitely do not want you going to Stoneheim to disturb my family."

"Your wishes are no longer my concern, if ever they were."

"I swear to you on my mother's grave and my father's heart, Runa is not our child."

"Then what secret do you hide?"

"Mayhap I will tell you one day, but for now it is my secret to keep."

"So be it!" He stood and was about to leave. First thing he was going to do was question some guardsmen.

"Wait," she said, and stood to face him, a hand on his arm. "For all purposes, Runa is my child, though I did not give her birth. I must needs protect her at all costs. If you promise not to ask any more questions about Runa, I will tell you my secret after you return to the city, afore you leave Miklagard for good."

He frowned. "Why would I make such a promise? What benefit is there for me?"

"If you will wait"—her face flushed—"I will . . . I will give you . . ."

He knew instinctively what she was going to offer in return for asking no more questions. "Forty-two nights in my bed furs?"

"Or until you leave the city for good."

"At which time you will tell me your secret?"

She nodded.

"This must be *some* secret you hold close, princess. You would give me your maidenhead to protect a child. A child you seem to think I might endanger." He wondered now just who the father might be. Obviously someone of importance. He would find out, eventually. But he was not about to let her off the hook so easily. "You are twenty and nine years old, Drifa. How do I know your female parts are not withered up, like a raisin?"

Her face flamed, but she shot back, "You are thirty and one. How do I know your dangly part is not shriveled to a winter-soft carrot?"

He laughed. "My dangly part is just fine, I assure you, especially with that head drilling that was forced on me."

"Would you prefer they left you for dead?"

"As you did?"

She rolled her eyes. "Do we have to discuss all that again? Will you accept my offer?"

"Agreed," he said finally and turned to walk away. But then he stopped. "Come here." He motioned her toward him with a forefinger.

He saw her warring with herself, wanting to tell him what to do with his finger. But then she gave in and walked up to where he stood waiting.

"Put your arms around my neck and seal our bargain with a kiss."

She did so with an awkwardness that touched him, despite himself. At first he let her press her lips against his in a kiss that was more suited to a child.

"Have you forgotten everything I taught you?" He hauled her up against him, chest to chest, groin to groin, causing her to be on her tiptoes.

"It was five years ago."

"Still arguing with me, sweetling. That is no way to persuade me to do your bidding."

She said a foul word under her breath. "What do you want me to do?" They were so close he felt said breath on his mouth.

"Open for me." He took over the kiss then, and it turned out Drifa hadn't forgotten much at all. Soon they were both panting with excitement. He could tell she was astonished by her quick response to him. He was astonished, too, and pleased.

"Oh my gods," she whispered, putting the fingertips of one hand to her lips.

He smiled. "Be in my chambers afore nightfall and do not plan to leave until dawn. Another thing. Do not bother to bathe afore coming to me. We will bathe together in my bathing pool."

He could tell she was shocked at first, as he intended, but she quickly shuttered her expression with a cool look of disdain. "Good. Because you stink."

Lifting an arm, he sniffed. No problem. Of course there wasn't. He had washed and put on a clean uniform before coming to court. He realized two things then.

Drifa was gone.

And the witch had gotten the last word in.

 chapter twelve

Let the lessons begin . . .

Drifa had hours to prepare for her "meeting" that evening with Sidroc, but she waited until the last moment to tell Ivar her plans.

"I will be spending the night with Sidroc," she said without preamble.

"Princess! You cannot do that."

"I can and I will, Ivar. With all due respect, I am twenty and nine years old, well past the age for maidenly protection of my virtue."

The shock on his face pierced her. "I promised your father to protect you, m'lady."

"And you do so, well and good." Seeing that he was unconvinced, she said something she knew she should not, but it preserved at least a bit of her self-respect and might convince her guardsman to relent. "Sidroc and I are betrothed."

She was therefore in a stormy mood by the time dusk rolled around and she arrived, with Ivar, at Sidroc's quarters. And, yea, Ivar would be standing guard outside the door all night. That was the concession she'd had to make to his demand that she allow him to speak to Sidroc first. She knew what "speaking" would entail. Fists, at the least. Blood, at the worst.

When she knocked on his door, Sidroc opened it immediately, raised his brows at Ivar's scowling presence and raised them even farther when she shoved him aside and slammed the door behind them, leaving Ivar behind.

"That was rude."

"Do not speak of rudeness, you arrogant lecherous libertine. Do not pretend to—" She stopped speaking on getting her first good look at the cad. He was wearing only *braies*, low slung on his hips, and naught else. Even his big bare feet with their narrow toes reeked sex. If she were not so blistering mad, she might have been tempted by his handsomeness. She might have put a hand to the light dusting of reddish-brown fur on his chest. She might have pressed a fingertip against his hard male nipples. She might have done so many wicked things. Instead she snapped, "Expecting a heat wave?"

"Nay, just you."

She could tell he was amused by her fury, which had not been her intention. If there were a pottery pitcher nearby, she would hurl it gladly.

"Is Ivar going to stand out there all night?"

"Yea. Feel free to go out and remove him, if you will."

"His presence does not bother me. Just do not do too much squealing with bedjoy, lest he think I am killing you."

As if I even know what bedjoy is! She shot him daggers of revulsion.

He just smiled. "How did you convince him to allow you to come stay the night?"

"I told him we are betrothed." She raised a hand to halt what she knew would be some insult or other about how he would not marry her now if she were the last female this side of Asgard. "Do not worry that I am deluding myself about your intentions. I will not be begging you to make a virtuous woman of me."

"Virtuous?" he scoffed.

The donkey's arse! "What do you want me to do? Let us get this farce over with as soon as possible."

"You are so anxious for us to begin."

"Nay. I am so anxious for us to end."

"Sweetling." He laughed. "We have at least nine hours to while away, by my guess. I have even lit a timekeeping candle so you can keep count. We have plenty of time."

Drifa gulped, unable to imagine what could possibly last for nine hours. He was probably just teasing her.

"I thought we might start with a light repast," he said, pointing to a low table where there was fruit, cheese, and a flagon of wine.

"My stomach heaves at the thought of sharing food with you at the moment."

He should have been offended, but instead he just shrugged. "Perchance later you will have worked up an appetite."

She hoped not.

He handed her one of the goblets of wine, though. When she tried to decline, he said, "Drink

it, Drifa. You need to soften your sharp edges."
She was about to argue that her sharp edges were
her only weapons against this untenable situation,
but he put his fingertips to her mouth. "Enough.
Come, let me show you around."

Sidroc's bedchamber was small, containing only
a raised pallet with a thick mattress against one
wall, several pegs on the wall for clothing, and a
large chest. His bedchamber had another door, on
the opposite side from the entrance door, which
opened onto a bathing pool with floating lotus
blossoms. It was situated in the midst of a small
garden. There was also an antechamber with a
table where soldiers could get massages to work
out their weary muscles. Another table sat in the
garden, this one for dining or playing the board
game *hnefatafl*, which lay open as if a game had
been interrupted.

"They give such splendid accommodations
to all Varangian soldiers?" If her mind were not
consumed with what was to come she might have
enjoyed investigating the garden more thoroughly.
Right now flowers were the last thing on her mind.

"Nay. Those in command of divisions, as Finn
and I are, get separate quarters. And we share." He
pointed to five other closed doors arranged next to
his in a semicircle.

Drifa was appalled, but not by the bathing pool
or massage area. "These men could come out at
any time and witness what you . . . what I . . ."

He smiled. "Your modesty is safe, Drifa. Those
doors are locked, at my request."

Thank the gods!

"The men know I am entertaining a lady, but not whom."

Oh good gods!

"However, Ivar standing guard in the outside corridor might be a clue to some."

There was naught she could do about that. Ivar would not budge without her, she knew that sure as sin . . . the sin she was about to commit.

"This is a good life you have here," she remarked, sipping at the wine. Unlike Sidroc's reason for giving her the wine, she needed it for courage. "Are you sure you want to give up all this luxury?"

"For a certainty. Finn and I had a conversation on this very subject recently. Vikings are not meant for such a soft life. It weakens us."

She nodded her understanding. "My father always says that the coldness of the north hardens a man's muscles."

"And other body parts," he commented dryly.

If circumstances were different, she might have laughed with him.

"Don't you feel guilty betraying Ianthe?"

"Nice try, Drifa, but you cannot make me feel guilty. Ianthe and I did not have that kind of relationship. In fact, we have none now, except for being friends." She must have gazed at him doubtfully because he added, "Are you looking for fidelity from me, Drifa?"

"Nay, that is not what I meant."

As if she hadn't spoken, he said, "Well, you have it. Yours will be the only bed furs I share until I leave this country."

"Even Ianthe?"

"Even Ianthe," he agreed. Then laughed. "Guess who is visiting her this evening?"

"Who?"

"Alrek, your clumsy Viking."

This was news to her, though she shouldn't be surprised. Alrek had talked about nothing but Ianthe since the emperor's feast. "Visiting? Do you mean that in a carnal sense?"

"I doubt it, but not for lack of the young man's wanting. 'Twould seem he has fallen in love with my former mistress, or so he claims."

"And how does Ianthe feel about that?"

He shrugged. "Mostly she is amused, I think. He is quite a few years younger than she is."

"And you don't care that Ianthe would be with another man so soon?"

"Nay. We are friends and always will be. I wish her joy in her life, wherever it comes from, or whomever it comes from."

That was amazing to Drifa. *I wonder if he will care so little about me once he ends this game of his. Will he discard me like stale ale because, in truth, we are not even friends?*

Sidroc sat down on a low bench near the pool, his long legs extended and crossed at the ankles. "Take off your gown, Drifa, so I may see what I have 'bought.'"

And so we begin. "You have not bought me, knave. We are equal in this bargain."

"Take it off, Drifa."

She downed the rest of her wine, feeling the heady liquid rush to all her extremities, dulling her brain. But not nearly enough. She was fully aware of what she was doing as she removed her garments and soft shoes. She raised her chin but could not make herself look at him. She knew that her blush covered not just her face but her entire body exposed to his scrutiny, and that was evidence enough that he was humiliating her.

"Unbraid your hair and comb it out with your fingers." His voice was huskier than usual.

She raised her hands, thus lifting her breasts, which were much too full for her slim frame, in her opinion. Combing through the long strands required her to not only raise her arms but twist her shoulders from side to side, which in turn caused her breasts to bob. In the process, she inadvertently looked his way. Then looked again. Not only was he flushed, too, but there was a large bulge sticking up from his *braies*.

Before she could bite her foolish tongue, she asked, "The head drilling?"

"Nay, this is all your doing."

Mine? My nude body has that effect on him? She was both flattered and gratified by his remark.

"Come closer," he demanded, and spread his legs.

You can do this, Drifa. Think of Runa. You can do this. When she stood between his thighs, he ran his fingertips over the outside of her arms that she'd pressed rigidly to her sides. Every fine hair on her body rose to attention, including some unmentionable places.

"Oh nay, no hiding. Open your eyes."

Think about planting bushes. And manure. Do not let him see your feelings. When she opened her eyes, she noticed immediately the haze of arousal in his eyes, which were more gray than green at the moment. "Good girling," he said, and leaned up to kiss her briefly before setting her back so he could see her better. "You are so beautiful."

She was not, but 'twas not the time to argue. In truth, she doubted she could put two words together as he lifted her breasts from underneath, then ran his thumbs across the nipples, bringing them to hard points. *Manure, manure, manure. Horse manure. Cow manure. Oooooh!*

Sensing that she was about to swoon, he put his hands to her waist for a moment. "It is all right if you moan your ecstasy here and there."

"I swear, I am going to hit you over the head with a pottery jug first chance I get."

"Do not be angry with me because your body betrays you, Drifa."

And then her body betrayed her some more as he played and played and played with her breasts. Tweaking the nipples. Running his knuckles across them. Pinching them, for Asgard's sake! But it was when he put his mouth to her that it became too much. He suckled her, he actually suckled her. Hard. Rhythmically. Interspersed with flicks of his tongue. Then he moved to the other breast and did the same.

"So much for manure!" she muttered.

"Huh!"

"I am thinking about manure so I can resist you better."

"Don't you dare." He licked one of her nipples, and a shock of pleasure rippled throughout her body. Her knees gave way and he caught her with a chuckle, placing her on his lap. But not just on his lap. She was astraddle his lap, wide open and exposed to his scrutiny. And he was scrutinizing her, all right.

"Oh, this is not normal. Let me up."

"Not a chance."

"But . . . but . . . I need to visit the privy. I think my bladder is leaking."

His lower body lurched, and he made a low moaning sound at the back of his throat before pressing his forehead against hers, as if trying to catch his breath. "Drifa, dearling, that is not piss. It is your woman dew readying itself for my penetration."

"I must be as perverted as you are!" she exclaimed when she understood what he meant. *Can this situation get any more embarrassing?*

"That is not perverted, silly woman. 'Tis the way the gods . . . or the One-God . . . made women. It will aid in your pleasure."

"Pleasure! I do not intend to get any pleasure from this act. Not at all." *If I can help it.*

"Tsk, tsk, tsk! Do you not know better than to dare a Viking?"

"I was not daring you."

"Sounded like a dare to me." To demonstrate, he put a fingertip right into her wetness and fluttered it once, twice, three times.

She almost flew off his lap.

But he put both hands to her hips and held her in place. In fact, he moved her flush up against his cloth-covered bulge.

"You are torturing me," she said on a moan.

"Sweet torture, I hope."

He began to kiss her then, and, oh, he was a good kisser. She'd always known that Vikings were masters of the art of sailing and fighting. She'd had no idea that some were also masters of kissing. In truth, she'd never known there was an art to it, but there was. There definitely was.

He framed her face with both his hands and moved his lips over hers, slanting and pressing, licking and moving from side to side until he got their alignment right. And then, praise gods and goddesses, he kissed and kissed and kissed her until she was open and ready for his tongue, which he used like an instrument of sexual assault.

"You are too good at this," she murmured during one of his brief breaks.

"Kissing?"

She nodded.

"I practice a lot."

"I'll bet you do," she said, and nipped at his bottom lip.

He laughed and nipped her back.

Her entire body felt as if it were humming, waiting for something momentous to happen. "Are you going to tup me now?"

He made a gurgling sound. "Nay, Drifa, sex is like a good boar stew, best left to simmer and simmer."

"I have simmered enough. Do it. Now."

"Nay. First, I am going to bring you to peak, with my fingers alone. Do you know what peaking is?"

"Not exactly."

"Remember the time in your garden?"

"Oh." *How could I forget?*

"Have you ne'er brought yourself to peak with your own fingers?"

"Are you demented?" *Get on with it, for gods' sake.*

"I guess I will just have to show you then."

"Wait. Are you going to be peaking, too?"

"I hope not. Leastways, I will try to forestall my pleasure until you have had yours. That is why I am keeping my *braies* on. Otherwise, I fear you would cause me to lose control."

Drifa rather liked the idea of her being able to make Sidroc lose control. She eyed him speculatively.

Sensing her thoughts, he chuckled. "Put your hands on my shoulders, Drifa."

She could do that, though she wasn't sure why.

She soon found out.

"Lean back. More than that. Ah, just so."

If she hadn't been holding on to his shoulders, she would have fallen backward. *Acrobatic sex? The man really is perverted.* But she was unable to think after that. About manure. Or acrobatics. Or anything else.

He was touching a part of her body between her legs, a spot where all the nerve endings in her body seemed to be centered. She began to keen with the mounting tension filling her from head to toes to the tips of her fingers, but especially *down there*. If she hadn't been so focused on what the fingertip was doing, she would have realized that the middle finger of his other hand was stuck up inside her. She yelped and tried to rise up, but he would not let her.

"Press downward, dearling. Lift and press. That's the way. What a good learner you are!"

And then she screamed. She actually screamed with the pure white-hot flames of bliss that overtook her in wave after wave after wave. It was the most horrible/wonderful thing she had ever experienced in all her life. Better even than the time she'd managed to grow a bloodred rose.

When she came back to her senses, she was slumped against him, her face pressed into the curve of his neck, his hands caressing her back in a soothing manner. She was mortified, not by what Sidroc had done to her, but by how she had reacted.

He drew back slightly and kissed her softly. Then he said the last thing she wanted to hear right now.

"That was a good start, sweetling."

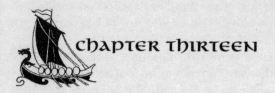

CHAPTER THIRTEEN

He was a regular Marco Polo . . .

When Sidroc had first "coerced" Drifa into coming to his bedchamber, he doubted that he planned to carry through with his threats, just give her a bloody damn scare into revealing her secret. But now . . . Holy Thor! *Now* . . . He couldn't stop now if he wanted to.

Not only had she caused him to spill his seed in his *braies* like an overeager youthling with his first maid, but his enthusiasm was at high pitch again. He was almost afraid to show her the size of his cock lest she go running for the gates.

Fortunately she was in a daze as he carried her into his bedchamber and laid her on his bed. He'd already lit an oil lamp when he'd been readying for her visit.

He went back out and got the wine and goblets. When he returned, she was no longer in a daze. She stood at the foot of his bed, wrapped in his bed covering like a shroud. She was holding the cloth together with one hand, and in the other she had his broadsword dragging on the floor. The weapon was heavy for a man. A woman, especially one of her weight, would scarce be able to lift it with two hands, let alone one. Of course she could drop her shroud. That was a picture he'd like to have in his memory . . . a naked Drifa wielding a sword. "I fulfilled my part for tonight," she said.

"Oh nay, you little schemer. That little bit of diddling did not count for one night."

" 'Twas sex," she argued.

" 'Twas foresport. Do not think to get off so easily."

"Easy?" she nigh shrieked. "That was not easy."

"Put the sword down, Drifa, afore you hurt yourself. And have some wine to calm your nerves."

"My nerves are just fine, but this charade is ending. You've had your fun, and now 'tis time—"

"Drifa, Drifa, Drifa, does it look like I have had enough fun yet?" He gave a meaningful glance downward. "They have contests in the Hippodrome for every blessed thing. If they start having them for the man with the biggest cockstand, I would win easily."

"This is beyond embarrassing." She was staring at his bulge.

She's embarrassed? I'm the one who should be embarrassed. Well, not really.

"I feel like a small child who wet the bed, and you are a rude dolt for calling attention to it."

"Huh?"

She dropped the sword with a loud clank on the marble floor. He hoped she didn't put a crack in the stone. He would check later. Then she waddled along, almost tripping over the dragging bed covering, to the stand where he'd placed the goblets and took several big sips out of one of them, hoping to get brave with drink, no doubt. Only then did she explain by motioning with her goblet toward the dark spot on the crotch of his *braies*. "I dampened you."

She'd dampened him, all right, but not in the way she imagined. "Pfff! That is mostly from me, not you."

Tilting her head to the side, she watched as he lowered his *braies*, gingerly, and began to wash himself with a small cloth he'd moistened in the pottery bowl of water.

She gasped.

He glanced over and saw her eyes riveted on his manpart that, if anything, was even bigger. But really, was there ever a greater compliment to a man than a woman's gasp when he dropped his *braies*?

"Why is it red on the end? Does it hurt?"

He started to speak and choked. After a short bout of coughing, he said, "It hurts good."

"What kind of male illogic is that. Oh! You mean like that sweet torment you just inflicted on me."

Sweet torment. He liked the sound of that. "Precisely."

"Give me a cloth so I can cleanse myself."

"You would have to drop your shroud to do that," he pointed out. *Please do.*

"You could turn your head."

"Or not."

"Give me the damn cloth."

He laughed and held the cloth away from her. "I like seeing the woman dew glistening on your curly hairs." *Come closer, my little bug. This spider would like to spin some more dew in you.*

"I don't have curly . . . Oh, good gods, that is perverted."

"Not even nearly." He walked over to the bed and lowered himself to lie with his arms folded under his head.

"You look ridiculous," she said.

"So do you."

"I meant you look ridiculous because of that . . . that thing standing up in the air."

"Dost think so?" He gazed down at himself. It looked mighty impressive if you asked him.

"Surely you do not think it would fit."

"I know it would fit." *Come closer, little bug, and I will show you how.*

She shifted uneasily from foot to foot, probably wondering if she should run.

That would be a sight to titillate the jaded courtiers. *A naked Varangian chasing a naked Viking princess down the halls. Mayhap we can try it later. Or not.*

"There is still time to end this farce, Sidroc."

Thor's breath! She is still talking. "Only if you tell me your secrets."

"I cannot. Not yet."

He shrugged. In truth, he would rather have her than her secrets at the moment. "Come to bed, Drifa, and fulfill your bargain, or could it be you have some special entertainment planned for me?"

She made a snorting sound that should have been disgusting, but, on the contrary, was rather adorable. "Like what?"

He shrugged again. She made being a spider so easy. "Nude dancing. Nude acrobatics. Nude self-pleasuring."

Her jaw dropped with each of his suggestions.

Hmmm. Those ideas sounded pretty good to him, if he did say so himself. Mayhap later.

Suddenly he reached out a long arm and yanked on the edge of her covering, thus causing her to lurch forward. He caught and lifted her all in one motion, ending up with her lying atop him, her shroud on the floor. "Got you!" he crowed.

She gasped and tried to squirm out of his embrace, to no avail, of course. Instead he adjusted her so that her breasts nestled in his chest hairs, and his favorite body part nestled in her nether hairs. A perfect fit, in his opinion.

He was caressing the soft skin of her back, from shoulders to buttocks, over and over.

A full-body shiver rippled over her.

He was fairly certain it was due to his touch and not distaste.

In one last-ditch effort to change his mind, she said, "You will hate yourself in the morning if you do this thing."

How little you know! "On the contrary. I will hate myself in the morning if I do not. Now, sweetling, like all good Vikings, 'tis time for us go exploring."

She perked up at that suggestion. "Where? What are we going to explore? The palace? The garden?"

"You." He flipped the foolish woman over onto her back so that he could lean over her.

He could see that she wanted to argue, that she

waged a silent war within herself. Sex or secrets. Sex won out, thank Odin, Thor, Frey, and every other god in the Norse universe.

"Oh. If you must." She closed her eyes and laid her head back on the pillow and her arms at her side, like a corpse, or a martyr.

Not for long, he vowed.

"Get it over with quickly, if you don't mind."

"I do mind. This exploration is going to be long and slow with many discoveries along the way, that I assure you." For now he was enjoying a visual exploration. Drifa had aged well, he observed. He had expected more softness and sagging, but she was nigh perfect, curves in all the right places. And no signs of childbirth that he could see, but mayhap not all women showed outward signs.

"Why? Why can't we hurry?"

Blather, blather, blather. She asks more questions than a boyling on first learning about sex. "You would not want me to rush my voyage and miss something important, would you?" *Where to start? Where to start? 'Twas like sitting before a feast and not knowing which delectable dish to try first.*

"Gods forbid!"

"Dost think sarcasm is wise at this point, lily of my heart?" *I have no idea what she is gods-forbidding about. Pfff. It does not matter.* He caressed her jaw with a fingertip.

"Please, don't start with the flower nonsense again. I can take only so much torture." She was still in her corpse pose, but the hands at her sides fisted when he used the same fingertip to draw a path from her collarbone down her chest, all the way to her navel. He interpreted the fisted hands as a good sign that she was getting aroused. On the other hand, perchance it was just a sign that a pottery pitcher would be welcome to her about now.

Enough with talking. Time for action. "The first thing a good explorer does is map out his territory."

And he did.

"Ah, the North Star," he said, tracing her lips with the tip of his tongue. The top, the bottom, the seam. When she was glistening and parted for him, he edged his tongue inside. At first he just basked in the pleasure of filling her, thankful that she hadn't bitten him, but then she sucked on him—a reflex, no doubt—and he groaned into her mouth. Drawing away slightly, he remarked against her lips, "Methinks I have discovered a new fjord. Its waters are wet and warm and delicious."

She murmured, "Fool!" but then she belied her insult by sighing.

An invitation, if he ever heard one.

"Look here what I found, you clever woman. Two islands. One on the east, and one on the west. They're pretty and not too small, either."

"They're too big," she said, cracking one eye open.

"Nay. Just right." In truth, her breasts were big for her slim body, but that's what made them so attractive. To a man, leastways. To him, especially. "And here is the best part. There are berries on your islands, and I am very hungry."

Her hands were still fisted at her side, her eyes

scrunched tight, and her body braced for the assault she expected him to launch. Silly maid! He was Lord of the Bedplay. There were no defenses.

He blew against one breast, then the other.

Her eyes opened with surprise. "What in bloody hell are you doing?"

"Tsk, tsk, tsk! Such language!" He blew again. "A strong north wind is crossing your islands." And that's all he did for a while. Just blowing. But then he licked around each areola, never touching the nipples, just the rosy circles, which he then blew dry. Lick and blow. Lick and blow. "A rainy north wind," he explained.

When she began to arch her chest slightly, as if seeking the wind, he knew he was succeeding. But it was still too soon, in his opinion. So he added another feature to his island exploration. He lifted both breasts from underneath, and continued to lick and blow.

Finally she swore under her breath, grabbed his head, and yanked him down. "Eat the damn berries, you slime-sucking son of a troll."

"Endearments will get you everything, sweetling," he said, laughing against her breast where she had planted his face. Time to give his teasing a rest, he decided, and concentrated on her lovely nipples, already hard as pebbles . . . or berries . . . and begging for his attention. Without warning, he began to suckle her hard, then drew away through puckered lips so that a moist, popping sound echoed in the room. Before she had a chance to smack him for the vulgar sound, he did the same to the other breast. "Your berries are sweeter than honey."

She was breathing heavier now. In fact, her arms were raised above her head in a relaxed position of readiness. Too easy! This was supposed to be a "punishment" of sorts. He rolled off the bed and walked to the bottom.

"Wha-what?"

There was no headboard or footboard; so, before she could say, *Wha-what?* again, he grabbed her ankles and tugged until her buttocks and the bottoms of her feet rested on the edge of the mattress. "Are you ready for a different kind of exploration?" *Best you agree because, ready or not, you are getting it.*

"What kind?"

Thank you for asking, little bug. "Well, my fingers are getting rather tired, and I thought I would use another body part for my discoveries." He paused for a moment so she could imagine the worst.

"Your palm?" she guessed, hopefully.

Think more "perverted," my innocent flower. "My tongue."

She was slow in understanding his meaning, which gave him the opportunity to quickly kneel on the floor and spread her legs wide. *By thunder! Was there ever a sight prettier to a man on a mission? A seduction mission?*

She yelped and tried to sit up, her arms flailing.

He shoved her back down. None too gently, either.

"I knew you were depraved, but this passes all bounds. You toad. How dare you? How . . . oh! Oh my gods!"

He had just pressed his tongue against the secret bud of pleasure all women had, and he knew without a doubt, he had her now. "Dost like that, Drifa?"

Her only response was a gurgle, but her legs went limp, and she allowed him to spread her farther.

"I must be the best explorer in the world, Drifa. Mayhap I will go exploring with Erik the Red to that new world beyond Iceland. Mayhap I have discovered a secret waterway to paradise. There are all these shoals, of course, and hidden channels, but mayhap there will be a dam up ahead. Never fear, my longboat can make it through, that I assure you."

"Mayhap, mayhap, mayhap. If your longboat gets any longer, it will be stuck in the shallows, of that *I* assure you," she countered.

"I love a woman who can make jest in the midst of bedsport." And that was the gods' truth. Life was too hard and unmerciful at times. Laughter and smiles eased a man's life path.

"That was no jest. That was . . . Frigg's foot! . . . What are you doing now?"

"Just using my paddle to explore the water." He laved her with his tongue in long stokes. He flicked certain parts with the tip of his tongue. By the time he began to kiss her sweet spot, she was arching off the bed. He could not have that, so he looped her knees over his shoulders and suckled her bud as he had her nipples.

She peaked and peaked and peaked. He could feel it against his mouth, if he hadn't already come to that conclusion by her almost continuous moaning.

"No more, no more," she protested as he moved her back up the bed and laid himself over her.

"Shhh," he said, "I will take care of everything." He pushed the stray strands of hair off her face and kissed her lightly.

"That is what I'm afraid of. It's not supposed to be like this."

"Oh really? How is *it* supposed to be?"

"Quick."

"Quick is good betimes. At others, 'tis best to make the journey last a long time, to enjoy the scenery along the way, to prolong the bliss."

"My scenery is supposed to be private, and I do not think I can stand any more bliss. Must you do that?"

"Do what?"

"Rub your chest hairs across my nipples. It is . . ."

"It is what, Drifa?

"Unsettling."

He did a mental punch in the air of triumph. "That is because your body yearns for more."

"You are making that up."

He rose up a bit and made more of a production of rubbing his chest hairs over her nipples. When her eyes glazed over, he said, "See. But now it is my turn. Wrap your legs around my hips." He put his hands under her buttocks and raised her up, positioning himself at her woman-portal. "This might hurt the first time, sweetling. Do you want it fast or slow?"

"Fast."

That was all he needed to hear. She was more than moist enough, but she was tight. Very tight. It took three thrusts before he breached her maidenhead and was in as far as her body could take him. He was the one who moaned then, so intense was his pleasure. And not just the tight fit. Her inner muscles were clasping and unclasping him in welcome.

When he was able to speak above a whimper, he rose up on extended arms and looked down at her.

She appeared stunned, her eyes huge and unblinking. Her mouth formed a little circle of astonishment.

"Are you all right, Drifa?"

"I think so."

"Are you in pain?"

She shook her head. "It pinched at first, but now it just feels odd. Are we done?"

Was she really this naïve? Must be. "I am just waiting for you to recover."

"Recover what?"

He tried to smile but found he was unable to, so consumed was he with another activity. Moving out slowly, he relished the drag of her inner muscles that resisted his withdrawal. Then he thrust back in again. This time he went in a little farther.

Surely the way women were built for men was a gift from the gods.

Surely the sex act was a gift from the gods.

Surely Drifa was a gift from the gods.

She blinked up at him and said, "Do that again."

Definitely a gift. He did smile then. "With pleasure."

Drifa might have been a virgin moments ago, but she soon learned the rhythm. She met him thrust for thrust until he was embedded in her to the hilt, and they were both panting on the climb toward what he hoped would be a joint peaking.

For the next three short strokes he made sure he hit her sweet bud, and suddenly she was convulsing around him down below and screaming with joy up above. It took the most painful discipline for him to pull out and spill his seed onto her thigh.

As his breathing slowed and his heart no longer felt as if it would burst from his chest, he realized that he lay heavily atop Drifa, who was surprisingly silent for once. He should move. But he hated what he knew sure as sunshine would happen next. Drifa would begin to berate him for this and that. He was not yet ready to spoil what had been the best swiving he had ever engaged in, and being one and thirty, there had been plenty.

He was also not quite ready to examine what had just happened. Surely it was more than sex. What that more might be, he feared to think. Not with Drifa, with all her secrets. Not with Drifa, who might kill him in his sleep.

The witch surprised the spit out of him then by biting him on the shoulder and instead of saying something like *Are we done yet, you loathsome lout?*, she purred. She honest-to-gods purred. And she bloody damn licked the inner whorls of his ear.

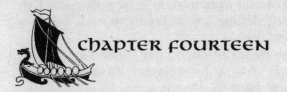

CHAPTER FOURTEEN

A Viking cowgirl?

Who knew? Drifa certainly hadn't. And why had none of her sisters explained, in detail, exactly what would happen in the sex act, and how mind-melting pleasurable it would be? Even with a dolt like Sidroc. She would have a thing or two to say to them when she returned to the Norselands.

"Did you like that, Drifa?" the dolt inquired in a drawl that reeked of male satisfaction as he rolled off her and wiped her thigh with an edge of the bed linen. Then he had the audacity to kiss her thigh on that very spot. Insufferable man! As if sensing her imminent rebellion at his lewdness, he tucked her into his side with her head on his shoulder.

She bit his shoulder, just to show she was not that enthralled by his talents. "I swear, if you smirk, I will . . ."

"What? Hit me over the head with a pottery jug?"

"Mayhap."

"Admit it, Drifa, you enjoyed your first sexplay?"

"Of course I did. Damn the Norns of Fate who made it be with you."

"Be careful when maligning the goddesses. They may just destine you to repeat the act, over and over and over."

If he meant to imply that would be a punishment, he was in for a bigger surprise than she planned. *Time to show you, Varangian troll, just which woman you are with at the moment. I will not be your sex puppet.* "So, this exploring business . . . does it go both ways? Does the woman get to explore, too?"

Sidroc stiffened and turned further to stare at her. "Are you suggesting . . . ?"

She shrugged. *Let's see how you like having a woman pull your erotic strings.* "I might have a yen to go exploring myself."

"A yen?" he choked out.

'Twas a good sign that she could make him choke, Drifa believed. "Yea. The only problem I have is that I have no expertise with steering a longship over the seas. Methinks I would have to explore mountains. Aha! What do I see here? A forest." She ran her fingertip over the silky chestnut-colored hairs on his chest, same color as on his head. She ran her fingers through the curls and was gratified to hear his sharp inhale.

She had to admit, he was a fine specimen of a man, even for a Viking. He was long, and lean and well-muscled, with a smile that the jester god Loki must have graced him with to beguile women.

"Drifa," he cautioned with that damn beguiling smile. "Be careful when putting your head in the lion's mouth."

"Betimes lions are just big cats, you know."

"Do not underestimate me."

I already did. Otherwise I would not find myself in your bed with my woman-dew weeping for another bout of sexplay. "Would I do that?" she inquired sweetly, glancing meaningfully to his manpart that was already rising again. *Fool thing! Tempting fool thing,* she immediately amended.

"Lie still and let me explore," she ordered.

"Whate'er you say, m'lady."

After that she spoke to him in her most sexual voice, if in fact she had one. Her discovery of a gully in her travels, midway between his waist and his thighs. The two immense boulders covered with moss through which emerged a tree, its trunk straight and true. The thick veins that protruded were its bark and the bulging top was a mushroom, she declared, the kind that sometimes emerged out of tree trunks.

By that time, Sidroc was laughing and enjoying her attention immensely if the size of his "tree" was any indication.

"Methinks your exploration on this mountain is getting too tiring for you," he said finally. "You need a horse to ride." With those words, he lifted her so that she straddled his hips. He put his fingertips to her cleft and declared in a raw voice of wonder, "You are wet for me Drifa."

"'Tis just your leftover seed, no doubt." Her heated face had to be flaming.

"Nay, your fjord overflows to ease my long-boat's passage."

"Enough with your fjord longboat nonsense!"

"It means you are ready for me. Come, Drifa,

take my longboat . . . uh, thirsty tree in hand and guide it inside your body where it may be quenched. That's the way, dearling, lower yourself slowly."

Longboat, tree, staff of torture, it was all the same to her. If anyone had told her hours ago that she would do such a thing and sigh with the bliss of being filled by the lout, she would have laughed. Now she could scarce breathe.

With hands on her hips, he guided her. "It really is like riding a horse, isn't it?"

He grinned.

If there was anything more tantalizing than his smile, it was his grin.

"How are you at galloping?"

Are we having fun yet? . . .

Sidroc sat on a shallow ledge of the bathing pool across from Drifa, who had her eyes closed, pretending to be asleep. As if she could escape his attentions so easily!

It was a small pool; he could touch her with his toes if he stretched out his legs. The pool was filled with warm or cold water, or emptied, with the mere flick of a lever. Right now the water was slightly warm and soothing to the overused muscles. And he had overused some of Drifa's muscles, for a certainty.

"When will you leave for your mission?" she asked, her eyes closed, her head resting on the lip of the pool.

"Early morn. I will meet Finn in the stables of the tagmata."

"And when you return, you will leave Byzantium. For where?"

"I am not certain. Finn and I will surely discuss this very subject whilst away. I have a longship that has been beached outside the city. It will be made sea ready in my absence. Mayhap the Orkneys. Mayhap somewhere in the Norselands. Mayhap even some estate near Stoneheim."

Her eyes shot open, and she glared at him for bringing up the subject he'd promised to avoid.

"Just teasing. Just teasing."

She gave him an extra glare for good measure and closed her eyes again. Sinking deeper in the water, she sighed and ran her fingers through the waters. She was relaxed. Too relaxed.

"You are not to worry, dearling. We will still have nights together on my return."

"But not forty-two. Rather forty-one."

"Come, Drifa, you have rested enough. Time to dry off and try something new."

Her eyes were open now, and wary. "New?"

"'Twill be a surprise." He rose from the water and used a long linen for drying himself, taking extra care as Drifa studied his body, despite herself. Then he walked to the other side and drew her upward. As he dried her body, he admired and commented on the various parts.

"Your skin is softer than Byzantine silk," he said.

"But it is ofttimes grimy when I am gardening," she said.

"Your breasts are the size of pomegranates and twice as sweet," he said.

"More like overripe melons, squishy," she said.

"Your maiden hair is like the combed fleece of a golden-haired sheep."

"There is no such thing as a golden-haired sheep. Besides, raw wool is coarse and rough."

"Your buttocks make me breathless."

"Buttocks! Enough!" she finally protested. "Next you will be making praise odes to my toe-nails."

"Now that you mention it . . ."

She groaned.

He smiled. And he knew, because she'd told him so in a weak moment, that his smiles made *her* breathless. "Come, Drifa, there is something special I have planned for you." *For us, actually. For me, particularly.*

He led her to the far side of the bathing pool where there was a wall panel that could be pushed inward. When it revolved, a massive slab of polished brass was on the other side, now facing them. It was taller than a man and twice as wide.

She gasped in wonder. "I have ne'er seen a brass mirror this size afore or one so highly polished as to be like a mirror." Momentarily, she forgot that she stood nude before it. He knew the moment when she realized the state of her undress. "Oh, good gods!" She tried to cover herself with an arm across her breasts and a hand over her groin.

"Nay, Drifa, put your arms down. See yourself as I see you whilst I gather some things."

Though continuing to gape at the wondrous

mirror, she was still trying to cover herself when he returned with several oil lamps, two fat candles, and a small carved olivewood chest, inlaid on top with an ivory longship.

If she only knew, the view from the back was almost as good as from the front. Her legs were long and muscled from all her gardening, no doubt. Her buttocks were high and deliciously round. The curve of her hips accented her small waist, and the small of her back was indented and lovely. Sidroc had a particular fascination with the small of a woman's back.

He lit the candles and lamps and arranged them on either side of the mirror, which added to the moonlight streaming into the room. It was almost as good as daylight.

"Dost think I would be able to purchase one of these brass mirrors here in Miklagard?"

She might not want a reminder after this night was through. "Probably, but it would cost a fortune."

"I have a fortune."

He shrugged. "'Tis time to try something different," he said then.

Drifa jerked, having just realized he stood behind her, very close. "How different?" she squeaked out. "Will it be perverted?"

"Drifa, Drifa, Drifa, what is it with you and perverted?" He forced her arms to her sides and wrapped his arms around her waist. "But, yea, this time it will be perverted, by some people's standards."

She made a small whimpering sound, but did

not argue with him. She'd learned that he liked overcoming her arguments.

"Look how nice we look together, Drifa."

"We are naked!"

"That is the best part."

"I do not think I will ever forget the things you made me do tonight."

"Uh-uh! You do not get away with blaming it all on me. I may have led you on a sensual journey, but you were with me in the end. Besides, I like the memory pictures we are creating."

"You would."

"Lean your head back to my shoulder and put your hands behind your back," he said then.

"Why?"

"And do not talk. You are my sex thrall, remember. You must do as your master bids."

She rolled her eyes, but did as he asked. Before she realized what he was about, he tied her wrists together with a scarf.

Her posture caused her back to arch and her breasts to push forward. The nipples were flushed and erect from his earlier ministrations. Still, he pinched them, then soothed them with soft caresses of his palms.

"The thing I would have you learn in this bout of sexplay is that there is a fine line betwixt pain and pleasure. When you are aroused, as you are now, your breasts and other erotic spots on your body respond to both. For example, I am about to put some jewelry on you which should demonstrate perfectly."

He reached down to the chest at his feet and

took out two small gold rings. They were made of gold so thin it was malleable. He put one on her right breast and pinched it tight, and then tighter so that the nipple was encircled totally by the wire, leaving a small loop below.

"Ouch!" she said, and tried to struggle out of his arms, which caused her breasts to bounce and the pressure on her nipple ring to dig in farther.

"Some women, and even men, have their nipples pierced to hold the rings, but I would not do that to you."

"You're hurting me," she complained.

"Shhh. It will be fine in a moment." He did the same to the other nipple before she realized what he was about.

"You look beautiful, Drifa. Look how much bigger your nipples are now, and red as cherries."

"First pomegranates and now cherries. What next?"

"This," he said, "a little syrup for your cherries."

He took a stopper from a small vial of oil and dribbled it on her breasts, then worked it in with his fingertips. "How does that feel?"

She refused to answer but her beautiful eyes were glazed and her nostrils flared with rising enthusiasm. His enthusiasm was rising, too, and pressing against the cleft of her buttocks.

"You can wear these nipple rings when I am gone, under your *gunna*, to remind you of me."

She made a snorting sound that translated to *Not in a Norse lifetime*. He would wager she would be tempted, though.

"Let me show you something else," he said then.

"Oh gods, is this not enough?"

"Not nearly." He chuckled and attached several dangling beads from both rings, giving them weight, and added titillation, he hoped.

Her only response was a whimper and leaning her head back farther on his shoulder, exposing her neck and arching her breasts even more.

"How does it feel?" he asked against her ear.

"Wicked."

"And wonderful?"

She nodded.

"We are going to sit down now, Drifa, so that I may teach you something." Before she could protest yet again, he sank down to the marble floor and arranged her between his thighs, then he spread her wide so that she might see her womanparts. He doubted she had ever looked there afore. "Dost see how wet you are for me?"

He used the fingertips of both hands to part her farther. "And see that bud there that is swollen and more ruddy than the folds around it? That is the seat of a woman's pleasure. Just strumming it can bring some women to peak."

"Are you going to strum it?"

He shook his head. "I am going to grow it bigger and warmer 'til you are so hungry for a peaking you will beg me to enter you."

"I do not like this game." She tried to close her legs and rise, but he would not allow that. Instead he reached for yet another vial in his chest, and told her, "This is a special oil that makes whatever skin it touches grow hot and throb. It takes only one drop to . . ." He let the stopper hang over her open folds, and one drop fell exactly where he wanted.

Almost immediately she was gaping at what was happening before her eyes. "Do something. Oh, oh, I burn, I yearn. Nay, I throb. Oh, do something, you brute."

"In a moment." He dipped the stopper back in the vial and put one droplet on each of her nipples. They grew before his eyes and became even redder.

"Release me. I must touch myself."

That remark caused him to about peak, which was way too soon. "Mayhap next time."

He put his middle finger between her fold and spread the fluid back and forth over the bud, which was now twice its original size. Then he used the same fingertip to caress her folds and enter her inner channel itself.

She was weeping and crying her ecstasy in almost a continual croon now. He released the scarf from her wrists and guided her down so that her hands and knees were all on the floor and she was facing the mirror. Then, after hesitating only a moment, he added two more beads to each nipple ring, causing her breasts to be drawn down slightly.

"Look at you, Drifa. Look at us."

"I look like a wild woman," she whined. "I look like a wild dog."

"Nay, you look beautiful."

He took her, from behind. When he thrust into her, her breasts bobbed with their weights. He soothed and aroused them further with his fingertips, flicking back and forth across them. Then he did the same to the bud betwixt her legs.

"Do you want me to stop, Drifa?" He paused with the tip of his cock barely inside her. "Tell me what you want."

She tried to wriggle her behind against him to draw him in, but he would have naught of that. "Tell me," he demanded.

"I want you," she finally begged. "Now."

"Whate'er you want, dearling." He pounded her then with long and slow strokes, alternating with short and hard. She peaked not once, or twice, but thrice afore she was satisfied, and he was able to take his own joy.

Later, as he soothed her body in his bed, and her eyes drooped with weariness, he said, "Thank you, Drifa."

"For what?" she murmured against his chest and nestled closer, one leg thrown over his thighs.

"For giving me such pleasure. For taking your own pleasure in sexplay that was a mite . . . extreme."

"At least you admit it was extreme." She paused, drawing circles in his chest hairs with a fingertip. "Would you have done these kinds of things to me back then, five years ago?"

He shrugged. "Probably not. I have developed an appreciation for . . . other things . . . in my travels to other countries. That does not mean there is no pleasure in 'regular' sex. I shouldn't have pushed you so far so fast."

"Does that mean you release me from my . . . obligations?"

"Hah! I can't wait to see what we will do next."

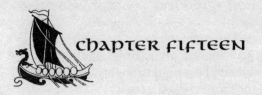

CHAPTER FIFTEEN

A good man is hard to find . . .

Two more hours left by count of the timekeeping candle until Drifa's night of horror ended.

The worst thing, though, was that Drifa wasn't as horrified as she should be. She had enjoyed herself too much, even the depraved things Sidroc asked of her. She could pretend until all the Valkyries went home to Valhalla that she had been forced, but she was a truthful person at heart, and truth was, she had been a willing participant in the end. Seduced, yea. Forced, nay.

What did that make her? Wanton to the bone? Or susceptible to this man only? That latter was a horrible prospect. If she allowed the lecherous lout any inroads into her emotions, he would use the weakness against her. Best to gird her loins against him. And she needed to be strong for that moment when she told him of his daughter and her hopes that he would allow Runa to continue living with her at Stoneheim.

"Why are you stiffening up?" Sidroc whispered against her ear. She'd thought him asleep beside her in his bed, finally depleted. "Are you going to play the corpse again? If so, you will not be wearing a shroud."

She stuck her tongue out at him, although he could not see, tucked up against her back as he was. If he did see, he would probably consider it an invitation for more wicked activity.

But his thing was not prodding her behind, so she figured she was safe. For now.

Belatedly she answered him. "I am asleep."

He chuckled, and she felt his breath against her ear, which was sensitive due to all his ministrations. And, yea, she had to admit it. The man had made love to even her ears. "Then why did you stiffen in your sleep? Bad dreams?"

Nay, a nightmare. "Go back to sleep. We must rise soon, and you will have a long day of riding ahead of you into the mountains." Although he had told her that he and Finn were to be engaged on a military mission into one of the many Greek mountains, he had not told her where or why.

"I can sleep in a saddle, whether it be horse or camel. 'Tis a talent I learned when traveling up one coast of the Saxon lands and down the other in endless battles for King Harald Bluetooth. We gained so much *danegeld* that betimes we horse soldiers walked so the horses could carry our plunder. I got a blister on my big toe the size of an onion."

She giggled at the picture, despite herself. Big bad soldier felled by blister. Too bad it hadn't been on his arse.

"Drifa!" he chastised her.

She realized that she'd inadvertently spoken aloud. *Oh well.*

"What will you do today?" he asked, smoothing her hair off her face. It probably looked like a bird's nest with all the rolling around she'd done.

"Sleep."

He pinched her shoulder lightly in reprimand.

"After I sleep, I will go see Rat Face."

"You must be careful."

"I will. My four *hersirs* as well as the guardsmen will accompany me. Plus, methinks it would be a good idea to make arrangements for my meeting with the empress so that I may remind the eparch that I can stay for only so long because the empress is expecting me."

"Smart woman!"

"I am not King Thorvald's daughter for naught."

He chuckled. "After that, what will you do?"

"Well, I am not certain about today. But I want to meet with the head gardener of the Imperial Palace, for a tour and just to talk. To learn new things."

"Have I not introduced you to enough new things?"

She slapped him playfully. "Mayhap the gardener will direct me to those gardens best suited for my study. I like to sketch and paint what I see. So these will not be short visits. And of course I will go to the Hippodrome to see the races. And Ianthe has promised me roots."

"Roots?" he exclaimed.

"Iris roots," she explained. "To take back to the Norselands for planting. I already have Judas tree seedlings."

She could feel him shaking his head at her seeming hopelessness.

"Mayhap I could give you some roots and seeds to plant at your new home, wherever that might be. To remember me by," she said. And, yea, she was fishing for information.

"Drifa, I need no reminders. This night is firmly *planted* in my memory." She could hear amusement and something else in his voice. Something like wonder. "You like Ianthe, do you?" He seemed pleased.

"Actually, I do. Very much. What I don't understand is why you do not marry her and take her with you when you leave."

"First off, Ianthe would not want me for husband. Ianthe is one of those romantical souls who waits for love . . . a love like she had with her husband. And, truth to tell, I want no wife. I come from a line of evil men. My father, my grandfather, my brothers . . . they all abuse their women and children. The fist or the whip suits them better than words, not that their words cannot flail, too."

Drifa tried to picture a young Sidroc growing up in such a household, and her heart wept for him. Even worse, Runa, who thrived at Stoneheim, would have withered away with such harsh treatment. "You are not the same, Sidroc. Were you not the man willing to suffer marriage to me for the sake of a child?"

Sidroc turned her over on her side to look at him. "I do not think marriage to you would have been such a hardship, Drifa. You took my foolish words to Finn too personally. While I have long maintained marriage is not for me, I had an obligation to my daughter. Finn told you that. And I failed her. In the end, however, 'twas probably for the best that she died. I might have been as harsh with her as my father."

Now would be the time for Drifa to tell him that Runa was alive. But fear . . . not of physical harm . . . but that he would take the child from her, held her back. *He deserves to know. I will tell him when he returns,* she vowed silently. *I will convince him that I make a good mother. I will tell him how Runa thrives in a loving household. But I need time to do that.* In the meantime, she said, "Sidroc, you are a beast in bed, and you make me do bad things and like them, and insult me way too often, and your teasing tongue is not amusing by half, but you are a good man."

"That is the most half-arsed compliment I have ever heard." He squeezed her tight against him in mock punishment.

She smiled up at him. "You would no more strike a woman or child than you would cut off a limb, of that I am convinced a hundredfold."

He did not appear convinced. Still, he said, "I thank you for that."

There was silence after that as she lay nestled against him, her face on his chest. His one arm held her loosely about the shoulders, the other was thrown over his head. Soon she felt his breathing slow, and he fell asleep.

For a long time she just lay against him, unmoving, contemplating this brutish man she should hate, but could not. Heartache lay ahead, of a certainty. But she could no more avoid that fate than stop time from passing. She thought of a dozen things she should do. Like slide out of the bed and escape. Like hit him over the head with another pottery jug. Like enumerate in her mind all the bad things about him. But she did none of these.

She fell asleep.

And then they heard bells . . .

The sky was already turning gray and the time-keeping candle almost burned out when Sidroc awakened Drifa with a soft kiss. "Wake up, sleeping violet. 'Tis time to leave."

"Grmpfh," she said against the crook of his neck.

The vixen was attached to his body like a vine. Her face against his collarbone, one arm holding on to his waist, and a leg twined around one of his thighs like an erotic rope.

There was still another hour before dawn, but she should go back to her apartments before others were about. Though why he should care about her reputation was beyond him.

She had been a total surprise to him. A pleasant surprise. He had asked things of her that were shocking, especially to a virgin, but she'd met him at every step, and challenged him, too. She would make a formidable mate, if he ever wanted one. Which he did not. This was the type of woman that could bring a man to his knees.

"Pssst! Morning glory, wake up lest your guardsman come in and see that delicious, naked arse of yours."

Her eyes shot open. "Wh-what?"

" 'Tis time for you to go," he said.

She glanced around. " 'Tis still nighttime."

"But not for long." He kissed the top of her head and rose, dragging on a pair of *braies*.

She stared up at his naked form for a long moment, forgetting that she was naked, too. When she did, she jumped up with a little squeal and began to pull on her *gunna*, which he'd earlier laid across the chest at the foot of his bed. While she donned her apparel, her face flamed. She kept glancing his way, no doubt recalling all they had done throughout the night. He helped her braid her wild hair, and it was oddly satisfying to him.

"Come," he said, taking her by the hand. "Do you want something to eat or drink afore you leave?"

She shook her head.

Just before they got to the outer door, he picked up a piece of rolled fabric. "Wouldst do me a favor, sweetling?"

"What?" She was immediately suspicious, as she should be.

"When I come back, we will resume our nightly visits, but I want you to do something for me."

"What?" she said again. This time she had her arms folded over her chest.

"Wear this on my first night back." He handed her the fabric, though she tried to shove it away, no doubt suspecting what it was.

"Nay, I do not want it."

"But I want you to have it."

"Nay."

"Yea."

The back and forth passing of the garment caused it to unroll and make a sound. Tinkling bells.

Beware of men with rat faces . . .

A shame-faced and silent Drifa, the hood of her mantle pulled forward, walked beside Ivar back to her quarters. To her surprise, she was not the only one scurrying home through the silent corridors under cover of darkness.

She told her maid Anna that she needed no help undressing when she was back in her own bed-chamber. Sidroc had marked her good and true inside, that was for sure. Gods only knew what marks he had had left on the outside of her body.

She would never be the same.

And she could not blame him. Not entirely. She'd entered this arrangement of her own accord to protect her secret, a secret she had no right to keep. And she could not deny she had enjoyed the love-making, both the dark and the light side. Sidroc had revealed passions in her she was not sure she liked.

For now, though, she fell into a deep, untroubled sleep and did not waken until noon when Anna reminded her that she had an appointment with the eparch today, and that both her *hersirs* and guards-men awaited her.

Despite having purchased Greek garments, she wore her traditional long-sleeved Norse garb to hide the whisker and finger and even teeth marks on various parts of her body. A tight-fitting silver torque about her neck covered a red spot the oaf had inflicted on her with a sucking kiss. The worst part was that he probably carried as many of her marks, as well.

When she opened her door, Wulf grumbled, "What in bloody hell took you so long?" Then he looked at her and his jaw dropped.

Can I crawl back into bed and cover my head for a sennight?

Ivar, in his protective mode, frowned at the Saxon and said, "M'lady was out in the sun too long yesterday and . . . and a bee stung her lips."

The gods must be punishing me.

Jamie let out a hoot of laughter, then slammed a hand over his mouth.

Thork was not so shy about expressing himself. "Looks like someone got lucky at the tupping barrel." Wulf clouted Thork at the side of the head with a palm but that did not stop the rascal, who continued, "Really, Princess Drifa, you should not be embarrassed. Many a Viking has done the morning-after walk of shame, not that you have anything to be ashamed of."

Do you want to place a wager on that?

"Hah! We Scottish lads ha' perfected the walk of shame, except ours is through the moors on the long way home," Jamie added. "Have ye ever smelled heather on a heaving stomach?"

Huh? What do flowers have to do with . . . oh.

"I crawled through me front door one time," Farle, one of the guardsmen, said. "Me wife made me sleep in the cow byre for a sennight." He beamed as if he'd done something to be proud of.

Men! "I have not been drinking to excess," she protested.

"I know." Jamie winked at her.

"There's more than one kind of shame," Thork informed her. He winked, too.

I need one of those mantles that Eastern women wear, ones where only the eyes are visible. Of course my eyes probably speak of my shame, too. Drifa's only saving grace in this whole situation was that Sidroc was absent. He would have surely added to her humiliation by showing off to one and all her love marks on him.

"Her father is going to kill me," Wulf said to no one in particular.

"You and me both," Ivar muttered.

"Where's Alrek?" she asked, wanting to change the subject.

"He did not return last night," Thork announced gleefully. "Methinks he got lucky at the tupping barrel, too."

Jamie elbowed Thork and hissed. "Psssh, you dumb dolt. Have ye no wits in yer fool head?"

Drifa had a fair idea where Alrek had spent the night. Apparently Ianthe wasn't as attached to Sidroc as Drifa might have thought. Sidroc had assured her of that fact. Still . . .

It was under ominously gray skies—a storm was brewing from the east—that they arrived at the Praetorian, where much of the city business was conducted under the watchful rat eye of the eparch Alexander Mylonas. Hundreds of people worked in beehive-like chambers of the huge building, many of them with scrolls, quills, and ink. The hallways buzzed with folks in a hurry to get somewhere. Occasionally there were shouts or once a scream coming from the bowels of the structure where Drifa knew a prison was located.

Once they arrived at Mylonas's headquarters, they were made to wait in an antechamber for what seemed like a long time while aides came and went, none of them looking particularly happy. When it was finally their turn, a man in uniform of the tagmatic army informed them, "Only two of you may go in with the princess. Eparch's orders."

They were not happy about that order, but Ivar and Wulf went in with her while the rest of the men stood guard outside after ascertaining that it was the only entry or exit out of the eparch's office. Still, they glowered their disapproval at everyone who passed by.

A rather chilling atmosphere of austerity filled the eparch's chamber. Despite his being a wealthy man, there was no sign of riches or high station here. Just a table, behind which Mylonas sat with two men on either side of him scratching notes on crisp parchment. One of them, a defeated-looking man of Slavic origins, wore a slave collar.

"Princess Drifa," the eparch greeted her. He did not rise as a sign of respect, which was telling. Then he addressed the others, "Lord Cotley. Ivar of Stoneheim." Was it ominous that he recalled their names? "Sit," he said, motioning to the hard chairs in front of the table.

"I welcome you once again to Constantinople,

Princess Drifa. You have only been in the city a few days, but I wonder . . . have you given thought to declaring goods to be sold here?" There was intelligence and craftiness in his expression. His two front teeth protruded slightly, enhancing his rodent appearance. This man was not and never would be a friend.

"I have no goods to sell," she said. "I have come to study the gardens of your fair city. I am here purely for my own pleasure."

At the word *pleasure*, his head shot up and he gave her a studied, insulting scrutiny, mostly centering on her bruised mouth, as if he knew what she had been about the previous night. Surely he could not know. Could he?

"Those were fine gifts you gave the emperor and empress. Are you sure you do not bring into my country items for sale or barter? The penalty for smuggling undeclared goods into Byzantium is high."

"I have already said that I do not. Is it against your Greek law to give gifts?"

Mylonas narrowed his eyes at her sharp retort. "Of course not. But already you have established contact with one of our craftsmen, rather craftswoman. The jewelry maker. I hope you do not intend to supply her with stones?"

"I have no intention of doing such. If I ever did, I would declare myself, as your law prescribes."

"Tell me, Princess Drifa, do you intend to contact your Arab family while here?"

That question came out of nowhere and took Drifa totally by surprise. "What? Why would I do that? How would I do that? I know of no Arab family."

"Your mother . . . ?" he prodded.

"My mother was a slave afore she wed my father. She died when I was born. As far as I'm concerned, I am Norse and always will be."

Mylonas shrugged.

"What is this about?" Wulf demanded. "Is Princess Drifa accused of some crime?"

"Did I say that?" Mylonas made a ridiculous-looking moue of innocence, which caused his teeth to stick out even more over his pursed lips. "If you must know, Princess Drifa came to the attention of some Arab dignitaries at the feast two nights ago."

"Arabs were invited to a Greek feast?" Ivar asked incredulously. Everyone knew of the ongoing battles between the Christian and Moslem nations.

"While we are at war with most of the infidels, who have declared a *jihad* against all Byzantines, there are some who are friendly," the eparch revealed. "Those who are not number far greater, of course, and they include your possible blood relatives."

Drifa and her companions reeled with shock.

"What are you inferring?" Wulf wanted to know.

"I infer nothing. There are three great caliphates of the Moslem world at the present time, one of which is the Abbasid, whose capital is in Baghdad. I merely ask if Princess Drifa could possibly be the granddaughter of the most celebrated of the Hamdanid emirs, Saif ad-Dawlah, best known as Sword of the State, before his death. His daughter was abducted many years ago in Egypt. 'Twould seem there is a resemblance."

"Even if there was this connection, what does it matter?" Wulf was clearly annoyed by the eparch's veiled threats.

"Saif ad-Dawlah's family still has many supporters. They, along with his enemies, could use her for their own ill purposes."

Drifa assumed that Mylonas was among those who might use her. Her already low opinion of the man sank lower.

"My mother's name was Tahirah. I have no idea if that was her birth name or not. My father purchased her at the slave marts in Hedeby. He brought her home as a concubine, then married her. That is all I know."

"And you have no intention of traveling to the Arab lands whilst here, mayhap to establish relations between the Norselands and our desert enemies?"

"Good gods, nay!" Drifa wanted nothing to do with politics or centuries-old feuds.

"You make many accusations. Dost have any proof of this?" Ivar demanded to know.

Mylonas put up a halting hand. "I make no accusations. Sorry I am if I have offended you with my questions." The rat wasn't sorry at all. He was fooling no one.

"Does the emperor know you are interrogating one of his honored guests in this manner?" Wulf added.

"Forgive me if I have shown disrespect, Princess Drifa. It is my job to ensure the safety and financial well-being of the city. Ofttimes threats come from the high, as well as the low born."

Did he place her in the high or low born class? It mattered not. "I am no threat," she said through gritted teeth.

"Let us hope so. Have a pleasant visit here in Constantinople." He waved a hand in the air. They were obviously dismissed.

"Well, that was interesting," she said after they'd left. "What do you suppose was the purpose?"

"Intimidation," Wulf declared, and updated the others on what had happened behind the closed door.

"Would you want to meet your Arab family?" Thork wanted to know.

"It never occurred to me that might be possible, but, now that it's been suggested, I don't think so. I have thought of myself as Norse for too many years."

"I wouldna mind meeting some harem lassies," Jamie mused in a deep Scottish brogue that seemed to come and go at will.

"Harem *lassies*?" Thork scoffed.

"I still think you should return to Stoneheim, Princess Drifa. Even with your guardsmen . . . well, I have a bad feeling." Wulf was frowning with concern.

"I do, too," Ivar surprised her by concurring.

She arched a brow at the older man, and he said, "I am confident of my abilities in a front-on fight. Even a sneak attack. But we are in a foreign city, and normal rules do not apply."

"Listen, I understand your concerns, and I even

concede that the dangers may be greater here than
if I were in Jorvik, or Birka, or Dublin, but I am
not a lackwit. I will cultivate a friendship with the
empress. I will never go about without a guardsman. I have all the seamen who man my longship
to back us up, if need be. I am here to study gardens, and I will make that abundantly clear to one
and all. In fact, I will even inform the eparch of
Ianthe's plant roots that I intend to take home."

All seven of the men accompanying her shook
their heads hopelessly.

"If that be so, our longships will be leaving in
two days," Wulf said.

"Then let us all enjoy ourselves today," she said
cheerily. "Shall we go to the Hippodrome?"

They all agreed, though some of them had already visited yesterday. Apparently there was
something new to see every day.

When she returned to her chambers later that
day, Anna told her there had been a delivery for
her in her absence. It was the harem garment, and
there was a note.

> *Drifa:*
>   *Until I return. Miss me.*
>   *S.*

She already did.

chapter sixteen

Sex in the Golden City . . .

Drifa was sad to wave off the four *hersirs* two mornings later as their longships rode the waves away from the Golden City harbor. They had been her companions for months and had come to feel like brothers to her.

But she did not remain sad for long. Today she was going to witness a truly spectacular event . . . an imperial Byzantine wedding. And Empress Theodora, whom she had spent an hour with yesterday in her separate wing of the palace, had invited her to have a special placement in the cathedral and at the wedding feast. Much to Ivar's displeasure, by the by. If he had his way, she would stay put in her own palace quarters. He worried about her safety in the crowds that would come to witness the historic event.

But then Ivar worried about every location or happening. For example, yesterday he and Farle had stuck to her like burrs on the hem of a *gunna* when the head gardener of all the palace gardens, a Greek monk named Father Sylvester, gave her a tour that lasted all afternoon, thanks to the empress's influence. While she'd been fascinated by the monk's vast knowledge, her men had been bored nigh to tears, if their constant yawns were any indication. When she'd asked Ivar later if he didn't find the tour interesting, he'd stared at her as if she were daft and compared it to watching his toenails grow.

"Not even the tamarisk grove?"

"Pfff! Not even the lotus petal fountains, or the statue garden, and I do not care what you say, that Greek senator's manroot was the size of a radish."

With a smile behind her hand, Drifa pretended affront. "Some men have no taste for the finer things in life."

"The finest thing I could appreciate right now is a cool horn of mead."

Drifa had been captivated with plants for most of her twenty-nine years and only now realized how much she did not know. The benefits of terracing and trellising. Ways to graft certain trees and cross-breed flowers. How to increase the number and quality of roses on one bush. Best times for pruning and thinning plants. Edible flower petals and roots. Even different types of manure, some very unusual, like camel dung.

But then, Drifa was able to teach Father Sylvester a few things, too, especially about the hardy plants that were able to grow in her snowy climate and ways to improve a species for survival.

The priest had given her permission to return and sketch in the gardens in the future, as long as she made arrangements ahead of time. They were, after all, mostly private oases in the busy palace. And he'd given her roots and cuttings and seeds to take back to Stoneheim with her. Those, on top of the iris roots Ianthe had already dug up for her, the flowers having quit blooming early, made a nice collection for Drifa, so far.

But now Drifa must ready herself for the wedding events. Ianthe had accompanied her to the harbor, along with her new guard, a burly Nubian eunuch named Joseph Samuel hired by Sidroc. Ianthe was coming back to the palace with her to help Drifa dress in her best finery. Ianthe herself had chosen not to attend. Having no special invitation, she would be crushed in the crowds.

"I noticed you spending some time with Alrek this morning before they set sail," Drifa remarked as they walked along.

Ianthe blushed. "He is too young for me."

That is a revealing answer if I ever heard one. "Oh? And if he were thirty and two, and you were twenty and two, then it would be all right?"

Ianthe shrugged. "It is the way of the world."

"Pfff! I admire the way you live so independently, Ianthe. I've told you that before. You defy conventions in so many other ways."

"That is different. The heart is not involved in a business. Well, not in the same way. I fear making a fool of myself."

Don't we all? "My friend, it is obvious that Alrek has developed an attachment for you. I've known him since he was only ten and single-handedly raising his two younger sisters and a brother. He was old for his years even then. And I can tell you this, I have ne'er seen him fall in love the way he appears to be with you."

"So he says." Ianthe was pleased, despite herself.

"It is to Alrek's credit that he raised three fine siblings. His brother serves honorably in my father's *hird* of soldiers, and his two sisters are of marrying age and free to choose, thanks to the dowries Alrek has amassed for them."

"His honor was never in question. Nor his fine form," Ianthe added mischievously.

"He is clumsy," Drifa had to point out. After all, Ianthe lived in a confined space and worked with sharp objects in her jewelry making.

Ianthe appeared insulted by Drifa's observation. "I think Alrek's awkwardness is adorable."

An adorable Viking? Every Norseman in Valhalla must be laughing in his ale. "You *are* considering his suit," Drifa guessed, smiling at Alrek's good fortune. Ianthe's, too.

"We shall see. Alrek says he will return after his mission against the Saxon king."

"And?"

"I will say this, when Sidroc asked if I wanted to leave Byzantium with him, I did not hesitate to decline. But with Alrek, the temptation is great."

Sidroc asked her to go with him? To marry him or as his mistress? It must be why their relationship ended. Ianthe must have been the one who severed it, not Sidroc. Drifa wasn't sure why it mattered to her, but it did.

But then another idea came to her unbidden. If Sidroc married, whether it be to Ianthe or some other woman, he would almost surely take Runa from her.

She did not want to think of that now. Later.

She would think on it later, knowing that when he returned, she must tell him her secret, as promised, regardless of the consequences.

"Now let us decide on your garments," Ianthe said.

They were in her chambers back at the palace where Anna had balked but finally heeded her request that she leave them to prepare for the festivities without her help. Not for the first time, Drifa wondered if the sly-eyed Anna reported her doings to someone higher up, like the emperor, or the general, or—shudder—the eparch. For what reason, she would have had no idea . . . until the recent meeting with the eparch. Now she suspected everyone around her.

Ianthe was examining the various *gunna*s she had laid out over her bed, then held up a white silk one.

Drifa shook her head. "We will be walking to the cathedral. The hem would be black afore we returned to the palace."

"You are right." Ianthe chose a crimson one then, also in silk, with a stiff-pleated train and gold braiding about the tight sleeves and round neckline. It matched the crimson, open-sided apron she pulled over it, except there was gold-threaded embroidery in a writhing wolf design along its edges, instead of braiding. She clipped gold wolf brooches at either shoulder. Placing a gold filigree fillet on her head, Ianthe then experimented with a hairstyle that involved twisting strands of Drifa's black hair over and under the band so the crown appeared part of her hair, the gold peeping out from the ebony. A wide swath of hair hung down her back.

Drifa, watching in a small hand mirror, was impressed with the results. She did not dare think about how much easier it would be to prepare herself if she had a large mirror like the one at Sidroc's Varangian quarters. It brought up too many images. Wicked images. "The hairstyle is wonderful. I never would have thought of doing that."

"But wait, this silver does not go with the rest." Before Drifa could see what Ianthe was about, she undid the silver neck torque, saying, "You need something gold about your neck. This silver is beautiful, but it does not suit your . . ." A heavy pause followed, in which Drifa knew that Ianthe had discovered the red mark on her neck. To her surprise, Ianthe burst out in giggles, which soon escalated to side-splitting laughter. "Sidroc . . . You and Sidroc . . . Surely you didn't! . . . You couldn't possibly! . . . Oh my!" she choked out. "I cannot believe you allowed the cad within touching distance of your person."

I can't, either. Drifa should have been offended, but she burst out laughing, too. It *was* funny, and not just the silly mark, which she had grown fond of, truth to tell, but the fact that Sidroc's mistress, or former mistress, was the one to discover her shameful mark. "You must think me a total wanton," she said finally as she swiped the moistness from under her eyes.

"What? Do you jest? Am I so pure that I could cast stones?"

"Oh, I did not mean—"

"Please, Drifa, you must stop apologizing to me. I am not so easily offended. Surely, even in your lands, friends can say anything to each other without fear of insult."

"Ha! Vikings are known for their blunt tongues. You would not believe the things that come of out my father's mouth. My sisters, too."

They smiled at each other, then rooted through Drifa's jewelry chest and agreed on a gold filigreed torque with a hanging ruby in the center. There were matching rubies for her ear rings.

"Too bad I didn't bring one of my spiderweb necklaces for you, although I don't think I have one with rubies at the moment."

"Much as I would have liked that, I do not think it wise for me to call attention to your work at the moment." She told Ianthe of the meeting with the eparch.

"Mylonas is definitely a cruel man," Ianthe said, casting a glance here and there to make sure she was not overheard. "And dangerous. You are right. Best not to call attention to oneself when his rat nose is on the scent."

Drifa laughed.

"But thank you for the warning. I will be extra diligent in reporting my business activities. His spies are everywhere."

They walked out to Drifa's small garden, where there were cool cups of lemon water that Anne had left for them. It would be an hour or more before Ivar and her other escorts arrived.

In the meantime, Drifa had to clear the air of one thing. "Ianthe, I am uncomfortable about

Sidroc. 'Tis true we have a history, and there is
more to come, I fear, though I would avoid it, but
he is . . . was yours."

"No, no, no! I keep telling you that ours was
never a love match, and whatever we have is over.
If you suffer guilt, please let it not be because of
me. If anyone should feel guilty, it is me. Sex without marriage . . . sex without any intention to ever
wed . . . that is a sin in my religion. At least you
were betrothed to the man."

*Not anymore. I really have no more excuse
than you do. In fact, my sin is probably greater
to your God, compounded as it is with lies. Nay,
the sex, wicked as it was, is not my greatest guilt.*
Although a maidenhead was prized afore marriage
in the Norse culture, men and women were looser
in their sexual activities. The word *sin* did not even
exist when it came to bedsport, as far as she knew.
That did not mean Vikings were without morals.
Just a different kind. But she could not dwell on
that at the moment.

"Ianthe, I would ask . . ." She hesitated to speak
what was on her mind. "Never mind."

"Tsk, tsk, tsk! You cannot stop now."

She took a deep, bracing breath before beginning. "I have four sisters who are married, all to
virile men whom they love dearly. So I know that
women can enjoy sexplay, but by the gods!" She
rolled her eyes.

"That good, huh?" Ianthe grinned, taking way
too much pleasure in her discomfort.

Drifa thought about lying, but what was the

point? "I do not consider myself naïve, but I never imagined!"

"I, on the other hand, can imagine. The dolt should know better than to try such nonsense on an inexperienced woman."

"I'm sure he just wanted to shock me." *And shock me, and shock me, and shock me.*

"Were you shocked?"

"For a certainty. Do normal women enjoy such things?" *I certainly did, to my shame.*

"I am not about to ask you what things you refer to, but I will say this. If two people care about each other, and no one is hurt physically . . ." She shrugged. "The things my husband and I used to do! I still blush. And we were virgins together when we wed."

The difference was that she and Sidroc didn't "care" for each other.

Or did they?

Rather, did she?

Even if Sidroc did have some faint feelings for her, how would that change when he found out she withheld knowledge of his daughter? She wished there were a way to find out how he would react regarding the child. Certainly, he would be happy that she was still alive, but the big question was whether he would insist on raising her himself. Without her. If only her sisters were here to help her decide the best course to follow!

Hesitantly, she said, "Ianthe, I need your advice about something."

"Of course."

"You must promise not to repeat what I tell you."

"Of course."

Drifa explained everything, with Ianthe interrupting her with pertinent questions here and there. When she was done, Ianthe summed the situation up succinctly. "What a mess!"

"Do you see what my problem is?"

Ianthe nodded.

"Will Sidroc be so joyous over Runa's being alive that he will want what is best for her?"

"Meaning: allow the child to live with you?"

She nodded eagerly.

"You cannot be serious."

Her shoulders drooped. "He will kill me."

"He will consider it, at least at first."

"But it was just a misunderstanding."

"One you have failed to rectify since you arrived in Constantinople."

She had hoped that Ianthe would reassure her, not be so judgmental. Her sentiments must have shown on her face because Ianthe reached out and squeezed her hand.

"Look at the situation from Sidroc's perspective. Yes, he insulted you by his marriage proposal, but you struck what could have been a mortal blow to his head. Then when he very well might have been facing death, you left for what he believed was a pleasure journey. After that he discovered that his daughter was gone . . . to him, that meant dead. Now, five years later, he meets you again, and the first thing out of your mouth is not, 'Sidroc! What good news I have for you!' as it should have been.

Now you want him to hand over his daughter to you."

"That is not the way—"

Ianthe held up both hands to stop Drifa. "Wait. I have spoken of Sidroc's possible view of the situation. Now, let us look at your view."

Yea, let's.

"Yes, Sidroc behaved like a pig when discussing his betrothal to you. Men ofttimes act like pigs. Nothing new there. You reacted emotionally when you hit him over the head with the pitcher. I would have done the same. But you are a woman with heart, and when you heard about his daughter, you acted according to your conscience and rescued the child. It was never your intention to hide the child from Sidroc. In fact, you tried many times to locate him over those first few years. Sidroc might say you should have tried harder, but that is neither here nor there. You took care of his daughter these many years and grew to love her. To me, and I suspect to Sidroc, your biggest crime will be failing to tell him now. Each hour, each day, that has gone by while he is kept in ignorance, your innocence loses its . . . innocence."

"So it is hopeless?"

"Not at all. 'Tis obvious that Sidroc has an attraction for you. Oh yes, he does. I saw the way he looked at you during the feast and while you visited my shop. You must use that attraction to your advantage."

She frowned in confusion.

"You must marry the man."

"Whaaat?" she squealed.

"If you are wed, Runa will live with you both."

"But he does not want to marry, and especially not me."

"Then you must seduce him."

Drifa groaned. "I am as far from a seductress as a rowboat is from a longship."

"Drifa, Drifa, Drifa. All women have the tools. I will teach you how to use them."

Was Drifa really about to get sex lessons? From the former mistress of the man to be seduced?

If her sisters ever heard about this, they would be hiring a skald to write sagas about her escapades.

If her father ever heard about this, he would have her baptized and locked in a convent for life.

If Sidroc ever heard about this, he would probably laugh himself silly, or kill her, or both.

"Well?" Ianthe tapped her foot impatiently.

Drifa took a deep breath and said, "Let the lessons begin."

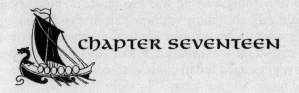

chapter seventeen

**It wasn't the wedding of Kate and
Prince William, but still . . .**

For the days that followed, Drifa felt the presence of someone watching her. A stranger. Not
Ivar and the other guardsmen. Never in a private
place.

The wedding procession from the Great Palace
to Hagia Sophia cathedral was led by a hundred
Varangian Guardsmen in dress uniforms; she'd
seen them earlier lounging about playing dice as
they awaited their duties. The Varangians were followed by another hundred tagmatic troops, also in
dress uniforms. All wore plumed helmets and rode
black stallions with silver trappings. She assumed
Sidroc and Finn would have been among them if
they were in the city.

After that were several dozen priests and monks,
hands folded together in front of their chests in a
prayerful attitude. Drifa was glad she wasn't close
to their aromatic bodies since so many of them dis-
dained bathing as a lust of the flesh.

Then came choirs that sang beautiful hymns
in Latin, followed by drummers and lute players.

The only thing missing was the acrobats, but they would probably come with the exiting procession.

Emperor John was already in the cathedral with his entourage awaiting his bride, who rode in an ivory, gilt-edged sedan chair with curtains of spun gold mesh. She was carried by eight Ethiopian men of equal height, whose muscular skin had been oiled to look like polished ebony. Camel guards surrounded the chair, and behind rode the patriarch on a snow-white mule, an attitude of humility and purity, Drifa supposed. After that were the empress's eight ladies-in-waiting with their kohled eyes, rose-pomaded lips, and chalk-powdered throats and bosoms riding two apiece in their own sumptuous sedan chairs. What a contrast to the churchman! How the nun-like Empress Theodora must hate all this pomp!

The people who crowded the city streets kept shouting, "Long live Empress Theodora!" followed by cheers. Occasionally she would reach out a hand and toss coins to her subjects, causing near stampedes.

Princess Drifa and her four guardsmen—who looked especially handsome dressed all in black, tunic and *braies* of softest wool tucked into their waists by heavy etched silver belts, with silver-hilted swords scabbarded at their sides—walked behind the procession, along with several hundred other dignitaries and emissaries from other countries. In all, the procession along the short distance from the palace to the church took more than two hours.

Halfway through their walk, Drifa was bumped from behind. When she turned, dark eyes stared at her intently from beneath the burnoose of a desert-style robe, the kind she'd seen her brother-by-marriage, Adam the Healer, and his aide Rashid wear on occasion. "Begging your pardon, mistress," the man said in heavily accented Greek and bowed away. It happened so quickly that her guardsmen saw her stumble but hadn't noticed the man, who'd no doubt pushed her. She decided not to alarm them, leastways not until later.

Once inside, all thoughts of danger melted away under the most magnificent splendor. Drifa was not a Christian, but she could appreciate the heavenly sense of beauty dedicated to their One-God. The high central dome had dozens of arched windows that let in sunshine to reflect off the marble pillars and mosaic walls, many with colorful lapis lazuli, telling stories in art about their One-God and saints and angels. It was enough to turn a heathen Viking into a believer.

"Holy bloody hell!" Ivar murmured beside her, and it did not sound at all sacrilegious. All of their jaws were gaping open with astonishment.

At the altar the emperor stood in a pure white silk robe. The empress, whose face was veiled, wore pure white, too, except her gown was of brocade with raised designs in silver and gold. Extremely ornate and heavy crowns were held above their heads by attendants as they spoke their vows and exchanged rings.

Various high church and civil dignitaries presented themselves before the emperor and empress by prostrating themselves on the floor in front of them in a position of obeisance called proskynesis.

It was an extreme sign of allegiance to not just the emperor but his new wife, who just stared stonily forward.

A totally inappropriate-for-a-church thought came unbidden to Drifa, a picture of Theodora doing those things with John that she had done with Sidroc. Almost immediately, she knew. It would never happen. *What does that say about me? Mayhap just that I was never destined to be a nun? Or an empress?* She put a hand to her mouth to prevent herself from laughing aloud.

Ivar slanted her a questioning look.

She pretended not to notice.

But Drifa did notice everything she saw and heard, hoping to imprint it on her memory so she could tell everyone at home about it all. If only she had a real talent for painting!

Once when he glanced around during the lengthy rituals, she saw Eparch Mylonas staring at her from across the aisle. A shiver of apprehension raised the fine hairs on her body.

It wasn't that the eparch looked at her with lust, as some men did. Nay, it was more like dislike. Rabid dislike. What had she done to engender such animosity in the man? Ah, she realized. Her half-Arab ancestry. To some Greeks, just being Arab was reason for hate.

And that reminded her of the man in the Arab burnoose who'd bumped her earlier in the procession. She must tell Ivar about both these happenings, not that there was much to tell. Just an uncomfortable feeling.

Later at the wedding feast, in the Hall of Nineteen Couches, Drifa was seated at a table of strangers. Her guardsmen were permitted to stand off to the side under the colonnade, but they were not invited to partake of the feast itself. There would have been no room, if nothing else.

The people she dined with were pleasant enough, though none of them spoke Greek as a first language, and the conversations were ofttimes stilted. Toward the end of the evening, though, the man from the Rus lands on her right side leaned closer to her and said, "I have a message for you from your cousin."

"Cousin? What cousin?" She tried to recall if she'd ever heard her father mention a cousin. Nay, she decided. He had not.

"Bahir Ahmed ad-Dawlah, your cousin thrice-removed."

"Huh?"

"He saw you today in the procession and he is pleased."

The man in the burnoose? "That's nice."

"Mayhap a wedding will be in your future." The Rus man winked at her.

"What? You cannot be implying what I think you are. Impossible!"

"Who knows what Allah has in mind for us?"

Ah, so this man, though of Rus background, was a Moslem. That was fine, but she was not, and no god was proclaiming a marriage for her, especially not with a stranger.

"Do not be afeared, m'lady. Bahir is young and virile. He has already produced ten sons and six daughters with his other wives."

"Other wives?"

"Of course. What kind of man of wealth would he be at forty and one if he did not have at least three wives? Bahir has five."

"And I would be number six?"

The Rus man nodded. "And most favored."

"Sorry I am to decline this most unusual proposal, if that is what it is. But I have more than enough 'favors' back home in the Norselands."

"No, no, no, princess. Baghdad is your true home, and the desert your garden."

Ha! Some gardens I would be able to plant in the endless sand.

"A fair maiden like you does not belong in the icy land of the barbarians."

"My father is not a barbarian." Not often, leastways. "And let me repeat: Thank you, but nay, I am not interested."

The man just smiled and turned to speak to the lady from Crete on his other side. The lady was a distant relative of the emperor.

Later, when she told Ivar about the strange proposal, she thought he would laugh. But instead he ranted and raved. "We should go home immediately. It is as I expected. More and more danger. Everywhere you step there are pitfalls."

"Ivar! It was a silly marriage proposal from afar. The man did not even ask me himself. And, besides, this is not the first marriage proposal I have ever received."

"More like fiftieth," he grumbled.

"What did you say?"

"Nothing," he grumbled some more. Then,

he straightened. "Methinks I should call in some seamen from your longship to help us stand guard over you."

"What? Nay! That is ridiculous. Four Viking guards is plenty. Any more and I will just be calling attention to myself."

"As if you do not already!"

"Ivar, I do not like your tone, not by half."

"I do not mean disrespect, m'lady."

She bowed her acceptance of his apology and put a hand on his forearm. "We will be careful, my good friend. And if there are any further 'problems' we will reassess the situation. I promise you, I will agree to go home if it is deemed a clear danger."

He nodded, but he was not happy. "The back of my neck is twitching all the time, a sure sign that something bad is coming."

The next sennight, the bad arrived.

For whom the bell tolls . . .

Sidroc and Finn had been at the mountain retreat of General Leo Biris for a sennight when they had to admit that the warlord was no imminent threat to the emperor. And they told him so.

"I ought to lop off both of your fool heads for sneaking into my camp under pretense of joining my guard," roared the big bear of a man with a mane of thick black hair and full beard.

"Please don't. You might get blood on my hair, and I just washed it. Rather, one of your pretty maids washed it for me." Finn finger-combed the long blond locks off his face in a preening fashion.

For a moment, Leo went slack-jawed at Finn's halfwit humor. Then he slapped him so hard on the back that Finn nigh went flying across the table where they sat following the evening meal.

"Leo, you must understand that Finn is a man like no other. He takes some getting used to."

"That is for sure. I swear, Finn, if I had not come across you tupping my wife's weaving maid behind her loom, I would think your bells gonged in a different direction."

Finn straightened with affront. "My gong goes in only one direction."

They all laughed.

"Have I mentioned that I have five unmarried daughters?" Leo inquired slyly, not for the first, or twentieth, time. If they were not careful, they would find themselves landlocked and wedlocked on a Byzantine mountain.

Sidroc had kept his *braies* tightly laced since he left Miklagard. For him, that was a long period of celibacy when there were willing partners aplenty. Finn, on the other hand, had tasted every other comely being with breasts that came within smelling distance.

"I have not touched one of your daughters," Finn protested.

"I know," Leo said unhappily.

He and Finn had discussed in private that neither of them should so much as find themselves alone in a chamber with one of Leo's daughters, aged from fourteen to twenty. Not that they weren't attractive. They were. But Finn was determined to find the most beautiful woman in the world, one to match his beauty. And, if Sidroc was going to be forced into marriage, he would rather it be with a woman of his choice. For some odd, infuriating reason, Drifa came to mind.

I should not have coerced her into doing the things I did.

She should not have complied.

An innocent maid deserves better than such rough handling.

But she rough handled me, too. I have the marks to prove it.

She was a virgin; so the child Runa cannot be hers, as I suspected.

Then why the big secret? Why has she refused to discuss the child, or its father, with me?

In any case, Sidroc had decided over this past sennight to end his threat over Drifa's head when he returned to Miklagard, as tempting as her charms were. Secrets be damned! Time to put the past behind him. If she came to his bed again, it would be her choice. But then, he expected to leave this land soon. Mayhap, as with Ianthe, 'twas best to cut ties and just be friends.

A strange laughter erupted in his head at the prospect of him and Drifa being just friends. But, nay, it was Leo laughing. Apparently the general had continued talking whilst Sidroc's mind had gone a-wandering.

Finn excused himself and went off to check on his horse, which had a hoof disease he was treating. It would have to be healed before they left.

"So, the bastard turned on me once he went from military tent to soft bed?" Leo mused about the emperor once it was just the two of them. "As a fellow soldier, if nothing else, I thought John knew me better." Leo appeared hurt at the actions of his old friend.

"I don't think it's so much the emperor as General Sclerus and Eparch Mylonas who have suspicions," Sidroc told him. "As you know, the empire relies on you border lords to hold off the Moslems. And they depend on the taxes you funnel to the capital. But it's your very strength that makes them fear you, meaning all the *dynatoi*. They're afraid you might use that strength for your own ends. Leastways that is how Sclerus and Mylonas see things."

"Pfff! Bugger the both of them! Just because I'm popular with my people and our lands flourish, just because more and more soldiers want to join my ranks, they figure I must be doing something wrong. Does it never occur to them that I am doing things right, as they should?" The general slammed a big hand on the table, causing the goblets of ale to teeter before righting themselves.

"I know this to be true, and it is what I will report to the emperor."

"Will they be sending you to investigate the other *dynatoi*?"

Sidroc put up both hands. "Not me."

"Are you sure you would not reconsider my offer to join my ranks? I would give you and Finn positions of authority. You would be well paid."

"Nay. 'Tis past time I established my own homestead."

"Why not here? I could give you land."

"Again, I thank you for your offer, but I am a Norseman. 'Tis time for me to go home."

And, actually, Sidroc had decided that his destination would in fact be the Norselands. He was tired of letting his father dictate his life. He would not settle in another country just to avoid proximity to his villainous family. Not too close, though. Mayhap he would seek an estate farther south in Vestfold. He would know the right place when he saw it.

Three days later, he and Finn were practicing swordplay with some of Leo's soldiers when a messenger came riding in from the south. The closer he got, the more Sidroc stiffened with apprehension. He soon realized that he recognized the man. It was Farle, one of Drifa's guardsmen.

This could not be good news.

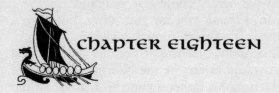

CHAPTER EIGHTEEN

The terrible trouble arrives . . .

Drifa had been in Miklagard for more than two sennights, and she'd seen only a tiny portion of what she'd planned. Still, she was missing Runa fiercely.

So she decided to spend some time with Ianthe, who had become a good friend. She was bringing her sketch box with her, not just to show off her work, but in hopes that Ianthe could fill in some of the blanks about certain flowers that grew differently in this climate.

Ivar had rolled his eyes when she'd informed him of her plans. "Gardening again!" he complained. Really, Ivar was better suited to fighting her father's battles with his battle-axe, not guarding her in yet another garden.

So she was not surprised that Ivar's boredom had led to sleep when she went out to the hall that afternoon to inform him that it was time to go back to the palace. The palace gates closed at mid-afternoon, so they must hurry.

"Ivar!" she yelled with distress when she was unable to wake him.

At the same time, Ianthe yelled at her, "Drifa, come here at once."

It was already too late. A masked man had come up behind her, lifting her off her feet and carrying her back inside.

"Oh my gods! You've killed my guardsmen," she said in Greek, since she assumed that was his nationality.

"He is alive. Just an herb-induced sleep in his ale," the man replied, also in Greek, but it was clear this was not his first language.

"But I brought him his ale," she said, her gaze catching with Ianthe's fearful one.

"The ale was tampered with. Your other guardsmen and my workers are 'asleep' as well," Ianthe told her. "Even Joseph Samuel."

"As you two will soon be, too," her captor said, then spoke in a foreign language to three other masked men who emerged from the balcony door, as well as the steps leading to the shop below stairs. Although she was not proficient in Arabic, she recognized bits and pieces of their words as ones Rashid, her brother-by-marriage Adam's healer assistant, had taught her when she visited their Northumbria home.

Drifa and Ianthe were bound and gagged then with some scarves the leering men found in a low chest in Ianthe's solar. Then the men dragged in Drifa's four guardsmen and Ianthe's shop workers with Joseph Samuel, all limp with the same deep sleep as Ivar; they bound and gagged them as well. The only one missing was Irene, Ianthe's elderly maid, and Drifa could only assume that she was the culprit who'd tampered with the ale and helped these men. Luckily Drifa and Ianthe had only drunk wine, or they would be in the same condition.

"We must wait for a few hours until it is dark," her captor said in heavily accented Greek.

"Shall we put these two to sleep, Hakeem?" one of the others asked the man who appeared to be the leader.

"We can wait, Faisal, as long as they are gagged. Did you put a sign in the shop window saying they are closed for a funeral?"

"Yes. I wonder whose funeral it will be? Ha, ha, ha!" Faisal must be the second man's name. By the gods, he reeked of garlic. Did no one ever tell him a little went a long way?

Drifa saw no humor in such a morbid jest.

"Shall we take both women with us when we go?" another man asked. "The Greek woman could act as translator."

"I do not think it will be necessary since the princess speaks Greek," Hakeem remarked. "Although we could use the Greek woman on our journey to sate our lust and then sell her in the slave marts in Baghdad."

Drifa's eyes shot to Ianthe's, which widened with even more fear.

Oh, merciful Asgard, she wished that Sidroc was still in the city. Who else would come looking for them? Other than her guardsmen, she did not think anyone would notice that she was missing. Leastways, not immediately.

"No. Best we follow orders directly," Hakeem decided, thank the gods!

It seemed like forever that they lay in their uncomfortable positions on the floor. Only occasionally could she make out the conversations taking place outside on the terrace. The name Mylonas came up a few times, but more often it was ad-Dawlah. That latter fit in with their earlier mention of Baghdad.

An awful prospect occurred to Drifa then. What if they took her to that city in the midst of Arab lands? She might never be found.

She knew her guardsmen, if they were allowed to live, would initiate a search immediately and mayhap even draw in the emperor, though gods only knew if he was in on this scheme. And her father would of course come with an army, but by the time word was sent to him, and he made the return journey, sennights, even months would have passed. Her fate might be sealed by then.

Sidroc . . . he was her only chance, she decided. *Please, Thor, and Odin, and even the One-God, let Sidroc return soon and care enough to look for me. And let these men leave my guardsmen and Ianthe alive*, she prayed.

When nightfall finally came, Hakeem, still masked but identifiable by his height, approached her with a vial of amber liquid. He took off her gag and ordered her, "Drink this."

"Is it poison?"

He laughed. "Nay, 'tis just a sleeping draught . . . to make you amenable on your journey."

"Nay!" she said, and turned her head. "Please don't do this."

Hakeem took her chin in a bruising hold. "I can

pinch your nose and force your mouth open, or you can drink willingly. Either you comply, or I kill off every person in this room, starting with the female jeweler."

"If I cooperate, what will you do to the others?"

"Give them more of the sleep potion so they will not awaken until tomorrow. No one has seen us without our masks. So no need to kill them, but I will if I have to."

Drifa opened her mouth immediately, and soon felt herself drifting off to sleep.

The next time she awakened it was to a loud, strident noise, *"Gronk! Gronk! Gronk!"* She soon realized that it was dark, and she was riding atop a camel, in front of a man . . . Faisal, she was pretty sure, by the garlic smell of him.

"She awakens," Faisal called out to Hakeem, on another camel.

The six camels holding her and the now un-masked Arab men halted, and she was lifted down. Her legs were weak and her knees folded, but Hakeem caught her with a curse at her "clum-siness." Just as rude was the camel, who spat at her. She'd seen camels from a distance before. Not up close. She hadn't realized what unpleasant crea-tures they could be. Smelly, for one thing, and they attracted hordes of flies.

In Greek, Hakeem advised her, as if she were a petulant girling, not a kidnapped woman, to go into some nearby bushes and relieve herself. When she returned, he ordered Faisal, "Give her more to drink."

She protested, but water was withheld until she complied. When the vial was held to her mouth again, she drank it and a cup of water thirstily, soon succumbing to sleep again under the soothing rhythm of the animal beneath her.

For the next three days and nights—leastways, that's how long Drifa thought it was—she was either riding on a camel's back, sleeping in a tent, or relieving herself in the bushes, her limp body propped ignominiously between two laughing guards since she was so weak with the drugs.

Finally, on the morning following her third night away from Miklagard, Drifa was conscious, though bone-weary, as they approached what appeared to be a small city of colorful tents.

She turned her head to ask Hakeem, whose camel she was on now, "Where am I?"

"The desert outpost of your husband-to-be, Prince Bahir ad-Dawlah."

"What? I am not betrothed to anyone."

"Yes, you are, Princess Drifa."

"I gave no consent to a betrothal."

"A woman's consent is not necessary in this land. Only that of a father or guardian, and your uncle, King Asbar, definitely approves."

"I don't understand."

"In time, in time."

She noticed that Hakeem spoke to her with respect now, something that had been missing back at Ianthe's quarters or during this long journey. He led her gently, a hand under her elbow, into one of the smaller tents, where he told a slave girl to prepare bath water and a meal for the princess. He never distinguished what princess he meant. She hoped Norse.

She was wrong.

She bathed and dressed in clean clothing . . . a demure Arab gown with face veil to be worn when out in public over a more revealing silk gown. Then she was escorted through the city of tents to the biggest of all, Prince ad-Dawlah's home away from home. A flag with a rampant sword dripping blood against a black field edged in red hung atop its center pole, emblematic of the "Sword of the State," she assumed. There was no breeze moving the flag in the oppressively hot desert heat.

Just then a *muezzin* burst forth with the *azan*, a droning call to prayer. One after another, she saw men drop to their knees and bow their heads to the ground. Meanwhile, others picked up the *azan* so that it was like a haunting echo of rising crescendo all around her. Hakeem had told her earlier that the call went out to the faithful five times a day. When she'd asked if women participated, too, he'd been horrified.

The interior of the desert prince's tent was surprisingly luxurious. Persian carpets on the ground. Incense burners in the four corners. Big, fluffy pillows scattered about. A low table with solid gold platters holding figs, dates stuffed with walnuts, and flaky honey cakes.

Overseeing the activities of various girls working about the tent was an elderly woman with a hawk nose and piercing black eyes, sitting cross-legged on the floor. Although she wore no face veil, her gray hair was covered with a sort of head rail of pale blue, matching her plain gown of lightweight material in deference to the heat but running to her wrists and ankles. Although it was hard to tell under the voluminous gown she wore, the lady appeared to be as wide as she was tall, which was not very. On her calloused feet were sandals. Her fat, gnarled hands were petting a large gold and black cat on a leash. A leopard, for the love of Frigg!

Drifa froze in place, but Hakeem whispered in her ear, "Not to worry. The animal has no teeth, and it has been castrated and declawed."

A eunuch leopard. Rather than being relieved, Drifa was horrified that such a beautiful, wild animal should be so treated. 'Twas like turning a Norseman into a scullery maid. Luckily, her face veil was still in place, and her expression was hidden.

The woman eyed her with a sneer, then said something to Hakeem in a rapid, biting flow of Arab, too quick for Drifa to understand.

"Queen Latifah would like you to remove your veil and outer gown."

Drifa doubted that such a request had been made. At least not so politely.

But it was not necessary for her to react because with a great flurry of activity outside the tent, a man soon entered, gave her a passing glance, then went to the old lady, who was smiling of a sudden. The leopard growled its displeasure, and Drifa had a suspicion that the man might have been the one to emasculate the cat. The prince leaned down and kissed the woman on both cheeks. "Mother, how bide you?" he asked warmly.

"Pains here, pains there, my son," she said, shrugging. "How went the horse breaking?"

The man smiled. "Fifteen wild stallions now ready for market."

"My talented son!" The woman nigh beamed with pride.

They were speaking in Arabic, of course, which Drifa was able to understand now that the words weren't all jammed together. For some reason, she'd let no one know of her linguistic abilities thus far. Instinctively she sensed it was the wise thing to do.

"I told Hakeem to take the woman's *abayah* off but he is slow to obey," the old lady whined. "Too long in the Christian lands, I think."

Hakeem gasped, especially when the man, whom by now Drifa assumed was Prince ad-Dawlah, walked up and slapped Hakeem across the face. "Do you disobey my revered mother?"

"No, master," Hakeem said, bowing his head. Then to her, in Greek, ad-Dawlah said, "Take off your veil and *abayah*. At once."

Drifa's gaze locked with the prince's then. Oh, how she wanted to refuse, but she feared what he might do to Hakeem, who was innocent, in this instance anyhow.

She removed her veil and the outer gown, letting both drop to the ground. Raising her chin haughtily, she demanded of the prince in Greek, "Is this how Arabs treat guests in your land?"

At first he stiffened with affront, and his mother could be heard sputtering with outrage at her tone, no doubt, but then he put a genial expression on his face and bowed to her. "Forgive my manners,

Princess Drifa. Welcome to our land. Your land, too, of course. The birthplace of your mother."

As he spoke, his dark eyes surveyed her figure, much as he would if he were at a horse fair, contemplating a purchase. So she did the same to him.

He was not a bad-looking man, what she could see of him in the white robe he wore, tucked in at the waist by a heavy twisted rope belt. No jewelry, except on his left hand there was a heavy, jeweled ring on his middle finger. He was only slightly taller than she, but well built, with wide shoulders and narrow hips. His black hair, slicked back off his face wetly, or greasily—she wasn't sure which— was threaded with a few strands of gray; he was after all forty and one years old, according to the man from the Rus lands she'd met at the wedding feast. A meticulously trimmed mustache adorned his otherwise close-shaven face. Drifa suspected by the arrogant way he carried himself that he and Finn would make great comrades-in-vanity.

"Why have you kidnapped me?" she demanded.

He seemed taken aback. "Kidnapped. No!" He turned to Hakeem, "If you mistreated the princess in any way, I will have your head on a pike afore nightfall."

"No, no, no!" she interrupted. "Hakeem did nothing wrong, other than bringing me here against my will, at your orders, I presume."

"What does she say?" his mother demanded to know.

The prince told her.

And his mother ordered him, "Beat the woman for her insolence."

Also in Arabic, he replied, "Later, Mother. We must get her consent first."

His mother nodded.

Oh, so my consent is needed, after all. Drifa was having trouble with this swinging back and forth between the two languages and having to not react to the Arabic one.

With a peremptory wave of his hand, ad-Dawlah indicated to Hakeem that he should leave. The man bowed and backed out of the room. She hoped the lout didn't expect the same obeisance from her.

But nay, he turned to smile at her, an oily smile that must charm some women. Not her. She'd been around men too long not to understand when a devious seduction was in play. "Princess Drifa, you are more beautiful than a thousand sunsets."

Oh please, spare me the nonsense.

"She is skinny as a winter-starved chicken," his mother remarked.

Drifa schooled her face not to show that she understood.

"You can fatten her up afore the wedding," the son replied with an ingratiating smile.

I have got news for you. There will be no wedding, and the only fattening will be of your smirking mouth when my fist makes its mark.

"She is old," his mother observed.

"Not so old that she cannot bear me many sons."

His mother shrugged.

Drifa thought, *When dragons fly and birds talk!*

Turning back to her, he said, "My mother remarks on my good fortune in finding such a glorious bride."

You are such a bloody liar.

His mother glared at her.

"Allah must be smiling on me today," he concluded.

Or Loki, the jester god, because the joke is going to be on you, my high and mighty halfbrain. There will be no wedding with me, that I guarantee. "Prince ad-Dawlah," she began, forcing her voice to remain calm and polite.

"Call me Bahir," he said, and led her to the table, where he indicated she should sit on a fat cushion next to his equally fat mother. Instead she moved to a cushion on the other side of the table.

He slid down beside her.

Subtly, pretending to adjust her cushion beneath her, she placed a small cushion between the two of them.

"Bahir," she started again, "you must understand that I cannot marry you."

"Why not?"

"For one thing, we don't know each other."

He flashed her a lecherous smile and said, "We can get to know each other after the wedding. This I promise you, my dear. Despite commitments to my other wives and concubines, I will devote three full weeks to you alone." He smiled then as if he'd gifted her a great boon.

Some gift! "In my country, a woman's consent must be given." That wasn't entirely true, but he did not need to know that.

"This is your country now, Princess Drifa." By his tone, she could tell that her protests were annoying him.

Good!

"I know this is all strange to you now, but you will become accustomed to our ways. Women here yield to the greater wisdom of their men."

"Are you serious?"

"Watch yourself, Princess Drifa. You may be my betrothed, but that does not give you leave to cross the line of what is proper."

"Is it proper to force me into marriage?"

"Enough on that subject!" he proclaimed in an icy voice. "The wedding will take place in three days' time, with or without your consent. In the meantime, you will be taken to my harem to prepare yourself."

Prepare myself? How? Do not ask, Drifa. You do not want to know. "You have a harem here in the desert?"

"Of course."

What? He cannot suppress his base urges for even a short time, she thought snidely. "So, does your whole entourage move with you wherever you go?"

"Entourage?"

"Harem. I understand you have five wives, but—"

"How do you know I have five wives?" he asked sharply.

She wasn't about to get Hakeem in any more trouble. "Someone mentioned it at the palace. The eparch Mylonas, I think, when he insinuated that I might have Arab kin." *And that you had been watching me.*

"Mylonas! What a pig!"

More like a rat, but pig works as well. "In any case, aside from your wives, how many concubines do you have? I believe that is what you call the harem occupants. Or is it houris? No matter."

"I have six concubines here. Twelve in my Baghdad harem. Four in my mountain harem. We could go to Baghdad for the wedding, where my father would be able to attend . . . he is not well, but, no, that would take too long and I am anxious to taste your charms." Once again the oily smile.

"My father will arrive with an army to rescue me. Do you want to risk a battle with two hundred Norsemen?"

"By the time your father arrives, you will be big with my child."

"You are so sure of yourself?"

"Indeed! I have thirty-one children already, twenty of them sons. Sixteen of them legitimate children! You have nothing to fear when it comes to my virility." He winked at her as if he'd imparted some deliciously lascivious comment.

"My father will not force me to stay, even if I am breeding or already have borne a child."

"I suspect you will convince your countrymen that you stay here by choice, unless you wish to leave the child behind."

What a loathsome, evil lout! "You are a despic—"

He pressed his fingertips to her lips. "A team of strongest horses cannot pull a word back once spoken. Take care what you say to me."

Her opinion must have been reflected on her face because he leaned over and patted her hand. "You are not to worry. I will take care of you henceforth. Now eat. You will need your strength for the days ahead. And nights." He winked again. As an afterthought, he added, "Allah be praised."

Drifa did eat, although she almost tossed the contents of her stomach when she was given fermented goat's milk, a prized beverage here. Its stink was almost as bad as its taste. Queen Latifah reluctantly handed her a glass cup of grape juice to wash it down, at the direction of Bahir.

The queen served her son the choicest pieces of sliced lamb, cutting them up for him like he was a small boyling. She even mixed some raisins in a plate of rice, topped by orange segments, which she passed to him. "I picked the oranges for you myself just after dawn," she told him in Arabic.

"You are the best mother in the world."

Drifa felt like gagging, and not just because the taste of fermented goat milk was still on her palate.

But then, she had more to worry about when his mother remarked, "Are you sure she is a virgin?"

The question seemed to startle Bahir, and he looked to her, as if her virginity or lack of it would show on her face. "I had not considered that possibility, but she *is* twenty and nine," he said hesitantly. "And she *is* part Norse. You know how immoral those heathens are."

Have I told you how handy I am with a pottery pitcher, you slimy son of a toad?

"Never fear, my son," his mother said. "I will determine for myself if she still has a maidenhead once I take her to the harem."

He nodded, his obvious concern placated.

But she had to wonder: Exactly how did one determine if a maidenhead was still intact? And what happened when they discovered it was not?

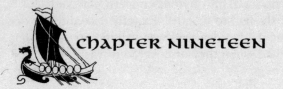

chapter nineteen

Lawrence of Arabia he was not! . . .

"**B**loody damn woman!"
   "Bloody damn delay!"
"Bloody damn Arabs!"
"Bloody damn Greeks!"
"Bloody damn camels!"
"Bloody damn heat!"
"Blood damn flies!"

Sidroc was so bloody damn mad he could bloody damn spit. Which he did because, of course, there was sand in his mouth. In fact, there was sand in every opening and crevice in his body. He no doubt had sand in his piss; he would have to check next time he relieved himself.

When he arrived in Miklagard a sennight ago, having arrived back in the city in record time, he discovered that Drifa had been kidnapped by some Arabs believed to be members of her mother's family. Mylonas had alluded to it in her meeting with him, according to Ivar.

"What are you complaining about now?" Ianthe asked with irksome cheerfulness from her camel, which walked with irksome slowness beside his own irksome camel.

Her camel was a pleasant beast. His, on the other hand, had bitten him twice, attracted every flying bug in the desert, and broke wind repeatedly, usually when there was a back wind. He'd named his camel after the Christian religion's Lucifer, equivalent to the Norse god Loki, whose name he hadn't wanted to use for fear of further angering the Norse gods.

"He is always complaining, Ianthe," Finn said from his other side. To no one's surprise, Finn had found the most beautiful camel, with long silky fur. A female, no doubt, who batted its long camel eyelashes at him every chance it got. "Truly, if he keeps frowning like that, his face may freeze into furrows so deep Drifa will be able to plant roses in them."

"We must be indulgent," Ianthe told Finn. "Sidroc is grouchy because he is so worried about his ladylove."

He choked on a mouthful of sand.

Ladylove? Finn mouthed silently to him.

"Drifa is not my lady, nor is she my love," he insisted hotly. "Get that idea out of your fool heads right now."

"Whatever you say," Ianthe said, clearly thinking otherwise.

In truth, Sidroc wouldn't let himself question why he was so concerned over Drifa's welfare that he'd appointed himself her savior, and that was the bone of his increasing self-induced irritation.

So what if she had gotten herself into trouble? So what if she was injured or being assaulted? So what if he never saw her again? He could not care less.

Which was a total lie.

He cared.

Too much.

"Why don't you two drop back and entertain the rest of the 'troop'?" he suggested.

That was another thing that made him bloody damn mad. Once he and Finn had reported to the emperor what they'd discovered at the border lord's estates, and once Sidroc had spoken his mind to Mylonas over what he suspected was the eparch's involvement in the plot against the Norse princess, and once he had made plans to rescue her—though why that was his responsibility he could not understand—he was faced with a mob of people wanting to come with him. The mob being Finn, Drifa's four bodyguards, who were nigh prostrate with guilt at losing her, and Ianthe, who claimed to now be Drifa's best friend. If Drifa hadn't come to visit her, it never would have happened, in Ianthe's remorse-ridden mind. It was all Ianthe's fault. No, it was everyone's fault, they each proclaimed. Except Finn, who came along to enjoy the debacle. Nay, that was unfair, Finn was a good friend, and a soldier always wanted a comrade with weapon-skill at his back.

In any case, the bunch hadn't ever asked if they could tag along. They'd insisted. And when he'd repeatedly refused, they'd said they would follow after him anyhow.

He was particularly intrigued by Ianthe's comment that Drifa would need female companionship when he uncovered her secret. And then the infuriating woman had sealed her lips, refusing to say more. 'Twas galling to think the princess witch had a secret, which apparently involved him, which she shared with a person who was almost a stranger, but not with him.

"Will I be angry when this secret is revealed?" he'd asked. Surely Ianthe could tell him that at least.

Ianthe had shrugged.

Gods, I am coming to hate shrugs.

"Happy and angry at the same time. I am hoping happiness will overwhelm anger."

What a load of feminine ill-logic!

They camped that night around a fire at an oasis, which meant a puddle of water with one single palm tree and about a million hectares of sand. *Oh joy!* Hopefully they would arrive on the morrow at the desert tent city Mylonas had reluctantly mentioned to him, under pressure from the emperor.

"What is your plan?" asked Ivar, who was dipping a hunk of *paximadi* into his cup of ale. *Paximadi* was the hard bread the Greek military carried on all their missions. It lasted forever because it was hard as a rock.

He was saving his to feed to Lucifer at the end of this mission in hopes the devil would choke to death. His luck, the beast would turn the bread into vomit and spew it at his face.

"Are you listening, Guntersson? What is your plan?"

What plan? "First, we must discover where Drifa is being held." *That sounds like a plan, doesn't it?* "It makes no sense for us to go storming into an enemy encampment, and that is how we must view this Arab tent city. Believe me, they will not welcome us." *You would think I had actually thought this out, instead of barreling ahead on the steam of my emotions. Emotions? Me?*

"I can go in, dressed in Arab garb," said Gismun, one of Drifa's guardsmen. "My dark hair and complexion look least like a Norseman of us all."

"It could be dangerous," Sidroc warned.

Gismun's chin shot upward. "I am a Viking."

That said it all.

Sidroc nodded. "Once we locate Drifa, we must attempt to remove her with stealth. Our numbers do not warrant an all-out attack."

"I know where Drifa is," Ianthe said with certainty. "She is in a harem."

Everyone turned slowly to stare at Ianthe.

"Mylonas inferred to us in our meeting with him that Drifa had an Arab cousin who might wish to marry her for purposes of an alliance," Sidroc mused aloud.

Ianthe waved a hand dismissively. "Does not matter. That is where she would stay. At least at first."

"How would you know that?" Sidroc asked.

"One of my shop assistants had a cousin who had been kidnapped by a tribe of Arab nomads at one time and ransomed for coin. She told us many stories."

"And?" Sidroc prodded. Why had Ianthe waited

until now to tell them this? Did she not realize that every bit of information was necessary for this mission to succeed?

"Even if the ad-Dawlah cousin plans to marry Drifa, she would first go to the harem where she would be prepared for marriage," Ianthe explained. "That could take days or even weeks."

Sidroc did not dare ask how she would be "prepared." He had enough to worry about without that bound-to-be-alarming enlightenment. And in the back of his mind he had a picture of Drifa wearing the revealing harem garment he'd bought for her. For no logical reason, he did not want anyone else seeing her in that manner.

Drifa's fourth guardsman, a mostly quiet, mid-aged man named Ulf, said, "As long as the princess is a virgin, she has naught to worry about. They will treat her with respect and gentle care."

Ivar exchanged an accusing, horrified look with Sidroc.

Through a tight throat, Sidroc asked, "What happens to those women who are not virgins?"

"They do not marry them, that is for sure," Ulf said. "They are either cast into a harem for life as a concubine, or they are sold on the slave market."

Finn tilted his head and gazed at him with questioning eyes that asked, loud and clear, *You didn't, did you?*

Oh, that was wonderful. Now Sidroc joined those who were weighted down with guilt.

"Once Gismun steals into the tent city and discovers Drifa's whereabouts, I think I should slip into the harem tent, assuming that is where Drifa is located. With veils and such, and the protection of the Blessed Virgin, to whom I have been praying, I will not be recognized." This from Ianthe, of course. "We must warn Drifa to be ready to escape on a moment's notice."

"I have an idea," Finn said. "This particular ad-Dawlah is a noted horse breeder. I could locate where his herd of horses is being held and release them. That should create a furor calling all the men to help round them up, distracting attention away from the harem tent."

"That sounds like a good plan, depending on what information Gismun brings back to us," Sidroc said.

Everyone began talking at once then as they discussed the various paths this rescue might follow. 'Twas impossible to hear oneself think until Finn clapped his hands for attention.

"Just one question," Finn said, a forefinger upraised. "Can I bring one of the harem girls back with me?"

They all laughed, assuming he was making a jest.

Sidroc hoped he was jesting.

In any case, a bit of humor was like sauce on a bad piece of meat. They needed to laugh, or else they would weep at the bad situation they were in.

What was it about men and virgins?

The first day, Queen Latifah stuck her grubby fingers up into Drifa's female parts and announced with glee, "Not a virgin!"

Drifa didn't know what outraged her more, that two males witnessed her humiliation, albeit eunuchs ordered to hold her down on the bed, or that the prince who proposed to marry her would allow his mother to go at her with such rough handling. The only thing that could be worse was if Bahir had stood there himself as witness.

Even so, Bahir was furious when he entered the harem tent, which was actually a series of interconnecting tents, containing everything from soft pallets for sleeping, to bathing chambers, to salons. A number of the concubines, some as young as thirteen, scurried out of the way of their storming master, no doubt having suffered from his fury in the past.

Stalking right up to her where she sat on the edge of the bed, her gown thankfully tugged back down, he yanked her to her feet by a pincer hold on her upper arms, then backhanded her so hard she fell back down. His ring had cut into her face and she felt the blood gather and leak down to her chin.

"You lying bitch!" he yelled in Greek.

"I never said I was a virgin. Mayhap you should have thought of that afore having me taken." Sometimes Drifa did not know enough to keep her thoughts to herself.

"You dare to talk back to me?" he spat out and pulled her back up by her hair so that she stood so close to him she felt his spittle on her face. She had to turn her face to accommodate him or lose a hunk of hair. Even then, he slapped her other cheek. She would be black and blue afore morn. "You will pay, whore. You will pay." He shoved her back down.

"You can always send me back," she suggested. *You better, because I swear I will put a dagger through your slimy heart eventually. A pitcher over the head would not be good enough for the likes of you.*

"Never! You were brought here for a purpose and that purpose still exists."

"And that is?"

"The Moslem tribes must unite to fight the Greeks. We have been splintered apart of late, since the defeat of our beloved Saif ad-Dawlah a decade ago. Our marriage will accomplish that. An added bonus will be your Norsemen joining our battles."

"Do you think my father would align himself with you, even if I bore your child, if all I am is a prisoner in your harem?"

"Prisoner? My concubines are not prisoners. They are here willingly."

She arched her brows in doubt.

Which further infuriated him.

At this point, she did not care. She was furious, too.

"Who says there will be no marriage?" he asked with an evil expression on his face. "We will wait until you get your bloody flux, or not. If you are not with child, I will wed you, and may Allah protect you from my rage, for I will not. If you *are* breeding, nothing will protect you from my wrath."

Drifa should have been scared, but in fact she was jubilant. She was not pregnant, having evidence of that soon after Sidroc left the city. It would be at least two sennights until her next monthly flow. Time, that was what Bahir's decision gave her. Time for Sidroc to come rescue her.

Please, gods, let Sidroc care enough to come after me.

But does she have to belly dance? . . .

Two days later, Sidroc was preparing to send Ianthe into the tent city to become a harem houri.

She was dressed in a black robe with a hood and veil that covered everything except her hands and eyes that were heavily kohled. She was taking the place of a young Slavic woman they'd intercepted on the way to the privy tent. The woman, named Marizke, praised God for her rescue after five long years in the harem.

Gismun had reported back to them last night after one full day in the tent city, pretending to be a horse trader from one of the distant Arab tribes. He was offering a fine stallion for sale, one that Sidroc had actually been given by the emperor some time ago.

Gismun was able to tell them where the harem tents were located, and, to everyone's distress, he said that he'd seen Drifa in passing. And she had fingermark bruises on both sides of her face.

When asked, Marizke told them that the prince was in a rage over Drifa's lack of virginity, although no one was supposed to know about it except him and his mother, the evil queen. Apparently the queen mother had taken a dislike to Drifa, mocking her Norse background in front of one and all, and jabbing her with a cane every chance she got. Further evidence of the woman's cruelty, she forced Drifa to sleep with her pet panther. Did not matter that the panther was harmless, Drifa had to be terrified.

Sidroc swore he would kill Bahir and his mother, once everyone was safely away from the tent city.

"You must be discreet. Never speak unless spoken to, and then only in one word, if possible," Sidroc advised Ianthe.

"Get Drifa alone as soon as possible and inform her of our plans.

"Neither of you should do anything to draw attention to yourselves."

"Sidroc! We have gone over these instructions already. You do not have to remind me."

He wasn't so sure about that. He was just so worried, leaving the fate of their plans in the hands of these two women. He should be more trusting, he supposed, but he knew how unpredictable Drifa could be. And Ianthe was growing more like her by the day. Finn, he trusted implicitly, but anything could go wrong in a situation like this.

"Pray," Ianthe advised them all when dusk finally came. "Drifa and I will expect you after everyone has gone to sleep."

He nodded, then pulled Ianthe aside. "Tell Drifa—" He stopped to clear his throat. "Tell her that I promise to return her to her little girling." But then he realized when he saw the stunned expression on Ianthe's face, how lackwitted that sounded, and added, "Tell her we have unfinished business."

A woman is expected to do *what*? Eeew! . . .

Drifa was sitting cross-legged on the carpet along with the other harem "prisoners," which was how she chose to regard the concubines. They were getting yet another lecture from the Imad, the head eunuch, on "How to Please the Master."

"Eeeew!" murmured Marizke, the Slavic thrall-concubine, who folded herself down beside Drifa after returning from the privy.

"He is still discussing 'licking the tree,'" Drifa whispered to Marizke, who had her head bowed slightly as if listening intently to Imad. "I am a gardener, but I have ne'er licked any tree. Who wants to swallow . . . bark?"

Marizke put a hand to her mouth to suppress a giggle. "Or sap?"

Drifa's head shot to the right. "Ianthe?"

Ianthe put a fingertip to her lips.

"How? When? Thank the gods!"

"Princess Drifa, since you are in such a talkative mood, would you like to come forward and demonstrate for us," Imad requested in a voice that was not a request, but an order.

Imad spoke in Arabic, but another young eunuch, Habib, translated everything he said into several other tongues represented in the harem: Greek, Italian, even Saxon English.

"Uh, my apologies. I just wanted to make sure Marizke's stomach ailment is better."

Habib translated for her.

Imad arched his brows with suspicion, but just then the stomach growled in the heavy concubine sitting in front of them, and everyone laughed, thinking it was Marizke.

"Isobel, then," Imad said, smiling at the woman in front, a favorite of Bahir's from the Saxon lands. They soon found out why. "Isobel will demonstrate the correct way to 'Milk the Tree.'"

Isobel stepped forward and took from Imad's hands a long marble phallus, similar to the ones Drifa had seen in the Miklagard marketplace.

Several of the women giggled.

Imad cast them frowns, and they immediately stopped, knowing the head eunuch had methods of punishment that did not show, like whipping the bottoms of their feet or making them wear a small metal rod inside the body for an entire day. One young woman even had a rod put up her backside, a particularly painful punishment for daring to defy the queen mother, who'd ordered her to disrobe and sit on the lap of a visiting horse breeder the prince wanted to impress.

Drifa had been here only a week, but she knew the best course was to make oneself as inconspicuous as possible. Even then, it was only her high status as a Norse princess, and possible sixth wife, that saved her from some agonizing or humiliating chastisement.

Everything the harem concubines did was intended for the master's benefit. The way they dressed (scantily when in his private quarters) or ate (root vegetables presumably making them lustsome, though carrots never made Drifa think of sex) or cared for their bodies (shaved nether parts being a preference), even the thoughts in their heads (nothing of substance), were intended to please this one man only.

But wait, Isobel was doing something amazing with the marble phallus. She was kneeling with her head bent back so that her neck was arched. Little by little, she eased the entire bloody manpart all the way in. Then out. Then in.

"It is all in the art of relaxing the throat muscles," Imad told them. "Let the master touch your hearts."

From the inside? Is he demented? "Good gods!" Drifa murmured, despite her resolve not to speak.

Ianthe's jaw had dropped with astonishment.

"Now, notice how she milks the tree on the end before easing it in again. And sometimes the good concubine will let the tree do all the work." He smirked and stepped forward, taking the phallus in hand and thrusting it in and out of Isobel's receptive mouth, mimicking the sex rhythm.

"She deserves every accolade Bahir gives her," Ianthe whispered in amazement.

"Better her than me," Drifa whispered back.

Imad patted Isobel on the head when he was done with her, almost as if she'd performed the act on him. "You may have the rest of the day to yourself, sweet one."

Isobel smiled coyly, but as she was leaving the tent, Drifa noticed the look of desolation on her pretty face. She also noted the livid scar on her one cheek, the kind left by the tail of a lash. How many punishments had Isobel suffered to reach this state of compliance?

After their lesson, they went off for the midday

meal of fruit and olives. Drifa and Ianthe had only a few moments of privacy, not wanting to draw any attention to themselves.

"Tonight," Ianthe said.

Drifa nodded.

"We must wait for a signal. There will be a distraction."

She nodded again. "Who is here?"

"Seven of us."

"Huh?"

"Sidroc, Finn, Ivar, Farle, Gismun, and Ulf."

"Sidroc wanted to be gone from Byzantium. He is angry, isn't he?'

Ianthe grinned. "A mite piqued to be so inconvenienced."

"I can imagine."

"Not to worry, my dear. I think the man has strong feelings for you."

"Like hate, mayhap."

"He said to give you a message. He promises to deliver you back to your little girl."

She groaned.

"Also," Ianthe said with a note of mischief in her voice, "he said there is unfinished business betwixt you."

Oh gods, she thought. *Now I will owe him even more nights of passion.*

Imad entered the dining tent then and clapped his hands for attention. "Come, ladies, time for more pleasure lessons."

As they walked sedately through the chain of tents, their faces demurely covered lest they run into an unwary male—gods forbid!—one of the concubines asked the eunuch, "What do we learn next, Teacher Imad?"

"Today we henna our flower buds."

"Flower buds?" Ianthe mouthed to Drifa.

"Nipples."

CHAPTER TWENTY

My hero! . . .

The horses were released, and the tent city went into a frenzy of yelling and running, giving Sidroc and Finn the opportunity to approach the harem section. The others stood guard at various points, including Ivar, who was determined to blood his battle-axe this night. Sidroc planned the same. Hopefully his weapon would have royal Arab blood on it.

Finn made an owl cry three times. Stopped. Then hooted again. This was the signal he'd practiced that was intended to show Ianthe and Drifa where the men were waiting for them. What they hadn't taken into account was the noise and whether their signal could be heard over the panicked voices and screams inside and outside the tent.

Just when he heard a female voice say, "Sidroc?" an Arab guardsman approached them from behind.

Sidroc motioned with his head for Finn to release the women by cutting the tent fabric with a sharp blade, while he raised his broadsword high overhead in two hands. Within seconds, despite the dodging miscreant and two failed attempts, his third wide arc nigh severed the man's neck. Blood spurted everywhere, including onto Sidroc's body, but he had no time to worry about that because others soon followed.

He scarce noticed as Finn led the two women—nay three women, for gods' sake!—by him, but he did hear a cry of distress from Drifa, followed by a warning of "Be careful, dearling."

Dearling?

No matter! He now faced two other men with those ancient curved sickle swords called *khopeshs* in hand, shouting Arab obscenities at him. He dropped his broadsword and used his short sword in one hand and lance in the other to fight. It was a particular technique he had perfected where he distracted the enemy with a swing of the lance toward their knees and then lunged with the sword.

Finn was back and Ivar was with him. The three of them worked well together, raising the death throes from five more and raising the sword dew on three others who managed to run away when he paused to ask Finn, in that brief moment of respite, if the women were safe.

"Yea, except for Marizke, who ran back inside the tent. Apparently she prefers the devil she knows to the ones she does not."

"Meaning us?"

"Precisely. In any case, we have to get out of here, too," Finn said.

They were all breathing heavily, but the berserk lust was still in Sidroc. Fighting was what he was trained to do, and he did it well. It was not easy for him to walk away from a fight.

"You and Ivar go first. I'll meet you in a few hours at that oasis where we rested last night."

"Nay! I'm not leaving without you," Finn insisted.

"Do not be demented, Guntersson," Ivar added. "There are too many of them and too few of us."

"I want to kill Bahir first. I *need* to kill the bastard."

"Save that for another day," Finn advised.

"I cannot let the prince escape punishment for his misdeeds."

"Shall I hit him over the head and carry him out over my shoulder?" Ivar asked Finn. He was talking about Sidroc, not ad-Dawlah.

"If you must," Finn agreed.

"Idiots!" Sidroc said, realizing once he calmed down that it was foolhardy to stay. Bahir would send his men for him. The coward would not engage himself lest the odds were greater in his favor. Nay, Sidroc would be taken captive. So, with several foul words, he joined Finn and Ivar in rushing toward the area where their camels were waiting. Gods, he hoped the camels could gallop because if Bahir and his men came after them on horseback they would be in dire trouble.

But, thank Thor, god of war, the second part of their plan erupted just then. From three different areas of the tent city, he saw fires break out. The dried tent fabrics soon went up in flames and spread fast. Hopefully the Arabs would care more about saving their tents and goods and any people left inside before chasing after them.

By the time Sidroc and his two comrades-in-arms caught up with the others, they'd had to fight off more of the Arab soldiers on two different occasions. Once four men, the other time, three. For now, the battle lust had passed in Sidroc, replaced by the survival lust. No one spoke, just galloped as long as the animals would allow, and for once Lucifer was not balking or farting.

He no sooner dismounted from Lucifer than Drifa launched herself at him. He caught her just in time as she wrapped her arms around his shoulders and wept into his neck. He had no recourse but to hold her about the waist, her legs dangling above the sand.

"Thank you, thank you for saving me, I got my monthly flux and if you hadn't come I would have had to marry the slimy prince even though Ianthe said not to worry, but they were going to make me practice tomorrow with the marble phallus, and, oh, I think I would have killed myself first, but they already hennaed me and Ianthe, we couldn't stop them, and the queen mother is more vicious that a maddened warrior, and she made me sleep with her bloody panther whose breath smelled like rancid meat, and I need a bath so bad, and did you know that fermented goat's milk is considered a prized drink like mead, and what took you so long, not that I am complaining, but . . ."

On and on she blathered, never stopping to take a breath, with Sidroc only understanding half of what she said. In the end, he began to laugh. He couldn't help himself.

Soon the rumbling of his chest must have alerted her to his mirth. Drawing her head back, she stared at him. Her face was dirty and tear-tracked, her hair snarled, and her nose red. In total, she looked nigh adorable, even with the ignoble bruise marks on both sides of her face.

"You are laughing at me?" she asked, hurt limning her voice.

"Well, you must admit, you were talking without taking a breath. I must ask, though, what exactly were you going to practice with a marble phallus?"

She blushed and tried to squirm out of his hands, but he wasn't letting go. Not yet.

But then she noticed the dark stains on his tunic and face, and now on her night rail, as well. A very nice night rail, by the by, one that gave him shady glimpses of not-so-hidden delights.

"You are hurt. Oh my gods! Were you wounded? Where?"

He should release his hold on her, but he didn't want to. Still, with a sigh of regret and a quick squeeze, he did in fact do so. This was not the time or place.

She slid to her feet and began undoing his belt in an attempt to raise the hem of his garment and check his injuries. Everywhere she moved her hands, he checked her, but she just tried another spot.

He started laughing again, especially when she slapped at him each time he kept her from revealing his skin. "Later, Drifa. Later you may have access to my body. I am not hurt. It is my foeman's sword dew."

"Oh," she said, stepping back. Then, "Eeew!"

as she noticed the front of her garment, now hugging her breasts wetly. He should be repulsed. He was not.

Ianthe came up with cloths for both of them to wipe off the mess, the best they could do until they got to a water hole. Then Ianthe leaned up to kiss his cheek. "I kept telling Drifa that you would come, but she was worried."

"You doubted me, princess? Tsk, tsk, tsk!"

" 'Tis not that I doubted you. I knew you would try, but—"

"How did you know that I would try?"

"That is the kind of man you are. A man of mettle."

He felt oddly elated at that compliment.

"—but I worried that you wouldn't succeed . . ."

Not so elated, after all.

" . . . not with so many guards. There are some women who have been captive there for ten years and more. Like poor Isobel." She looked over to the woman talking with Finn. She was attractive, but thirty if she was a day, and thinner than his friend usually preferred. Plus there appeared to be a livid scar on one side of her face. He had to peer closer to see if his eyes were playing him false, but, nay, Finn was indeed gazing at the woman as if he'd discovered gold.

He and Drifa exchanged an amused glance.

It was decided to split the nine of them into three groups heading in different directions, but with the ultimate destination being Miklagard, where both Sidroc and Drifa had longships that could take them away, if it became necessary. They hoped to confuse any enemy followers and weaken their ranks. No one was surprised when Finn chose Isobel and Ulf to ride with him. Farle and Gismun would travel with Ianthe. And he would be with Drifa and Ivar.

They all sat about the oasis, having a last cold meal together before separating. The skies were still dark, which would be an advantage if their escape was to succeed. It would be hours before dawn.

"I want to go home," Drifa told him.

"To Byzantium?"

"Nay, to the Norselands."

"Mayhap you should. Leastways everyone has been advising such from the beginning."

"Are you going to gloat?"

"Just a little." He smiled. "If Ivar rides ahead later and gets there before us, he can make ready your longship. If we get there first, I can put you in the hands of your seaman."

"Where are you going? Aren't you leaving, too?"

"Eventually, but I refuse to leave without getting my Varangian pay for the past year. The emperor owes me."

"Well, that is all right because I am not leaving without my sketchbooks and paints, and the roots that Ianthe saved for me, plus seedlings and grafts that the imperial gardener promised. The jewelry I left in my palace chamber is worth a fortune. And I still need to buy a gift for my father. When I said I want to go home, I didn't mean immediately."

Sidroc rolled his eyes, as did Ivar, who had heard it all from her other side.

"Do what you will," Sidroc said on a long sigh. "You will anyway."

"Nay, you misspeak me, Sidroc. What I meant is that I can wait for you."

"Did I ask you to?"

"Aaarrgh!" She seemed to brace herself. "I want you to come to Stoneheim with me."

Her pronouncement was met with his silence.

The Big Reveal was really big! . . .

Lackwit! Lackwit! Lackwit! Drifa berated herself for her clumsy words and was about to try again in a more subtle fashion, but Gismun yelled, "Men coming! Men on horseback coming!"

While properly shod horses could travel across the desert just fine, they could not go long distances without water or rest. Camels, on the other hand, could last for long stretches without stopping.

While Drifa hid behind the camels with the two women, their six men fought valiantly for an hour or more, leaving on the desert floor ten enemy dead, and only minor wounds on Finn, which Isobel was already tending. All the men in her group, but especially Sidroc, were skilled swordsmen. She had to admire their talents. In truth, the six of them were comparable to twice or thrice their number of other fighting men. She could see why Sidroc and Finn had been recruited for the Varangians. She could see why her father had chosen these four particular guardsmen for her safety.

"No more dawdling," Sidroc said to her a short

time later. "Time to get up on Lucifer and get out of here."

Dawdling? She had been waiting for him. The lout! "Lucifer?"

"My camel. The camel from hell. You know, the One-God religion's evil one." He pointed over to where one particular camel stood apart from the other five.

"For shame! You can't call that lovely camel Lucifer."

"Why not?"

"For one thing, 'tis a nasty name for such a beautiful animal." They walked toward the animal and Drifa stroked its snarled pelt. In truth, it was a smelly beast, and not at all comely, despite what she'd said to Sidroc. But she had always held that animals had feelings, too, and 'twas not nice to speak ill of them in their presence.

"Are you referring to the selfsame beast that likes to spit on me and fart to the beat of its plodding hoof steps?"

Drifa stifled a giggle as the camel gave Sidroc the evil eye but seemed to purr at Drifa.

Sidroc gaped with incredulity.

"For another thing, it is a girl, not a boy."

"What? It is not! Is it? How do you know?"

She put both hands on her hips and gave him a look one might lay on an ignorant boyling. She glanced down at the camel's nether end, then over at another camel's nether end. A vast difference!

"Oh. How could I have missed *that*?"

Ivar was laughing so hard he almost fell off his

camel, which he'd already mounted . . . his very male camel.

"So, no Lucifer. You could name her Lucy, though. For St. Lucy, or St. Lucia, the Christian patron saint of blindness. Even Norsemen pray to her betimes to be able to withstand the darkness of the long winters."

"Are you going to talk the whole way to Miklagard?" He was doing something with a switch to get the camel to kneel so that they could mount.

"Does someone have a thorn in his paw?"

"Huh? You mean the camel?"

"Nay, not the camel. Methinks *you* are grumpy."

"I'll give you grumpy," he said, pinching her bottom just before lifting her in front of him so that they both mounted the saddle at the same time, both of them astride, with her in front of him. With another light tap of the switch, the animal rose gracefully to its feet and began to follow after Ivar's camel.

Drifa waved to the others, who were also departing in other directions.

Once they were comfortable, or as comfortable as one could be atop a walking longship, she said, over her shoulder, "You will notice that I did not protest riding back to Miklagard with you. Don't you wonder why?"

"I cannot say that I do."

"Dumb dolt!" she murmured. "There are things I need to discuss with you."

He groaned. "You *are* going to talk endlessly, aren't you?"

"Don't be rude."

"I am not going to Stoneheim with you, if that is where this conversation is leading."

"Why not?"

"Could it perchance be that I have unpleasant memories of that place?"

"We need to talk about that."

"Why must women talk everything to death? What's done is done."

"Not according to you and your forty-two nights of sensual torture."

She could feel him smile against her hair. "Perchance I had a thorn in my paw then, too."

"I meant to tell you. There will be no more of that."

"*That?*"

"Bedsport."

"Is that so? Actually, I had the same thought . . . I intended to tell you that your nights of incredible passion are over. I have decided not to hold you to your bargain. Do not beg me. I will not be moved."

"What? Beg? Me? You are deluded."

"You cannot deny you enjoyed it, too. All of it."

"Be that as it may, whether you hold me to our bargain or not, I have decided to save myself for my husband."

He laughed. The brute actually dared to laugh at her. "A little late for that, isn't it?"

Really, the man needs another head thumping. "It is never too late for new beginnings. You should try it."

"Do you perchance have any particular man in mind? Oh, nay, do not tell me that is why you want me to come to Stoneheim. You wish to lure me into a marriage trap."

"Don't be ridiculous."

"Why is that ridiculous? You called me dearling when I rescued you."

"My mind was overwrought. It meant nothing. I take it back."

"There are some things you cannot take back, *dearling*."

"Why do you argue with every bloody thing I say?"

"Perchance because I enjoy doing so."

"Immature youthling!"

"You certainly have a way of convincing a man to do your bidding, princess."

"Aaarrgh! Can you not listen without baiting me for just a few moments? Is it not obvious to you that I have something important to tell you?"

"Uh-oh! Perchance is the big secret about to be revealed?"

"It must be at some point, but I had hoped to get you to Stoneheim afore telling you."

"Ah, so that is where this roundabout conversation is leading. And why would you want me there for the big revelation?"

"Stop mocking me, and listen well. It is not so much what I must tell you, but who I must show you."

"Who? This is gets more and more confusing." She could practically hear his brain working. "Oh, nay, if you are perchance thinking of providing me a new bride to make up for your leaving me nigh mid-wedding rites, forget about it."

"You are driving me barmy with all these per-chances. Let me turn around so that I can look at you. What I have to say should be said face-to-face."

"Now you are scaring me," he said, and turned her so that she sat sidesaddle, with her legs over one side of the camel, and her rump on Sidroc's lap, rather on Sidroc's rising enthusiasm. It was sad but true that teasing Drifa aroused him. "Stop squirming," he ordered, "lest you want to have sex atop a camel."

Lucy farted her opinion. Sidroc cringed. Drifa pretended not to notice.

"All right, I am listening. What is so important that you nigh shake at the prospect of telling me?"

"Your daughter is alive."

"What daughter?"

"Runa is your daughter, the one you thought had died whilst you were in your death-sleep."

He frowned. "Signe?"

She nodded. "I changed Signe's name to Runa."

"Why? What? Who?" he sputtered. "Are you telling me that the baby did not die five years ago, and that she has been alive all this time, but you failed to tell me?"

"Yea, but—"

His heart thundered in his rib cage. His blood raced. He felt light-headed. Little by little, one at a time, the facts registered in his dumbstruck brain. Signe was not dead. Drifa had somehow rescued her. All these years of guilt and grief, his daughter had been alive . . . a daughter whose name had been changed, for gods only knew what reason. And Drifa had failed to tell him.

"You bitch! You flailed me with remorse for taking your virginity and introducing you to unnatural bedsport. All the time you cast insults at my honor, you were living the biggest lie. Have you no idea the guilt I have suffered all these years for failing to rescue Signe? And you waited until we were in the midst of a dangerous desert escape that might very well end one or both of our lives?"

"I did try to find you."

He made a snorting sound of disbelief.

"I sent Rafn to Jomsborg and all the market towns, Norsemandy, the Saxon lands, even Iceland. We believed you were dead."

"And since you arrived in Byzantium? What held you back since then? What feckless excuse do you have for that outrage?"

"Fear."

"Of what? I have ne'er beaten a woman."

"Not that kind of fear. I feared . . . I feared you would take my baby from me."

"*Your* baby?"

He yanked on the camel's reins, pulling it to a stop, then called out to Ivar, "Princess Drifa will be riding with you now. I need to go on ahead. Alone."

Ivar looked surprised, but stopped his camel and made quick work of transferring her from one camel to the other. The whole time Drifa just barely held back her welling tears. The whole time Sidroc refused to look at her.

Still, she persisted, "There is more I need to say if you will only—"

He cut her off with the slice of his hand in the

air. "No more! If you say anything else, I cannot guarantee I will not go berserk with rage at you."

She decided to tell him one more thing, anyway, despite his warning. "I love your daughter as if she were my own. She is adorable. Everyone thinks so. She has everyone at Stoneheim under her little thumb with just a smile."

"Is that supposed to convince me to give up rights to my own child?"

"That's not what I said."

"How would I know? You jabber, jabber, jabber, and what is the point? How would I know what are lies and what is the truth with such as you?"

"Here is a truth for you. Runa looks just like you, and I have told her about you, her father, and how you saved her life. And, yea, you did save her life, Sidroc, by forcing your father to give you time."

He froze, closed his eyes for a long moment, then rode away in silence.

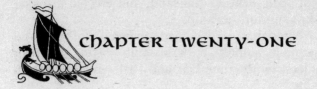

CHAPTER TWENTY-ONE

The saddest words: What might have been . . .

It was evening before Sidroc was in Drifa's presence again. He'd ridden all day, never stopping, until he found a small watering hole that was too tempting to pass up, especially since a large, tattered but useable tent had been left behind. He'd first had to evict a snake, two lizards, and a hairy spider.

Despite keeping his distance, he never went so far in advance that he couldn't see Ivar and Drifa to make sure they were in no danger. The whole time he pondered and pondered what little Drifa had told him about his daughter. That event—the death of his daughter—had been such a turning point in his life, and he was having trouble getting past the implication of her being alive.

Skinning and roasting the snake for dinner was a possibility, but then he snared a skinny lamb that had managed to survive somehow here in the desert, probably lost from some passing caravan. He packed the snake meat in wet palm leaves with hot coals beneath the sand, and erected a make-shift spit for the lamb.

After that, he'd bathed, changed clothing, and set up a campfire, with the lamb spitting succulent juices, by the time Ivar and Drifa caught up with him

He saw immediately by Drifa's puffy eyes and red nose that she had been weeping profusely. He did not care.

He saw immediately that Ivar was furious with him for making his princess cry and probably for riding separate from them. He did not care.

Sidroc helped a glaring Ivar unload the camel and told the man, but for Drifa's benefit, that the watering hole was clean enough for drinking and there was enough for buckets to bathe with. She walked silently past him, her red nose raised pridefully.

Ivar shook his head.

"What?" Sidroc snapped.

"Fools! The two of you are fools!"

"You don't know the half of what she's done."

"And neither do you."

Whatever that meant! If there were more secrets, he didn't want to know about them. Not yet. Not until he'd digested the other deceit.

The old man stomped off to some nearby bushes to relieve himself. Drifa filled a bucket and went into the tent to bathe.

When they sat about the fire after both Ivar and Drifa had bathed as well as they could out of a bucket and donned clean clothing, Sidroc asked Ivar, "Did you have any trouble today?"

"Lot of good it does for you to ask now!"

Sidroc felt his face heat. It had been immature of him to ride off alone.

"Nay, there was no trouble, just not being able to stop and rest our weary bones for trying to keep up with you. What were you trying to prove, boy?"

Boy? Oooh, Sidroc had done bodily harm to men who gave such insult to him. "I needed to prove I could hold my temper when stabbed in the back."

"I didn't stab . . . oh, what's the use?" Drifa cast him a disgusted look. "You won't believe anything I say anyhow."

"Talk," he demanded. "I am ready to listen now."

"Well, mayhap I am not in the mood to talk now."

"Uh, I think I will go set up my sleep furs in the tent. You two can argue all night for all I care. I am so tired my bones hurt."

"Mine do, too," Drifa said, and was about to stand and follow Ivar.

"Sit!" Sidroc ordered.

She arched her brows at his command, but sat back down on the stump she'd been using for a chair. He and Ivar had been sitting on a fallen tree.

"You know, Sidroc, I would think you would be pleased that your daughter is alive."

"I am."

"Then why are you so furious?"

"Because you kept this news from me."

"I already told you, Rafn traveled far and wide at my beseeching, trying to find you, but you were nowhere to be found. He even went to Vikstead to ask your father if he had seen you, telling him that you had suffered a head wound and we were worried about your condition."

"I can imagine my father's distress over news of my possible demise."

"Your father is not a nice man."

He almost smiled at her understatement.

"Rafn spent months looking for you, and after that whenever he went trading or a-Viking, he would ask after you, to no avail. You seemed to have disappeared, or—"

"—died," he finished for her. "And that is why you were so distressed when first you saw me in Miklagard. I was alive and it did not fit in with all your plans."

"Nay, that is not how it was. Not exactly."

"Be honest for once, Drifa."

"What will you do now?" she asked, abject fear in her dark eyes.

He could not allow himself to be moved, even when tears welled and streamed down her face. "I will get us back to Miklagard, meet with the emperor, make ready my longship, and go to Stoneheim to recover my daughter."

"You will take her then?" she choked out.

"How could you think otherwise?"

"She will be frightened. She does not know you."

"And whose fault is that? Nay, forget I said that. I do not blame you for that. I blame you for not telling me the instant you saw me on the steps of the harbor when you arrived in Byzantium."

"That, I concede. But betimes a sin is balanced

out by a good. Can you not forgive my sin by ac-
knowledging my good intent and the loving care I
have given your daughter for five years?"

"Forgiveness? Mayhap in time. But I cannot
forget. You have no idea how the loss of my child
has affected my life, how guilty I have felt. I never
should have left the baby at Stoneheim, not for a
moment, let alone sennights. I knew my father was
not to be trusted. I knew."

"Where will you take her?"

He noticed that she did not mention a refusal
to give up rights to the girling, to say she had the
Stoneheim *hird* at her back. That was wise of her
because, in his present frame of mind, he would
welcome a battle. "I am not sure. Wherever I
decide to settle, that's where she will be."

She began to sob then, big, blustering, nose-run-
ning, gasping cries of pain. He could see that she
cared for his daughter and that separation would
hurt.

But what could he do? Even if he forgave all,
what could he do?

Ivar stuck his head out the flap of the tent to see
what was going on. Then he just shook his head at
him, and returned to his bed furs.

For one brief moment, Sidroc wondered how
different his life might have been if he'd married
Drifa as he'd planned and they'd raised Signe, or
Runa, or whatever her name was now. What might
they have been by now? Would they have their own
estate, other children, a good life? Or would he
have become a cruel husband and father like the
men in his family seemed prone to be?

It was a hopeless exercise to contemplate all those possibilities.

Fury and compassion warred inside Sidroc. Fury won out. He walked away.

In love with a loathsome lout . . .

Drifa allowed herself one whole night of weeping and self-pity before raising her prideful chin and saying, "Enough!" to herself.

Marching outside the tent the next morning, she saw that the cold camp fire had been scattered, the camels packed, and both Ivar and Sidroc preparing to leave.

"There is cold fare laid out for you," Sidroc told her, pointing to a slice of hard bread, a slab of left-over snake, and a piece of cheese.

If he thinks to intimidate me with the snake meat, he underestimates the stubbornness of a Viking woman. We surpass our menfolk tenfold in that regard. I can out-stubborn him any day. She bit into the meat and stared at him, daring the lout to make a remark. It was hard swallowing the food, even mixed with a bite of bread and washed down with ale, but she refused to show any weakness.

A wasted effort because neither Sidroc nor Ivar was watching her. Therefore, she dumped the snake meat under the log, and ate only the bread and cheese.

When she went over to Ivar to share his camel, Sidroc said, "Nay! You ride with me."

"Why?"

"Because I say so."

She turned to Ivar for help, but he just shrugged.

"If you are going to continue insulting me, I'd rather walk."

"Good thing it is not raining. Or you would drown with your nose so high in the air."

"Does boorishness come naturally to you?"

"Must be," he said, and lifted her without warning into the air. For a long second, he didn't set her over the camel's saddle, but held her in the air and stared at her. "Your eyes are bloodshot and your mouth is puffy from all your wailing."

She stiffened.

"Are you done crying?"

"I am."

"Good," he said, and that was all. If it was intended as an apology, it fell flatter than a glob of gruel on a hot plate.

Puzzled by his odd demeanor, Drifa remained silent for the first hour of their journey. To her consternation, she was very aware of the man against whom she was nested. The scent of his clean body and clothing, the movement of his muscled arms as he steered the reins of the camel, his breathing against her ear, his heartbeat against her back, his thighs cradling her hips, and his manhood pressing against her backside. It was hard to maintain her anger, or her grief, or any other emotion, when she was being assailed by all these physical reminders that Sidroc was a man, and she was a woman.

Finally, out of nowhere, he said, "Tell me about my daughter."

Drifa thought about refusing, but decided that Sidroc, despite his boorishness, deserved to know. "Runa was a difficult baby, at first. She'd been barely fed by her wet nurse, and her little bottom was raw from lack of cleaning. It wasn't Eydis's fault. Your brother Svein demanded she spend all her effort and milk on his baby."

She felt Sidroc stiffen behind her.

"That is not meant as a condemnation of you. Merely a statement of your father's order to do only what was necessary for the baby."

"How did you get the baby out of Stoneheim without my father knowing? What does he think happened?"

"This will sound terrible."

"And everything you did before was not?"

"If you are going to start insulting me again, I am going to stop talking."

"Go on," he said grudgingly.

"There was a baby in the village who died of the coughing ailment. We managed to slip inside your father's keep—"

"Wait. Stoneheim is well-guarded. 'Tis not an easy task 'slipping' beyond its defenses."

She shrugged. "My sisters and I are clever. Besides, Tyra is a seasoned warrior."

He snorted his opinion.

"She is. Besides, we took no chances."

Sidroc swore a long streak. "Took no chances?" he sputtered. "Forget about what my father would consider 'stealing' his grandchild, do you realize that going within a hide of my father was taking a chance."

"I thought your father didn't want to let the baby live."

"He didn't, but he would consider it his decision to make, and sure as his soul is black as sin, he would resent anyone else impugning his honor, not that he has any."

"We rescued the baby. The manner in which we did so does not matter," she argued.

"Are you really so thick-headed you cannot understand. Dost know what my father would have done to you . . . before killing you or sending to your father for ransom? He rapes at will, and makes sport of giving innocent women to his men for public fornication."

Drifa cringed. "I see, but why make such a fuss when the deed is done?"

"Because I suspect you will continue to make such foolhardy decisions in the future."

"'Tis not your concern. You are naught to me, as you have reminded me on more than one occasion."

He inhaled and exhaled loudly several times, as if to garner patience. Men did that around her and her sisters all the time, especially her father. "Go on, then, continue this wondrous tale of how you managed to sneak into my father's castle unnoticed."

"Your sarcasm is unnecessary."

He pinched her bottom. "Continue."

"Whilst Vana flirted with one of the guardsmen, Breanne located the chamber where the wet nurse was caring for not just your baby but your brother's as well. When the wet nurse went to the garderobe, Breanne put a flagon of strong Frankish wine in the room. Once the wet nurse was *druk-kinn*, I came in with the dead baby and substituted it for the live one."

"Are you demented? Do your sister's husbands know what things they do? You should be beaten. You should be locked up for your own safety."

"A mere thank you would suffice."

"Your sarcasm is unnecessary, as well."

She shrugged. "Anyhow, we managed to escape, with the baby, and no one had any reason to think other than your child had died."

"Is that everything?'

"Well . . ."

He groaned.

"We did kidnap the wet nurse, and Tyra did have to clonk one guardsmen with the flat side of her broadsword, and Vana kneed one man in his dangly part, and methinks there might have been a tiny fire in the kitchen for a distraction."

First she felt a rumbly sound, then a shaking, and realized that Sidroc was laughing and trying to hold it back.

"What is so funny?" she demanded finally.

"You," he gasped out.

"A mere thank you would be welcome," she said once again.

He paused, said, "Thank you for saving my baby," then brushed his lips against the curve of her neck.

That mere whisper of a kiss sealed her fate. She was in love with the loathsome lout.

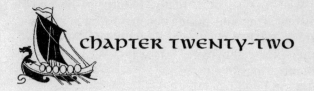

ChapTER TWENTY-TWO

**He could think of one way to shut the
woman up . . .**

Sidroc was no longer bone-melting angry with
Drifa, but he did not trust her any farther than
he could throw her. Not that he had any plans to
throw her anytime soon, *unless* she continued to
prattle about how happy his daughter was at Stoneheim and how unhappy she would be if forced to
leave.

In truth, Sidroc was conflicted and did not need
Drifa's harping to add to his agitation.

"I want my daughter with me," he insisted.

"But you do not know Runa. You would be
strangers."

"Whose fault is that?"

"You have no home yet for yourself, let alone
Runa."

"I will get one, and stop calling her Runa."

"It is the only name she knows. Best you get
used to it. Who would care for Runa? You have no
wife or female staff."

"I will."

"Get a wife?" she asked in an oddly choked voice.

Well, not so odd, really. He knew she feared his marrying and taking the girl to form his own family for her. And why wouldn't he? "Nay. No wife. Not right away, leastways. Why? Are you volunteering?"

"Good gods, nay!"

"Methinks you protest too much. But get that idea out of your head right now. Marriage is not on offer for you."

"Aaarrgh! As if I would accept!"

"Women always say 'Aaarrgh!' when they are losing an argument."

"This is not an argument."

"You could have fooled me. Just to be clear, I meant a female companion for the girling, not a wife."

"Do you know anything about things a little girl likes to do?"

He thought of his own boyhood . . . those times when he'd been able to escape his father's heavy hand and just be a child. He had to grin. "I could teach her how to spit long distances, or sing bawdy songs."

Instead of making her usual tsking noises at him, Drifa grinned and said, "I'll wager I can spit farther than you, or skim pebbles farther on a fjord. My father taught me."

"Come to think on it, you and your sisters were raised by your father, no mothers around, and you seem to have survived just fine."

"Humph!" Another of her usual retorts when she was bested in an argument. She stomped off to say her final good-byes to Lucy.

They'd traveled for three days by camel, and were now out of the desert and within the borders of Byzantium. That did not mean they were safe. At the moment, they were trading the camels for horses to be used for the remainder of the journey.

"Ivar, can we speak in private?" he asked.

Ivar nodded and walked over to the side of the stable in the village where they'd stopped.

"I am concerned about Princess Drifa reentering Miklagard. There are those within the city who aided in her being taken captive."

Ivar nodded. "I have the selfsame concern."

"I think you should ride ahead. We have made good time, and I don't think there is any way ad-Dawlah's men could have gotten word of her escape to those in the city so soon."

"How much time do you think we have before that happens?"

"Two days' lead time, at most. Hopefully Finn and all the others will have arrived by then, too."

"What is your plan?"

"I will keep Drifa with me, and I will prolong our journey long enough that you can gather together all of her belongings from the palace and from Ianthe's. You can make her longship ready to sail, but take it to the harbor near the Gate of St. Barbara. That way, once we arrive, I will take Drifa directly to her longship, and you can set sail immediately north up the Bosphorus. Quickest way to leave the city behind."

"The princess will not like being denied a last visit to Miklagard. She will say there are more gardens to study. More people to say her farewells to. More sights to see."

"I know, but this is a decision we must make for her."

Ivar nodded. "Her father would want it so." Ivar smiled then, "I do not envy you. When the princess finds out what you plan, she shall be furious."

"I can handle her," he said.

But Drifa walked up then and remarked, "I hope it is not me that you are referring to."

"Of course not," he lied. "I was referring to that mare over there that I am thinking of purchasing. She is skittish, but I can handle her, don't you think?"

Drifa looked dubious.

Ivar made excuses to go purchase some food supplies, and Sidroc knew he would take this opportunity to leave. Sidroc must occupy Drifa so that she would not suspect. Yet. "I have a surprise for you, Drifa," he said.

She eyed him cautiously.

"How would you like a bath and a soft bed for tonight?"

She sighed. "Is that possible?"

"The stable master told me of a farmstead where they have a small pond, which is private, and he offers clean hay stalls for travelers. How does that sound?"

"I cannot imagine anything that would give me greater pleasure."

I can.

"You think of everything."

You have no idea.

Where's a chaperone when you need one? . . .

It was early evening when Drifa realized that Ivar was missing.

Sidroc and Ivar had taken her outside the village to a farmstead where an elderly Greek couple, Stamos and Vera, gave them a hearty meal of lamb and lentils with warm bread, then directed them to a nearby pond that they assured them was clean. In other words, their farm animals were kept away from this section so there was no runoff of their waste. They'd even given them soap and drying cloths.

Drifa had gone first, and, yea, she had probably taken longer than she should have, luxuriating in being clean once again, from squeaky hair to shiny toenails. And she'd used the opportunity to wash her dirty clothes as well, laying them on a bush to dry.

Of course, this was the first time she had been naked since leaving the Arab tent city, and she got her first good look at her hennaed nipples and areolas. They looked ridiculous to her, although the harem eunuch had assured her and Ianthe that it was considered beautiful to many men. It would be months before the dye wore off. Good thing she wasn't married. It would probably give a Norseman a good laugh, or a fit of heart pains at the shock on first seeing them. Skalds would compose poems and recite them up one end of the Norselands and down the other, "Ode to Painted Nipples." And folks would whisper with questions about what other intimate body parts of hers had been painted. None, thank the gods, though they probably would have been if she hadn't escaped.

After bathing, she went to the barn where they planned to sleep that night, and Sidroc went off to bathe by himself. She was sitting on a clean wool blanket on clean hay in a clean *gunna*, combing her clean hair, marveling at how it was the simple things in life that gave the most pleasure.

But then Sidroc returned.

It wasn't that he took away those pleasurable things. 'Twas just that he unsettled her.

He, too, had bathed and donned clean clothing. He'd even shaved. And he looked more handsome than any man had a right to, even a Norseman.

While she continued to comb her hair, he braided the long strands on either side of his face. 'Twas not an exercise in vanity, she knew. Viking men favored long hair, but they did not like it swinging onto their faces, blinding them. Even so, the braids added to his attractiveness, and he probably knew it.

"Where are you and Ivar going to sleep?" she asked as she put her comb away and smoothed out the blanket. When he didn't answer, she turned to look at him.

He averted his eyes and busied himself checking over the horses they had purchased, which were in nearby stalls.

When he returned, she tried again. "Sidroc? You never answered my question."

"Ivar has gone."

"Gone where? The man has not left my side

since we arrived in Byzantium. Like barnacles on the underside of a longship he has been to me."

"I will be the barnacle on your underside for the time being."

Surely he did not mean that the way it sounded. Especially since he seemed to harbor a hatred of her most times, and indifference the rest. "Why? Where has Ivar gone?"

"Ahead to Miklagard."

"Why?"

"To make preparations."

"What is going on?"

"We decided that there might be danger for you in the city. Mayhap Mylonas. Mayhap some others. We do not believe ad-Dawlah arranged his misdeeds on his own."

"We. We. We. What is it with all this 'we' business? Why was I not consulted as well?" *I have a bad feeling here. A very bad feeling.*

"Men's work," he murmured.

If I had a pottery pitcher, I cannot say I would not use it over the fool's head. "What. Did. You. Say?"

"Not. A. Thing." He sighed deeply. "Do not make this difficult, Drifa. It is for the best, and we will catch up with Ivar in no time at all."

Drifa narrowed her eyes with suspicion. "Let me repeat my earlier question. Where do you intend to sleep tonight?'

"Right here," he said.

I knew it, I knew it. The troll! "Nay, you are not. I am not coupling with you again."

"Mayhap you should wait until you are asked."

Her face flamed. "Go find another stall to sleep."

"None are clean. Do not worry, I will not touch you."

She should have been assured by his promise, but then he added something else.

"Unless you ask."

He proceeded to remove his clothing. Every single stitch. Then he stretched his arms overhead, yawned widely, and laid himself down on her blanket.

"Good night, Drifa."

He really means to stay away from me? She would have been fooled, except for one thing. His enthusiasm was sticking up like a bloody flagpole.

Laughter bubbled up in her and erupted in a guffaw as she pointed at it. She continued to alternately snicker and giggle, even as she laid herself down, fully clothed, at the farther edge of the blanket.

"Good night, Sidroc," she said when she finally calmed down. *Isn't it wonderful that this is a game two can play?*

She was almost asleep when she heard him mutter, "It's not funny."

"Yea, it is."

" 'Tis not nice to make jest of a man's . . . um, manhood."

Drifa fell asleep with a smile on her face.

She awakened in the middle of the night to a chill in the air and a light that should not be there. She realized that a torch had been lit and placed in one of the secure wall brackets. And, somehow, her clothing had melted away.

Most amazing of all—though she was a dunderhead for letting down her guard—the biggest scoundrel in all the Norselands was leaning over her, staring slack-jawed at her hennaed nipples.

'Twould seem the joke was on her.

He wasn't an artist, but he painted pictures in his mind . . .

Sidroc didn't know whether to hoot with laughter or shout with joy at the wondrous sight before him. He was kneeling at the side of Drifa's nude body, taking in the view. A most incredible view, by the by.

Drifa had suddenly grown reddish-brown nipples and areolas. *Bright* reddish brown! They were either a virile man's fantasy-come-true, or a monumental jest. He was leaning toward the former.

"Why am I naked?" Drifa asked, her eyes shooting open suddenly.

Was there ever a more foolish question asked by a woman? "You were moaning in your sleep and I thought it best to check for hidden wounds."

"Do you expect me to believe that?"

"It was worth a try." He turned his attention back to her chest, not that it had ever left. "Uh, what happened?" he asked with as much subtlety as he could muster.

"I already told you before that the harem eunuch hennaed all the flower buds, even Ianthe's."

She reached for her *gunna* that lay beside the blanket.

He reached it first and tossed it to the far side of the stall.

Flower buds? Does she mean . . . ? "You told me before? Never! I would have recalled *that*."

"When you rescued us, I distinctly remember telling you about the marble phalluses and the hennaed flower buds."

"I must have been dazed with delight over seeing you again." *Or something.*

"Are you being sarcastic?"

Who? Me? "Not at all. You must understand . . . nay, do not cover yourself. I am not done admiring the artwork." He drew circles around the outer circles of both areolas with his forefingers.

She smacked his hands away, and he retaliated by pinning both hands to her sides so he could look to his heart's content, which should be a good long time.

"As I was saying, you must understand that men see things differently than women. We like to look, and while there are so many bits on a woman's body that are a delight to the male eyes, these"—he waved a hand at her red-tipped breasts—"are like flags waving at a man, saying, 'Look at me. Touch me. Taste me.'"

"That is the most ludicrous thing I have ever heard. Especially about my ridiculous breasts. Anyhow, I thought we decided not to do this anymore."

What? Look at red nipples? Best he check her meaning. "This?"

"Sex."

Think quick, Sidroc. "Uh."

"I am saving myself."

Oh, good gods! "I have news for you princess, you have nothing to save. You already lost it to me." *I should feel guilty. Do I feel guilty? Not even a little, after what she has taken from me. But I am not going to think about that now.*

"I'm not talking about my maidenhead, you lout, and it is not nice of you to remind me of that misstep of mine."

"Misstep?" he hooted.

"Shhh. You will wake the cows and horses."

And I should care about that . . . why?

"Stop staring at my breasts."

Are you gone barmy, princess? How could I not look at your breasts? 'Tis like placing a roast boar in front of a starving man. Um, mayhap I won't share that with her. Reluctantly he raised his eyes to her face. It did no good. He still had the image in his head. "If not your virginity, what is it you are saving? And for whom?"

"I have decided that lovemaking is too special for lust-sex."

"Lust-sex?" *Mayhap I am the one gone barmy.*

"Yea, lust-sex, as compared to love-sex."

Now she is an expert on sex?

"Sex is best saved for a man and woman who care about each other and are either married or about to be married."

That woman refrain! 'Tis the monks' fault. We ne'er should have allowed the monks into the Norselands.

"Ianthe and I discussed it and we both came to that conclusion."

I am going to kill Ianthe. After about a hundred bouts of lovemaking, Ianthe is going to turn into a nun. And turn Drifa along with her. I do not think so!

"Sex without caring is like a bath without soap."

Huh? "I care," he said.

"Liar," she retorted.

"Anyhow, I am the one who said we would end our sex deal." *What? Now I am talking myself out of sex?*

"And?"

I regained my sanity. "I changed my mind."

"When was that?"

I cannot believe this. She is naked. I am naked. And we are discussing when we had a particular conversation. Lack of sex must be affecting my brain. "When you sat bouncing on my lap for three days, causing me to have a continuous enthusiasm for you."

"That was not me bouncing. It was the camel."

He shrugged. *Now we will converse about camels?*

"I do not appreciate lying here naked whilst you ogle me."

I am appreciating it, though. Very much. "If we are not going to tup, I must get my pleasures in small ways. Can I taste?"

"Taste what?" she asked dubiously.

"Your nipples." *But other body parts might appease my appetite, too.*

"Absolutely not."

"Does it wash off?"

"Do you think I would still look like this if it could be washed off? Stop grinning."

"Mayhap you should let me try washing it off for you. My hands are calloused, and with some soft soap, I might be able to wear off some of the color." *Or stir your ardor.*

She actually seemed to consider the suggestion for a second, and he suspected she might be getting aroused. A little bit. "Actually, one of Bahir's concubines told me that a mixture of olive oil and salt might fade the color."

"See. Calloused hands with my skin's oil and saltiness. Perfect." He released his hold on her arms, which he still held to her sides, and reached for her breasts.

She used the opportunity to duck under him and roll to her stomach, then stand. Her *gunna* was sliding over her head before he could react. The witch was enjoying the chase, immensely.

In truth, he was, too.

"There is one other way that the color can fade," she told him with a mischievous grin. "If I lie outside with my bare breasts exposed, the sunlight might leach out the color."

Oh, the wicked idea you stir in my brain, princess. Wicked, wicked, wicked! "A great idea," he concluded with as serious an expression as he could muster on his face. "You can ride naked on your horse on the morrow, and then when we stop to rest, I will rub olive oil and salt on them, just to make sure we have covered all remedies."

"Are you always this lecherous?" She was staring at his cockstand.

"Only around you." *And that was the gods' truth.*

"Blow out the torch so I can go back to sleep. That way you won't be able to see my ridiculous breasts, and your undangly part can go back to being dangly again."

"I have news for your princess, my undangliness is going nowhere." *Without your help.* He stood to do her bidding and noticed her staring not just at his cockstand, but at his rear end, as well. And she liked what she saw.

Once he lay down beside her again in the pitch black, he said, "See, I can still see your flower buds in my head. I have mind pictures of you wearing the harem girl garment I bought for you with your red flower buds showing through the sheer fabric. Then I have mind pictures of your hennaed nipples growing even bigger and redder with the nipple rings. And then, whoa! I have this most scandalous mind picture of you—"

"Stop! Enough with the mind pictures!" She rolled over on her side, turning away from him. The tip of his dangler was touching the tip of her buttock.

Oh joy!

But then she ruined the mood, or enhanced the mood, depending on one's perspective, when she muttered, "Bloody hell! Now I have mind pictures, too."

"Of your nipples?"

"Nay, not of my nipples, you idiot. Of me riding a horse naked."

He put the same mind picture in his head and

was musing over it, erotically, when she added something else.

"And the horse is you."

He groaned aloud.

He would never sleep tonight. Is this what they meant by that old saying, "Impaled on his own lance"?

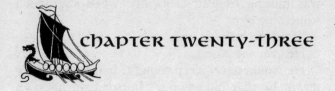

CHAPTER TWENTY-THREE

It wasn't Appomattox, but it was a surrender . . .

Drifa hadn't slept much at all the night before, and by the sounds of Sidroc's grumbly mood, he hadn't, either. He started picking on her as soon as they arrived at the stable where coins were being paid for the horses, above the trade value of the camels.

"What in the name of all the gods and goddesses are you doing now?" he bellowed, nigh knocking her to the ground with surprise.

"What does it look like I'm doing, lackwit?"

"Shoveling camel shit into a leather bag?"

"Yea. I am taking it back to the Norselands with me. The gardener at the Imperial Palace told me it makes a wonderful plant fertilizer."

Sidroc was standing, hands braced on his hips, staring at her as if she were demented. "Do you honestly think I am going to allow you to carry shit in a bag for the two or three days it will take us to return to the city?"

"Do you honestly think you can allow or disallow me to do anything? It's not like I'm carrying it on your horse anyway."

He shook his head as if she were hopeless while she continued to shovel up the piles. She was holding her breath as she worked; so, at first, she didn't hear what he was saying. Then she saw him handing her some garments.

"These should fit you. They belonged to the stable master's son."

"Boys' clothing? For me?"

He nodded. "Disguise yourself as best you can. Wear the cap, too, and tuck all your hair under it. Try not to pucker your lips in that flirty way of yours."

She ignored the flirty-mouth remark and took the items he handed her. "Dost think it necessary?"

"Why take chances? At some point we will be followed, for a certainty. Let us just hope we make better time than they do."

She couldn't argue with that, and so a short time later she emerged from the bushes, no longer Drifa, but a slim boyling in tunic and *braies*.

"Drifa!" Sidroc exclaimed on first seeing her.

"Not Drifa. My new name is Askell. I always liked that name."

"Pfff! More like Ass-kill. That would be more appropriate for our situation."

She just smiled at his mispronunciation and showed him all sides of the new attire.

He groaned, which was what she'd intended, knowing how tight the *braies* were across her buttocks. He deserved the torture after what he'd

put her through the night before with his "mind
pictures." This morning, too, truth be told. Every
time he shot her one of his hot glances, she felt the
heat all the way down to her bones. That must be
why she gave her bottom an extra wiggle as she
walked away from him.

His muttered curse was her reward.

They rode steadily that day, avoiding villages or
farmsteads because Sidroc said, and she agreed,
that the less notice they garnered, the better. They
stopped only occasionally to water and graze
the horses, and eat their own cold repasts. The
smoked snake was long gone, thank the gods!
Now they had slices of mutton, hard cheese, and
bread, which Stamos and Vera had given them on
their departure this morning from the farmstead,
washed down by the cool water of a stream cupped
in their hands.

The entire day—and this was what caused her
tension and abetted her exhaustion—attraction
sizzled between the two of them. And it went both
ways, she knew it did.

He would glance her way as they cantered side
by side, and her nipples would harden.

She glanced his way and saw the bulge betwixt
his thighs, which seemed to be always present.

When she bent over to get a drink, she noticed
his eyes riveted on her bottom.

When he bent over to get a drink, her eyes
latched on to his bottom.

He licked the excess water from his lips, and she
imagined those lips in other places.

When she put her hand to the small of her back

and stretched her aching muscles, he watched her with what could only be described as hunger.

She would be hair-tearing barmy by nightfall if she didn't do something. So, as they rode side by side through the mountain path, she tried to divert herself with conversation. "Tell me about your plans," she urged. "Oh, not what you intend for Runa. What were your plans when you decided to leave the Varangian Guard, before you knew about your daughter?"

"Finn and I had both grown tired of Byzantium. The endless fighting in a war that was not our own. The climate. Yea, we actually yearned for deep snow and blistering cold on occasion. And it was too soft a life for a Norseman."

"And what did you decide was preferable?"

"Well, when I came to you for marriage, I was without home or coin, my home and belongings having burned to the ground the season before that. My situation is different now. I plan to settle in my own home."

"In the Orkneys? Is that not the site you mentioned one time?"

"Nay. I had considered the Orkneys, and whilst many Norsemen live there, I prefer the Norselands. Nowhere near my father, but still in my homeland. And that is all I will say on the subject. So do not consider asking how my daughter fits into that picture." She could tell that his inadvertent use of the word *picture* brought forth thoughts of those other "mind pictures" they had discussed yestereve. Thus he asked his own questions, to divert their already aroused attentions. "Why have you ne'er married?"

She shrugged. "I always intended to, but every time a man offered for me, I found some reason to decline. And they were not all bad, either, though some of the specimens my father paraded before me would make the most desperate maiden cringe."

"And you were not desperate."

As you were when you proposed to me? "Not even when you offered for me."

"Why did you accept me, then?"

How much of the truth can I tell him? How much of my emotions can I spill like fallen blood? She hesitated. They were entering dangerous territory. Dangerous for her, leastways. "I thought you were a man I could love."

"And you thought I loved you?" The tone of his voice was incredulous and, yea, insulting. But honest, she had to give him that.

"I assumed you had a warm regard for me and hoped that it could perchance grow into love, over time. Foolish of me, wasn't it?" *Do not laugh. Oh please, do not laugh.*

After a long pause, he said, "Not so foolish. My time constraint for regaining my daughter was too desperate for me to think of much else, but methinks my attraction to you, even then, could have grown into something more." He shrugged. "Who knows?"

Drifa didn't know whether to be dismayed or hopeful.

He grinned at her then. "You said something else when I rescued you. Not just about hennaed flower buds. You mentioned marble phalluses. Like the ones in the marketplace?"

"Just like," she said with an air of disgust.

"What did you do with them?"

"Not a thing, but I would have been forced to if I'd remained there much longer. Mainly they were used for teaching tools."

"Phalluses for teaching tools? Now I am really intrigued."

"Don't be. 'Tis not what you are thinking."

"How do you know what I am thinking?"

"Hah! I've known what you were thinking, all day long. It does not take an experienced harem houri to know what has been on your mind."

"Your mind, too, m'lady. Do not place all the blame on me."

And so they rode, mostly in silence, toward their destination.

Drifa was in torture. The coarse material of her tunic abraded her nipples. The undulations of the horse between her thighs caused her woman-dew to weep. Sidroc's smoldering gaze gave her ideas . . . erotic ideas.

By the time they stopped for the night in a secluded clearing near a stream, Drifa was so aroused she could scarce stand. She glanced over at Sidroc, whose glowering demeanor told her, without her asking, that he was in a similar condition.

She moaned.

He groaned.

And before she could say, "I yield," she was lifted and braced against a tree trunk with her legs wrapped around his waist. He kissed her voraciously, and she met him with wet, openmouthed kisses of her own.

At one point he drew his head back and stared at her through passion-glazed gray eyes. And all he said was "I care."

That was enough.

It was the Perfect Storm . . .

Sidroc was shocked at the intensity of his arousal.

He'd been aboard a longship one time during a violent sea storm that buffeted the boat and all the seamen about like specks of dust. That's how he felt now. A fleck of lust-dust on the wind. Totally under the control of an erotic storm, unable to fight its power. Uninterested in fighting it, truth to tell.

"Should we lie down?" he gasped between kisses.

"Can't wait," she gasped back, and surprised the spit out of him by beginning to unlace his *braies*.

That works for me. He was a quick learner and began to unlace her *braies* at the same time.

Without any foresport, he surged up into her wet channel and pounded her against the tree. She didn't seem to mind. In fact, she was rubbing her breasts back and forth across his chest and making keening sounds of satisfaction.

For a moment Sidroc rested, in her body to the hilt, his ballocks touching her body. He felt the vise of her slick glove shift to accommodate his size and seize at him, as if to keep him inside. He could swear he grew even more.

Sidroc had been with more women in his thirty and one years than he could recount. He'd engaged in some interesting exercises with a few of them, way beyond what Ianthe, or Drifa, would call perverted. But this . . . this act of bliss with Drifa . . . was like nothing he'd ever experienced.

Even though it was his cock plundering her narrow sheath, every part of his body was involved, from his ringing ears to his tingling toes. He could no more have stopped swiving her than he could have stopped breathing.

In the end, he roared out his peaking in harmony with Drifa's sweet screams of ecstasy.

Well, that was short and sweet.

And belatedly realized that he'd forgotten to withdraw at the last moment.

And possibly disastrous.

Was this how he was to be trapped into matrimony? Was this something Drifa had planned? Nay, no one in the world could have planned something this spontaneous.

Carefully he eased himself out of her and lowered her legs until she could stand. She stared at him dazedly. "Was that another perversion?"

"Nay, Drifa, that was normal sex. Almost boring."

Her eyes widened. "Were you bored?"

"Hardly. More like so interested my eyeballs might have been rolling back in my head."

She smiled then. "Good. I was worried that I would only like perverted sex."

He could swear his heart expanded as he smiled

at her. Was there anything better than a woman who could make a man smile during sex?

"Can we do it again?"

Mayhap he'd smiled too soon.

Stepping back from her, he noted both of their *braies* pooled at their feet, as if they were overeager youthlings. He toed off first one, then the other of his half boots, and shrugged out of his *braies*. Then he took a blanket off his horse and shook it out on the ground.

"You. Blanket. Naked. Now."

He half expected that she would balk at his order. But instead she licked her kiss-swollen lips, cast him a sultry look from slanted eyes, and said to him, "You. Blanket. Naked. Now."

Gods help me. I think I am falling in love. A little.

A short time later, after Drifa demonstrated something to him that the harem ladies had been taught about phalluses, he *knew* he was falling in love. A little. Milking the Tree, indeed! What man wouldn't develop an attachment to a woman who could do *that*? He couldn't wait to see what she would do next. Wait. It was his turn to surprise her.

"Driiiiifffaaa," he drawled out.

She was lying sprawled on her back, arms thrown over her head, legs spread. She claimed that he'd depleted her. Hah! She was the one who'd depleted him; he'd only returned the favor.

She slitted her eyes at him. "What?"

"Have you ever heard of Riding the Rolling Log?"

Here comes a total eclipse of her heart . . .

Sidroc had told Drifa at one time that she would be his love thrall, but she never realized that she would enter that thralldom so willingly. After two days and nights of lovemaking, Drifa was good and truly enthralled by the man.

And she didn't dare tell him. One word of love and he would be running off to the horizon. With her daughter. Rather, his daughter. Leastways that's what she feared. Even now that they'd been so intimate, the future loomed before Drifa. Uncertain. Frightening. Empty. Dark.

Best not to think of what-ifs. What would happen would happen. And soon. Because they should arrive in Miklagard sometime on the morrow.

To give him his due, Sidroc seemed as enthralled with her as she was with him. In fact, more than once he'd murmured in the sex-husky voice she'd come to relish, "What are you doing to me, princess?"

As much as I can, sweetling. As much as I can.

They made love often and every which way but upside down, and every one of them was unique and satisfying to her, even the "normal" ways. But then she no longer knew what was normal and what was not.

He touched her all the time, even in passing. And she was like a kitten that preened and rubbed against him, begging to be petted. Pitiful, really, except she could tell he liked her constant touching, too.

He regaled her with wicked words of what they would do next as they rode their horses ever onward toward Miklagard. Twice they'd had to stop because he'd aroused them both so much. With words!

She'd even ridden her horse naked from the waist up one afternoon to test the theory of the sun fading hennaed skin. She didn't know if it had done any good, but it did arouse her to the point of lust madness. When they'd stopped to rest, she'd nigh jumped him for sexual favors.

"Are you sleeping?" he whispered now.

"I just woke up," she lied, and nestled closer into his embrace. It was the way they slept now, wrapped in each other's arms, as if afraid one or the other would skip off during the night. Or mayhap just because they fit together so well.

"We should be in Miklagard soon," he told her, not for the first time.

"And then what?"

"Ivar knows the route we will follow into the city. He should connect with us soon and let us know whether it is safe, or not."

"You expect trouble."

"I do. Leastways, 'tis best to plan for the worst. Then if naught happens, we have only lost the time spent on caution, not a life."

She smiled. "That reminds me of the proverbs Rashid used to quote all the time. Rashid was Adam's healer assistant. 'Pray to Allah, but ride a fast camel.'"

"Precisely." He squeezed her tighter against his side.

"Honestly, Sidroc, I think if I go to the empress and tell her what happened, she will place me under her protection."

"Do you ever listen?" he chided her. "In the past hundred and fifty or so years, more than a third of the emperors have suffered violent deaths. I mean, dozens, Drifa. Not just a handful. And empresses have not been immune, either. When politics is involved, no one is safe."

"Is it not the same at every court?"

" 'Tis worse here because it is such a rich country. Greed corrupts. But more than that, when religion is involved, any means are justified, or so assassins think. And do not doubt that the Byzantines think they are fighting a holy war against the Moslems, and the Moslems are equally certain Allah is on their side."

He was probably right. For a long while she remained silent, and he did, too. But other things were on her mind, as well as her safety.

"Sidroc," she broached carefully, "were you in love with your wife, Astrid?"

He stiffened for a moment. "Where did that question come from?"

"I just wondered. You are so determined to take Runa and raise her yourself, I thought it might be because you loved her mother so much."

"Must I remind you, we decided not to discuss Runa for the time being."

You decided. Not me. "Sorry I am, but the question just popped out."

She felt him smile against her hair. He was probably thinking of other things that had popped out of her mouth. Like her tongue. On his manpart. He did answer her, though. "Nay, I was not 'in love' with Astrid. I do not think I even 'loved' her.

But I did care about her, best I could. Let's face it, I am not a man for loving."

And care is all he ever offered me. She wanted to argue that everybody was capable of loving, but now was not the time. Arguments erupted between them with the least spark. The only fire she wanted to ignite at the moment was the bedplay kind. Love fires.

"As for Runa, I have an obligation. She is my daughter. I am honor bound to care for her. Mayhap in time I will grow to love her, but if not, I can at least ensure she will be safe and well cared for."

Cringing at the prospect of Runa in a loveless household, Drifa blinked back tears. Despite her wish to avoid a battle, she had to state her opinion on that prospect he laid out. "The future you plan would be as cold as your own upbringing, without the physical pain. Do you not see that coldness can be a cruelty, too?"

He gasped at her words and began to shrug out of her embrace. To stand and walk away, she suspected.

She would not release him, clinging tightly to his shoulders. "Nay, do not go, Sidroc. I meant no offense. Truly I did not."

"You rail at me for shortcomings I cannot help, Drifa. Because I do not gush soft words and proclaim undying love does not mean I have no heart. I am *not* in the same mold as my beastly father."

"I never insinuated such. Never!"

"Then let us drop the subject. We have only a few hours left, alone. Let us make the best of this precious privacy."

They made love then, and it was tender and poignant, probably because it would be their last time together. At least until Miklagard. Mayhap forever.

So Drifa showed him with kisses and caresses and sighs of pleasure how much she cared. She never said the words *I love you*. Not out loud. But every whispered caress held that hidden message.

If he understood, he never said. But he made sweet love to her, which she chose to interpret as a sign of his unconscious feelings for her. If that made her a fool, so be it.

Once they were together in Miklagard, she would tell him of her love and suggest they stay together, if not for their sake, then for Runa's.

They had plenty of time.

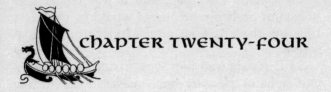

CHAPTER TWENTY-FOUR

Could he perchance be colorblind? . . .

Sidroc felt like one of those timekeeping candles. His time was wearing out.

They were an hour outside the land gate into Miklagard when Ivar connected with them. He sat atop a horse in a stand of olive trees off to the left side of the road. At a jerk of his head, Sidroc and Drifa followed him farther into the grove, where they dismounted.

Drifa launched herself at Ivar with a hug about his middle, which Sidroc could tell disconcerted the older man, whether from being unused to such contact or from the princess/servant separation, he could not tell. In any case, Ivar hugged her back after his initial shock, then set her away from himself and nodded to Sidroc.

They soon learned that neither of the other two groups had returned to the city yet, and that was a concern. Of more concern, though, was Ivar's news about the happenings within the city.

"There are guards and spies all about Ianthe's shop and living quarters," Ivar informed them. "Whether they are from Mylonas, the Arabs, or someone else, I do not know. But they are there, and in the palace, too, of course."

"I do not understand. I am no one of importance. Why would these people go to so much trouble?" Drifa's brow furrowed with puzzlement.

"Actually, you are of much importance, dearling," Sidroc said, and noted Ivar's raised brows at the endearment. "Not you yourself, but what you represent as a tool of war."

She still frowned with confusion.

"They would use you for leverage, Princess Drifa," Ivar explained. "You would be of value to the Greeks in their war against the Moslems. You would be of value to the Arabs in uniting the tribes. And others have their own greedy uses for a woman of your stature."

"What a mess!" she said. "What should I do?"

"I have removed all your belongings from the palace, and I managed to get into Ianthe's home by the secret door Sidroc told me about to gather any items you left behind," Ivar told her.

Secret door? Drifa mouthed at him. Then she turned back to Ivar. "Where are my things?"

"I stored them on *Wind Maiden*. I figured that is the safest place until we decide what to do next."

She nodded hesitantly.

Sidroc and Ivar exchanged meaningful glances, and Sidroc understood that the longship was ready to sail on a moment's notice. The only thing remaining was to convince Drifa to fall in with their plans.

"Let us go to your longship where we can discuss the situation in more detail," Sidroc suggested.

"I would feel better if Ianthe and Isobel and the others were here, too," she said.

They all would, but for the moment Drifa's safety was paramount. And there was more.

He'd avoided for days now talk of the future. Their future. And that of his daughter.

In truth, he did not have any answers. Mayhap he would not know what to do until he'd met his daughter face-to-face. Mayhap even then he would be confused.

He had reached a turning point in his life once again, just as he had on his daughter's birth. Which path he took was so important he could not act hastily.

Would he make a good father? Without love?

Would he make a good husband? Without love?

Drifa seemed to think not.

He was a soldier, a commander, who made decisions daily. There was black and there was white. No wavering.

Why then did his life feel so gray?

But how do I live without you? . . .

Drifa was in the hold of her longship, checking over her belongings, making sure Ivar had gathered everything, when she heard a clunking noise. The vessel appeared to be pulling anchor. An accident?

She moved toward the ladder, and it was not there.

"What in bloody hell is going on?" she yelled up.

Sidroc peered over the edge. "You are going home, princess."

"What? Nay! I am not ready yet."

"Sorry I am to inform you, but the decision is out of your hands, sweetling."

"Do not 'sweetling' me, you louse. Drop the ladder so I can climb up."

"Only when you are well away from Byzantium."

A heartening thought occurred to her. "You are coming to Stoneheim with me?"

He shook his head. "I will be jumping to shore any moment now, before the holding ropes are released."

"Why are you doing this?"

"I must ensure your safety. Only then can I take care of the villains in this case. The emperor needs to be informed of snakes in his midst. And Ianthe has to be protected afore I can leave."

"I am not your responsibility."

"I beg to differ."

"I do not want to be your responsibility then."

He shrugged.

"Where is Ivar, the traitor? He obeys me, not you."

"Not this time."

"But I am not done with my plant studies. And the imperial gardener is supposed to give me saplings from various trees to try in the Norselands. And unique rosebushes. And trellises for training ivy."

At his stubborn demeanor, she went on, "And we have to wait for the other guardsmen. And Isobel . . . I promised Isobel to help her get home."

"They will come with me later. And I will bring the bloody damn bushes."

"You will come to Stoneheim?"

"Of course I will. Eventually."

She wanted to ask if he was coming for her or to take Runa, but she was too cowardly. It was a question she had put off for too long, and now her time had run out.

"I will ne'er forgive you for this."

"Just add it to my other sins, then."

"Have these last few days meant naught to you?"

"They have meant everything, Drifa. You must know that."

"I know nothing," she wailed.

There were shouts up above, and Sidroc told her, "I must go now."

"Not yet, not yet," she begged.

"Be safe, princess, and . . . and tell my daughter I am coming."

"And if you don't come, if something happens to you to prevent your return . . ." *Oh gods! What if he should die afore I can tell him how I truly feel? Not that I am certain how I feel. Oh gods!* "You face danger all the time, what if you should die, what then should I tell Runa?"

Pausing to clear his throat, he choked out, "Tell her I cared."

He walked away then, leaving her stunned. *Words for his daughter, but none for me?*

But then his face popped back into the space. "One more thing, heartling," he said in an oddly raw voice, "I am not as cold as you think I am."

Dithering: the bane of a busy Viking's life! . . .

With one bothersome thing and another, it took Sidroc more than a month to be ready to leave Miklagard. Most of it due to the boring, dithering, nonsensical requirements of an imperial court and imposing women.

The other two groups arrived safely back in the Golden City soon after Drifa's departure, and all of them were being housed at Ianthe's, despite the cramped quarters. It seemed easier to protect everyone in that confined space. He and Finn stayed in their Varangian rooms at the palace, though ever watchful for sabotage.

Then he ended up in Mylonas's prison after confronting the bastard over his treatment of Drifa. To his immense satisfaction, he'd broken the rat's nose afore two of his guards dragged him off. He would have been doing the world a favor if he'd managed to kill the miscreant, and he'd later told the emperor just that.

Of course, he would be limping for the next century or so over the thigh wound he suffered, at his own hands, for the love of Frigg! He'd swung his battle-axe high in the air in Mylonas's office, hoping to lop off his loathsome head, but instead the evil toad ducked, and the sword struck deep into the wood of the eparch's worktable. When he'd yanked back, the blade flew off the handle and into his leg. Everyone thought he was wounded by Mylonas. He let them think so. Of course, if his axe had cleaved the rat's head between his beady eyes, Sidroc would probably be decorating a pike somewhere by now, food for the carrions.

The emperor eventually ordered his release from the dank cell, and the royal physician tended his injury, but only after letting him stew for two days. The emperor was furious with both him and Mylonas . . . with his eparch for his dastardly deeds and with Sidroc for failing to come to him for aid, right off. The emperor was particularly offended that Sidroc thought he might have been involved in the plot.

Even so, the emperor walked a fine line between appeasing his valued eparch and the safety of the empire on one side, and offending all the Norsemen in his Varangian Guard on the other side. It would be disastrous for the empire if the Norsemen pulled out of his elite forces, and they just might if they felt one of their own had been targeted.

Most surprising of all, it turned out that the new empress was not the quiet mouse they had all thought her to be. She had berated one and all for their treatment of a royal guest, meaning Princess Drifa, not him, and as a result, she was the one who made sure Sidroc's longship carried all the plants Drifa had requested. And then some!

And that was another thing. Drifa had never even hinted that there would be so much! Saplings, she had said, not full-blown trees, in some cases. And who knew there were so many different, thorny, bloodletting rosebushes in all the world? He scarce had room for supplies in his hold with all her dirty plants.

And who was going to water them and make sure they did not die at sea on the long journey back to the Norselands? *Me, no doubt.* Everyone else was just laughing too hard.

He arrived at Ianthe's now for his final farewells to find yet another reason for delay.

"I have decided to go with you," Ianthe declared.

What? He could see that her entire living quarter had been nigh gutted. Carpets rolled up. Furniture stacked as if for carrying out. Trunks—many trunks—piled high with furnishings, and clothing, and jewelry-making tools and supplies.

He recalled having asked Ianthe—what seemed ages ago, but must have only been a few months— if she would like to leave Miklagard with him, to settle in a new land. But things were different now. Bloody hell, did she think his offer to take her with him as his ongoing mistress still held?

What would Drifa think about that? He, Ianthe, and his daughter? Hah! Drifa would stab him with a kitchen knife in his other leg, or another body part.

"Uh," he said.

Ianthe gazed at him, waiting for his answer. Then she swatted him on the chest with the palm of her hand. "You idiot! I did not mean *that*."

"Oh?" He was developing a talent for one-word lackwit responses.

"I no longer feel safe in this country, despite everything the emperor has promised. For all we know, he could be murdered in his sleep, like some before him."

"Shhh!" One did not even whisper such thoughts for fear of being overheard.

"Drifa once mentioned to me a lovely section of Jorvik, in Northumbria."

"I know where Jorvik is," he grumbled.

"She said craftsmen and traders have their own homes and shops and stalls right in the Coppergate section. Methinks I could be happy there."

His fuzzy and, yea, relieved brain registered only one fact. "You want to go to the Saxon land. But I am headed for Stoneheim, not Northumbria."

"Are there not ships there that go to the market towns?"

He nodded hesitantly.

"Besides, Isobel wants to go back to her homeland. We can travel together."

He groaned. Another passenger. "Ianthe, with all of Drifa's trees and plants, and her three guardsmen, where would I fit all this?" He waved to the mountain of items piled about the room.

"That is the best part. I have bought another longship for you with the funds I raised selling this building."

"You. Bought. Me. A. Longship?"

"Yes, isn't that wonderful?" She beamed at him, as if another longship was the best gift in the world.

But all he could think was *More delays!*

"You are not to worry about a thing. Finn is helping me. A crew has already been hired."

Not for the first time in these past two sennights had he considered killing his good friend. Finn was moping about like a lovesick bull. Apparently Isobel wanted naught to do with him, and this was a new happenstance for the man far-famed for his woman-luck. Sidroc wasn't sure if Finn was more upset by his unrequited love or his damaged reputation. Ianthe told him that the Saxon woman had suffered much abuse at the hands of men in the ten years she'd been in captivity, and she probably had no interest in any male, not just Finn.

So it was that four and a half sennights after Drifa left Byzantium, Sidroc left the Golden City shores, for good. Hopefully he would be at Stoneheim within another two sennights.

But he hadn't anticipated an underwater volcano erupting just outside Byzantium, causing them to have to reroute their journey, causing further delays.

Nor had he anticipated pirates.

Or a mutiny on one of the ships over rosebushes.

Or a fight among two of Drifa's guardsmen over a missing harem girl garment.

Or Ianthe and Isobel's need for constant stops to piss and bathe.

Or his heart-hammering fear of what he would do when he arrived at Stoneheim, because gods only knew what that would be. He didn't.

Was there anything worse than a confused, impatient Viking?

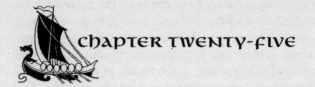

CHAPTER TWENTY-FIVE

**Absence just makes the heart grow
asunder . . .**

Drifa had been up out of her day-long entrap-
ment in the hold of the longship for two sennights now, but still she was hurt, and more than
that, she was blood-churning angry. The troll! The
toad! The slimy, dirt-crawling, lying, traitorous,
loathsome snake.

Despite all that, she loved Sidroc.

And he'd sent her off like so much bothersome
baggage.

Oh, she knew that he nursed a modicum of concern for her well-being, but he would no doubt feel
the same for any woman. Like Ianthe. Or his dead
wife. Or any passing fancy.

So he "cared" for her. She did not want his
caring. She wanted his loving.

So much for that!

When would she learn? He'd nigh broken her
heart five years ago. And he'd done it again now.
And, gods help her, he would do it again when he
came for Runa.

She would not think of that now. *Wind Maiden*

was skimming down the fjord toward Stoneheim, and she could see a small crowd awaiting their unexpected return. The tall man with the flowing white hair would be her father, and the little mite jumping up and down was sweet Runa.

After many hugs and kisses, Drifa was walking up to the keep with her father on one side, filling him in on all that happened, with Runa on her other side, singing a little song she'd made up which was composed of one word, "Present, pre-sent, preeee-seeent," and all its variations. Drifa had made the mistake of telling Runa that she brought presents for her.

Many sennights later Drifa sat with her father; Ivar, whom she was still angry with; and her sister Vana on benches in the great hall before a cold hearth, it being a warm autumn day. Runa was outside playing her marble game with some of the other children on the hard dirt of the back courtyard.

"I still say that the Arab bastard should not go unpunished. I should put together a *hird* of two hundred or so of my best warriors and go after that ad-Dawlah *nithing*," her father said, not for the first time since she'd come home and told them of her captivity.

The possibility of her father going off to war at his age, and engaging the enemy in a remote territory, was foolish and unacceptable to Drifa. She shivered at the image of him atop a camel leading his troops.

"Nay, Father!" she and Vana said at the same time.

Even Ivar, who had served King Thorvald well

for many years, shook his head. " 'Tis too far away, and there are too many of them."

Drifa reached over and put a hand on her father's big one. "Bahir ad-Dawlah is a vile man, and he should face the raven, no question about that, but I am alive and was not physically harmed. What I hate most is that my trip to Byzantium was cut so short."

"There will be other trips," her father assured her, but Drifa knew it to be untrue. She would be nigh a prisoner here at Stoneheim from now on.

"Besides that, ad-Dawlah and his men are not the only guilty ones," Ivar pointed out.

The king let loose a long string of expletives, then snarled out, "And you can be sure that I will let the emperor and all his Greek underlings know that I am unhappy with how his court failed to protect my daughter. The Byzantines rely on an ongoing supply of Norsemen for their Varangian Guard. If I let it be known that a princess of the Norselands was so abused, believe you me, he will have to look elsewhere for replacements."

She started to say, "Now, Father—"

But he cut her off. "Another thing, daughter, do not think I am so feeble that I am ready for a straw death yet. Bahir the Bastard will die, and soon. It does not take an entire *hird* to accomplish that goal. And the blood eagle he will suffer, too."

Which meant that he was sending soldiers to do the job for him, probably in the disguise of traders. She couldn't argue with that.

But enough for now! Her father's color was getting high. She and Vana exchanged glances, both agreeing it was time to change the subject.

"It has been two months, sister. Dost think Sidroc will still come?" Vana asked.

That wasn't quite the change of subject she wanted, but Drifa nodded. "Unless something has happened to him, he will come for Runa." She had already told Runa of her father, and the girling was anxious to meet him, although Drifa wasn't sure she really understood what having a father would mean to her. Just another person to do her bidding, Drifa supposed. "Will he bring presents?" was Runa's biggest concern.

"Does Sidroc not come for you, too?" Vana interrupted Drifa's musing.

Vana had trouble believing any man would disdain Drifa's favor. A biased sister's view.

"He said naught of that when last I saw him."

"How could he say aught when you were screaming at him?" Ivar offered.

"Where do your loyalties lay, Ivar?" she snapped.

"You wound me with your words," Ivar said. "Have I ever been disloyal to you?"

She ducked her head. "Mayhap not."

"Besides, you misread Sidroc. Methinks he cares for you."

"Care, care, care!" She threw her hands in the air. "Who wants 'care'?"

Everyone stared at her as if she'd gone barmy.

"Do you want the man, Drifa? I will get him for you, if he is your choice for husband." Her father patted her arm with comfort.

"Don't you dare! I will not have a man forced to marry me."

"You would let your pride stand in the way of keeping your daughter?" Vana posed the question softly, but it stung nonetheless.

"You above all others know what it's like to be wed without love," Drifa pointed out. Vana's first husband had been a cruel man. No love there, but a far cry from Sidroc, and their situation. Drifa immediately wished she hadn't made the comparison.

"You could always go with Sidroc as his mistress to stay close to the child," Ivar suggested.

"What?" she exclaimed with affront.

"What?" Ivar repeated back at her. "His bed furs were not objectionable to you in the past."

A silence pervaded the group as Ivar's words sank in.

Belatedly realizing what his loose tongue had revealed, Ivar groaned.

She cringed.

And her father did the least expected thing. He smiled. "That settles it. If the man has taken your maidenhead, he will wed you, or face the flavor of my wrath."

"Father! I am twenty and nine years old, soon to be thirty. What matters if my maidenhead is lost from carnal use, or lost by withering away from lack of use."

Vana giggled behind her hand.

"Be that as it may, I will have words with the rogue, you can be sure of that. What say you to Evergreen as a dower for you, dearling? 'Tis a small estate I own south of here. Still in the Norselands, but somewhat warmer in climate. Your flowers would grow better there."

"And you could get some of that camel shit out of the stable," Vana, the traitor, added. "It smells worse than horse manure."

As if no one else had spoken, the king went on, "I have promised Stoneheim to Rafn and Vana, as you know, Drifa, and a steading cannot have two jarls without enmity."

Who said anything about two jarls, or that there would be a wedding? My father's head is thicker than a berserker's shield, despite his having been drilled.

And still her father went on, "That way, you and Sidroc would have your own home at Evergreen."

Drifa put her face in her hands.

"You could give Sidroc more children, preferably sons. You are not breeding now, are you? Do not scowl at me so. I am just asking. In any case, you could pop out babies, and Sidroc could go on being a warrior, or a farmer, or a trader, or whatever he decides for his future. But a husband he will be. What think you, Ivar? Last time you were at Evergreen, what was its condition?"

As her father rambled on, she grew more and more furious. Why wouldn't he listen to her? "Aaarrgh!" was the best she could get out.

Just then, Rafn walked in. "I have news," he said.

A maid handed him a cup of mead, and he sat down beside his wife. "A ship heads this way. 'Tis Jarl Gunter Ormsson from Vikstead."

"Drop the drawbridge," her father whooped joyfully.

Never mind that they had no drawbridge. Or moat, either.

" 'Twould seem I am going to get my battle, after all." To a passing *housecarl*, he yelled, "Where's my favorite sword? Nay, bring me Skull Crusher, instead. And my helmet and shield. Call up the troops."

Drifa would have been concerned, except that it was more important that she go hide Runa. And any evidence of her trip to Vikstead five years before, like Eydis, the former Vikstead wet nurse, now chambermaid at Stoneheim.

Why couldn't her life be nice and calm and boring, like other princesses?

He made Simon Legree look like Santa Claus . . .

It was a lost cause, hiding Runa, because Gunter Ormsson knew full well that his granddaughter was alive and living at Stoneheim. Apparently some passing traveler had noticed Eydis one time when visiting Stoneheim and mentioned her being here. The jarl figured out the rest.

If only Sidroc were here to protect his daughter, and Drifa and her sisters, from this evil man, who was demanding not just Runa, but restitution for the stealing of his grandchild.

Gunter and two of Sidroc's older brothers, Svein

and Bjorn, had been here since yesterday morning, and a sorrier lot there never had been. Maids complained about gropings and outright demands for bedmates. Various Stoneheim soldiers had been insulted and were threatening violence.

They needed to get the vile miscreants out of Stoneheim. Without Runa.

"Your daughters committed a crime, and should be forced to pay *wergild* for their crimes, just like anyone else," Gunter said, sitting across from them, with his sons, at a table in the great hall.

Her father, Rafn, Vana, and Ivar bracketed her on the other side. Runa had been brought forth to meet her grandfather earlier today, but like a dog that sensed a bad person, the little girl screamed and cried to get down from his lap. Ormsson had muttered something about "Females need to be put their place. All the child needs is a good switching to teach her what is what."

Drifa shuddered to think of what Runa's life would be like in this man's household. "Our crimes are no worse than yours. In fact, some might say we prevented your far greater crime."

"What crime?" Ormsson and his sons sputtered.

"You were going to kill the baby," she said.

"Says who?"

"Your son Sidroc."

Ormsson made a dramatic show of glancing all around the hall. "I do not see Sidroc here. In fact, he has not been seen for some time. Some say he died, mayhap even at the hands of your healer, King Thorvald."

"You go too far, Ormsson," her father said, his voice steely with outrage.

"Besides, the law says a man has a right to do what he wills with his own family," Ormsson continued. "Let us call out a Thing-bidding over the land. Let the Thing court decide what is just."

"What is legal and what is right are two different things," Drifa argued.

"You exceed yourself, bi— girl."

"No more than I should. And, for your information, I have seen Sidroc." *And he is more than alive.*

"Me too," Ivar said.

"In fact, he is on his way here now, from Byzantium where he has been a Varangian," Drifa added.

"So you say." Ormsson emptied his horn of ale, belched, and motioned to a maid for a refill.

Drifa and Vana exchanged glances of disgust.

"What exactly do you want?" her father asked.

"The child, of course."

"The child stays here, awaiting her father's return."

"Which might never happen," Ormsson remarked. "And I want a hundred gold coins for *wergild.* Return of the wet nurse Eydis. And thirty lashes to the backs of each of the princesses."

That last was so ludicrous that Drifa let out a burst of laughter.

Ormsson gave her a look that said if he got her alone she would not be laughing.

"You touch one of my daughters and you will leave Stoneheim in pieces," her father threatened.

"There is an alternative," Bjorn said, eyeing Drifa in a rather crafty manner. "I would take your youngest daughter to wife."

Drifa and everyone on her side of the table gasped.

The king held up his hand to stop Drifa from speaking.

"I thought you were already wed."

"So?" Bjorn said. "The *more danico* is an accepted practice in the Norselands, as you well know."

"I was ne'er married to more than one woman at a time," her father said. "Nor will any of my daughters be second wives to any other. Besides, my daughters choose their own husbands."

"That is ridiculous," Ormsson scoffed. "No wonder your females behave so badly when you give them free rein."

"I see no husband here to Princess Drifa. She has been on the shelf long enough." Bjorn licked his lips, staring at her like she was a choice boar steak.

"That is not for you to say." Her father eyed the three men as if they were manure under his boot.

"Leastways, Drifa is betrothed."

Oh nay, not that again!

"That is the first we have heard of this." Ormsson appeared set back by this knot in his plans. "Methinks there is no betrothal. Name the man, if there is one."

Her father beamed as he announced, "Sidroc Guntersson."

Now it was those on the other side of the table who gasped.

"You risk war with us," Ormsson said, "over a split-tail."

Drifa didn't know if he referred to Runa or her. Either way, it was an insult.

"If that is what it takes." Her father stood to his full height, which was intimidating even to other tall Norsemen. He was a majestic figure with his clean, flowing white hair and still sturdy body.

Ormsson, on the other hand, was of the same age, but his dissolute lifestyle showed on his lined face and unkempt body. There was naught of Sidroc in him that she could see, thank the gods.

Just then a *hersir* walked up to Rafn and whispered something in his ear. With a smile, Rafn stood next to his king and father-by-marriage. "'Twould seem there are more visitors coming to Stoneheim." With a dramatic pause for effect, he said. "A longship was spotted at the curve of the fjord that leads into the North Sea. 'Tis Sidroc Guntersson."

"Well, I guess this disagreement will be settled, after all," her father said, gloating at his adversaries.

Drifa was filled with joy that Sidroc had finally come, but then Rafn, his expression dire, leaned closer to her and said, for her ears only, "He has two women with him."

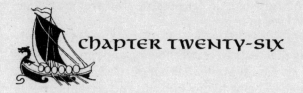

ChAPTER TWENTY-SIX

**There's nothing like a good fight to raise a
man's sap . . .**

Finally, finally, finally Sidroc arrived at Stoneheim. Much longer and he would have pulled
out every hair in his head, and his nose and ear
hairs, too.

"Never, never, never travel with women," he
advised Finn, who stood beside him, gloomy as
usual.

"I have given up women," Finn said dolefully.

Under any other circumstances Sidroc would
have fallen over with laughter, but he had been listening to Finn's moaning and mooning over Isobel
for too long. "You need a tun of good Stoneheim
ale and a woman or two to restore your spirits,"
he said. "Look. Over there. Is that Drifa and, oh
my gods! That little girl. Her braids are reddish
brown, just like my hair, and did she—yea, she
did—she stuck out her tongue at the little boyling
scooting behind her." For some reason, that impish
act struck him as admirable.

The closer they got, the better he could see. The
little one even had his gray-green eyes. Not much

of Astrid's blonde fairness or frail frame that he
could see in her.

He raised his eyes to Drifa, and noted immediately that tears were overflowing and running down
her cheeks. Was she that happy to see him? He ad-
mitted to being happy himself, and certain parts of
his deprived body were happier than others.

Ianthe and Isobel came up to stand beside him
at the railing. Finn immediately shuffled away, like
a whipped puppy. He'd been rebuffed too many
times.

"Oh, this is lovely," Isobel said.

Huh? There was nothing of beauty that he could
see in the hodgepodge castle up on the hill. Thanks
to Drifa's builder sister, Breanne, additions had been
put on to the building over the years in a manner to
make the whole appear lopsided. Of course there
were Drifa's flowers to add their charm, if flowers
on a Viking fortress could be called charming.

"I did not think I would like it here in the North,
but this is nice," Ianthe continued.

"You will enjoy my home near Winchester even
more," Isobel assured her. "I cannot wait to show
it to you, and Jorvik as well, of course."

They had learned that Isobel was the daughter
of an English earl, stolen when she was scarce thirteen. Sold in the slave marts of Hedeby, she'd lived
in the Arab lands for more than ten years. How she
would be accepted among her class was unclear, but
'twas not promising, in Sidroc's opinion. A woman
was judged harshly in such circumstances. Women
forced into sex slavery were deemed harlots. The
best that they could hope for was a nunnery.

In any case, once they'd disembarked here at Stoneheim, after a rest of a day or two, Finn would be taking the women to Britain on the other longship.

What Sidroc would be doing remained to be seen.

He glanced landward again and recoiled at what he saw. Walking, nay, swaggering down the hill from the keep, were his father and two brothers.

A blood-boiling, nigh-berserk rage overtook him, and the longboat had scarce butted against the plank wharf when he jumped off and stalked toward his family, if they could be called that. Luckily Drifa had gone off with Runa. He did not want his daughter to witness what was to come.

"What in bloody hell are you doing here?" he demanded of his father.

"Greetings to you, too, my son. Taking care of family business, which you have neglected to do," his father replied, casting him a scornful scrutiny.

"You stay away from my daughter, old man. You failed in killing her once. Do not think I will allow you near her again."

His father waved a hand dismissively. "You misunderstood me when the girl was born. You always did overreact to the least little thing." He looked to Svein and Bjorn on either side of him for affirmation. Both of the halfbrains nodded.

"I am here to demand payment from King Thorvald for my suffering," his father said. "After all, the girl is my granddaughter, and they stole her from me."

Sidroc let out a hoot of humorless laughter. "Go

home, Ormsson," he said finally, refusing to show the respect of the name Father.

"You don't give me orders, whelp. I brought you into the world. I can send you out of it."

A melee broke out then, with his father, two brothers, and more than a dozen Vikstead men on one side, and an equal number on the other side with Sidroc, including Finn, King Thorvald, Rafn, Ivar, and a dozen others.

For an hour and more they fought, with others joining in. It was a silent battle, except for the grunts and growls of soldiers at giving and receiving sword wounds, the clang of steel upon steel, the whistle of arrows, the slap of leather, and the occasional death scream.

In the end, before they scurried off like rats in a sinking ship, his father lost an ear to him, Svein appeared to have sustained a possibly mortal gash in his belly, and two Vikstead warriors were dead. Panting heavily, but smiling at the pleasure of a good fight, Thorvald was assessing their casualties. None dead, but quite a few injuries, some serious.

"Shall we make pursuit?" Rafn asked the king.

He paused to consider, then said, "Nay, let the scoundrels go. They are not worth the effort. Me, I could use a horn or five of ale. What say you?" The latter was spoken not just to Rafn but all the men still standing, some dripping sword dew, and not just from their swords.

"To the hall!" a chorus rang out. "A feast! A feast!"

Sidroc limped over to Finn, the limp being from his prior self-inflicted accident in Mylonas's Praetorion chamber, not a new one today, though it hurt like hell from all this activity. He felt something wet on his face and realized he had a cut on his forehead, but it did not appear to be deep.

Finn was sitting on the ground against a boulder, holding a blood-soaked rag to his face.

"Are you injured, my friend?"

"A broken nose. Can you believe it? After all these years of safeguarding my good looks, I am now ruined by a disfigured nose."

Sidroc smiled.

"You have blood on your teeth," Finn observed with distaste.

Sidroc licked his lips and realized that he must have bitten his tongue during the fight. That sometimes happened. Back to Finn, though. "Some women like the looks of a broken nose. They say it makes a man more masculine."

"If Isobel did not want me when I was perfect, she will not want me when I am not."

Only Finn would describe himself as perfect. "Desist with the Isobel nonsense. She will not have you, Finn, and that is that."

"I do not notice Drifa hanging on you with adoration, either. Methinks we are both out of woman-luck."

Sidroc glanced around. Finn was right. Drifa was nowhere to be seen. Nor was his daughter. Which was a good thing, though. 'Twas not proper for women to see the gore of battle.

Heading toward the castle, he saw Drifa's sister Vana speaking to her husband, Rafn. "Have you seen Drifa?" he asked.

"Bloody maggot arse hole!" Vana snarled, shocking both him and her husband before stomping off.

He looked to Rafn, who was grinning. "Ne'er mind my wife. Betimes she speaks her mind in an earthy way. Comes from living in a fortress with so many fighting men."

"Why is she angry with me?"

"She is angry on Drifa's behalf. Do not expect any less from Drifa."

"Huh?"

"Are you really so daft?

"Speak plainly, you smirking cur."

"Didst really see naught wrong with sailing into Stoneheim, not to seek your ladylove, but to bring with you not one but two beautiful women?"

Ladylove? He tilted his head to the side. "She's jealous?"

"Do dragons piss?"

He pondered the idea for a long moment and decided he liked it. As he was walking away, Rafn called to his back, "Oh, I should warn you. King Thorvald is planning a wedding."

He glanced back over his shoulder to see that Rafn was still grinning.

"Whose?"

"Yours."

First came the sweet, then the bitter . . .

Drifa was sitting on a bench in the back garden with his daughter. They were waiting for him.

He'd washed his face and changed his bloody tunic, not wanting to shock or repulse the child. He stood frozen, taking in the sight.

The child cocked her head to the side, listening to words Drifa spoke to her softly. He thought he heard the little girl say, "But Mother . . ."

My daughter calls Drifa Mother, he mused. For some reason, that did not bother him as much as it might have at one time.

He was filled with so much joy, and fear, and anger. Emotions shot around his head and in his heart, confusing him. He had not expected to feel so much.

At a prodding from Drifa, the little girl rose and started to walk toward him, hesitantly. She wore a bright green *gunna* with a pale green, open-sided apron over it. Her reddish-brown braids hung midway down her back. When she smiled tentatively at him, he saw she had two missing front teeth. She seemed rather tall for four and a half years, but he knew little about children in general and nothing about girls.

As she drew closer, he dropped down to his haunches to put himself at her level. The pain in his thigh caused him to teeter for a moment, which prompted a giggle from his daughter.

"Are you my father?" she asked.

"I am," he answered without hesitation, his heart thundering with such a strong feeling of possession. *Mine*, he kept thinking. *Mine*.

"Where you been? Dint you want me?"

"Oh, sweetling, I have always wanted you."

"Mother says you were lost."

He chuckled. Lost. As good a word as any, he supposed. "I guess you could say that, but I'm not lost anymore."

"Did you bring me a present?"

He laughed, having been forewarned long ago by Drifa that it would be the first thing Runa asked.

"Let me think. I might have brought one present. Or . . . hmmm, could it be five presents?"

Runa's eyes, mirror images of his own gray-green ones, went wide as she silently marked the numbers on the fingers of one hand: one, two, three, four, five. "I love presents."

"I guessed that was the case." He smiled at her.

"You have red on your teeth," she pointed out.

He'd thought his mouth had stopped bleeding, but mayhap not. He rolled his tongue over his teeth. "I bit my tongue today."

She nodded knowingly. "I bit my tongue one time when I was skipping too fast. Can you skip?"

"I do not know. I haven't done it since I was a boyling."

"I could show you how."

Wonderful! A Viking warrior skipping. "That would be . . . delightful."

"My mother doesn't like to skip because it makes her bosoms jiggle."

He was sure Drifa would appreciate Runa having shared that. He thought about telling Runa that he liked jiggling bosoms, but decided it would not be appropriate. He would have to do that a lot from now on, question whether something was appropriate or not.

"Can I give you a hug?" Runa asked suddenly.

He could swear his heart grew thricefold. "You never have to ask. Hugs are always welcome."

She launched herself at him then, almost knocking him over. With her little arms wrapped tightly around his neck, and her face pressed against his throat, she was choking him, but he could not care when she was giving him such delicious, wet kisses.

He returned her embrace, inhaling her little-girl fragrance of soft skin and the honey she must have eaten recently. Standing with her still in his arms, he turned to see Ianthe approaching.

"Oh, Sidroc, she is adorable," she said, placing a hand on his arm and smiling up at his daughter, who was enjoying the height. He knew that Ianthe was barren, and seeing his little dearling must evoke pain in her. He reached out and drew her closer for a quick kiss on the top of her head.

He thought he heard a gasp, but when he turned to take Runa and Ianthe with him over to the bench, he saw that it was empty. He'd forgotten in the excitement of meeting his daughter for the first time that Drifa had been there, in the background.

But now Drifa was gone.

Some swearwords survive the test of time . . .

For hours, Runa led Sidroc around like a puppy on a leash. First he had to see the new kittens in the stable. Then her bedchamber, where she showed him her collection of colored stones. Then the pond, where there was a bullfrog that she described as huuuuuggggge!

Another hour or more was spent with him showing her the presents. A set of carved wooden farm animals. A miniature longship. A Greek girl's gown with butterflies embroidered along the edges. A small box of marzipan candies. And a rope of colored stones, recommended by Ianthe; it could be wrapped around the neck as jewelry, or used as a belt. Runa was wearing it now across her forehead, tied in back, with tails hanging down past her neck.

The whole time he was getting acquainted with Runa, he kept looking for Drifa. She should be sharing this experience with him.

After that, King Thorvald enticed him into the great hall, where numerous toasts were being made to the heroes of the day. Not that Sidroc considered himself a hero. If he'd killed his father, deprived the earth of his cruel being, mayhap that would have been heroic, but all he'd done was slice off his father's ear.

Dinner was about to be served when he'd had enough.

"Where is Drifa?" he asked the king.

"Is she not with Runa?"

Sidroc shook his head.

"Mayhap she went to the garderobe."

"For four hours?"

The king shrugged. "One never knows what women do in there."

He stomped off and saw Ianthe, who was just coming downstairs from the chamber that had been assigned to her and Isobel. "Have you seen Drifa?"

"I have not seen her since we arrived. She was standing on the shore last time I saw her," Ianthe said.

"Nay, she was in the garden when I first met Runa. Remember?"

She shook her head. "I did not see her there."

Sidroc was starting to get a bad feeling.

"What? Why do you have that odd expression on your face?" Ianthe asked him.

"Vana hinted that I might have done something to make Drifa jealous."

"Jealous? Of what?"

He ducked his head sheepishly, then set his gaze on her.

"Me?" Ianthe squeaked out.

"You *and* Isobel."

"Why would Drifa be jealous of . . . oh, can you be such an idiot? Drifa was expecting you to come for her, wasn't she?"

"She was expecting me to come for Runa. Same thing." *Isn't it?*

"Men! Tell me true, Sidroc, does Drifa know that you love her?"

"How would she know that if I don't know it myself?" *I mean, I do know, but 'tis hard to put it into words. Bragi, god of eloquence, has ne'er blessed me.*

Ianthe threw her hands up in the air, as if he were a dunderhead. He was beginning to share her assessment.

"Sidroc, what did Drifa say when you greeted her today? How did she receive you?"

"Uh."

Ianthe put a hand on each hip and arched a brow.

"I haven't had an opportunity to talk with her yet. I thought to settle other matters first so I would have time with Drifa." *To show her with my hands and body what my clumsy words could not.* "I had to first fight my father and get to know my daughter."

She shook her head at him. "What have you been doing that was so much more important? Never mind. What makes you think she's jealous?"

"Vana. She asked what I was thinking, bringing not one but two women with me to Stoneheim."

"And what did she say when you set her straight?"

"I never got a chance—"

Ianthe rolled her eyes. "Aaarrgh! No wonder Vana treated me and Isobel with such cool regard. You must find Drifa and make things right, and you must do so afore her grievances have time to fester. Oh, and you should plan on groveling. A lot."

"I think not! I have had more than enough of chasing my tail over that woman, the very one who clobbered me over the head with a pitcher and left me for dead, the very one who kept my daughter's existence from me. And what did I do in return? I saved her from a life of harem servitude. I put off my departure from Byzantium to take care of her business. I filled the hold of my longship with half-dying trees and bushes. I brought her new best friend to visit. What need have I to grovel?" Somehow, Drifa's sins did not seem so bad in the telling.

Just then, Vana was about to swan by them with her arms piled high with bed linens, but he put a hand to her shoulder to halt her progress. She stopped, but stared at his hand as if it were leprous, until he let go.

"Where is Drifa?" he demanded to know.

"As if I would tell the likes of you!"

Some women should have been born tongueless. "Drifa would want you to tell me," he lied.

"And that is why she wept as she left?"

Wept? She wept? Oh, I am in big trouble. "Left? Left for where?"

Instead of answering him, Vana said snidely, "I see you and your mistress have found each other."

"I am not his mistress," Ianthe said at the same time he protested, "She is not my mistress."

Vana arched her brows skeptically. "Never?"

He could feel his face heat with color. "Not for a long while." *And what business is it of yours, anyhow?*

"How long a while?"

Ianthe was blushing now, too.

He did not want to answer, he really didn't, but Vana appeared as stubborn as . . . as Drifa. "Three months."

"So long?" Vana's voice reeked with disdain.

"Your sarcasm ill-suits," he told her. *Even if it is warranted.*

"Your arrogance ill-suits," she told him, then walked away, muttering, "Bloody maggot arse hole!"

But then another thought seeped into his muddled head, and he mused aloud, "Drifa went away and left Runa here for me. Does she intend to give up that child of her heart? To me? Is that why she has gone away? What would prompt such action? Certainly not jealousy. It must be . . . could it be . . ."

"Of course it is, you thick-headed fool," Ianthe said.

" . . . love?"

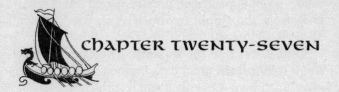

CHAPTER TWENTY-SEVEN

The only thing missing were the violins . . .

Drifa had been at Evergreen for several days, assessing its worth as her new home. She could see where it had gotten its name. It was overridden with pine trees, even up to the back courtyard.

The timber fortress castle was small in comparison with Stoneheim, but that was fine. She did not need anything bigger for herself.

It was the hardest thing she'd ever done, leaving Sidroc and Runa, but it was the right thing to do. Sidroc deserved to have his daughter with him, wherever that might be. And he had every right to choose the woman who would be with him, even if it wasn't she.

And, really, with the scare that had been posed by Jarl Ormsson, wasn't this the best for everyone? Things could have been so much worse if Runa had been taken to Vikstead.

Still, she never realized that love could hurt so much. She suspected it was something she would have to abide for the rest of her life. A solitary life, she vowed. No longer would she let her father cajole her into marriage.

She would spend her time restoring Evergreen. Hopefully she would be too busy to think about all she had lost.

Thus it was that she was sitting at a table in the small solar off the great hall, making lists of all she must do. There was only a small staff in residence, but she had set them to raking old rushes, scrubbing tables, and laundering bed linens. Many more would be needed. *Housecarls* protected the estate, but only a dozen or so. Then she would need gardeners to help clear out the deadfall and pines that encroached on the keep. Carpenters to make repairs to the roof. Kitchen and chambermaids.

It would make a good home. Perchance one day she could even open her home to other women who wished to escape captivity, whether it be from a harem or from a bad marriage. Divorce with good cause was acceptable in Norse society, but usually the women had no place to go.

But wait, she heard a ruckus outside in the front courtyard. It better not be the housemaids arguing again over who should clean the privies.

As she walked out of the solar and across the hall toward the huge double doors, which had been opened to air the dankness, she saw two figures approaching from the fjord. One tall and one small.

She put a fist to her mouth to stifle a cry. It was Sidroc dressed to high fashion in a pewter-gray tunic over black *braies*. His face was clean-shaven, and his hair combed sleekly off his face into a queue secured with a leather thong.

He was holding the hand of Runa, who was also dressed as if for some great event. The blue

Greek-style *chiton* left her shoulders and arms bare to expose a strand of colored crystals wrapped around like an endless arm ring from her wrist to her elbow. The blue gown was embroidered with butterflies along the edges. There were also crystal beads woven into her inexpertly braided hair. Had Sidroc bought the gown for his daughter? Had he actually combed her hair for her? She knew what a difficult task that could be with a squirming child.

At one point, Runa skipped to keep up with her father's long strides, and she could have sworn she saw the big Viking take a skipping step as well, but she was probably mistaken.

By the time they came up the stone steps leading to the keep, tears were streaming down Drifa's face.

"Mother! You are crying!" said Runa, who was about to rush up to her, but Sidroc held her back and whispered something to her. The little girl nodded.

"Drifa, how could you have left me alone with your demented family?" Sidroc spoke chiding words, but his eyes were giving a different message, one she did not dare interpret, it was too precious.

"I do not take offense at your characterization of my family. I have been living with them for almost thirty years and betimes feel a bit demented myself." *Like now.* "What exactly have they done now?"

"They are planning what they call the wedding of the century. At last count their guest list measured a thousand from nine countries."

She did not need to ask whose wedding. Stone-heim must be a total madhouse. "I will put a stop to it at once."

"Will you now?" he drawled.

She nodded, unable to speak over the lump in her throat. She leaned against the door frame for support.

"And your father is the worst of all. He wants to sell head drillings to any Vikings who are interested during the wedding feast."

Drifa's mouth dropped open. "That is awful, even for my father. Don't worry. Adam would never consent to such foolishness."

"Your father seems to think anyone will do. He's already hired the blacksmith." He smiled at her then.

The rogue! He knows what his smiles do to me. I might just melt into a puddle at his feet.

She could not stand the tension any longer. "Why are you here, Sidroc?" And she glanced meaningfully at Runa as if to say, *Is it not enough that I left you the child of my heart?*

Runa whispered loud enough for even the seamen down at the fjord to hear, "Now, Father? Now?"

"Yea, sweetling. Now," he said.

Runa turned her attention to Drifa. "We have come to pro . . . pro . . ." Runa looked to her father for help.

"Propose." He held Drifa's eyes as he spoke.

Drifa whimpered.

"We want you to marry us," Runa explained, as if Drifa hadn't understood.

Drifa tilted her head in question at Sidroc. Something was not making sense here. "Where is your mistress? Or should I say mistresses?"

"Women? More than one? At one time? Tsk, tsk, tsk! You flatter me." He shook his head at her. "If you refer to Ianthe and Isobel, they were on their way to Britain. *As they always intended.* But when they heard about the wedding—the *potential* wedding—they delayed, in case you wanted them there."

"Why would I marry you, Sidroc?" *Foolish question! But then I am feeling foolish.*

"I know, I know the answer to that, Mother." Runa was jumping up and down. She glanced up at her father, as if looking for a cue.

"Go ahead, rosebud," he said.

Runa preened. "Because we love you."

Drifa let out a sob and turned tearful eyes to Sidroc.

He smiled again, one of those I-can-make-you-do-anything smiles, and said, "Because *I* love you."

She was so mad at him for so many things.

He was so mad at her for so many things.

But what did it matter if he loved her?

"Well, Drifa, are you suddenly without words? Pray Odin the sky does not fall down."

She launched herself at him, and he caught both her and Runa in an embrace. Against his neck, she whispered, "I love you, too."

And the lout said, "I know."

READER LETTER

Dear Reader:

Well, Drifa is the last of the Viking princesses. Did you like her story?

I smile sometimes to think of where I have placed my Vikings over the years. The Norselands, of course, which would be all the Scandinavian countries. Norsemandy (Viking Age Normandy). Britain. Iceland. Scotland. The Baltics. America. And now Byzantium.

What next? you may very well ask.

Well, how about Transylvania, Pennsylvania, and a group of Viking vampire angels? Talk about tortured heroes with a sense of humor! This Deadly Angels series will begin in May 2012.

That doesn't mean that I will discontinue the historical romances. Wulf, and Jamie, and Thork, and even clumsy Alrek deserve their own stories some day. I'm thinking these so-called Viking pirates need their comeuppance, maybe even capture by a group of Amazon-like female Viking pirates. And in the back of my mind, there has always been a story calling to me: *The Harlot Bride*. Maybe Isobel from *The Norse King's Daughter* would fill that role well.

Keep in mind that the previous books in this series are still in print, either as new books or as reissues: *The Reluctant Viking, The Outlaw Viking, The Tarnished*

Lady, The Bewitched Viking, The Blue Viking, My Fair Viking (retitled *The Viking's Captive*), *A Tale of Two Vikings, Viking in Love,* and *The Viking Takes a Knight.* I have made sure to update the reissues, giving them new, funny scene tags, as well as new reader letters and glossaries.

For the record—in case you thought I was guilty of an anachronism—trepanning, or head drilling for medicinal purposes, did take place in the tenth century. In fact, ancient (meaning before the time of Christ) skeletal remains show drilled holes in skulls. Archaeologists tell us they were made for a variety of purposes: to release evil spirits, to alleviate headaches, or to relieve the pressure of swelling on the brain. There is no evidence that head drilling had the sexual side effect mentioned in my book (grin).

And just for a note of interest . . . there's a reason that I wanted Drifa to have an interest in irises. My aunt Eliza was a great gardener, and her favorite flower was the iris. Over the years, every time anyone in her small town traveled around the world, they would bring her back roots (or rhizomes) from some special species. In the end, she probably grew hundreds of different kinds. Unfortunately, when I went back to that town a few years ago, an art gallery was located in her former home, and all the gardens dug up and planted with grass.

Keep checking my website at www.sandrahill.net for more information on my books, genealogy charts, free novellas, and contests. I love hearing from readers at shill733@aol.com, and, as always, I wish you smiles in your reading.

SANDRA HILL

GLOSSARY

Abayah—long loose robe with built-in head cover.

Asgard—home of the gods, comparable to heaven.

Augustaion—public, ceremonial square in Constantinople.

Azan—call of faithful to prayer.

Berserker—an ancient Norse warrior who fought in a frenzied rage during battle.

Birka—Viking Age trading center in Sweden.

Blood eagle—a method of punishment whereby a sword was placed on the victim's spine to hack all the ribs away from the backbone down as far as the loins, then the lungs pulled out as an offering to Odin.

Braies—slim pants worn by men.

Chalmys—in ancient Greece, a cloak clasped on one shoulder, leaving the weapon arm free.

Chamberlain—high steward, person in charge of managing a household, sometimes a high official at court.

Chiton—gown or tunic without sleeves, worn by both sexes in ancient Greece.

Christogram—symbol for Christ using Greek letters.

Concubine—a woman who cohabits with a man who is not her husband.

Danegeld—in medieval times, especially Britain, a tribute or tax paid to Vikings; in other words, you pay or we plunder.

Danelaw—northern, central, and eastern parts of Anglo-Saxon England in which Viking law prevailed.

Dynatoi—border warlords similar to later-day samurai soldiers.

Drukkinn (various spellings)—drunk, in Old Norse.

Ealdorman—a royal official who presided over shire courts and carried out royal commands within his domain. Comparable to later earls.

Ell—a linear measure, usually of cloth, equal to forty-five inches.

Eparch—next to the emperor, the most important official in Constantinople; alternately called the prefect; served as chief magistrate, chief judge, chief of police, supervisor of immigration, and trade commissioner.

Fillet—band worn around the head.

Garderobe—latrine or privy.

Gunna—long-sleeved, ankle-length gown for women, often worn under a tunic or surcoat, or under a long, open-sided apron.

Hectare—unit of land measure equal to 2.471 acres.

Hedeby—market town where Germany is now located.

Hersir—local military commander who owes allegiance to jarl or king.

Hird—a permanent troop that a chieftain or nobleman might have.

Hnefatafl—a board game played by the Vikings.

Houri—beautiful woman, often associated with a harem.

Housecarls—troops assigned to a king's or lord's household on a long-term, sometimes permanent basis.

Jarl—high-ranking Norseman similar to an English earl or wealthy landowner, could also be a chieftain or minor king.

Jihad—religious duty or holy war deemed a sacred duty by Moslems.

Jomsvikings—elite group of Viking warriors who banded together as mercenaries, often for noble causes, and lived together in military fortresses.

Jorvik—Viking Age York, known by the Saxons as Eoforwic.

Khopesh—type of curve-bladed sword, a sickle sword.

Komvoskoini, or *chotki*—prayer beads.

Léine—a long, full shirt down to the knees, resembling an undertunic, often of a saffron-yellow color.

Logothete—chief minister, the person who introduced important visitors to the emperor during public sessions.

Loki—blood brother of Odin, often called the trickster or jester god because of his mischief.

Midden—refuse dump.

Miklagard (various spellings)—Viking name for Constantinople.

More danico—Norse practice of multiple wives.

Muezzin—person or persons who call the *azan*.

Nithing—one of the greatest of Norse insults, indicating a man is less then nothing.

Norns of Fate—three wise old women who destined everybody's fate according to Norse legend.

Norselands—early term referring not just to Norway but all the Scandinavian countries as a whole.

Norsemandy—tenth-century name for Normandy.

Northumbria—one of the Anglo-Saxon kingdoms bordered by the English kingdoms to the south and in the north and northwest by the Scots, Cumbrians, and Strathclyde Welsh.

Parapet—low wall along edge of roof.

Patriarch—the bishop of an ancient see, such as Constantinople, in the Greek Orthodox religion.

Paximadi—very hard Byzantine bread, often carried by ancient armies because it lasted so long.

Pennanular—a type of brooch, usually circular in shape, with a long pin crossing it in back for attachment to fabric.

Pladd (or *brat*)—large length of fabric like a blanket, which was fastened on the shoulder with a brooch; a mantle of sorts, looped under the sword arm for better maneuverability, and secured at the waist with a leather belt. Men usually wore it over the *léine* or long shirt, which left the legs exposed.

Porphyry—hard, purplish-red rock that contains large crystals of feldspar.

Portage—act of carrying a boat overland from one navigable waterway to another.

Praetorion—the building that housed government offices, including that of the eparch.

Sagas—oral history of the Norse people, passed on from ancient history onward.

Sennight—seven days; one week.

Skald—poet or storyteller.

Straw death—to die in sleep upon a rush mattress, shameful for Vikings.

Tagmata/tagmatic—troops that were assigned to the emperor. These were separate from the Varangian guardsmen.

Tamarisk—a tree or shrub with feathery needles and numerous small pink flowers, also known as salt cedar.

Thane—a member of the noble class below earls but above freemen, usually a landowner.

Theme/thematic—Byzantium was divided into separate military districts called themes, which had their own native garrisons and governor generals.

Thing—an assembly called to discuss problems and settle disputes, similar to a district court.

Thralls—slaves.

Tun—252 gallons, as of ale.

Valhalla—hall of the slain, Odin's magnificent hall in Asgard.

Valkyries—female warriors in the afterlife who did Odin's will.

Wergild (various spellings)—a man's worth.

Turn the page

for a sneak peek

at the first book in Sandra Hill's

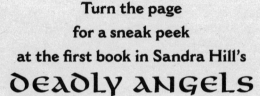

DEADLY ANGELS

series.

Coming in May 2012

from Avon Books.

TRANSYLVANIA, PENNSYLVANIA, 2012

Welcome to my world, sweetling . . .

"I need to taste you," Vikar said, and almost immediately wished he'd bitten his tongue, except his fool fangs had come out in anticipation of—*what else?*—a taste.

Son of a troll! How he hated these fangs! They were embarrassing, really. And inconvenient. In fact, they seemed to have a mind of their own. Like another part of his body.

But wait. Something strange was happening here. The air fair crackled, and he could swear his skin tingled. Tingled, for the love of a cloud! Every hair on his body was standing at attention, like bloody antennae.

The woman backed up a bit, but he was between her and the door to his castle office where he'd yanked her after seeing her alarm on first viewing his fellow VIK members. There was a telling silence on the other side of the door now, as if all twenty-seven vangels in residence so far were attempting to listen in on how he would handle this latest disaster.

He wasn't sure if she sensed the same chemistry in the air, or if it was his rude behavior that frightened her. Probably both.

"Taste . . . taste . . . ?" she sputtered, her green

eyes sparking anger at him. "In your dreams, buster. I'm here for an interview, and nothing else. I don't appreciate your manhandling me, either."

"I 'manhandled' you for your own safety. The tasting must be done, for your own safety."

"'For your own safety,'" she mimicked him. "That's a new line, right up there with 'I have to have sex or my blue balls will fall off.'"

She has a mouth like a drukkinn *sailor. I like it.*

"You have a coarse tongue, m'lady."

"Yeah, well, *m'lord*, you put *your* tongue, coarse or otherwise, anywhere near my private parts, and you will be very sorry."

"What? That is not what I meant." *But, now that you've planted the picture in my mind, I wonder if it fits in with Trond's "near sex" idea?* "You missay me. 'Tis your blood I must sample in order to—"

"Whoa! The only taste you're going to get is of the mace I'm going to blow your way."

"A gun and mace? What are you, some kind of bounty hunter?" He was fairly certain she referred to the eye-blinding substance, not the medieval ball and chain weapon. So he put both hands up in mock fear.

She made a snarling sound and was already digging into a briefcase-style purse the size of a boar's behind. As she bent forward, he relished the sight of her reddish-blonde hair falling forward out of the knot at her nape. He also relished the sight of the cleavage exposed under her flimsy upper garment, a wisp of flesh-toned silk and lace. Immature? No doubt. But when a Norseman had been celibate for a hundred years, he got his kicks wherever he could.

"Ah, here it is." She held up a pocket-sized canister that might fell a dwarf, but not a man his size, and certainly not one with his supernatural composition.

He tried but failed to hide his grin. "Blow away, but the only effect it will have is to make me sneeze. You do not want to see a vampire angel in a sneezing fit. Last time, my fangs turned my lower lip into bloody pulp, and feathers flew everywhere." That was not quite true, his not being winged yet, but exaggeration was a God-given Viking prerogative, in his opinion.

"Angel?" she scoffed. "First you're a vampire. Now an angel. I can't wait to hear what else you claim to be."

"Viking."

"Huh?"

"I'm a Viking vampire angel. A vangel. My brothers and I, Viking to the bone, are called the VIK, leaders of the vangels."

She rolled her eyes.

"Are journalists usually so cynical and . . . discourteous?"

She blushed. "No. Let's start over here. I'm Alexandra Kelly, *World Gazette* magazine." She extended her hand toward him.

"And I am Vikar Sigurdsson." He shook her hand, but only lightly, fearing a recurrence of the current that flowed betwixt them. "I mean you no harm, that I do swear." He placed a hand over his heart for emphasis.

She studied him for a moment, then set her canister on the desk that was piled high with bills and account books and wallpaper samples, a Bible, and two empty bottles of Fake-O. Cobwebs hung from every corner. Mr. Clean, he was not.

Apparently she'd decided he was no longer a threat. How humbling was that for a fierce Viking warrior? But then humility was part of his ongoing penance.

"How come you're being so open now, when a few minutes ago you were refusing my interview?"

"Because I saw the fang marks on your neck."

"I beg your pardon."

Enough! There was no way to convince this woman that he needed to suck out a bit of her blood to test for a demon infection. No quick way, leastways. And time was of the essence.

So, with a speed faster than any human could comprehend, he grasped both her wrists and held them behind her back with one of his hands, his hips propelled her back against the floor-to-ceiling bookshelves, and his other hand grasped her chin, forcing it to the side so that her neck lay open to him. With a reflexive hiss of anticipation, he sank his teeth into her skin where she'd already been bitten.

He'd done this hundreds of time before. He could do it in his sleep. He could do it and recite the *Poetic Edda* in his head. He could be cool, calm, and as collected as any Viking vampire angel in the midst of a fanging. But this was different, he recognized instantly.

The taste of her washed over him like a tidal

wave. His cock shot up without warning and went lance hard without any forewarning. It was a thickening so exquisitely orgasmic that he felt his knees begin to buckle.

Jerking backward, he released his hold on her and put the back of his hand to his mouth, rubbing. Staggering to the other side of the desk, he plopped down to the swivel chair to hide the continuing erection that tented his shorts, the thigh-length *braies* men wore in the summer months.

At the same time, she appeared more stunned than angry, although the anger was sure to come. Gingerly picking up a dirty tunic from another chair, she dropped it to the floor before sitting down to stare across the desk at him.

"Who *are* you?" they both asked at the same time.

Was that arousal hazing her green eyes? Was she feeling as shocked as he was? And why, after being dead for one thousand and sixty-two years, was he being sucker-punched with this kind of temptation?

Mike, he immediately thought. St. Michael the Archangel, their heavenly mentor.

On the other hand, what if the fiendish Jasper, head of all the demon vampires, had a hand in this? What if this strawberry-blonde vision was actually a Lucipire? Hmmm. He would have to tread carefully. At least the pole between his legs was unthickening.

"I am Vikar Sigurdsson," he repeated. "I am the owner . . . um, developer of this property." A seventy-five-room, run-down castle built by a coal baron in the Pennsylvania hills. Well, 'twas true. To a point. He was developing . . . something.

"And a vampire?"

The smirk on her face was not pleasing to him. Not at all.

Still, he advised himself, tread carefully. "Not precisely. The word *vampire* implies dark. Evil. I am neither of those."

She arched her pretty reddish-blonde brows in question.

"I am a Viking vampire angel. A vangel, to be precise."

"Do you have wings?" The snide tone to her voice betrayed her disbelief, but she must have realized how impolite she sounded for a person requesting a favor . . . an interview. "Sorry. Sometimes I have trouble suspending disbelief. Let me rephrase that. Do you have wings, Lord Vikar?" This time she asked the question without mockery.

"Not yet."

"Seriously, what's going on here?"

"Seriously, you wouldn't believe me if I told you."

"Try me."

"Are you a Lucipire?" he blurted out.

"Huh? No. I already told you my name is Alex."

"Lucipire is the name for one of Lucifer's vampires. You know, fires of hell, burn and sizzle, and all that."

"Sizzle? Hah! Don't blame me for this sizzle between us. I didn't create this fire. That's your magic crap." She slapped a hand over her mouth, realizing how once again she'd failed to rein in her tongue.

But sizzle? She feels the sizzle, too. Her blood is on fire for me. Oh, I am in big trouble. "Lucipire. L. U. C. I. P. I. R. E. One word."

Her face turned a lovely shade of beet.

"A demon vampire."

She rolled her eyes. "You people in this town really do take this whole vampire charade a bit too far. I understand why. The tourist attraction and all that. But I'm not writing a promo piece for you in my magazine. If you're not going to be straight with me, you're wasting both our time. And, frankly, I don't appreciate your biting me, either." She put a hand to the bite mark on her neck, but the way she rubbed it was almost a caress.

Which caused the air to crackle again and ripples of electricity to shoot right to . . .

Down, thickening! Down!

All right, so maybe she wasn't in league with the devil. But how much information could he trust her with? On the other hand, she said Mike had sent her. Besides, there wasn't any way he could let her leave after having tasted her blood. She'd definitely been infected. He had work to do on her if she was to be saved.

"You've been bitten by a Lucipire, not a mosquito. That's why I had to sample your blood, to evaluate the extent of your infection."

"Oh, please . . ." she started to say.

He held up a halting hand. "The Lucie must have been interrupted in the midst of feeding on you." He tilted his head in question at her.

"The Yoders' dog did start barking wildly, now that you mention it. I slapped a hand at my neck at the same time I heard Mr. Yoder walking down the hall to call the dog in. But it was a mosquito," she insisted, "not some dumb-ass devil bloodsucker."

She is going to have to do something about her language before Mike gets here. "Are you sure?"

"Of course I'm sure."

The warrior in him recognized that 'twas best to surprise the enemy with a sudden attack. Not that she was his enemy. So he launched his big question point-blank: "What big sin have you committed?"

"What?" That question certainly got her attention and caught her unawares, as he'd planned.

"You are clearly in a state of mortal sin."

"How dare you make such a personal statement about me, a perfect stranger?"

"The Lucipires only attack those who have committed some grave sin, or are contemplating such." Plus, the sin-scent teased his enhanced sense of smell, as well.

"Oh." That one word said it all, guilt personified, along with another beet blush.

So, the sin has not yet been committed. That is good. Although even the small amount of demon infection is already heightening her temptation to evil. He tented his fingers in front of his face, his two forefingers resting on his forehead. Finally he came to a conclusion.

"You have to tell me everything so that I can save you," he said.

"Save me?" she sputtered. "Like you're my guardian angel?"

"So to speak," he agreed. Time enough to explain later.

"That's it. I'm out of here." She stood and walked to the door. When she tried the doorknob, it was, of course, locked. "Unlock. This. Door." She glared at him over her shoulder.

"Sorry, m'lady, but you are going nowhere."

She gasped. "You'd force me to stay?"

He shrugged. "I prefer to say you are the first guest of the Hotel Transylvania."

"Are you people escapees from a mental hospital? Is this the vampire version of *One Flew over the Cuckoo's Nest*? Am I going to see Jack Nicholson popping out of the woodwork with an axe in hand like he did in *The Shining*?"

She was going to see an axe or two, that was certain. Battle-axes. Lots of them. Along with swords. Maces. And any number of modern weapons, including his favorite Sig pistol. But he did not need to inform her of that just yet.

"Aren't you a little old for these kinds of silly games? How old are you anyway?"

"You do not want to know."

"Which means you're older than you look. Let me guess. That's a weave you're wearing to hide your receding hairline. And they say women are vain about their appearance!"

He hated that she'd hit his sin right on its unruly head. Vanity, ever his downfall! Still, he attempted to defend himself. "I shaved my head one time so I could avoid the sin of pride. Mike made it grow back even better. He said cloistered virtue was no virtue at all."

"The poet John Milton was the one who said that."

"He did? Wait 'til I tell Mike about stealing someone else's quote."

"Who's Mike?"

Would you believe St. Michael the Archangel?

"Saint . . . I mean, Mike Archer. My . . . uh, agent."

"And he told you not to shave your head?"

"I have a thing about hair." He shrugged.

She went on to discuss just about everything that was wrong with the male gender, from plagiarism, to comb-overs, to infidelity, to sex obsessions, to selfishness. On and on she went, lumping him in with the worst.

He let her vent for a while longer, then asked politely, "I don't suppose you know how to cook? We have a side of beef in the kitchen that we got from a local Amish farmer, and our cook has not yet arrived. No one knows how to cook it without building a fire, and that would surely ruin the new floor tile." He was teasing, of course, just wanting to stop her tirade.

She told him to do something to himself that he knew for a fact was physically impossible. "I take that for a no."

"Correction. That would be: Hell, no!"

"We don't mention that place here."

She gave him a look, the one women have perfected over time that essentially said of their menfolk, *Dumb dolt!*

He widened his eyes with innocence, pretending not to understand.

"I need a drink. A dirty martini would go over

great about now. Even a Bloody Mary, minus the blood. I don't suppose you vampires have any alcohol?"

"M'lady! We are Vikings. We practically invented beer."

"Angels who drink beer," she muttered as she followed him out of the office. "And vampires, besides. I suppose you only suck on beer-sodden alcoholics."

"Ha, ha, ha!" he said. "You have much to learn, wench. Much!"

He wondered if her obvious sense of humor would be intact after a day or two in VIK land.

USA TODAY AND *NEW YORK TIMES*
BESTSELLING AUTHOR

Sandra Hill

"Her books are always
fresh, romantic, inventive, and hilarious."

New York Times bestselling author Susan Wiggs

The Bewitched Viking

978-0-06-201900-4

The Blue Viking

978-0-06-201901-1

A Tale of Two Vikings

978-0-06-201912-7

The Reluctant Viking

978-0-06-201910-3

The Outlaw Viking

978-0-06-201909-7

The Tarnished Lady

978-0-06-201913-4

Visit www.AuthorTracker.com for exclusive
information on your favorite HarperCollins authors.

Available wherever books are sold or please call 1-800-331-3761 to order.

HILA 0411

Give in to Impulse . . .
and satisfy your every whim for romance!

Avon Impulse is

- Fresh, Fun, and Fabulous eBook Exclusives
- New Digital Titles Every Week

The best in romance fiction,
delivered digitally to today's savvy readers!

www.AvonImpulse.com

AVONIMPULSE

IMP 0711